These Broken Pieces

Pieces

Karen Ramsey

Also by Karen Ramsey

Enjoy the Little Things
Making Lemonade

These Broken Pieces

Karen Ramsey

This is a work of fiction. Names, characters, businesses, schools, and incidents are either used in a fictitious manner or the product of the authors imagination.

To my Uncle Steve

I know you are so freakin' proud of me!

Miss you tons

TRIGGER WARNING

This book contains content that might be triggering to some readers including depiction of anxiety, depression, negative self-talk, thoughts of suicide, thoughts of self-harm, and talk of attempted suicide. Reader discretion is advised.

CHAPTER ONE

Katelyn

I'm pretty sure my brain is broken. I mean, what other explanation is there as to why I have not typed anything new in the past two hours?

I peel my eyes away from my laptop screen and glance around the quaint little coffee shop I found on my walk this morning. A high countertop runs along the front windows, allowing guests to look out at the boardwalk. A few small round tables, all occupied, fill the middle of the seating area, and then there is the long brown leather bench where I'm seated. Besides my table, there are three other tables that run the length of the bench. Each had another chair on the opposite side. I didn't even notice my table didn't until now.

I take a sip of my coffee, tilting the cup to taste the last few drops. Nothing comes out. Frowning, I set it aside and focus back on my screen. I type a few lines and then re-read them.

"Stupid," I mutter, hitting the delete button furiously.

Someone clears their throat. I peer up to see a gentleman in a wheelchair staring at me. His hazel eyes seem to be trying to solve a puzzle. "Mind if I…?" He gestures toward the table. I narrow my eyes, my brow scrunching in confusion. "This is a handicap table. Do you mind if I join?"

Oh. No wonder there wasn't a chair. "Oh my gosh. Yes—I mean no. I am so sorry. It was the only free table when I walked in. Umm…" Hitting save, I close out of my document and slam my laptop closed. Progress was eluding me anyway. I gather my scattered notes, shoving them into my notebook, and toss everything into my bag. I grab my cup and scoot out of the bench.

"I didn't mean to interrupt. You can stay. You looked very"—he pauses—"focused."

If by focused he means completely failing, he would be right. My throat tightens. "No, really. It's fine. Sorry again. Have a good day."

"What were you working on?" the gentleman asks.

"Nothing," I say over my shoulder, heading for the trash can. I toss my cup and when I turn he's still staring at me, that same perplexed look on his face.

As I pass by him toward the exit, he mutters, "It didn't look like nothing."

At that I pause as my thoughts bring me back to another time I sat in front of my computer. *I don't know why you're investing so much time in this. I mean, none of this is real life. They are just stupid stories!*

Letting out a small, humorless chuckle, I say, "Trust me. It was."

"I'm Dom. And you are?"

Dom looks at me expectantly. His espresso brown hair falls across his forehead, into his eyes.

"Nobody. Have a good rest of your day." I give him a little nod and walk out. When I get to the rental car, I throw my bag into the back seat and then climb into the driver's seat. I drop my keys in the cupholder and hit the start button. Letting out a long sigh, I back out and try to decide what I want to do with my last day here.

As I drive, my mind wanders back to the handsome gentleman, Dom. *And you are?* Why couldn't I have just said Katelyn? It would have at least been a polite response. His scrutinizing gaze left me a little speechless. It felt like if I answered honestly, he would continue to ask more questions. What scared me is that he might truly be interested. How long would that interest last? With the exception of one or two people, everyone else eventually walks away. Why would he be any different?

After the coffee shop, I stop at a few bookstores, wander around Target, and then pick up pizza. Entering my hotel room, I cross the small space, setting my pizza on the bedside table and dropping my bag on the plush gray chair. My suitcase lies open in front of the ottoman. I change into my sweats quickly, then grab the TV remote and channel surf until I find a re-run of *Friends* and eat my pizza.

This trip was supposed to be a chance for me to make real progress on my manuscript. Instead, I'm still stuck with writer's block at one hundred and twenty-seven pages of nothing. There's not even a good ending. Those pages lead nowhere. I've been stuck at the same spot for weeks and I can't seem to get unstuck. When Wheelchair Guy said I looked focused today I wanted to both laugh and cry. Laugh, because there was no focus, there was simply wishing any decent words would appear. Cry, because I had sat there for hours today hoping to create just a few good sentences—something—and I had nothing.

After I devour the pizza, I grab the wine glass—because who wants to drink wine out of a paper cup?—and the wine bottle I purchased earlier at Target and head for the balcony. I push the curtain as far back as it will go and let the light from my room illuminate the little space. I situate the end table closer to my chair and then stare out at the San Diego Bay. The *USS Midway* is easy to spot with the red, white, and blue string lights along with the giant illuminated 41 on its side. Beyond the *USS Midway* is Seaport Village, a charming tourist trap filled with shops and dining spots.

Eventually, I set down my half-empty wine glass and pick up my laptop. I open the document I stared at all afternoon and begin staring again. *Mazey looks out over the never-ending chasm, wondering what, if anything, is on the other side.* I reread the line for the millionth time, trying to decide where to go next. Mazey has been looking at this chasm for weeks. I know why Mazey needs to learn what's on the other side, but how do I get her this information? Does Mazey go talk to some villagers? Does she find a way to cross the chasm? Maybe fly over it? She has a dragon and could do that. But why hasn't she done that already? Is there something stopping dragons from flying over the chasm? The problem could be that I know just as much as Mazey does concerning the chasm.

"Ugh, this is ridiculous." I pick up my wine and take a sip. "You are smart, you can figure this out," I tell myself. *Great, now I'm literally talking to myself.* My eyes dart around making sure there is no one else out. I finish my wine, setting the glass down on the table. For a few seconds longer I stare at my screen and then start typing.

Mazey steps to the chasm's edge. The rocks crumble beneath her feet and she plummets down, down, down...

As I try and think through what could occur next, my thoughts whisper, *Nothing happens. As you said earlier, you are nobody. You are going nowhere. You are nothing.*

Tears prick my eyes and I blink hard, not letting any fall. I quickly hit save, not wanting to lose those few words, and shut my laptop. In the distance, the dark water laps at the shore. I collect all my belongings and head inside, brushing my teeth and washing my face before crawling into bed. Tomorrow, I go back to the real world with my real job and real responsibilities. I don't know why I ever thought I could be something more.

When the tears come this time, I don't stop them.

CHAPTER TWO

Dom

I thought I was ready for big life changes. I didn't expect to run into the most intriguing girl on the planet, studying her laptop with such laser-focused intensity that if she had stared any harder, it might have spontaneously combusted. I desperately needed to know what she was working on.

The whole interaction has played through my mind over and over since she walked out of the coffee shop. When I realized she was sitting at the handicap table and it would be an easy opening to speak with her, I was elated, but she seemed upset when I interrupted and I felt a little guilty. Her comment about being "nobody" struck me hard. She wasn't just saying it to blow me off. The sadness in her tone and the look on her face made me think she actually believed it. Why on earth would she feel that way? I had wheeled after her, but I was too late. I lost her in the crowd on the boardwalk. I didn't want to be the creepy guy stalking her, so I let it go and went back in.

Pushing the beautiful brunette out of my mind, I try to focus on what I came for. I pull up the email that I've already read a dozen times and read it again.

Dear Mr. Renner,

Congratulations on your promotion to Director of Creative Marketing effective July first. This position is hybrid, allowing you to work remotely and in office. Please note, you are required to be in office two days a week.

Attached you will find an updated contract containing new employment terms, compensation package, and benefits. Please review and sign all documents and return via email to Human Resources by June twenty-first.

I review all attached documents. The raise is substantial. Since our company has a location in Arizona, I could move in with my two best friends and former roommates, Jeremy and Tyler. They moved out there a little over a year ago and have been begging me join them.

When my company posted the position, I applied instantly. Mainly because I had been working toward a more senior level position for the past year and a half. When I realized there was an opportunity to relocate, I thought it was icing on the cake. That is, until I really started to think about it. I was somewhat settled into a new normal after a car accident two and a half years ago left me needing a wheelchair to get around. Moving meant finding a whole new team of medical professionals, including doctors, physical therapists, and counselors. A move would likely require making modifications to a house too, which are costly, not to mention I'm the only one who needs them. Any changes made to accommodate me will inconvenience others, and I hate that. Not that Jeremy and Tyler would mind. They would bend over backwards to make sure

I have whatever I need. It's just a little infuriating that a couple years ago this was a non-issue.

Now, staring at the contract, I consider turning down the offer for a whole new reason. What if there's a chance I run into the brunette again? Maybe with a different approach, I could get her to open up. That is a long shot, though, and this job opportunity is right in front of me. It would be stupid to pass up. I complete all the paperwork and send it in.

After I finish my coffee, I take a lap around the boardwalk. Part of me hopes the woman from the coffee shop had hung around, maybe did a little shopping. Eventually, I have to give up. I run a few errands and then head home.

Once I get comfortable on my couch, I message Jeremy and Tyler letting them know they're getting a new roommate. Immediately, my phone buzzes.

"Dude! It's done? It's official?" Jeremy asks. Excitement radiates through the phone.

"It's done," I say flatly.

"Well, don't sound too excited. Jeez. What's up?"

"What if this is the wrong move?" I ask.

"What if this is the best move ever? You've been working at this for the past year, and you did it. This is a good thing." His words bring a small amount of reassurance.

I sigh.

"Come on, man. Talk to me. What's going on?"

"It's nothing. I just…met a girl this morning and I guess, I don't know." There is no way I can tell Jeremy that the small, seemingly meaningless conversation triggered some haunting memories I would rather not relive. I know all too well that when one feels like they are nobody, broken, they can sometimes take drastic measures to *not* feel that way anymore. *And you let her walk away. Way to go!*

"Dom?" Jeremy breaks through my thoughts.

"Huh?"

"Did you have a life-altering conversation with this woman?"

"No. I didn't even get her name," I say.

"There ya go. You had a brief interaction with someone who really is nobody—"

Nobody. Have a good day. Her words replay in my head. "She's not *nobody*," I snap.

Jeremy is quiet for a moment. "—to you," he finishes. "What's going on?"

"Sorry. It's just been a long day. Lots of big changes. I'm good."

Sitting up, I transfer to my chair and make my way to the kitchen. "So, do you two have potential houses or did you give up?"

Jeremy and Tyler have been roommates in a two-bedroom apartment for the past year, but have always kept some potential homes in mind for when, as they put it, I inevitably moved out there.

"Oh, we still have a few contenders. While you're out here, we'll have to talk about what accommodations we need to make," Jeremy says.

"I don't need many. Most things can stay the way they are."

Jeremy starts to refute that, but I assure him I'll be fine.

CHAPTER THREE

Katelyn

I'm driving home from work when my phone rings. I suck in a breath before I answer.

"Hey." I force my tone to sound chipper.

"What's wrong?" Eliza asks immediately.

"Why do you think something's wrong? All I said was hey."

"I've known you for almost your whole freaking existence. I know when you're not okay." I swear I can hear her eyes roll at the end.

She's not wrong. Eliza and I met in preschool. All those memes on social media about how introverts make friends because extroverts claim them is totally true. Eliza sat down next to me in class and when it was time to play, she dragged me to the toy bins with her, and she has been dragging me along ever since. That is, until she met her boyfriend, Marc, and followed him across the country. I low-key hated Marc for a solid four months for taking my best friend away from me. But when I was able to fly out and visit him for the first time, it quickly became apparent that he treated my favorite person in the whole world like she was his whole world. It was hard to stay mad after that. Ever since the move, we text every day, with calls peppered in throughout the week.

Sighing, I admit, "It was just a long day. What's up with you?"

"You know I'm not letting this go, right?"

I roll my eyes. "Yes, I know. But please, can you just tell me about your day and give me a moment?"

"Fine. Work was decent. Good tips today."

She continues detailing her day as I make my way home. I'm listening to her recount the gossip of the kitchen staff and busboys as I unlock my door. My burnt orange IKEA couch is pushed against the wall. A small black coffee table sits in front of it. My television is mounted on the wall opposite the couch. The faux wood floor squeaks as I head to the bedroom, kicking my shoes off before flopping onto my disheveled bed. I don't understand people who make their bed every morning—you're just going to mess it up again when you go to sleep at night. What's the point?

I listen as Eliza finishes up her story. "Okay, your turn."

Inhaling a deep breath, I hold it a second before blowing it out. "Work was work." I shrug. I don't find accounts receivable for a small label company a thrilling job. It is a paycheck, though. "I sat in my cubicle all day, ate a salad for lunch, and finished my day calling clients about their overdue balances. Oh, and my mom messaged me. Fun times."

Thinking of my mom's texts, I put Eliza on speaker and navigate to my messages.

1:40—*Hey sweets, checking in. Call me when you can.*

1:47—*In a bind. Hoping you could help. Call me.*

2:12—*NM. You're taking too long. I'll talk to you later.*

"What did your mom need?" Eliza asks.

"Not sure. Whatever it was, I wasn't able to assist fast enough. I'll check in with her later."

"Remember, it's not your job to take care of her. You're not her parent."

I sigh. I know Eliza's right, but it's a hard habit to break. I've been the acting parent in our household for most of my life. My parents had me when they were in their teens. My dad bailed before I turned one. Part of me understood. I mean, becoming a father at sixteen is a big life change. Even though he wasn't in the picture he sent a Christmas card for my first Christmas. To this day he still sends a card with money or gift cards and a little life update every year.

My mom was fifteen when I arrived. She had quite a bit of help from my grandma in the early years of my life. We lived with her until I was six and then my mom moved us to a small apartment. Even though we were out of my grandma's house I still slept there often because my mom wasn't home. She claimed she was working a second job to make ends meet. When my grandma caught her in the lie, she refused to babysit. She wanted my mom to step up and be a parent. Throughout the rest of elementary school and junior high, she made some improvements. There were times I felt like I had a normal mom.

Once I got to high school, I guess she thought I was grown enough. She began staying out late most nights and when she did eventually come home, she was inebriated. I always stayed up until she stumbled through the door. I'd get her to bed and make sure she had everything she needed for the morning hangover. She started treating me like I was her roommate and not her child. I helped with groceries, cooked dinner most nights, and made sure our bills were paid on time. I also became her confidant. She would come home and tell me about her day at work or the latest relationship drama, oftentimes asking me for advice on what she should do.

Being an extrovert, my mom usually teased me for always sitting at home. I tried to convince her I was happy being a homebody. Once, I even showed her what I was working on during my nights in and she laughed at me.

"Oh honey, there is a whole world out there and you're sitting here writing about mythical creatures? That seems a little crazy, don't you think? I mean, what do think you're going to accomplish here?"

I didn't know what to say. She shook her head. "You need to get a life," she muttered.

That was the last time I confided in her about anything.

"Katelyn?" Eliza's voice brings me back to the present. "Your almost forty-year-old mother can take care of herself. She shouldn't be relying on her twenty-four-year-old daughter to swoop in whenever she's in trouble."

"I know," I mumble.

"Once more, with feeling."

"I know," I state.

"And look, I know you don't love your job but just remember, this is temporary. A placeholder until you become a world-famous author."

Tossing a glance at my olive green laptop bag, tears prickle my eyes. When I returned home from my trip, I threw my bag in the corner of my room and haven't touched it since. I wish more than anything that Dom had been right, that I was focused. I wish I could have told him I just completed one of my favorite scenes and my readers were in store for some amazing things. Instead, my manuscript lies dying and I'm not sure it's worth resuscitating. It's probably better to let it go at this point.

"Katelyn?"

I peel my eyes away from my bag. "Sorry. What do you have planned this weekend?"

"Well, Marc and I are thinking of going to the beach. I'll probably have to do some adulting at some point too and clean the house, do some laundry."

I'm jealous of Eliza sometimes. She lives in Georgia about two hours from the Atlantic Ocean, and the two of them are constantly visiting the beach.

"You're not the only one," I say, thinking of my overflowing laundry basket and pile of dishes in my sink.

"Are you going to do some writing this weekend?" Her words are gentle.

"Maybe. I don't know."

"What if you sent me what you have? Maybe I can help?"

"Yeah, we are dying to know what your latest project is. Let us read it!" Marc yells from the background so I can hear him.

I suck in a breath. "Was I on speaker this whole time?"

"No! He just walked in."

There's commotion on the line and then Marc yelps. More rustling, and then Marc says, "Don't be mad." The echo lets me know I'm now on speaker. "I heard something about writing and knew who she was talking to. I figured I'd throw my two cents in. I really do want to know what you're working on."

No one can know what you're working on. It's not worth sharing. All it shows is your lack of talent. Your lackluster writing skills will be laughed at. My brain spews these thoughts at me, bringing fresh tears to my eyes.

"Katelyn, you still there?" Marc asks.

I clear the knot in my throat. "Yep. You know what? I'm super hungry. I'm going to let you go and find some food."

Eliza takes control of the phone again. "Oh, sure."

"I'll talk to you later."

"Yes, you will. Bye."

I say goodbye and end the call. My stomach grumbles and I shuffle to the kitchen to find something to eat. After scouring the fridge and cabinets, I decide there is nothing edible in this place. Groaning, I grab my purse and head to the grocery store.

CHAPTER FOUR

Dom

"I don't understand why there aren't basic necessities at the house," I say as Jeremy and I enter the local grocery store. Jeremy slides a cart from the row and we proceed inside.

"There are a few. Plus, the three of us always shopped together. It's just like old times." Jeremy smiles.

Jeremy and I were roommates during our junior year. Senior year, we lived in a suite and Tyler was our suitemate. After graduation, Jeremy, Tyler, and I shared a small condo. Jeremy was the only one with family in the area and could have easily moved back home after graduation. Tyler and I thought he was crazy for not taking advantage of the basically free rent situation.

"I don't see either of you jumping at the chance to move in with your parents," Jeremy had argued.

He had a point. I put my degree to use as a marketing specialist for a bank. Jeremy was hired as a security guard at a shopping mall, and Tyler took a job that allowed him enough flexibility to spend time at the skate park working on stunts with either his skateboard or bike. We lived together just under a year before the accident happened and changed everything. I spent almost three weeks in the hospital before moving to a rehabilitation center. Tyler was in the hospital for a week before he was able to go home, but he still had physical therapy three times a week. Jeremy wasn't with us that night so he bounced between hospital rooms, keeping each of us company.

Jeremy and Tyler remained roommates, but the condo was no longer conducive to my situation, and I didn't want to inconvenience either of them with all the modifications I would need. Instead, I found an apartment that was completely handicap accessible and began living on my own.

I was nervous about moving back in with them, but they assured me everything would be fine. We already agreed I could have the master bedroom with the attached bathroom to make all the modifications I need. That way, I won't disrupt things for Jeremy and Tyler. Someone already came out to remove the carpet in the bedroom and replace it with faux wood flooring. Not that it was necessary, I'm able to maneuver on carpet, it's just a pain. Hardwood floors make things easier and we got a great deal on installation. They both argued with me about making modifications to the kitchen, but since I have some mobility in my legs, I can stand for short periods of time. I've continued working on my mobility and I'm hoping eventually, I can ditch the stupid chair. For now, the kitchen is staying as is. If we need to make adjustments in the future, we can.

One thing we always did when we lived together was shop for groceries. That way, there weren't duplicates of things. Making an exaggerated point of looking around, I shift my focus back to Jeremy. "Tyler isn't here."

Jeremy punches my shoulder. I grimace. "He will be. Man, you're hangry."

Hangry is an understatement. I'm starving and exhausted. No alarm should go off on a Friday morning before seven in the morning; mine started blaring at five. Not to mention the movers were delayed so all my stuff won't be here until tomorrow, Sunday at the latest. Good thing I packed a suitcase.

"So where do we start?" I ask.

"I don't know, man. We need everything," Jeremy remarks.

Groaning, I head first to the soup and condiments aisle. *This is going to take forever.*

We've made it a third of the way through the grocery store when Tyler walks up to us. "Yo, yo. Good to see you, man," he says, giving me a high-five.

"You too. How are you?"

"Can't complain."

He says that, but I notice a slight limp in Tyler's gait today. I wince, knowing the accident didn't leave either of us unscathed.

We turn the corner and I halt. Jeremy rams into the back of my chair and lets loose a string of profanities. I don't register anything he says, because standing at the other end of the aisle is the girl from the coffee shop. I sit frozen, studying the girl who's reading the list of ingredients on a box. Satisfied with her choice she drops it in the basket hanging from her arm, turns her back toward us, and disappears.

Immediately, I propel myself forward. Jeremy jogs to catch up with me. "Dude, what is happening? Where are you going?"

"She's here." Disbelief rings through my voice.

"Who's here?"

Taking the corner sharply, I nearly plow into an elderly woman. I grip my push rims to stop myself, leaning back a little to counteract the momentum. "Sorry," I mutter, trying to see past the woman.

"It's okay, deary. Maybe don't speed down these aisles. Be cognizant of your surroundings," she scolds.

"Uh-huh," I say, maneuvering around her and continuing my search.

"Who's here?" I hear Tyler ask from behind me.

"The girl from the coffee shop," I call over my shoulder.

"Who?" Tyler asks at the same time Jeremy exclaims, "No way!"

Rolling my eyes, I continue to scan each aisle, but then it occurs to me. Unless she's a thief, she is going to have to check out at some point. "You guys finish shopping. I'm heading up front."

"No way. I need to see the girl who had you questioning your life decisions," Jeremy protests.

Five minutes later, Tyler is now up to date on the coffee shop girl and the three of us are still standing near the cash registers, hoping to spot a girl with brown hair, which seems to be half the customers wandering around. We've been asked three times now if we need help. I'm starting to think that we missed her when I see her round the corner of the bakery section. I tap Jeremy in the stomach and point toward her. She glances up to the aisle signs and then heads down aisle three, frozen pizza and vegetables. My arms pump hard, carrying me quickly toward the aisle. I screech to a stop when I round the corner. She doesn't look up at the sound of squeaking wheels.

I watch as she studies one of the fridges, then opens the door and grabs a small frozen pizza. Just as the door falls shut, she catches it. She replaces the box and grabs a different one. She places it in her basket, and then finally turns and freezes.

"Woah. I would throw everything out the window to be with her. She's hot," Tyler whispers.

Coffee Girl still hasn't moved. I slowly roll myself forward. "Hey there." Her chocolate brown eyes widen as I draw near. "How goes it?"

"H-Hi," she stammers.

I didn't realize Jeremy and Tyler followed until I hear, "Hello, I'm Tyler. This here is Jeremy and this is—"

"Dom," she breathes. A grin tugs at my lips. She remembers me.

"And you would be?"

Her eyes shift over my shoulder. "Um…" She turns back, her eyes falling to me again. "Katelyn."

"Nice to meet you. Do you live in the area?" Tyler asks from my right. She nods. "Do you shop here often?" Again, she nods. "Cool, maybe we'll bump into you more often."

Through all the questions, her eyes don't stray from me. Like if she looks away, I'll vanish. I smile and wink, which seems to break the spell. She steps toward us.

"Were you visiting California?" she asks.

"No."

"So, you're here visiting?" A slight frown pulls at her lips.

"Nope, I actually just moved."

She wrinkles her nose. "Here? Why?"

I shrug. "Why not?"

"It's like moving to hell."

"I've been thinking that all day," I remark, bursting into laughter.

She lets a little giggle escape, and the sound sends shivers through my body. It's the most delightful sound I've ever heard.

"Hold up, it's not that bad. Don't listen to her. She doesn't know what she's talking about," Jeremy says.

"Actually, I do." Her tone grows defensive. "Lived here all my life, and I would argue that besides the outrageous cost of living, California is better."

"Because of the beaches," I pipe up.

She smiles. "Exactly."

"Okay, well, we just got him here and we aren't looking to send him back anytime soon. So don't go making Arizona sound like it's the worst," Jeremy argues.

"Fine." She shrugs.

"All right, can you just get her number already? We have shopping to finish and I'm sure she wants to get home before her dinner thaws out," Tyler says.

I glance behind me and see he is favoring his left leg, which means he's probably in pain and ready to call it a day. I look back toward Katelyn. "Well?"

"What?" she asks.

"Could I get your number? Then we can maybe meet for coffee without these two bozos interrupting." Jeremy gives me a light smack on the back of my head.

She watches us, wary. "Um…" She slides her phone from her pocket, then studies the three of us. She bites at her lower lip for the longest thirty seconds of my life before she closes the distance between us and hands me her phone. "I'll take your number."

I immediately enter my name into her contacts—Dominic, a.k.a. Handsome Coffee Guy—and hand her phone back to her.

Without looking, she double taps her screen, turning the phone off and sliding it back into her pocket. "Awesome. I'll text you." She looks at Jeremy, then Tyler, and then back at me. "Have a good night." She steps around us and heads toward the front of the store.

I spin. "That's it?"

"Enjoy Arizona," she calls over her shoulder. Then she's gone.

"What if she never texts you?" Tyler asks.

"Then I guess we will have lots of house essentials because I'll be here a lot." I push myself forward. "Come on. Let's finish so we can get out of here."

CHAPTER FIVE

Katelyn

Ever since Dom handed my phone back to me it's felt radioactive. It was easy to ignore through checkout, on the fifteen-minute drive home, and walking into my apartment. Now that the groceries are put away and a frozen pizza is in the oven, I can't any longer. I slide it out of my pocket and double tap the screen. I never closed out of the contact page, so his name and number are on the screen. *His full name is Dominic. Huh.* The little nickname he added for himself is both cute and a little cocky.

My thumb hovers over the message icon. Do I want to message him? Where would messaging him lead to? I know he offered to meet for coffee, but I have this feeling he wants coffee to lead to a date and I'm not sure I'm ready for that. My last relationship was a doozy and those scars are still healing. I close out of his contact and pull up my text messages.

I may have done something insanely stupid. I hit send and then wait for Eliza to respond. I glance at the clock and calculate what time it is in Georgia.

What'd ya do?

I roll my eyes. There's no way she's still awake right now.

I need Eliza, Marc.

She's busy. How can I assist? Marc replies.

For starters, stop stealing her phone!

Maybe I can help.

My groan echoes in my small kitchen. It's not like Marc is my first choice to have this conversation with, but he did reply.

Leaning against the counter, I type, *Okay. You meet a guy in the supermarket and he asks for your number but you don't give him your number. You do, however, hand over your phone and let him give you his number. Now what?*

Why am I getting this guy's number?

The oven timer rings as I sneer at my phone. I remove the pizza from the oven, quickly slicing it and scooping a couple pieces on a plate. I plop onto my couch, sliding my plate onto the coffee table, and return to my conversation with Marc.

Eliza wouldn't ask that.

I repeat, why am I getting the number?

Eliza would know exactly why I'm getting his number, I type, exasperated.

You're not going to tell me?

I'm saying I wouldn't have to if this was Eliza.

I'll let you two finish this in the morning. Marc follows it up with an eye roll emoji.

Trading my phone for the remote, I turn on the television and hit play where I left off on *Jane the Virgin*. The episode is half over when my phone buzzes. Ignoring it, I go grab another slice of pizza, putting the remaining pieces in a Ziploc bag to be warmed up later. I grab a bottle of water and return to the couch. When the episode ends, I check my phone.

Is it because the guy is hot? Marc follows it up with a fire emoji.

Sighing, I type back, *Maybe.* I add a winky face emoji. *Eliza will kill me if I talk to you about it first. Thx though.*

My phone buzzes again in the middle of the next episode. *Wow! Supermarket Guy must have been super-hot if there was an exchange of numbers. Smart move, by the way, for getting his number instead. If he's some creep, you won't have to worry about him bombarding you with messages every day. So proud of you for taking the leap, especially with a stranger.*

He wasn't exactly a stranger, I admit.

A few seconds later, my phone lights up with a call. I pause the show and slide the green phone icon to answer and then hit the speaker button.

"Back the train up," Eliza shrieks. Well, she's awake now, and sounding like she's about ready to have my head. "He wasn't a stranger? Who was he, and why haven't you mentioned him?"

I shrug, not that she can see. "It's not like I know him. I met him in California."

She gasps. "You've been holding onto this information for a whole month and you haven't said anything? Okay, details. Now."

"It hasn't been a whole month," I protest.

"Whatever. Where did you meet?"

"At a coffee shop I went to."

"And was this like a short glimpse of him and then a meeting of chance last night or…"

"No, he talked to me," I say nonchalantly.

"WHAT?" Her screech crackles through the speaker.

"He asked if he could sit at my table. I apologized and said he could have it. Then I left."

"Why would you apologize?"

"It was a handicap table. I felt rude."

"You were just sitting at a table. Why is that rude?"

"He was in a wheelchair, and I took one of the only tables available to him," I explain.

"Okay…but did he kick you out?"

"No, he said I could stay, but that would have been super awkward."

She sighs deeply. "Katelyn, you could have just stayed and talked to him. Asked him some questions. What's the worst that could have happened?"

My palms grow sweaty just thinking of the interaction. "You know me. I'm not good at small talk. It would have been a disaster."

"Yeah, but maybe you would've gotten his number sooner," Eliza points out.

"Well, that's not the way it happened," I argue.

"It doesn't matter how it happened. What matters is, it happened, and you got his number. So, text him. Now. Oh, also get his last name. Marc and I can internet stalk him for you. Vet him before you meet up with him."

"Oh, jeez. You're not doing that."

"Why not? Then you'll know whether it's even worth meeting up."

"I didn't vet Marc," I point out.

"Eh." The line goes quiet, which means she's thinking. "Free coffee. Who says no to free coffee?"

"Not me."

"That's the spirit. I'll expect a full report after."

"Eliza—"

"Katelyn, it's coffee. You get to decide if you stay for ten minutes or one hour. If you're absolutely miserable, you can leave. But he might surprise you, so give him a chance. How about this?" she adds. "Invite him to Espresso Yourself. You're there every Saturday. It's a place you're comfortable and you know the coffee will be good."

Espresso Yourself has become my favorite coffee shop for writing. Every other day, I usually stop at Starbucks and grab a coffee before work, but there's something about the quiet of the local shop on the weekend that makes it easy to work. I didn't tell Eliza that I haven't gone since my trip to California, but maybe she's right. I've let my manuscript sit long enough. I will never get unstuck if I don't work on it at all. Maybe looking at it now will spark an idea.

Eliza groans on the other line. "Great, now the only thing I'll be thinking about while lying on the beach this weekend is that I could be reading this epic fantasy, but the author is shy and stingy and hasn't shared it yet."

I shake my head at her poor attempt to get me to share my work. "She's super stingy," I reply teasingly.

"If it's anything like what you've shared previously, you know I'll love it," she says encouragingly.

"It needs a bit more work."

"It doesn't have to be perfect. You got this!"

"Thanks." We say goodbye and I hang up. I finish the episode I'm on and head for bed. Staring at my ceiling, I think of my previous writing project. I let Eliza read bits and pieces of it, and I also tried to share it with my ex. In the beginning, he seemed supportive, but when I expressed the desire to someday make this my career, he changed his tune. *Isn't the world inundated with little fairy stories?*

I roll over on my side and try not to relive the memory. He's not in my life anymore. His words shouldn't have any effect on me.

The next morning, I pull myself out of bed and head to Espresso Yourself. On the drive I practice the wording of the text I'll send to Dominic. *I wonder if he prefers Dom or Dominic?*

Maybe I can ask him when we get together for coffee. By the time I park, I'm no closer to a decent sounding text and I've put way too much pressure on this meet-up. Sweat stains my underarms and I'm not sure if it's from nerves or the extreme heat—probably both. I wasn't lying when I told Dom he moved to hell. It's hot enough during the summer to feel like it. Feeling myself chickening out, I switch to my conversation with Eliza.

This is the worst idea and I might bail on free coffee.

Her reply is instantaneous. *Don't you dare.*

CHAPTER SIX

Dom

Since none of my furniture had been delivered, Jeremy and I made a stop after the grocery store to pick up an air mattress so I would have somewhere to sleep. Every few minutes I checked my phone, hoping there would be a text from Katelyn. I went to bed hoping that when I woke up, she would have caved and sent a message. Staring at my screen now, there's still nothing.

I groan as I sit up, everything aching. I desperately miss my mattress and I'm praying it gets here today. There is no way I'm sleeping another night on this thing. Looking around the empty master bedroom, I try to map out the best layout for my furniture.

It takes effort to get into my chair and I'm hoping one of us grabbed a bottle of Advil or something. My back is killing me. I roll myself out to the living room where there is a recliner, a coffee table, and Tyler's giant flat screen. My couch was the winner in the who's-bringing-what-furniture game, so we're still waiting on it. Tyler, sitting in the recliner, looks up from his phone when he hears me.

"Morning. How'd you sleep?"

"These movers better be here today," I grumble.

Hinges squeak, and then Jeremy appears at the end of the hall. He glances around the sparce living room. "Well, this kind of sucks. I have nowhere to sit."

By some miracle, the movers arrive two hours early and by the evening we have about half the boxes unpacked. I take a break and find my phone on the kitchen counter. I briefly check it to see if I have any messages. Instead of obsessing over when or *if* I'm going to receive a text, I set my phone back on the counter and turn to the plethora of boxes still waiting to be unpacked. I'm hoping we can have everything unloaded by the end of this weekend. The one thing I'm extremely grateful for is my bed. It's like I can hear it whisper my name every time I go by.

When I wake up on Sunday, I check my phone again. Still no text. Tyler and I are lounging on the couch watching television when a phone buzzes. I jump, quickly searching for mine. Tyler chuckles. "Pathetic, man."

I toss a throw pillow at him.

"Why didn't you insist on getting her number?"

Why didn't I? Mostly because I saw how she looked at us— like she was ready to bolt. I knew if I pushed, not only would I never get her number, but I would also never see her again. None of these thoughts leave my mouth. Instead, I just shrug.

"So, what's the plan now? Are you seriously going to stalk the grocery store?" Tyler asks.

"That would be more pathetic than jumping at every phone notification," I say.

Tyler nods in agreement.

A loud clatter comes from the kitchen and we both turn. "Everything okay in there?" I yell out.

Jeremy pops his head around the corner. "All good. Dinner will be ready in five."

I transfer from the couch to my chair, wheeling into the kitchen. I grab a stack of plates and silverware and set the table for dinner. Out of the three of us, Jeremy is the best cook. Tonight is chicken alfredo, cheesy garlic toast, and rosemary roasted potatoes. All of which smell heavenly. The only sound is forks scraping against plates for the first ten minutes of dinner. I reach for another slice of toast when I hear a phone buzz. I left mine across the room, telling myself I wouldn't check it during dinner. Jeremy watches me for a moment and then slides his phone from his pocket. "Not me." He nods at Tyler quizzically.

"Nope."

All three of us look toward my phone. They whip their heads back toward me. Shrugging, I say, "I'll check it later."

Tyler's already made fun of me today, and I'm trying not to turn into a pathetic sap that is glued to his phone. However, everything inside of me is screaming to rush over and check my messages. I might hurt someone if it's not Katelyn.

Tyler hops up from his chair, instantly grabbing the table for support.

"Dude, you okay?" I ask, glancing at Jeremy in alarm. Jeremy studies Tyler for a second, brows furrowing. Tyler fractured his hip during the accident and had surgery to stabilize it. Tyler has always been super active and it drove him crazy just sitting around. When his hip was healed enough he was back to skateboarding and riding his bike. Of course, his doctors advised against returning to activities so soon, but Tyler figured he would be fine. It seems like the consequences of his choices are catching up to him.

"Never better." He limps over and grabs my phone. "I'm now deeply invested in this…whatever you want to call it, and I need to know if it's her," he says, dropping my phone in my lap.

I take a breath and then glance down. My eyes widen as I click on the new message alert. No name, just a phone number.

Okay. We can meet, but there are stipulations. We are not calling this a date. This is just a meet-up. In fact, it's not really a meet-up. I will be at Espresso Yourself on Saturday at three. If you happen to show up, I won't be rude and ignore you.

She follows up this message with a link to Espresso Yourself and directions. I'm on my fourth readthrough when Jeremy clears his throat. "So, when's your date?"

"I, um…what?" I say to my phone.

"I'm dying here, man." Tyler snatches the phone out of my hands.

His eyes scan the message, his forehead puckering as he gets to the end. "What does that mean?" He passes the phone to Jeremy.

Jeremy looks taken aback too. "'I won't be rude and ignore you.' What the hell?"

"Also, Saturday? That's a week away," Tyler points out, a fact that is not lost on me.

"You sure she's worth it? Why don't you just tell her you have other plans and let it go? She's clearly not into you," Jeremy says.

"I'm not doing that."

"Why not?" Jeremy pushes.

I think back to the way she said my name and the small smile she let slip. She's into me, but she's guarded. When I first saw her, all I wanted to know was what she was so intently focused on. Now, I want to know what walls she has built and if there is any way to make them come crumbling down. Instead of providing an explanation, I shrug. "I'm just not."

"This is going to be a long week," Tyler mumbles.

I throw him an annoyed glare. Reading her message one more time, I reply, *See you Saturday.*

CHAPTER SEVEN

Dom

I'm only a few minutes late but I feel horrible. It took a little longer to get ready today. Rolling up to the door, I realize there is a step to get inside. *Awesome.* I roll my eyes. I open the door and I'm trying to figure out the best way to do this when I hear, "Here, let me hold that for you."

An elderly gentleman in a light gray golf cap, hobbles up to the door. With his assistance I'm able to back up a little and pop a wheelie. Once I get my front wheels up, I push myself up the step. I look over to the man and thank him. Glancing around the seating area, I'm ready to apologize profusely for being late. The only person in the seating area is the elderly man who has returned to his table. Across the little lobby, a laptop sits open on a table.

The gentleman catches my attention. "There was a young lady sitting at that table. I think she went to the restroom."

"Thanks." I give the gentleman a polite nod and make my way over. I look around the seating area and toward the back. Off to the right of the counter is a small alcove to the bathrooms. I wait a minute before glancing down at the notes. I skim the first paragraph and then fully read the second. The third jumps a bit ahead in the story and I briefly wonder what happened—maybe I can inquire later. I'm fully absorbed in the small pieces of story when a hand slaps down on the table, blocking my view, causing me to jump.

"Sorry." I swallow. I'm greeted by furious brown eyes and scarlet cheeks. She is pissed.

"What the hell do you think you're doing? You have no business reading these." She hastily gathers her notes, tucks them into her notebook, and then shuts her laptop. She cringes when the lid closes, the muscles in her jaw tightening, before continuing to stuff everything into her bag. Maybe she hadn't saved her work? I know from college how painful that can be.

Way to go, Dom, I think.

"Katelyn. Please, I'm sorry. The page was out and at first, I was just skimming it."

"Is that supposed to make me feel better?" she bites out.

That's it, dig yourself deeper. You're killin' it.

"No. It's not an excuse. But—"

"But nothing. There is no defending this." She closes her eyes, taking a deep breath.

"It was good," I say.

She freezes. Her eyes slowly open and she glares at me. "You don't have to lie to me."

"I'm not. I seriously didn't realize you had come out of the bathroom until your hand slammed on the table. I was so engrossed in what I was reading."

I give her a pleading look. "It was exquisite writing. I would have kept reading." In my mind, I beg for her not to walk out. I have so many questions about the piece I read.

Some of her fire sizzles out and after steadying herself, she takes a tentative step forward. "Do you want coffee?"

"It's why I showed up," I quip.

She doesn't wait for me, just walks up to the counter and places her order. I think I hear her say something about cinnamon. Before she can tap her card, I shove my phone to the pin-pad. The register chimes and the barista smiles. "You're all set." Katelyn walks away without saying thank you. Either she has no manners whatsoever, or she is really mad. I try not to take offense. I mean, I did cross a line. I place my coffee order, a large iced americano with a splash of cream, and then join her where she waits at the counter. *Awkward silence anyone?*

When the barista calls out our drinks, Katelyn retrieves them and heads back over to the table she was originally sitting at. I move one of the chairs, making room for me to sit and then park myself across from her. She sits there, fiddling with her cup sleeve. Faintly, I hear, "You thought it was good?"

I stare at her, waiting for her to look at me. Her eyes are wide and full of panic when she eventually looks up. Maybe I should have just answered. Trying to defuse the situation, I joke, "Are you asking me or the sleeve?"

Her eyes stay fixed on mine. "You."

"Just checkin'." I wink. "Yes, I believe I used the word exquisite. A word I don't use often." I hesitate, making sure I ask this next question carefully. "Is this what you were working on when we met?"

"I didn't make progress." Her voice cracks and she quickly clears her throat.

I frown. "Was that frustrating?"

She shakes her head. "I don't want to talk about the trip."

There has to be something else to talk about. Taking a quick glance around the table, my eyes land on her coffee cup. "Okay, what do you usual—"

"Dom or Dominic?" she blurts out.

My brows furrow in confusion.

"In my contacts, you added your number under Dominic. Which do you prefer, Dom or Dominic?"

Boyfriend is the word that enters my thoughts, but I don't voice it. I shrug. "Either is fine. Most of my friends call me Dom."

"Oh, okay." She bites her lower lip. "Um, how old are you?"

"Twenty-seven. You?"

"Twenty-four."

The table falls silent. *Awkward silence, my old friend.*

I go back to my original question and ask her about her coffee order. She tells me she usually gets a cinnamon roll latte. Her eyes dart to her bag and she takes out her notebook, pulling out her loose notes. She inhales deeply and then extends them to me. Shock runs through me. I swipe my hair away from my eyes and reach for them. I begin to pull them toward me, but pause when I see the apprehension written all over her face. "You sure?"

Her breathing picks up, her complexion paling a bit. She nods warily.

"Hey." Taking her soft yet clammy hand, I give it a gentle squeeze. "I don't have to read these. We can talk about something else, or we can head out." We can do literally *anything* else, even return to awkward silence, if it means she'll relax.

"I'm not sure where you were, they're a little messy." Her voice wavers. She takes a trembling breath and throws out a tiny smile. Her hands are shaking as she picks up her coffee cup and she quickly sets it down.

She looks like she's about to have a panic attack and I'm not sure how to calm her down. "Katelyn, take a breath," I say soothingly.

She straightens. "In about two seconds I'm taking the notes back and that's it. So, now's your chance." I raise my eyebrows.

Okay, little firecracker. She snaps her eyes closed and I listen to her breathing even out. I search for the page I was reading before, skimming over the other ones.

"You reading?" she asks. I glance up to see her eyes still shut.

"Yes. You breathing?"

I focus on the notes again, but my heart stutters when I don't hear a response. "I'm going to need verbal confirmation."

"I'm okay."

I let out the breath I was holding. "Are you going to sit there with your eyes closed the whole time?"

I reach for my coffee, taking a sip as I flip a page. I skim through the last few notes and then slide them back to her. "How long have you been working on this?" The world building and character development is impeccable, and these are just her notes.

She's back to fiddling with her cup sleeve. "A few months. These are just snippets."

"I'd love to read more when you're ready to share. If you're ready to share," I reply, focusing on her.

Her eyes meet mine. "Really?"

"Really, really. Thanks for letting me peruse your snippets. I'm definitely intrigued."

A smile appears on her face, and I'm elated. It's gorgeous but quickly vanishes.

"Thanks." She slips all her notes back into her bag, not bothering to put them back inside the notebook. "Um, I think I should head out. I've got a few other things to do today."

"Oh, yeah. Okay." I undo my brakes and push myself away from the table. I return the chair to its spot and together we head toward the door. Since she was in the bathroom when I arrived, she didn't see how I got in. She steps to the door and holds it open. I pop a wheelie and ease myself down.

"Wow. That was kind of impressive."

"Thanks."

My navy blue compact SUV is closest, since it's parked in the handicap spot. I stop behind it.

"Thanks for showing up today," she says.

"Thanks for not leaving. Now, I know this sounds crazy, since this wasn't the best first impression, but would you please go on a date with me?"

She chews her bottom lip, but then softly says, "Okay."

"Pick you up Friday at seven?"

Her eyes shift to my vehicle, and I'm stunned. Does she seriously think I can't drive? I didn't have Katelyn pegged as the type of girl who would judge me. When her focus is back on me, I'm livid. "I can drive just fine. You'll be perfectly safe." My teeth clench together, and I try not to make another snide remark.

She's taken aback. "What? I'm not worried about that."

Good job, "okay" to "see ya" in two seconds. Pull it together, man. "So, seven?"

It takes her a moment to answer. "Yes. I'll text you my address so you can pick me up," she says forcefully.

I try to end the meeting positively. "Great. I look forward to it. Have a good afternoon."

"Yeah, you too." She turns and walks to her car. I'm already half expecting a text later tonight, or sometime this week, that says she has to cancel. I'm going to have to explain my reaction. I let out a huff of frustration, and once she is safely in her car, I transfer to the driver's seat and begin disassembling my chair.

You're such an idiot.

CHAPTER EIGHT

Katelyn

"This is a bad idea," I say as I swipe a pale pink eyeshadow stick across my eyelid. I glance over at my phone. Eliza has leaned her phone against her bedside lamp and is curled up in bed. Sometimes I hate the time difference. It may only be a quarter to seven here, but it's a quarter to ten where Eliza is, and for Eliza, that's late.

"No, it's not. You're getting out there. This will be good, whether it goes great or not." Her eyes close and I know I have precious seconds before she is out for the night.

"I don't even know what I did to make him mad. What if I inadvertently do something and he decides I'm the worst person on the planet? What if he just leaves me at the restaurant?"

"You aren't, and Uber." She shrugs.

Uber? Like, it's a possibility that he will actually leave me at the restaurant? *Do I even remember my password?* It's been so long since I've used the app. I quit primping my face and grab my phone. Minimizing Eliza's video chat, I find Uber in my apps and breathe a sigh of relief when I click in and it brings me straight to the home page.

"Katelyn, stop freaking out. It's going to be fine. At least you have one question for him."

"Why were you such a jerk? It's a horrible question on a first date." I look down at the right side of my screen where Eliza is now sitting up, holding the phone in front of her face.

"Hey, thought you were sleeping," Marc says from off screen.

Eliza shakes her head. "Giving Katelyn a pep talk. Any word of advice?" She turns the camera toward Marc, who's standing at the foot of their bed.

"Just be yourself. You're very likeable." To that, I roll my eyes.

"It's true though," she remarks, turning the camera back to her. "You just have to let him get to know you. Now, finish prepping. You have five minutes before he gets there. Call me tomorrow with all the details, 'kay?"

"Of course. Love you."

"Back at you." She winks and blows a kiss before ending the call.

Finishing my makeup, I step back and examine my reflection. I'm not sure why I care. A pretty face and freshly done hair will not make him any less of a jerk if I misstep. I replay our last interaction in my head for the hundred thousandth time since last Saturday. I looked toward the ground for two seconds as I tried to calculate if I would have enough time to get ready after work. When I shifted back to Dom, he was so angry, snapping at me about how he was a safe driver. Why would I think he wasn't? If I examine the meet-up overall, he was late and crossed a line when he read my notes. Granted, I left them out, but still. It's kind of a miracle I even said yes. However, sitting across from him at the coffee shop, I felt this sense of security. It made it easy to share my notes with him. Part of me thought it was better to keep my guard up and push him away, but part of me was curious to see what would happen if I let him in.

I grab my black, open-toed heels and head toward my living room. I'm buckling the last strap when my phone buzzes

Dom

This whole week, I expected a text canceling our date, but by some miracle, Katelyn never did. I know I have to make a better impression tonight. I check my phone for the thousandth time to make sure she hasn't reconsidered at the last minute.

"Lookin' good," Tyler comments, walking into my bedroom.

"Thanks," I say flatly.

"Thought you'd be a little more enthused." He plops down on the edge of my bed.

Turning toward him, I let out a heavy sigh. "Maybe I would be more excited if I hadn't almost blown it last Saturday. Maybe I'd be thrilled if I wasn't freaking out that she is going to cancel any minute. Then there is the issue with the chair. Tonight is a big deal and she's about to learn quite a bit about me. Enthusiasm is not very high on the list of emotions I'm feeling right now. In fact, I'm really hoping I don't puke." *Snap out of it*, I think to myself.

"Dude, it's gonna be fine. You know, how she reacts tonight is going to be a good gauge for how she'll handle other things," Tyler consoles.

I comb my hands through my hair then realize I added a bit of product to help keep it from frizzing and not look so disheveled. Shaking my head, I hurry to the bathroom to make sure it's not sticking up. There is one rogue lock and I smooth it back into place. When I roll back out, Jeremy has joined Tyler.

"How ya feeling?" Jeremy asks.

"Like I need to get this over with," I say, exiting my room.

They follow me out to my car. Instead of transferring to the driver's seat and taking apart my wheelchair, I roll to the back and open my trunk. I stand. Jeremy automatically reaches for my chair and places it in the back. "She's going to freak," I say. *Everyone does.* However, if I want her to be a passenger, my wheelchair can't clog up the front seat like it normally does. Now to figure out how to get my chair out on my own. Jeremy and Tyler are used to helping with my chair if we travel together, but not Katelyn, and I'm not going to ask her on the first date.

"Or she's going to think this is awesome. Let her surprise you. You're putting everyone's preconceived notions and your fears on her before you've even picked her up. It's not fair," Jeremy says.

He's right. I'm putting other people's reactions and my own insecurities on Katelyn, just like I did Saturday when I thought she made a snap decision about my driving. *You're the worst.*

I use the car for support to get into the driver's seat. "You gonna go up to her door?" Tyler asks as I sit down.

"It's too much work to get the chair in and out for a short trip and I don't think I can make it walking. I told her I'd text her when I arrive. Think that'll go over well?"

They both cringe. *Thought so.*

"I know the expectation is for the gentleman to go to the door, but if you overexert yourself, you'll be miserable and then she'll be miserable." Tyler shrugs. "Just explain everything when she gets in."

"*If* she gets in," I mumble.

"She'll get in," Jeremy states. I glance over at him. "She'll get in," he repeats.

They bid me good luck, and then I pull out. On the drive over I contemplate ways to unload my chair without having to ask Katelyn for assistance. The best process I've come up with is to lean against the back, disassemble the chair, and then reassemble it.

When I reach her apartment complex, I check the time. 6:58.

I take a deep breath and text Katelyn. *I'm out front.*

CHAPTER NINE

Katelyn

I glance at the message again. He did say he would text when he got to my apartment, but part of me hoped he'd change his mind and come to my front door. *I mean, how hard is that?* The thought stops me cold. How difficult *is* it for him? He was on time tonight, early even. I've never seen him get in and out of a vehicle, so I don't know how time consuming it is. I've left him sitting outside for five minutes now. I quickly send him a message, grab my purse, and head out the door.

His SUV is parked in a parking spot facing away from the building. I walk up to the passenger door and knock on the window. The doors click, unlocking. "Sorry," I say, climbing in and buckling my seatbelt. When I turn to him, he looks a little pale, slightly green.

He shrugs. "It's okay. Ready?"

"Yes."

His eyes catch mine and I give him a small smile. He turns and looks behind us, then checks all his mirrors before backing out. I watch as one hand maneuvers the steering wheel, while the other rests on a control off to the left. The steering wheel has a large knob on the lower right. *I wonder what that's for?*

"How are you?" he asks.

"I'm okay." My voice wavers.

"Look, I'm sorry I didn't come to the door. It's just kind of a process and—"

"I kind of realized that," I jump in before he can finish. "I mean, I guess I assume it's a process, because I've never seen you do it, but it's probably not as easy for you as it is for me. You don't have to apologize or explain. Sorry, I was kind of a jerk tonight," I ramble.

"You weren't. I haven't left you with the best impression."

Glancing over at him, I notice his knuckles are white from gripping the steering wheel tightly, and his jaw is tense. He's freaking out.

"I'm not scared," I blurt out.

His nose wrinkles and his brows furrow, completely confused. "I'm…glad?"

"What I mean is, I totally trust you. I never, ever thought you couldn't drive. I don't know why you think that, but I looked down for two seconds, trying to decide if tonight would work and then you were so mad and I don't know what happened or what I did, but whatever it was, you have to tell me because I don't want to upset you or make you think that I think any less of you and—"

"Woah, Katelyn. Take a breath." We stop at a light. He reaches over and rests his hand just above my knee. "It's fine. I should apologize to you." The light turns green, and he moves his hand back to the steering wheel. My skin feels like it's on fire where his hand had rested. "I thought you looked at my car. It's pretty common for people to judge my abilities. I'm fortunate enough that with modifications, I'm able to drive. I know others who can't. When I saw you advert your gaze, I jumped to conclusions, and for that I'm sorry."

Even after the explanation, he still seems tense.

I glance over and his eyes shift for a brief second to mine. "Okay," I whisper. "Can I ask where we're going?"

"Pita Jungle. I figured it had a lot of options, unless you don't like Mediterranean food. I should have asked what you liked or if there was anything we needed to avoid."

"I have a few food allergies. Dairy. Eggs. Pineapple. Pita Jungle has a ton of options though. Good choice," I reassure him.

When we park, I open my door and then look over at Dom. He hasn't moved. I glance in the back seat but don't see his chair. Suddenly, the back of the SUV pops up. Dom inhales deeply and then climbs—*climbs*—out of the car. I scramble to meet him by the trunk. Using the car for support, he comes around the vehicle. "Surprise."

My jaw drops momentarily before I quickly snap my mouth shut. Dom leans against the car, then turns and pulls the chair closer, popping a wheel off.

"Um, can I help?"

I don't miss the flash of irritation that passes over his face before he glances down at the wheel and then back to the rest of his chair. "No, it's fine. I'm good." He continues to dismantle the chair, wincing as he lowers the frame to the ground. Continuing to use the car for support, he reassembles the chair. As soon as he's clear of the door, I reach up and hit the button for it to close.

"Thanks," he says. He's staring at me, waiting for my reaction.

I blink a few times. "Hungry?"

He lets out a soft chuckle. "Starving." He wheels himself toward the restaurant and I quickly catch up. Questions zip through my brain, one after the other. How is he able to walk? How hard is it for him to walk? Does walking cause him any pain? How long can he walk? He was using the car for support, so can he walk on his own?

"You okay?" We've reached the restaurant and he pulls the door open for me. I hesitate before I walk in, feeling like it would be easier for me to get the door. Once inside, I tell the hostess two.

She looks at Dom and her face falls. "Um…let me go check something really quick."

Dom wheels up beside me. "We might have to wait a little bit for a table."

I glance down at him. "Oh, okay."

The hostess returns. "Is a half booth, half table okay? I can remove the chair."

"That's perfect." Dom smiles politely.

We follow her to a small table in the back. She removes the chair and I take my seat on the booth side. Placing the menus in front of us, she smiles. "Enjoy."

"Thanks," I call out.

When I look back at Dom, his hazel eyes are glued on me. "So, what do you want to know?"

Before I have a chance to answer, the waiter comes over to our table. He is super friendly and bubbly, telling us the specials and asking how our evening is going. Dom is patient, politely conversing with him, but I'm ready to yell at him to buzz off; we have important things to discuss. I quickly tell him my drink order, hoping he goes away. Once he writes down Dom's order he gives us a large grin. "Be back in a jiff."

I roll my eyes. When I look up, Dom is watching me. "Sorry," I mumble.

"So, questions?"

I shift my focus, studying the table intently. "Right. I guess the obvious one is, how can you walk? Or maybe the better question is, what is your injury? Well, no…" Biting my lower lip, I peer back up at Dom, whose eyes are still pinned on me. "I don't want to ask a question that sounds insensitive."

"You won't. To start, I can walk because I didn't lose total control of my legs. I have what is known as an incomplete spinal cord injury."

"How did it happen?"

"Car accident. I fractured the L1 vertebra, which affected my spinal cord. Essentially, that means everything controlled by that part of the spine doesn't quite work right." He takes a breath to continue but the waiter appears again before he can, setting our drinks down.

"Alrighty, what can I get started for you? Would you like a delicious appetizer to start with?"

I peruse the menu, then look at Dom.

"Up to you." He nods.

"Can we get the hummus trio?" I ask.

"Oooh, superb choice," the waiter says cheerily. "And for your entrée?"

"The chicken tikka masala," I answer. Dom orders the turkey pesto lavash wrap and with our order taken, our waiter spins and jaunts back toward the kitchen.

"Anyway, before we were interrupted, you were saying…" I gesture for him to continue.

Nodding, Dom jumps back into his explanation. "It affects hips, bladder, legs…" He pauses, clearing his throat. "And groin," he finishes quickly.

I sit there, not really knowing what to say. I replay the last sentence in my head. *Hips, bladder, and legs. But he seems embarrassed by…oh. OOH.*

My expression must give my thoughts away because he lifts his eyebrows and nods. "Just…fair warning."

Skipping over the myriad of questions that would lead us to a whole different conversation, I opt for, "When you say incomplete, what does that mean?"

"So, if your brain cannot send messages to and from your spinal cord below the area of injury, that would be considered complete. If your spinal cord can send and receive some messages, that is considered incomplete. Then they use a scale to see how severe your injury is. If I remember right, I'm a C or D on the scale, which means I have some sensation and mobility below the area of injury. It's why I can walk, just not well."

"Hence the chair."

"Yep." I stare at him, taking all this new information in. He swallows. "It's a lot, I know."

"Thanks for telling me." I smile at him. "So, what do you want to know about me?"

"How long have you been writing?"

It's like the question was on the tip of his tongue. I bite my lower lip. "A while."

"And you're working on a fantasy novel?"

I nod.

"Are you expecting it to be on all the Best 100 charts?"

HAHAHA! my mind cackles. *Top 100. She can't even finish the book. There will be no top awards for her. She is a nobody, going nowhere. She will never amount to anything.* I feel tears sting my eyes and I quickly shake my head.

"What just happened?" Dom asks gently, reaching for my hand.

I clear my throat, tucking my hands under the table. "Nothing. Um, let's talk about something else. What do you do for work?"

Dom tilts his head, eyes narrowing a bit, studying me, but he drops it. "I work in marketing."

"What all does that entail?" I ask.

"Well, right now I'm working with my team to make sure our branding is uniform across all of our platforms, from our website and socials, to what we present to our staff and clients."

I listen, absorbing every word.

"What about you, what do you do?" Dom asks.

I briefly explain my job. As we continue our conversation, the topic of writing doesn't come up again. The meal is delicious, and I'm stuffed. As we wait for the check, I ask what else Dom has planned for the evening.

"I thought about seeing a movie. I checked which ones are playing and made a list of ones I thought looked good." He slides his phone to me so I can see.

I examine the list of movies, feeling self-conscious about the two I decide on since they are both kids movies, but gravitate toward *Harold and the Purple Crayon.* "I'd be up for seeing number three or number five." I hand his phone back to him.

Once Dom pays the bill, we head back to the car. He stops at the back and hits the button to open the trunk.

"What would you do if it was just you?" I ask.

"I'd take my chair apart and it'd go in the front seat."

"And if you were with friends?"

He eyes me curiously. "It depends. Sometimes I take it apart, and other times we just leave it together and throw it in the back, like I did tonight."

"Do you usually get in the car first?"

"If Ty or Jer are with me, yeah. Why?"

"What if you get in and then I can put your chair in the back?"

To me, it makes logical sense. There is no reason he should have to lift his chair or walk around the car if it's difficult for him.

I'm perfectly capable of handling the chair, I think. He shouldn't have to work harder just because we're on a date.

But I sense that's not always the case.

His jaw has dropped and he looks at me, bewildered.

CHAPTER TEN

Dom

I think my brain short circuits. It takes a few seconds for me to remember to even breathe. Jeremy said to let her surprise me, but I didn't expect this. Her big, beautiful brown eyes are staring at me, waiting.

"Is the chair heavy?" she asks when I don't say anything, biting her lower lip. A nervous tick I've picked up on.

"It's pretty lightweight. If it feels too heavy, I can show you how to take the wheels off." I push myself out of the chair and stand.

"Wait, don't you want to get in the car first?" Her voice pitches up.

I shake my head, leaning against the vehicle. "I want to make sure you can get the chair in the car first. At least this time, and then when you feel comfortable, I'll let you do it on your own."

"You're okay right now?" Her eyes trail down my body, then back up to meet mine.

Keep staring at me like that and we can stand here all night, I think. In reality, my back is killing me, and my legs beg to sit down. "I'm good." I flash a smile at her. "Okay, the easiest thing to do is just pick it up by the frame and push it in." She bends, grabs the left side of the frame, and lifts it up.

"Woah, this is way lighter than I thought it would be." She gets the chair into the back and goes to push it the rest of the way in. The wheels don't budge.

"Shoot. I should have shown you where the brakes are."

She resorts to wiggling it the rest of the way in. "Next time," she says, pushing the button for the trunk to close. "Want help getting in?"

I shrug. "Sure." I turn, but my legs give out. Thankfully, I'm able to grab onto the back door handle, saving myself. Unfortunately, the car is unlocked and the door pops open.

Katelyn quickly steps to my side, grabbing my arm. "I got you."

In another minute or so, I'll be crawling to my front seat. Katelyn may be able to lift my chair, but she certainly cannot lift me. I push the door closed and then take careful steps, trying to keep most of my weight on the car.

"I'm not going to let you fall," Katelyn murmurs.

"Can you get the door?" I ask.

Katelyn scoots closer to me, pinning me between herself and the car. A brilliant move on her part. She opens my door and then steps back a little. I grab the frame and accept her extended hand to help position me in line with the front seat. A hiss of pain escapes as I sit and move my legs inside the vehicle. Out of the corner of my eye, I catch Katelyn flinch.

"I'm fine." I squeeze her hand in reassurance.

"Good." She squeezes back. "I'm going to get in now." She waits until I nod before closing my door and walking around. I use the time she can't see me to readjust, grimacing as I do. *And your brilliant self thought you could do this all night.* I blow out a breath of frustration as Katelyn climbs in.

She buckles up and then begins rummaging through her purse. My eyes light up when she pulls out a bottle of Aleve. It won't solve the problem completely, but it will at least help with pain and inflammation. Right now, even the slightest bit of pain relief seems glorious. She frowns. "I don't have water or anything."

"It's cool. I'll just take it when we get to the theater."

Once I've parked, Katelyn opens her door. "Wait here."

"You sure?"

She looks over at me. "I'm very sure. Sit tight and I'll be over momentarily." She flashes a smile at me and steps out of the car.

"Hey, wait," I yell out.

She peeks back in. "What?"

"Brakes."

"Oh, right. I'm sure I'll figure it out." She shrugs.

"I can get out and show you."

She shakes her head vigorously. "Is it hard to walk me through it?"

"I guess not. Once you get the chair on the ground there is a lever on each side, right below the seat. All you have to do is push each lever forward to release the brakes."

"Okay, sounds simple."

"Then you can just push the wheelchair to my door."

"Got it." She smiles again and disappears this time.

From the rearview mirror, I watch her open the trunk. My mind wanders to the movie options. I'm secretly jazzed one of her options was *Harold and the Purple Crayon* because it was one of my favorite books as a kid. It leaves me wondering if she doesn't like suspense movies or if she's as invested in the Marvel Universe as I am.

A clatter comes from the back and Katelyn curses. *Who knew cursing could sound so adorable?* Still, my heart rate accelerates when I lose her in the mirror. "Katelyn?" I call out.

"Don't you dare move!" she yells back.

It's another terrifying minute before her head reappears and I breathe a sigh of relief. I shift, my legs resting outside the vehicle when she comes around.

"Everything okay?" I ask, surveying her.

Nodding, she asks, "What's the best way to do this?"

"Angle it a bit so it's between the door and the side." She maneuvers the chair like I instructed. "Yep, perfect." She locks the brakes and then I transfer to the chair. Wheeling myself backward, I push my door closed and then turn. "Ready?"

"Yep." She smiles.

As we make our way across the parking lot, I notice her limping. The second we are on the sidewalk, I grab her wrist lightly, stopping us. "You're hurt. What happened?"

"It's really nothing. You don't have to worry."

She pushes forward again but I swivel to block her. "Katelyn, what happened?" I glance down and see blue and purple blooming across the top of her index toe on her left foot. The toes next to it look a little discolored as well. I swear. *This is why you should have been there!*

Katelyn pulls her foot out of my sight. "It's not that bad."

"You're sure? Can I see it?"

"Nope. We're going to be late." She nods toward the theater.

The movie is the furthest thing from my mind. She's hurt and it's my fault. A string of profanities run through my mind. I shake my head, furious with myself. "Katelyn—"

"Dominic," she snaps. Her eyes spark with frustration. "It's not a big deal. Are we going to see a movie?"

She uses full names when mad. Noted. I nod hesitantly and we continue toward the entrance.

Tickets purchased, we head to the concession line. I'm surprised when she declines popcorn. *Who doesn't like popcorn?* When I ask her that exact question, she explains. It's not that she doesn't like it, she just can't have it. She's never sure if the butter flavoring is safe. "I usually bring my own." She shrugs and opts for Haribo gummy bears instead.

As I stop to grab napkins, she says she needs to use the restroom. Watching her walk away, I notice her limp is more pronounced. Her foot must be killing her. I go back to the concession stand, find a free employee, and ask for a large cup of ice and an empty popcorn bag.

I'm extremely glad the theater has reclining seats. Even more happy when Katelyn immediately hits the recline button and brings her feet up. Her left index toe is completely black and blue and swollen. The other toes don't look as bad, but they don't look great. I gasp. This time, she doesn't try to hide it.

"It hurts a tiny bit," she admits.

"Here. Hold these." I hand over our snacks and then take the popcorn bag and line it with some napkins before dumping half the ice in. Rolling to the foot of the chair, I hold the bag inches from her toes.

She pulls her foot back a bit. "Wait, you don't have to do that. I'm fine, really."

"It's not a big deal, and I bet it will make you feel better." I move the bag a little closer. Biting her lower lip, she nods, cutting off with a whimper as I press the bag to her foot. *SHOULD HAVE BEEN THERE*, my brain screams. When I glance up, her eyes are red and she's fighting back tears. "I am so sorry."

"Don't be. I'm the klutz," she says, but her voice shakes. "Can you take these?" She gestures to the snacks.

I leave the ice resting on her foot and park in my spot. She hands over the treats, then leaning forward slightly, brings her knee to her chest. She unbuckles her heel, carefully slipping it off. I don't miss the tear that escapes down her cheek. She sets her shoe aside and then places the ice back on her toes. I reach over and gently rub up and down her back and her body tenses. The lights dim just as she glances over at me, apprehension on her face. My hand freezes on her back. Maybe this was the wrong move. But her eyes shift to the bag of ice and then back to me. *Thank you*, she mouths. I resume rubbing her back and, after a few minutes, she relaxes a little.

Throughout the first half of the movie, she alternates putting ice on her foot and letting it rest. She removes the ice again, which is more slush now, and leans toward me. The theater brightens as the characters step into bright sunlight on the screen, and I notice Katelyn's eyes are wide.

"What's wrong?" I whisper, leaning toward her, my pulse quickening.

"Are you okay?" she asks, worry lacing her words. "Do you want the Aleve?"

The moment I realized she was injured, I forgot all about me. I guess that's the power of adrenaline. A small chuckle escapes as I shake my head. "You should take some though."

"Already did. It's helping."

"Good." I take her hand, lacing my fingers through hers.

Her eyes shift, and a grin spreads across her face. She leans back, tightening her grip. The last forty minutes of the movie goes by too fast. I groan when the lights come back up. A drawback to the wheelchair is I can't walk hand in hand with her. *I hate this chair sometimes.*

CHAPTER ELEVEN

Dom

The second I'm through the door, the television is put on mute, Jeremy and Tyler both turning. "How'd it go?" Jeremy asks. He flips the footrest of the recliner down so he's sitting up straight.

From the couch, Tyler perks up and follows with, "Did you kiss her goodnight?"

"She broke her toe," I mutter.

"What?" Jeremy exclaims at the same time Tyler asks, "How?"

Tyler holds up his hand. "Start at the beginning. You got to her apartment and…?" He gestures for me to continue.

"And I sent her a text." *Had a minor heart attack when she didn't come out*, I think but don't voice out loud. "She eventually came to the car." I detail the beginning of the evening, Jeremy and Tyler listening intently. They are both leaning forward, completely engrossed in the story when I get to the part where the maiming happened. "There was a clatter and then the cutest cursing happened. Then she was at the side of the car."

"So, what happened?" Tyler asks.

I shrug. "She wouldn't tell me. Just said not to worry about it. She did eventually let me examine her foot and I'm one hundred percent certain she broke one, maybe two toes." I shake my head, huffing in frustration. "It never should've happened. I should've been there to help her or just to grab my chair. It's not her responsibility."

"Dom, dude. Breathe. I know you feel bad, but she was the one who willingly said she'd help," Jeremy consoles.

"She broke her foot!" I shout.

"Toes," Tyler corrects, and I shoot him a glare.

"Doesn't matter. She was *willing.*" Jeremy stares me down. "Did she help you the rest of the night?"

After the movie, when I stopped at the back of my vehicle, Katelyn shook her head and pointed to the driver's seat. When I opened my mouth to object, she crossed her arms. "I'm perfectly capable of getting the chair in the back." She, again, pointed to the driver's side. I reluctantly wheeled myself to the door and transferred in. Before I could challenge her or say anything, she unlocked the brakes and disappeared. I watched in the rearview mirror the whole time, not taking a full breath until she climbed in beside me.

Once I parked in front of her apartment, I asked to see her foot. This time she obliged, pushing back her seat and pulling her foot up. I gently slid my finger over her toe but even the slightest pressure had her wincing. She assured me she was fine, but it didn't make me feel better. I wanted to ask about a second date but the minute she put pressure on her foot getting out of the car, she grimaced and the words stuck in my throat.

"Yeah," I answer quietly.

"Good girl," Jeremy says approvingly. "So, when's the next date?"

Shrugging, I reverse and head to my room. "Would you wanna go on a second date after the guy doesn't show up at the door and then causes permanent damage to you?" I call out.

"Dramatic, much?" Jeremy yells back.

The creak of his recliner echoes down the hall, and a few seconds later, he appears in my doorway. "Do you really think it went bad?"

"No offense, I'm done tonight. I don't really want to dissect the date any further."

"Okay, but—"

"Jer," I snap. "I'm done." I wheel myself into my bathroom, slamming the door. This whole freaking day has been horrible, and even though the date went well, it could have gone much better. *You're such a loser.*

Groaning, I slip into the tub, letting the warm water relax my tense muscles. Waking up sore this morning, I knew the day wouldn't be particularly pleasant. I knew walking would be more difficult. Heck, I knew *everything* would be more difficult. Usually on days like this, I don't go anywhere or do anything. It was my first date with Katelyn, though, and I wasn't about to let anything stop me.

After a nice, twenty-minute soak, I get out, take some medicine, and climb into bed. As I wait for the meds to kick in and the pain to dull, I think about Katelyn. Tonight, she seemed more open than our first few interactions. She didn't seem to be trying so hard to make conversation. Still, when I asked her anything about writing, she clammed up. I couldn't figure that out. I mean, she only shared her notes with me, and I was enthralled. I didn't expect her big brown eyes to shine with tears, so when she asked to change the subject, I happily obliged. Hopefully, the more time we spend together, the more comfortable she'll be opening up.

The one thing that has been nagging at me since the movie theater is how Katelyn reacted when I tried to take care of her. *It hurts a little*, she had said, but I know it hurt more than *a little*. She kept insisting that it was nothing and she was fine. It's almost like she didn't want to be a burden.

Her attitude was very different when it came to me and my wheelchair. Part of me was grateful, but a bigger part of me wished this was a non-issue. I hated that I couldn't get out of the car, go to her door, walk with her hand in hand, and then escort her back to her apartment at the end of the night. Then, because of the chair, she got hurt.

Anger bubbles up. I grab a pillow, cover my face, and scream. *Stupid freaking wheelchair, stupid accident*, I think. *Thanks for making me the worst human ever!* Turning on my side, I feel a pull in my back and let out a few profanities. *I HATE my life!*

The next morning, I roll myself into the kitchen. Jeremy is finishing up scrambled eggs and I'm hoping he made extra, because they smell amazing.

"Hey," Jeremy says, eyes focused on the skillet as I stop beside him.

"Hey," I respond.

It falls silent, and I know I need to apologize for last night. I open my mouth to do just that when he pipes up, "You don't have to say anything. We're good." Jeremy focuses on finishing the scrambled egg. "Toast?" he asks.

"Um, sure." I stand so I can reach the plates but Jeremy stops me.

"I got it. You need to take it easy today." He grabs two plates from the bottom shelf of the cupboard.

"Jer, I'm perfectly capable of grabbing a couple dishes." Irritation colors my tone.

Finally, Jeremy looks at me, mouth set in a hard line. He slams the plates down on the counter and I cringe. He takes a deep breath—in through the nose, out through the mouth—before speaking. "I'm not trying to coddle you, but I'm not blind either. You had a rough day yesterday. When you came home last night, I could tell you were hurting, and your attitude was…"

"I know," I whisper.

"When have I ever babied you?" Jeremy crosses his arms, waiting for an answer.

"Never," I answer. Jeremy has always let me figure things out and jumps in only if I ask for help or if I'm in danger of hurting myself, which there have been a few close calls. *Because you're extremely stubborn*, my brain reminds me.

"Exactly." He grabs our plates, heading for the table as he continues, "Except, now we live together, and I see you all the time. And even though it's only been two weeks, I'm starting to pick up on things I didn't notice before."

I pull up to the table. Jeremy looks at me. "Like yesterday, for instance. You were short with Ty and me all day. When you were getting ready, there were a few times you grimaced a little, like your back or legs were bugging you. You were already so nervous, I didn't want to say anything." He shakes his head. "But at the car, I almost told you to call it off. That, or jumped in the car with you."

"What? Why?"

"You were struggling, dude. I doubted you would make it the rest of the night on your own. You also looked like you were about to barf, so I chalked it up to nerves, even though I knew it wasn't."

"Are you serious?" My voice rises and I take a calming breath. "You two were both so positive."

Jeremy chuckles. "Yeah, because we were both afraid you'd blow chunks. No one wanted to deal with that."

"Great." I roll my eyes.

"I was so relieved when you came home and told us she helped you." He smirks. "Even if she suffered a minor injury in the process."

Cringing, I reply, "I wouldn't call broken bones a minor injury."

"You have got to relax. It was her toe."

I inhale, glaring at him.

"We told you to let her surprise you. Seems like she did. Now, when's the second date?"

"We didn't get that far," I grumble.

"Well, hop to it. I can't wait to meet this girl, for real this time. She seems like a keeper." He winks.

Jeremy digs into his breakfast. After a few minutes, he clears his throat. "You know, we could make a few more modifications around here…" He trails off when he notices my death glare.

"I don't want modifications. They were great in the beginning, but I'd like to just go back to normal. I'm fine."

"Dude, I hate to break it to you, but you're going to have to accept that you have a—"

"Enough. The kitchen is fine. Just eat."

Tyler walks in, glancing at both of us. He grabs an apple and heads back to his room. "You two better kiss and make up before tonight," he calls over his shoulder.

CHAPTER TWELVE

Katelyn

Waking up Saturday morning, I smile thinking of my date last night. As I climb out of bed, my phone begins to ring. I don't even have to look at the caller ID to know who it is.

"You can't keep a girl waiting," Eliza says, exasperated when I answer.

"It's 8:34 in the morning," I reply.

"It's almost noon here. I need details. How'd it go?"

I look down at my neatly wrapped toes. Thanks, Google. When Dom and I pulled up to my apartment building, he asked if he could examine my foot. I reluctantly pushed back the seat and lifted it. He gingerly ran his finger along my index toe, and I bit my lip, trying not to make a sound. A myriad of emotions ran across his face; it was hard to catch all of them. Anger and guilt were the most prominent.

"It's probably not that bad," I had said, trying to make him feel better.

He let out a heavy sigh. "Katelyn, it's most likely broken."

"Dom, it's okay." I slipped my foot back down and readjusted the seat. Saying goodnight, I climbed out and walked to my apartment. I noticed his car was still in the parking lot when I turned to close the door, but as soon as it was locked, I ripped off my heels and then hopped on one foot to my kitchen to grab ice. I sat on the couch and googled what to do for a broken toe.

"Hello? Details, please." Eliza brings me back to the present.

"I broke my toe," I say, bursting into laughter.

"You what? Wait, back the train up. How did that happen? I need the whole story."

It takes several minutes for me to compose myself so I can tell her the story. I start at the beginning and the moment I say he didn't come to the door, Eliza mutters, "Oh, this is going to be great."

"It gets good. Just hold on."

She seems just as shocked as I had been when I say he climbed out of the car and walked to retrieve his wheelchair from the trunk. I speed through the explanation of dinner and the drive to the theater, then I reach the part where my clumsiness becomes the star. "I was so focused on getting the chair out and not scratching up his car, or his chair, that I wasn't paying attention to where my foot was. My grip slipped and the chair fell, and one of the small wheels slammed into my toes.

"It took me a moment to collect myself. I tried to hide my limp, but he caught on immediately and asked what happened. There was no way I was telling him it was because I was a klutz, so I shrugged it off and pushed us to get to the movie, if only for the pure fact that I could sit down. The initial shock of what I did was wearing off and my toe had a pulse of its own."

"Did he just let you walk around on a broken toe? What a jerk!"

"Liza, what was I supposed to do? Ride in his lap?" I quip. "He was actually very sweet. He got ice for me and comforted me throughout the whole movie. I swear he would have put his chair in the back afterwards, but I assured him I could handle it."

"Why? I mean, if he could do it by himself, maybe you should've let him."

Eliza's statement brings a wave of irritation. I recall getting to the car after dinner and the pain that had flashed across his face. There was also the fact he almost fell. "He didn't need to," I say defensively. "It was more work for him. Plus, putting the chair in the back isn't his normal routine. He usually takes his chair apart. He put it in the back for me."

There's a moment of silence as she digests that information. "A broken toe. I guess that's one way to remember your first date. How did the night end?"

"We said goodnight and then I hobbled to my apartment." I shrug.

"Are you going out with him again?" she asks.

Besides the toes that will take two to four weeks to heal, according to Google, the night was fun. Smiling, I answer, "If he wants to, I'd go out again."

"Eek, I'm so happy for you!"

I sip on my favorite latte at Espresso Yourself, laptop open and notes spread in front of me. Unfortunately, they're a hodge podge of scenes that aren't exactly linear. Anytime I had an idea I didn't want to forget, I wrote it down. However, I've been trying to type everything up linearly, connecting each scene as I go—to no avail. Maybe this isn't the best approach. I shuffle through my notes and wonder what page Dom was reading and what he found so interesting. *It's comical you think he found something compelling,* my thoughts snicker.

My phone vibrates and I flip it over, a grin instantly forming. *Hey. How are your toes?* Dom messages.

I move my foot out from under the table. The black strap of my flip-flop is a stark contrast to the white tape. I snap a picture of my taped appendages and send it to him.

Did I mention I'm sorry? That should've never happened.

Apparently, guilt still grips him. Shaking my head, I quickly type my response. *Well, if Miss Klutzy wasn't there, it wouldn't have. Really, it's not a big deal. Plus, now I can't say I've never broken a bone. Last night was a first for many things.*

YOU'VE NEVER BROKEN A BONE?! A shocked face emoji and the face palm emoji follow. *I'm the worst date.*

I'm doing a horrible job trying to make him feel better. *Seriously, I'm fine and already laughing about it. How are you?*

I stare at my phone for a minute. When he doesn't reply, I set my phone down and try to jump back into writing. *What atrocious scene are you going to butcher next?* I close my eyes, trying to block out all the negative thoughts, but when that doesn't work, I grab my phone again, typing, *Which part caught your attention? When you were reading my very private notes.*

"Come on, answer," I whisper. His response comes a moment later.

It's been a chill day at home. I think I started with them in a field, learning fighting techniques.

"Fighting techniques?" I say. The elderly gentleman from across the lobby, who is usually here Saturday afternoons, glances up. I shoot him a shy grin, turning my attention to my notes. When I find the page Dom is talking about, I skim through the sparse details. This scene isn't even close to where I'm at in the story. *You expect bridges. What bridges? You'll never make it,* my thought hurl at me.

Swallowing, I text Dom, *You're sure? This is the part that was decent?*

Decent? I wouldn't use decent to describe what I read. My heart seizes, until I finish the rest of the message. *I was hooked. It's cool that she's teaching him.*

I send him a smiley emoji, then open a new Word document and read through the scene Dom was talking about. Maybe starting in a different spot will break the writer's block. Slipping my earbuds in, I hit play on the playlist I created for this project and start typing. An hour and a half later, I'm just over one thousand words. I grin stupidly at the screen. *You do know this is all garbage, right?* Maybe that thought is accurate, but at this moment, I don't care. There are words on the page, and this is more progress than I've made in a while.

While packing up, I check my phone and find more messages from Dom. *Are you writing? Do I get to read it? Or does it remain secret?* Questions are broken up by time stamps. The most recent texts came in five minutes ago. *Would you be interested in trying again? No broken bones this time!*

My cheeks are beginning to hurt from all the smiling I'm doing today.

I'd love a round 2.

Dom and I arranged date number two to take place this upcoming Friday. Throughout the week, we've messaged back and forth. Simple texts just checking in with each other, but I now look forward to them. My phone buzzes again, and immediately, a smile breaks out on my face with the possibility it could be Dom. But it falters when I realize who's calling.

"Hi Mom," I answer, disappointment in my voice.

"What's wrong with you?"

I adjust my tone to sound happier. "Nothing. How are you?"

"Not too bad. Just checkin' in. I feel like I haven't talked to you in a while."

I roll my eyes. It's been a little over two weeks since she heard from me, and she usually only calls to "check in" if she needs something, or if she wants to rant about her most recent relationship or her crappy job.

"I know. I've been a little busy, but you have me now. What's up?"

My mom launches into a story about work and I try to listen intently. As she's ranting, a text comes through. I put her on speaker and check my messages.

Bad news. I'm not feeling great. Don't think tomorrow is going to happen. Rain check?

"Hello? Did you hear me?"

I sigh. "Yes, and I totally understand why you're frustrated. Maybe there's something going on you don't know about. Is there a way to ask what's-her-name about it?"

"I just said there wasn't. You clearly weren't paying attention."

"Sorry. If you can't talk to"—I think hard—"Maurine, is there someone else? Or what is your plan?"

"I've been putting feelers out. I think it might be time for a change."

My mom has thought on several occasions that *it's time for a change*. Usually, I try and talk her out of it. Today, all I say is, "If that's what you feel is best."

"That's all?"

"What do you want me to say?"

"I guess I was expecting your whole big speech about working it out and the longer you stay at a company, the more opportunities you have to advance. Yada, yada, yada."

I inhale deeply. "Yes, I still feel that way, but it's your life. If you think it's time to move on, then by all means, go for it."

It's quiet, so I begin to text Dom back.

"I'll think about it. So, tell me, what's up with you? Are you still writing your little fairy tales?"

"Yes, I'm still writing," I answer curtly.

"Now, now, don't go getting defensive. It was just a question."

Before she can comment any more about it or let me know that it's a cute daydream but not a career—ironically—I take a steadying breath. "I know. Thanks for checking in. Listen, I have an early day and a few more things I have to get done tonight. It was really good to hear from you and I'll check in soon, okay?"

"Fine. I'll talk with you later. Love you."

"Yeah, love you." I say goodbye and hang up.

Returning to my conversation with Dom, I'm bummed we won't be able to see each other this weekend.

Oh no. Is there anything I can do? Anything I can bring you?

That's sweet, but I'm okay. Just bummed I won't get to see you. We'll try another time. Get some rest.

CHAPTER THIRTEEN

Katelyn

It takes another week to get that second date, but finally, it comes.

My phone buzzes with a text from Dom, letting me know he's here. When I climb into the SUV, Dom smiles.

"How are you?" he asks.

Buckling up, I answer, "Good. And you?"

"Really good. How flexible are you?"

I tilt my head, confused by his question.

Dom chuckles. "How flexible are you with plans? I thought about changing it up a little bit."

"Oh, um…" I'd like to think I'm flexible, but others have said I suck at being adaptable when plans change.

"It's okay if you're not. It's just been a pretty good day and I thought we could do something other than wander around an aquarium."

I bite my lower lip, contemplating. "What's the new plan?"

"Mini golf," Dom states.

Smiling, I reply, "I could mini golf."

"All right, let's do it."

When we reach the indoor golf course, I glance toward the back seat, spotting his chair disassembled.

"Shoot. I was talking to Tyler as I was getting ready to leave and I guess I was on autopilot or something because I just disassembled it and Tyler put the frame in the back. I wasn't thinking about this." He takes a deep breath. "Um, okay. Sit tight and I'll get it assembled."

"Wait, I'm happy to help. Just tell me what to do," I say cheerily.

Dom hesitates, like he hates that he needs help. "All I need is for you to grab the frame. I can assemble it the rest of the way after that."

"Sure." I climb out, round the car to the driver's side, and open the back door, where his frame is sitting on the seat. As I slide it out, I accidentally hit the doorframe. "Sorry," I call out. When I close the door, Dom's looking at me. "Sorry," I repeat.

"No need to apologize." He gestures to his car, and I notice the plethora of nicks and scratches, even a couple dents. "It's just part of being a wheelchair user. Dings happen." He shrugs. "Go ahead and set it down on the left side, where the wheel is supposed to go."

While I get the frame positioned correctly, Dom reaches in the back seat and grabs the right wheel. He snaps it on and then adjusts the frame so he can put the other wheel in place. He then pops the back up and places a cushion on the seat of the chair. Once he's transferred into his chair, he shuts his door and turns toward me.

"Ready?"

I nod. As we make our way toward the entrance, I ask, "How long did it take you to figure out how to do all that?"

"All of what?"

"Putting the chair together, getting in and out of the car, all that."

"When I first started driving, I hated going anywhere because it took forever. The first few times, it was, no joke, twenty-five minutes, maybe longer to transfer in and then take my chair apart. Also, figuring out where to put all the pieces was a nightmare." He shakes his head. "Now, it's maybe five minutes. Super easy. It helps that I have a routine to take my chair apart, so it's like muscle memory."

He rolls himself easily up the ramp toward the automatic door button, but nothing happens when he pushes it. He tries again and still nothing. He bypasses the button completely and pulls the handle. It budges slightly but doesn't open. Frustration colors his features.

"Should I?" I gesture toward the door. The muscles in his jaw tighten, but he backs up to make room. Maybe because it's supposed to be automated, the door is heavier. I even have to pull hard to get the door open. He doesn't say anything as he passes me.

"Oh, oh dear. I'm so sorry about that. We've called someone to get that fixed," a lady in a green polo says, coming around a corner.

"It's fine," Dom comments. Even though his tense muscles and pursed lips tell a different story.

The lady joins her co-worker behind the counter. There is a group of three ahead of us in line. One of them turns around at the exchange and notices Dom. He looks at him like he has a third eye or something. I clench my fists until Dom rests his hand lightly on my forearm.

"It's fine," he whispers.

As the group steps away, I hear a few comments about a wheelchair and if it's even possible to play. I growl under my breath. Stepping up to the counter, I say, "Two for mini golf." The attendant plops two clubs on the counter, then glances up at me.

"Do you have a color preference?" He gestures to the ball rack behind him.

"Nope."

He slides a neon green and pink ball at me. "Good luck."

Grabbing all our gear, I turn toward Dom. He smiles at me and winks. "Ready to get your butt kicked?" he asks lightheartedly. However, I'm still irritated by the comments. The group wasn't that quiet and I know Dom heard them. I'm surprised he's not more upset. My face must convey something because Dom shrugs. "Happens."

I try to take his lead and let it go. By hole seven, it's hard to focus on anything other than the fact that Dom is a natural at mini golf. He sinks his shot in two hits.

"That's not fair," I pout. I'm on my fourth putt and still feet from the hole.

"You can do it," he says encouragingly.

After six hits, I give up, pick up my ball, grab his ball from the cup, and meet him at the start of number eight. He reaches up and pats my arm. "It's okay. Maybe you haven't had much practice playing with a disability." He nods toward my foot, my toes visible in my flip-flops. Most of the toes are back to their normal color, except my index toe, which is now a nasty greenish-yellow color.

I playfully smack his shoulder. "My broken toe is not the reason I'm falling behind."

"Some would call that losing."

"Shut up," I grumble, rolling my eyes.

He laughs and wheels himself to the tee mat. He putts and then follows the path, closer to the hole. At this one, you have to make it down the green and then up the little volcano. My ball makes it halfway up and then rolls right back to me.

"The trick to this one is—"

"Don't start," I shout, shooting again.

Five hits later, I'm still standing at the start. From behind I hear someone say, "Can someone in his condition even play the game?" I glance behind me to see a group of guys. One of them nods toward Dom. I try and ignore them, lining up my shot. I put a decent amount of strength behind my swing and end up launching my neon pink ball over the volcano and right at Dom. He skillfully catches it.

"I'll let you try one more time."

"Um, no. That's okay. Let's just move on." I walk over, extending my hand for my ball.

Dom nods back toward the hole. "Can you grab mine?" It took him three hits. I have to quickly stop the next patrons from playing so I can grab Dom's golf ball.

At hole fifteen, I watch Dom nearly make a hole in one. I'm practically fuming. My competitive edge is starting to peek through. I set my ball on the little mat and line up my shot, glancing down the green to the hole. I take a deep breath. Suddenly, hands slide down my arms.

"The trick is…" Dom says in my ear. His hands overlap mine. He teeters and I lock my knees so we don't fall. "To hit it gently. This way—"

I turn my head to look at him. "I don't need help."

He squeezes my hands and lets go. "Have it your way." He sits down in his chair, grinning at me. I narrow my eyes at him and then focus back on my shot. It takes me five tries. Dom gloats about his two hits as we move on to the next hole.

"Yo, look at this faker." I turn to see the same group of guys from earlier, staring at us.

"Wonder if he did it just for the good parking," another one calls out.

I whip my head back toward Dom. He's staring at me. "You gonna play?"

The guys are still making comments as I set my ball down on the little mat and putt. Instead of finishing the hole, I grab up both of our balls.

"Okay, rude. I wasn't done yet."

"Are you okay?"

His eyes flash to the group, then up to me. "No. You ruined my shot." His tone is light and joking.

"Sorry," I mumble.

Dom slides his hand into mine, interlacing our fingers. "That was a joke. Kind of." His eyes drift to the green.

"I think I remember where you landed. We can finish."

"Don't worry about it. Next?"

We finish the last two holes. I put no effort into the last one; I've lost anyway. It's quiet as we make our way back to the car. Dom opens his door and transfers in. He pops the left wheel off and sticks it in the back seat.

"It's a pretty common occurrence," Dom says.

"What is?" I ask.

He adjusts his chair, popping the other wheel off. He places it in the back and then folds the backrest down. "All the comments. The looks. People have their own opinions on how my life is."

"Does it bug you?"

Shrugging, he sighs. "It used to. I don't think I'm ever going to be completely okay with it. I've just learned to not let it get to me."

He reaches for my hand, but I step away. "I didn't mean to mess the night up," I whisper.

Shock flickers across his face. "You didn't. I should've warned you."

I shake my head.

"Katelyn, I do not want you to feel bad about any part of tonight. This is my every day. When you're with me, you'll have to deal with all of this too. I thought it was sweet that you immediately checked up on me. You anticipated that I might not want to stick around and made it so we could easily leave. Even though I also think it was a way for you to knock me down a few points." He gives me a cheesy grin.

There is no way to keep a straight face; I crack a smile. A genuine smile appears on his face. "There she is. Now, let's get this thing in the back and go grab food."

"Okay." I put the frame of his wheelchair in the back seat behind him, mulling over his words. People talk. However, he has let all the looks and remarks roll off his shoulders. Even now, he joked and made me smile. I may hate how people react but I'm going to have to let it roll off my shoulders just as easily. I climb in and buckle up. "Where to?"

CHAPTER FOURTEEN

Dom

"So, when do we officially get to meet this girl?" Jeremy asks, walking into the kitchen. He grabs a soda from the fridge and then comes to lean against the counter. The microwave beeps and I stand, removing the Hot Pocket I warmed up.

"You will eventually," I say, sitting back down. I roll over to the table so I can quickly eat before I pick up Katelyn. The OdySea Aquarium has Fish and Sips tonight, with cocktails, dancing, and access to the full aquarium. I'm supposed to be at Katelyn's apartment by 5:30.

"This is, like, your fifth date. You should invite her over."

I take a bite of my Hot Pocket, pretending to mull Jeremy's suggestion over.

Jeremy eyes widen. "Wait, does she not want to meet us?"

"No, she does. She has a rule."

"A rule?" he says flatly.

Nodding, I try to figure out a way to explain Katelyn's rule to him so he won't be completely offended. I was a little taken aback when she told me about it while we were out for ice cream.

"She doesn't want to meet friends until we are more serious," I start.

Jeremy purses his lips in contemplation.

"She thinks we can evaluate the situation once we've hit the six-month mark."

"What are we evaluating at six months?" Tyler asks, pulling out a chair and joining us.

"Katelyn's absurd rule," Jeremy answers.

Tyler scrunches his eyebrows in confusion. His mouth falls open when Jeremy repeats the rule. "Is she serious?"

"As a heart attack." I pop the last bite of my Hot Pocket in my mouth, toss my plate in the trash, and then wheel myself to my room.

"Who wouldn't want to meet us?" Tyler's voice echoes down the hall. Instead of focusing on their conversation, I quickly finish getting ready. Jeremy and Tyler are still discussing it when I call out a goodbye.

"Hold on, so you're saying she won't even come over? What if we bribe her with Jer's cooking? How could she say no?" Tyler says, following me out to my car. Jeremy trails him.

Incredibly easily, I think.

"This isn't up for debate, guys. I'm sure you guys will get to meet her. You just have to be patient."

"Have you met us?" Jeremy quips, earning him an eye roll.

I transfer into my car and disassemble my chair. Tyler stands outside the door and as soon as I fold the backrest down, he lifts it into the back seat. "How do you feel about the rule?"

"Look, I don't understand it. I want her to come over and hang out. I honestly think she would love you guys. I'd also, eventually, like to meet her friends."

"So, talk us up. Ask her again," Jeremy says.

I shake my head. "Dude, I don't know what happened, but whatever it was, it was bad. Like, kiss-this-girl-goodbye bad if I push." *She would bolt so fast. Whoosh, gone.* "I'm not willing to risk it yet. It sucks, but it is what it is. Deal with it."

Katelyn and I are standing at the edge of the dance floor watching everyone else dance. I'm contemplating asking her if she wants to join in when she looks over at me. "Shall we?" She nods toward the aquarium.

"Sure."

A blast of cold air greets us as we walk through the door. It's still a shock to me how cold establishments run their air conditioning. It's why I had to postpone our second date. I ended up with what they call a summer cold. I've now started bringing a sweater with me everywhere I go. Even Katelyn quickly crosses her arms, shivering, while watching a school of paddlefish. My eyes trail down her figure to her long legs, which look amazing in her black jean mini skirt. I bet they would look more beautiful if they weren't coated in goose bumps.

"Katelyn, are you cold?"

"Oh, I'm okay." She gives me a smile and moves over to the next tank. She's standing so straight, legs crossed, like she's trying to keep all her body heat in.

I tap her arm. "Could you do me a favor?"

"Of course," she says.

"In my bag, there's a sweater. Can you grab it?"

She steps behind me and I feel the straps of my backpack shift. She pulls the sweater out, extending it toward me.

"Awesome, now slip it on."

"Oh, I'm really—"

"Katelyn, you're freezing. Put the sweater on."

Hesitantly, she slides the sweater over her head. On her, it looks more like a dress, covering up the majority of her skirt. Her hands are lost in the long sleeves, and she keeps them buried inside. Standing by the last tank of the freshwater fish exhibit, I see Katelyn out of the corner of my eye pull at the collar of the sweater and sniff. A grin spreads across her face. We move on from freshwater fish to the sloth exhibit, and she looks way more relaxed.

"Thanks." She rests her hand on my shoulder.

"You're welcome." I wheel over to the parrots in the next enclosure, and she leaves her hand on my shoulder, walking beside me. *I guess if we can't hold hands, this will do.*

The exhibit changes to other freshwater creatures. Her eyes skim the plaques listing what animals reside in the tank. Her fingers tense, squeezing my shoulder. I look up, studying her. I'm not sure why she seems nervous. It disappears a second later when she glances over and spots the otters.

"Oh my gosh, look at them!" She lets go of my shoulder and beelines it to the tank where two otters are chasing each other. One dives into the water, and the other one quickly follows. The first one crawls out of the water, shaking itself off as the other pounces. Katelyn giggles. We stand there for several minutes watching the otters play.

The next section of the aquarium provides an aerial view of the large shark tank as well as an area where you can pet stingrays. "Have you ever touched a stingray?" Katelyn asks.

I shake my head. "Have you?"

"Not here. They have a tank at the Phoenix Zoo, though."

"Did you want to pet the stingrays?" I ask.

"Only if you do."

I roll toward the open tanks, where the stingrays swim along the bottom. When I reach the pool, I run into a concrete step around the enclosure, giving kids extra height to be able to reach in. The step is an obstacle for me, though, and I don't trust myself to stand. I'd most likely end up falling in. *The sign says pet, not swim.*

"Well, this is a bummer," Katelyn says, kicking the step.

I shrug, keeping my eyes focused on the stingrays. Just another thing normal people can do that I can't. Pressure on my shoulder draws me out of my spiraling thoughts, and I glance up. Katelyn smiles down at me. "Even if we can't pet them, they are so graceful, gliding through the water. It's peaceful to watch." She kneels, resting her knees on the step, making herself more my height. She doesn't reach in to try and pet one as they swim by, just sits, watching with me. After a moment, she turns. "Ready to move on?"

When we make it to the lower level, Katelyn seems nervous. At one point, I leave her observing an octopus while I venture over to see what animal lives in the tank in the center of the room. A moray eel pokes his head out of one of the numerous caves, eyeing me. I stare at it for a few seconds before glancing around to see if Katelyn has meandered over. I find her studying the facts posted about octopuses.

"Learning a lot?"

"Did you know they don't have bones?" she asks.

I shake my head. "I did not. You ready to move on?"

"Absolutely. Do you want to jump aboard the OdySea Voyager?" she asks, pointing.

"Of course." The OdySea Voyager ride takes you around in a slow circle to view several different tanks full of marine life. We join the line, Katelyn fiddling with the cuffs of my sweater sleeves until she eventually pushes them up, letting out a sigh. She glances over at me and I smile at her.

"Um, what was a career you thought would be cool when you were little?" I ask.

"Gosh, I think when you're little everything seems cool. I remember I wanted to be a teacher at one point." She shrugs. "You?"

"It's super generic. I thought I'd grow up to be a famous baseball player. I let that dream die after multiple tryouts for my high school team didn't pan out."

"And now? Do you like what you do?"

"I do, actually." I pause, knowing she might not answer my next question, but I'm curious. "When did your dream of being a writer start?"

"I don't know. Junior high, maybe?" She chews on her lower lip.

I press my luck with the next question. "And what you're working on now, is it your first book?"

She hesitates and then slowly shakes her head.

My eyes widen. "You've written something else?"

Inhaling deeply, she nods. She opens her mouth to say something when an attendant steps to the front of the line. "Welcome to the OdySea Voyager. You are about to embark on an exciting adventure." A large door opens and the line begins to move. As we approach the entrance, I notice it's a level transition into a staired seating area. I maneuver into one of the handicap spots up at the front and Katelyn takes a seat next to me. She stares at the track the ride must follow up ahead and fidgets back and forth.

"Everything all right?" I ask.

"I'm good."

The floor shifts, and a large floor-to-ceiling glass window comes into view alongside a large tank of water. The guide shares fun facts about sea turtles as one swims lazily by. I glance over at Katelyn, who is now furiously biting her lower lip. I'm not sure if our conversation has upset her or if it's something else. She's been on edge throughout the aquarium.

The first tank slowly disappears and another tank emerges, filled with large fish called groupers. "If we're lucky, Flotsam and Jetsam might make an appearance." Just as the guide finishes, Katelyn lets out a terrified shriek, covering her eyes, startling me and half the audience.

"Hey, what happened? Are you okay?" I ask, trying to pull away one of her hands.

I'm no longer paying any attention to the tank, but I do catch a snippet of the guide saying, "He is one of two."

An attendant stops by our seats. "Is everything okay over here?"

Katelyn drops her hands but keeps her eyes firmly on her lap. "I'm fine," she answers.

The attendant glances at me for confirmation. I slip my hand in hers, lacing our fingers together. "She's okay."

When the attendant walks away, I lean in close to her. "Are you sure?"

"Yes," she whispers. Her fingers tighten around mine and I realize her hand is trembling. "I'm terrified of eels."

The pieces fall into place. Flotsam and Jetsam. One of two. I didn't see a moray eel but my focus had shifted to Katelyn the moment she screamed, which means she saw it. It also explains why she kept studying the octopus and all their fun facts instead of joining me earlier.

"Can you tell me when we move on?" She doesn't look up.

"Yeah," I say, rubbing my thumb back and forth over the back of her hand. I peer up at the tank and spot a large green moray eel lounging at the top right.

Katelyn glances up when I give her the all clear and we've moved on to the tank with the playful sea lions. As we exit, she apologizes to the guide, her cheeks turning bright red. Katelyn takes a seat on one of the benches away from the crowds while the rest of the guests filter toward the shark exhibit.

"You okay?"

She lets out a soft chuckle. "I'm good." She sighs, shaking her head. "Guess I probably should have said something sooner."

"Nah, yelling on the slowest ride known to man and giving me heart palpitations was better," I joke.

She rolls her gorgeous brown eyes. "It's just so absurd."

"Everyone is afraid of something." I shrug, but think to myself, *Eels are a weird one though.*

"Ugh, I'm so embarrassed." She buries her face in her palms.

Chuckling, I maneuver my wheelchair to the side of the bench and loop my arm over her shoulders. "It just made for an awesome date night story that we will tell for years to come."

She grimaces. "Years?"

"Yep. There is no living this down." I wink and she groans. "Come on, let's get a souvenir to really remember this night and head home."

She cracks a smile. "Okay, let's go."

Placing a hand on my shoulder, we make our way to the elevator leading to the gift shop. I let Katelyn pick out anything she wants. She chooses a little stuffed otter. When she's not looking, I grab a postcard with a moray eel on it. Once I'm home and in my bedroom I write on the back of it, *The Great Scream of 2024. The moment you knew your heart was hers.* I tape it to the wall next to my bed. It might be the oddest decoration hanging in my bedroom, but it's the one that makes me the happiest.

CHAPTER FIFTEEN

Katelyn

Lying in bed that night, I keep thinking of Dom's comment. *The awesome date night story we will tell for years.* Years is a long time, and even though a part of me warmed at the thought of being together for that long, what happens when I'm not enough for him or he gets tired of me and my ridiculous fairy tales? Dom knows I write, but I haven't actually told him I'd love to quit my job one day and pursue this full time. He might feel the same as others have, that it's an impractical dream.

What makes your story different? My ex's words ring through my head. *Aren't there several books on the market with basically the same premise?*

I shut my eyes and try to think of something else. My train of thought switches to all the ways I'll fail Dom. I mean, even tonight, we received side-eye glances. I caught a couple people give him pitying looks while we were at the stingray pool. If he noticed, he didn't let on. I know he said that he was used to people judging his life, but I'm not yet. In fact, I want to shield him from it, or at least know how to make him feel better if it ever gets to him. I need to figure out how to do that.

It takes forever to fall asleep, and I toss and turn all night. I wake up exhausted. Sitting up, I look at my laptop bag. I should get ready and grab coffee and do some writing.

Why? Your story isn't unique. You can't even get past the midpoint. Just give up.

Groaning, I flop back on my pillow, but lying around all day is not going to do me any good. I force myself up and head toward my kitchen, brewing a small pot of coffee. While I wait, I load my dishwasher and take care of the dishes in the sink. I pause to drink my coffee and eat a Pop-Tart, then decide to tackle my bathroom.

The sleepless night catches up to me quickly. It couldn't hurt to take a nap, right? Maybe after some more sleep, I'll be able to focus more. *So you can what? Make headway on that* New York Times *best seller? That's comical.*

Thankfully, I'm able to rest a little bit, but don't have much motivation to do anything. I walk out to my living room, searching for my phone. When I finally find it, there are several missed texts and a missed call.

ELIZA: 3:14—*Hey, how are you? You seem to be a little down*

3:47—*Katelyn? Text me when you're free*

DOM: 3:38—*Did you go for coffee today?*

3:40—*How's your day going? Do you want to meet up later?*

I exit out of my messages without responding and check my voicemail. *"Hey, girlie. Just checking on you. Feel free to call me anytime. Marc and I are heading out to get groceries. Yay adulting, am I right? I'll talk to you later."* Even though she ended her message lightheartedly, there's still a hint of worry behind her words.

Ending the call, I glance at the time. 4:19. Great, it's too early for dinner but too late for lunch and I'm kind of hungry. As I head into the kitchen, I dial Eliza.

"Hi, you," Eliza answers.

"Hey, how was grocery shopping?"

"We're here now. What's up?"

Sighing, I reply, "Not much."

"What did you do today?" she asks.

"Nothing really."

"Those types of days can be relaxing. Is everything okay?"

You could share with her what a failure you are. That your book is unoriginal. It's a lost cause, really. This silly dream will never pay the bills. You need to think practically. I shove my berating thoughts back and say instead, "It's just been a rough day. I'm fine. I think I'm just going to order pizza and relax."

"Pizza sounds good. You could probably text Dom. I bet he'd hang out with you."

"I'm not in the mood to do anything." My words come out sharper than intended.

"It's only a suggestion. Just don't stay in your little bubble alone all weekend, okay?"

Eliza has my best interest at heart, and I know this.

"I won't," I murmur.

"Do you have any vacation time?" she asks suddenly.

"A few days. Why?"

There's a rustle and Marc grunts in the background. "You need to hear this," Eliza tells Marc before turning back to the phone so I can hear her clearly. "You should come out here. I miss your face and I want to see you."

I put her on speaker and pull up my calendar. Work requires two weeks' notice for time-off requests. To make sure the time gets approved, I figure in an extra week to be safe. "How long do you want me there?"

"Forever, but whatever time you can get is fine."

"What if I fly out on October ninth and stay until Saturday?" I suggest.

"Sold. Book the ticket!" Eliza squeals. "Oh my gosh, I'm so excited."

"Are you sure?"

"She's already searching for activities for you two. I'd say yes," Marc comments in the background.

"I guess I'll buy my plane ticket." A smile breaks through the gloom. Maybe a trip to see my best friend is exactly what I need right now.

"All right, send me the details of your flight as soon as you have them. I cannot wait to see you. Now go text Dom and get some linner."

"Linner?"

"Lunch slash dinner. Even though I guess you could consider this timeframe dinner now. A senior citizen dinner, but whatever floats your boat."

Our conversation only lasted a few minutes, but it's going to take me at least twenty minutes to get ready to go out. If Dom wants to meet up, we could go for an early dinner. Even if he already has other plans, getting out of the apartment might not be a bad idea. Sitting here alone doesn't seem like the best plan right now.

"Katelyn?" Eliza asks.

"Huh? Sorry, I was thinking I'm going to take your brilliant suggestion and text Dom. Thanks for checking in. Expect an email soon."

She shrieks excitedly. "It's going to be awesome. I'll talk to you later!"

I say goodbye and end the call. Pulling up my texts, I message Dom and then head to my room to find a different outfit.

Dom

Katelyn has been quiet most of the day so it surprises me when she messages and asks if I want to meet for dinner. It's an easy yes from me. I wheel myself into the bathroom to freshen up. When I roll to the living room, Jeremy looks up.

"Tell Katelyn I say hi," he quips. "Oh wait, she doesn't know who I am."

I roll my eyes. "She will eventually. This is going to work out."

"Dude, seriously, bribe her with a good meal. We can even lie and say you made it," Jeremy suggests.

"I'll think about it," I call over my shoulder. I doubt I'm going to but he doesn't have to know that.

When I get to the restaurant, Katelyn is standing out front, a frown on her face. She glances over, spotting me, and the frown disappears. I wonder what she was thinking before she saw me. I begin to assemble my chair as she comes up beside the car.

"Thanks for meeting me," she says.

"Of course. How was coffee today?" I know it's her Saturday routine, and I'm hoping she feels good about the writing she did today so I can ask her some questions, maybe coax her into telling me more of the story or sharing more details about her first story.

Her face falls. "No coffee today. Stayed home and did some cleaning around the house."

"Oh. That's good, though. Everyone needs a day for that, I guess."

She shrugs. "Sure."

I close my door and pivot toward her. "Shall we?"

She nods and turns toward the entrance of Freddy's, a delicious burger place. The fry seasoning they sprinkle on their shoestring fries is the bomb. The frown returns to Katelyn's face as I pull the door open, remaining as she passes. Katelyn and I order at the counter and then find a table to sit at.

"Is your apartment all clean?"

"Huh?" Katelyn looks at me.

"You said you cleaned today. Did you get everything you wanted done?"

She shrugs.

The gnawing feeling in the pit of stomach tells me there's something wrong. It's the same feeling I had when we first met, but now that I know her, I can't ignore it. I take a deep breath, ready to ask if she's okay when she looks toward the counter.

"We forgot our cups," she states and walks away from the table.

As we wait for our food, she asks how I spent my Saturday. I roll my eyes. "I listened to *Love Is Blind: UK* edition for a few hours."

"Why?"

"Because my roommate Tyler decided to make fun of his co-workers."

Katelyn tilts her head, confused.

"There are two girls that sit in his cubicle and they've been talking about the show all week. So, he sat down to watch it, just so he could walk in and join their conversation, maybe make a few jokes. He made a quip about people 'watching trash like this,' but now I guess he's one of the people." I chuckle at the irony, but Katelyn just stares at me.

Oh no, she's one of the people. You literally called the show she watches trash. Way to go, man. "Look, it's... I—" I have no clue what to say to fix this. "Sorry. I don't think it's a horrible show or anything. It's just not something I would choose."

"Okay." She shrugs. "It's addicting, though. I can see why Tyler got sucked in."

"I guess."

Our order number is called, and I go grab our food. I slide the tray onto the table. Katelyn pulls her basket of chicken tenders and fries to her while I place my basket with my burger and fries in my spot. Then I turn and deposit the tray above the trash can so it's out of our way.

I'm securing the brakes when Katelyn pipes up, "I'm all for social experiment shows. *Love Is Blind* is pretty good. My favorite is *The Circle*." She dips a fry in ketchup and pops it in her mouth.

"How bummed were you when they booted Milo out?" I ask.

"You watch it?"

"I would say *that* show is addicting, though I hate that they release three episodes at a time now. Granted, I won't stay up and binge the whole season now, but…"

"Oh, I know. I looked forward to Wednesdays. I hope there's another season." She smiles.

The knot in my stomach loosens a bit. That is a genuine smile on her face, and her eyes look brighter. I relax a little, hoping I can keep this up. As I think the thought, her smile falls a little and instantly the knot tightens.

I'm more than halfway through my burger, while Katelyn has only eaten a couple of her chicken tenders and a few fries. Chicken tenders are one of her favorite meals. If this was a normal evening, she'd be almost done with her basket by now.

"Katelyn, are you okay?" I ask.

Her eyes narrow. "Why wouldn't I be okay?" Her voice gains a hard edge.

Way to keep that positive attitude going. You're amazing. I take a moment, gathering my thoughts. She leans back in her chair, crossing her arms. A spark of anger lights her eyes and they don't drift from mine. "Maybe *okay* isn't the right word, but it seems like something is…"

"Off?" she offers, eyebrows rising.

"Yes."

She purses her lips, shaking her head slightly.

"Please don't be mad. I just noticed something seems to be wrong and I want you to know you can talk to me. About anything, okay?"

She assesses me for a moment before uncrossing her arms and picking up another fry, not saying anything. I take another bite of my burger, not really sure what else to do. If she had a bad day, maybe she doesn't want to talk about it in a public space. As soon as I'm done eating she asks if I'm ready to leave.

In the parking lot, she inhales deeply. "It was a rough day," she whispers.

I glance up at her, waiting, but she doesn't elaborate, and I'm not going to make her. Hopefully, one day, she will trust me enough to explain what a rough day for her means. I've had some hard days, and I know what my hard days have entailed. My gut feeling says her rough day is full of similar thoughts like mine used to have, and that makes me nervous. At least she reached out. I didn't. I shut everyone out and that ended in disaster.

We stop by my car, and she lingers. I open my mouth to tell her…what? That it gets better? I hated hearing that. She doesn't need platitudes right now.

"Dom?"

I look up to see her eyes shining with unshed tears. Reaching up, I lace my fingers through hers, squeezing her hand tightly. "I'm here."

She clears her throat. "I don't know what to say. There aren't really words."

"You don't have to say anything. You just have to know I'm here if you ever need anything."

Nodding, she leans down and gives me a hug. I wrap my arms around her and hold her as tightly as I can. Moving closer to her ear, I whisper, "I'm so happy I got to see you tonight. I hope dinner was a bright spot in your rough day."

She pulls away, quickly wiping a tear from her cheek. "It was. Thank you. Sorry I wasn't super fun tonight."

I shrug. "I'll take you any way I can have you. I don't care if it's an amazing day or a terrible, horrible, no good, very bad day." I smirk, remembering one of my favorite childhood books.

"Does that mean you'd move to Australia with me?" A tiny smile appears on her face.

"Absolutely."

She giggles. "Good to know. I'll talk to you later." She leans down, giving me one last hug before walking to her car. I don't move until I see she is safely inside.

CHAPTER SIXTEEN

Katelyn

I'm surprised when I walk into Espresso Yourself the following weekend and find Dom seated across from the elderly gentleman I see often. Dom glances over, smiling when he sees me.

"Hey, you."

"Hi," I say, looking at the elderly gentleman.

"Katelyn, this is Stan. Stan, this is my…" Dom pauses. "This is Katelyn."

Stan smiles, extending his hand. "It's nice to meet you."

I shake Stan's hand. "You too." I turn my attention to Dom. "What are you doing here?"

"Coffee sounded good and seeing you sounded better, so I thought I'd come crash your writing session. I hope that's okay."

A look of apprehension crosses his face. It's not like I don't want to see him, but I've viewed writing as a solitary activity. What will he do while I write? *He'll lose interest. He'll walk away*, my thoughts scream. I swallow, and my eyes flick to Stan. If I say no in front of an audience, that'll be rude. "Um, sure."

Dom studies me for a moment. "Awesome." He turns to Stan. "It was nice chatting with you. I hope you have a great day." He releases his brakes and then pushes himself away from the table, turning toward the counter. It's a silent walk to the register. I order my usual and today Dom gets their new fall drink, a maple praline latte.

Instead of waiting for my coffee, I go directly to my usual table and pull out my laptop. My hand freezes, my laptop halfway out of my bag. Maybe I should drink my coffee and visit with Dom first?

"I can take my coffee to go," Dom offers.

It's not like you'll write anything substantial today anyway. It's comical you thought you'd make progress. I close my eyes, throwing positive thoughts back. *I will make progress. I can do this.* Inhaling deeply, I open my eyes to see Dom watching me.

"No. Um, no." I remove my laptop from my bag and grab my notebook. Our drink order is called out and Dom picks up our drinks, placing them between his legs before returning to the table. I open my laptop and bring up the document I started a few weeks ago with the scene he had read from my notes. "Can you tell me what you think of this?" I guess while he's here, I can gather some feedback.

He slides over my drink, then adjusts the laptop so he can see the screen better. I watch his eyes move back and forth, my heart rate accelerating with each line read. *You're wasting your time. It's a dumb story. Now you're wasting his time.* He finishes and looks up, and I'm not sure I'm breathing. He reaches over, squeezing my hand.

"Can I ask a question?"

It sucks. It sucks. It sucks. Showing him was a mistake. This scene isn't even attached to any other part of the story yet, so why would I start with this?

Suddenly, I feel Dom's breath tickle my ear. "Katelyn, my little firecracker, it's okay. Take a deep breath for me. Try closing your mouth and breathing through your nose."

I try following his instructions, but exhale too quickly.

"Imagine you're blowing out a candle, nice and slow," he says. "In through your nose, and then slowly blow out the candle."

It takes a few tries for my breathing to calm down. I rest my head on the table, continuing to breathe deeply through my nose. Dom rubs my back in a slow rhythm. When I sit up, his hazel eyes are full of worry.

"Firecracker?" I ask him.

"Um, it just kind of came out. You have a tendency to be a little feisty at times. It seems to fit you. Sorry." He now looks panicked, like he did something wrong. I lean my head on his shoulder. It's just now dawning on me that he moved to the bench seat so he could help calm me down.

"I like that." I tuck myself into his side and breathe in his scent; it reminds me of standing by a bonfire on the beach. There are notes of driftwood, salty ocean, and a hint of smoke. This is the smell that lingered on his sweater on our date to the aquarium. I spent a good amount of time inhaling this scent. Curled up next to him now, the aroma makes me feel more at peace.

His arm wraps around me, holding me tight. "Are you all right?"

"I think so." I chuckle humorlessly. "I guess it's a little nerve racking sharing my work. It's not the best."

"Are you kidding me? I was only wondering if there was more so I could put the scene into context."

"I have more, but what I have and what you read don't connect yet. I can't do it." My voice cracks.

"You'll get there. Apparently, you've done it before. If you want, I can leave and let you work. I didn't mean to mess up your afternoon."

I shake my head. "Can you stay for a little bit?"

"Of course." He kisses my forehead and I freeze. Dom rubs his hand up and down my arm comfortingly. I take stock of my situation. He helped me calm down but I'm the one who leaned into him. I essentially gave the all clear for him to hold me. In the back of my mind, a warning bell tolls, telling me this is not a good idea. He's going to get tired of me and leave. However, the warning bell is drowned out by this overwhelming sense of comfort. Maybe it's a lie, but sitting here with his arms wrapped around me, I feel safe. I don't remember the last time I felt this—if ever—and I want this moment to last a little longer.

"I haven't shared this with anyone yet," I admit. "It's just some silly project and it's not that good."

"I don't think it's silly. Not many people can do this. Plus, if you don't let people read it, no one has the opportunity to tell you how amazing it is."

Dom has a point.

"You need practice letting others read your work." He's silent for a moment. "I have a thought. Do you trust me?"

I glance up into his hazel eyes already staring at me. Do I trust him? We've been seeing each other for a couple months now and he's done nothing to prove to me I shouldn't. I nod.

"You said you had more? Is it in your notes or typed up?"

"Typed." I give him a skeptical look then move and pull up the other document. "This is the beginning."

"Okay. I need you to close your eyes for a few minutes."

"Why?" A knot forms in my stomach.

"Just do it."

My hand stays resting on my laptop protectively. He probably wants a few minutes to read through the beginning without worrying about me passing out, I reason. I remove my hand and take a sip of my coffee before closing my eyes. I hear him shift back to his chair and then it's quiet. After several minutes, I ask, "Well?" Dom doesn't reply. My eyes fly open, only to find Dom's not at the table. He's across the lobby with my laptop—at *Stan's* table.

"Dominic!" I shriek.

He looks up, quickly rolling himself over, leaving my laptop with Stan. He parks himself between the two tables, so he's closer to me. "Don't be mad. I thought since Stan doesn't really know you, he could give an unbiased opinion about your writing."

"And if he hates it and I suck, I still have to see him," I counter. *Or switch coffee shops.*

"Katelyn, you have to stop telling yourself that it sucks. It doesn't," he says sternly.

Both of us glance over at the approaching footsteps. Stan shuffles over to our table and hands my laptop back to Dom. He looks over at me with a grin on his face. "I bet your favorite class was English, wasn't it?"

I nod.

"I was an English professor for thirty years. It's easy to tell when someone loves the writing craft. You, young lady, are very talented."

Dom smiles widely.

"Thank you," I say shyly.

"Is this what you've been working on when you come in?" Stan asks.

"Most of the time," I reply.

"My wife was the fantasy reader in our household. I bet she would've loved this book." Stan's eyes begin to water, and he blinks a few times. "She passed a few months ago."

"I'm so sorry to hear that," Dom says.

"It's okay. My children think I'm lonely, so they thought a pet might be good for me. It's how I ended up with Scout." Stan pulls his phone from his pocket. After a moment he turns the screen, showing us the most adorable picture of an orange tabby kitten. "She's a handful, I tell ya."

Dom's eyebrows scrunch in confusion.

"After Jean Louise Finch," I explain.

"This girl knows her literature." Stan beams. "You're correct. Scout is constantly getting into things she shouldn't be and always watching me, like she's trying to figure something out." He shakes his head. "I guess I should go figure out what she's been into while I've been away."

Stan turns to Dom, extending his hand. "It was good to meet you. Thank you for a wonderful afternoon." Then, he shifts his attention to me. "Katelyn, I may have read a little farther than Dom had asked. The beginning has an amazing hook. It really draws the reader in. If you ever have any questions or want to talk through a piece, I'd be happy to help. I'll expect you here often, seeing as how I expect you to finish so I can find out how it ends." He winks.

"Thank you," I breathe. I'm surprised at his offer to help, and even more shocked that he liked what he read. I'm still reeling as Dom says goodbye, the door already closing behind Stan before I can think to say it too.

"See? I told you. I hope those are the thoughts that live up here." Dom taps my forehead. "You're a great writer, Katelyn. Also, you now have multiple readers invested and dying to know how it ends. So, serious question."

I sit, waiting for whatever he wants to ask.

"Do you want me to leave so you can get some writing done?"

There are billions of people in the world. So what if two people want to read what you've written? That's nothing.

"Hey," Dom says softly. "What are your thoughts telling you?"

I swallow. "That it's just two people."

"That's two more readers than you had before. And it may shock you, but I have friends, and oddly enough, these friends read." He grins.

I can't help but return it. "You can stay if you want. What are you going to do?"

Dom shrugs. "I'll figure something out." He sets my laptop on the table and then reverses so he's sitting across from me.

I stare back at the Word document containing almost half of my story. Dom hasn't read any of this. *There is also the other story*, I think. Deciding to save the completed manuscript for another time, I quickly save a copy of my current work in progress as a PDF and open my email. He gives me a curious look but tells me his email when I ask. I add Eliza to the message as well and let her know she can share it with Marc. Before I lose my nerve, I hit send, hearing Dom's phone buzz seconds later.

Dom gasps when he realizes what I sent him. I stay focused on my screen, quickly copy and pasting the last few paragraphs from the original document to the second document with the fight scene. There has to be a way to fill the gap somehow and seeing the pieces together might help me.

"Woah, what?" Dom exclaims, causing me to jump. He holds out his phone. "This is—did you know about this?" I quirk an eyebrow, and he bursts out laughing. "Oh my gosh, I can't believe I just asked that. Of course you do, you wrote it. Sorry, keep working. I'll shut up."

Grinning, I return my focus to my laptop. I still have no clue how to connect the pieces, but I think I have an idea for a scene that could be sandwiched between events. Maybe I can ask if Stan has an email address and send the documents over to him to get his opinion.

"*To Kill a Mockingbird,*" I blurt out.

Dom looks up.

"Jean Louise Finch, a.k.a. Scout, is the little girl from the book. She's super curious and a total tomboy."

"Oh." Dom's silent for a minute. "Guess I should start reading more if I want to keep up with my girlfriend." His mouth snaps closed, and his eyes widen. He looks like he's seconds away from passing out. It's my turn to remind him to breathe.

"I don't want you to feel like I'm pressuring you. If it's too soon, I can just keep thinking of you as Katelyn." His words tumble out.

I stare it him. Words, I need words.

"Seriously, it's fine," he says when I don't respond. "Let's just forget I said anything."

Do I want to forget he said anything? He clearly is ready to take things a step further. Am I? If he introduces me as his girlfriend, then I can introduce him as my boyfriend. The idea doesn't freak me out as much as I thought it would. I cling to the sense of calm Dom brings and shove the fear that he'll eventually realize I'm nothing special as far away as possible.

"No, girlfriend is good." I smile. My cheeks feel like they're on fire.

CHAPTER SEVENTEEN

Katelyn

The amount of emojis Eliza uses when I text her that Dom is officially my boyfriend is insane. She then sends several GIFs of people cheering or jumping up and down, seconds before her name flashes on my screen.

"Hi, Liza." I grin, answering her video call.

"Boyfriend!" Eliza shrieks into the phone. A huge smile is plastered on her face. "Oh my gosh, I'm so happy for you. So, when do I get to meet him?"

I grimace. "About that…"

"No. You are not going to tell me that I can't meet him."

"I didn't say anything."

"Your face said it for you. Come on, you clearly like him. We could start with a video call and then, who knows, maybe he can join you the next time you're out here."

"I don't know. It feels too soon." I bite my lip.

"You're letting your past rule your present. It's okay to let him in."

I've let Dom in. Maybe not all the way in, but I've been sharing pieces. He's getting to know me little by little, but meeting friends, and then family… That's too much. The last time I got attached to someone, lived in their world, it ended badly. Suddenly,

I was left completely alone, and not just by my boyfriend. Several of my friends deserted me too. There is no way I'm going through that heartbreak again.

"Katelyn, from everything you've told me, Dom is amazing. I mean, *hello*, he got you to share your writing."

Marc appears behind her. "Holy cow, you've been holding out on us. I can't believe you haven't shared this sooner. I need more."

"She has more," Eliza informs him.

Marc's eyes widen. "Wait, seriously?" His eyes bounce between her and the phone. "Care to share?"

I shake my head. "Not yet. This is all you get for now."

"Well, what do I read to help soothe the reading hangover you've caused?"

"Any fantasy book. It's not like mine is spectacular."

"Yet." He points at the phone. "Not spectacular *yet*. I suggest giving it an ending and seeing what that does." He winks and then saunters off.

"He's right. People are going to devour this book. I'm dying to know what happens next," Eliza says.

"I'll see what I can do."

"You go, girl."

"All right, well, I'm going to go do some adulting. Ugh, and then tomorrow's Monday," I whine.

"Hop to it. I'll talk to you later. Just think, in a couple weeks, you'll be here."

"I know. I'm so excited. I miss you."

"Me too." She blows me a kiss then ends the call.

I take some time to tidy up my apartment and do a few loads of laundry. Dom texts me shortly after dinner, asking about my day. I give him a short summary.

How was your day, boyfriend? I text.

Okay. I didn't get to see my girlfriend, though. I think that would have made it perfect. He sends a wink emoji.

Maybe we can get together this week?

He responds with a cheesy grin emoji, and I'm sure the look on my face matches it. I've slowly let Dom into my life. Anytime alarm bells ring, I remind myself that Dom is different, and he is. He's always encouraging. He has yet to tell me my story is dumb, or cliché. In fact, he's always been quick to tell me it's captivating. When a situation feels overwhelming, he seems to know just what to do to help me manage it. He's a calming presence in my life. It's easy to be around him. Maybe, just maybe, things are turning around for the better.

Or maybe I spoke too soon.

When I wake up Monday, I have a slight headache. I stop by Starbucks on the way to work, hoping the caffeine helps. Instead, I feel nauseous halfway through my drink. Sitting at my desk and staring at my computer screen is only making my headache worse. By lunch, my whole body aches and I'm ready for a nap. Maybe if I work through my break since I'm not hungry anyway, I can leave early. I send a message to my supervisor asking if that would be okay and then lay my head down on my desk as I wait for a reply.

"Hey, hey," my coworker Jeff calls out, making his way to my desk. The noise makes my head pound and I flinch. "Woah, you look horrible."

I sit up. "That's what a girl wants to hear."

"I'm just saying, you don't look like you feel great. Is there something I can do?"

I shake my head. "Just a bad headache. Thanks, though."

"I'd be happy to grab something for you. Maybe a nice bowl of soup," Jeff offers.

The thought of food makes my stomach turn and I clamp my mouth shut, suddenly afraid I'm going to puke. I take a few deep breaths. "I don't think that's the best idea right now."

Jeff frowns. "Well, you know where to find me if you change your mind."

I nod and Jeff walks away.

Our office is usually cold and I'm always wearing a sweater. Today, the sweater has done nothing to take away the chills. Since I haven't heard anything from my supervisor, I keep working. To keep warm, I pull my legs up on my chair and tuck myself into the tightest little ball possible.

"Oh, dear."

I glance over to see my supervisor and, behind her, Jeff.

"Hey, I thought maybe a tea would help. I also brought a granola bar, just in case."

That does it. I bolt out of my chair and to the bathroom. I barely make it to the first stall before I hurl. When I return to my desk, Jeff and my supervisor are still standing there.

"Are you okay?" Jeff asks.

I shake my head.

"Do you need anything? Maybe I could give you a lift home?" He glances at our supervisor for approval.

"You don't have to do that. I'm fine."

"You are excused for the rest of the day and tomorrow," my supervisor says. "Please let me know if you will be out any longer."

I nod.

"Feel better." She looks over at Jeff. "Back to work."

With that, she turns and walks away. I give Jeff a small smile and pack up my things.

"I'd be happy to walk you out," he offers.

"Thanks, but I've got it. I'll see you later."

When I get home, I drop all my belongings at the foot of my bed and lie down, quickly falling asleep. I'm not sure what time it is when I roll over, still feeling lousy. It takes some effort to shower and get ready for bed.

I wake up again to a buzzing sound. Realizing it's my phone, I roll over to grab it. My stomach flips with me and I lunge toward the bathroom, barely making it to the toilet before I vomit. For the next few hours, I'm stuck hugging the toilet bowl. When it finally seems safe to move, I shuffle back toward my bed.

I'm not sure when my bedroom became the North Pole, but I'm freezing. I curl deeper into my blankets, but it's doing nothing to keep my body heat in. Slipping my arm out of the covers, I grab my phone to check the time. 1:27 a.m. The voicemail icon hovers at the top left of my screen. When I unlock my phone, I see a few texts and a missed call from Dom. By now he's probably sleeping. I send a quick text that I'm sick and then huddle back under the blankets. I'm dozing when my stomach somersaults, causing me to bolt for the bathroom again.

I officially live in here now, I think, curling up on the bathroom floor, which feels like an ice bath. If I wasn't afraid to leave the bathroom, I'd go grab a blanket. Instead, I opt for the towel hanging on the towel rack. It has to be early morning because streaks of sunlight dance across the portion of the living room floor I can see. As I watch the rays, my stomach tightens, and I pull myself up only to dry heave several times, nothing left in my system.

When I'm pretty sure my stomach is calm, I get up and grab a glass of water, but after drinking only half of it, I'm back in the bathroom again, sinking to the floor. I'm not sure what time it is when I hear a knock on the front door. Part of me hopes whoever it is gives up and goes away. I can barely move. The knock intensifies and I think I hear my name. In my bedroom, my phone buzzes. Groaning, I stand, using the sink counter for support. Someone pounds on the door, and then louder, Dom calls my name. It takes the rest of my energy to walk to the door. I don't even have enough strength to open it. I simply unlock the deadbolt, move to the side, and melt to the floor.

CHAPTER EIGHTEEN

Dom

When I wake up Tuesday, I check my phone and see Katelyn's text that she's sick. I message her back, asking how she's feeling. I'm not too concerned when she doesn't respond; she's probably sleeping. I get ready for work and head to the office. During lunch I send another text, but there's still no reply. By the time I'm heading home, I still haven't heard from her. Now I'm worried. I send a quick text to Jeremy, letting him know I'll be late for dinner and drive instead to Katelyn's apartment.

I'm lucky she has a ground level apartment. I knock on the door and wait for a moment. No answer, and I don't hear any movement inside either. With one hand I slide my phone from my pocket while knocking hard with the other, calling her name. She doesn't answer her phone either and my heart rate spikes. I pound on the door, yelling her name. *You have to find a way in there*, my brain demands. I hear the click of the deadbolt and try the door.

"Katelyn?" I call as I swing the door open. She is lying on the floor beside the door. "Oh my gosh, Katelyn."

I quickly lower myself down to the floor. Brushing stray strands of hair out of her eyes, I graze her skin. Pressing my palm to her forehead feels like I'm resting my hand on a brick wall that's been baking in the Arizona sun all day. I turn my hand over. "You're burning up."

"I said I was sick." She sounds like she swallowed gravel.

"What can I do? Do you want some water?"

She shakes her head. "Can't keep it down."

Groaning, Katelyn pushes herself up on shaky arms and heaves. I scoot back, anticipating vomit that doesn't come. She heaves several times before working up a minuscule amount of bile. When I look down at the tiny puddle, it's tinted red.

"Katelyn, when was the last time you had anything to drink?"

She shrugs, shivering violently.

"When's the last time you peed?"

She looks appalled by the question, but I don't care if I embarrass her right now. "Seriously, Katelyn, this is important. When was the last time you went to the bathroom?"

Closing her eyes, she purses her lips. "Yesterday?"

"You're sure?"

"I don't know," she mumbles. Her eyes remain closed and her breathing evens out.

I send a quick text to Jeremy and then hit the little phone icon.

"Yo, how's Katelyn?" Jeremy asks.

"I sent you directions to her apartment. She's bad and I can't get her to the car on my own."

I HATE this chair. Way to be helpful in a crisis, my thoughts quip.

"Sit tight. I'll be right there." Jeremy ends the call.

I climb back into my chair, wheeling myself to her kitchen. I grab a few paper towels and mop up the bile. Another shiver runs through her and she curls into a ball. I ease myself down beside her, trying to keep her warm with my body heat. I glance around the living room, but there is nothing to cover her up. After several minutes, I can't stand watching her shake. Pulling myself up to my chair, I wheel to her room, spotting a blanket on her bed. I've just entered her room when I hear a knock.

I breathe a sigh of relief as Jeremy peeks his head in. I back out of her room.

"Thank goodness! She's freezing. Can you grab the blanket off her bed and then pick her up? We need to get her to the ER."

"Sure."

Jeremy disappears into her bedroom. When he returns he's carrying a tote and the blanket.

"What's in the bag?" I ask.

"This probably won't earn me brownie points, but I grabbed her a change of clothes. I figured if she's admitted she might want clean clothes at some point." He shrugs, sets the tote and the blanket in my lap, and then scoops Katelyn into his arms.

I don't hear Katelyn's question, just Jeremy answering, "I'm the legs."

The response must not be what she wanted to hear because suddenly Jeremy is apologizing. He quickly glances at me, raising his eyebrows. *Yep, my little firecracker.*

"Seriously, why are you here?" Katelyn demands, sounding like she has smoked a pack a day for the last twenty years. It's disturbing. I open the front door for them.

"Just lending a helping hand," he answers, stepping outside.

Closing the door, I realize I have no way to lock it. It's probably not the best idea to leave the door unlocked all night. "Katelyn, where are your keys?"

"In my purse," she whispers, just as Jeremy utters a profanity.

"What?" I ask, eyes darting to Katelyn.

"I drove my truck which you can't climb into." Jeremy's truck is lifted, making it nearly impossible to climb into. I'm willing to figure something out in this situation, though. Katelyn's complexion is pale, her lips are chapped, and I have no idea when the last time she attempted to drink water was. If she keeps dry heaving, only to expel what little fluid she has, she's going to be in trouble. She's already in trouble. I want to get her to the ER—now.

Jeremy steps back into the apartment. I'm impressed Jeremy was able to get the door open and not drop Katelyn, but then he lays her down on the sofa, disappearing into her room.

"Dude, what are you doing?" I yell.

He comes out holding a brown leather purse. "Is this it?"

Katelyn glances up, nodding.

"Do you care if I grab the keys out?"

She shakes her head. Jeremy rifles through her purse, pulling out keys with a little pink fluff ball attached to them. He tosses them to me, loops her purse on his arm, and then lifts her up again. He looks at me and says, "We're going to make sure she's taken care of. Breathe."

I lock the door and turn to see Jeremy standing by my car.

"I've got to work tonight. Figured it'd be best to take two cars. I'll follow you." I open the passenger door for Jeremy. He sets Katelyn in the passenger seat and takes the blanket from me, draping it over Katelyn's legs. Shutting the door, he turns to me. "I'll follow you to the hospital. Need help with the chair?"

"Can you just stick it in the back?" I ask, wheeling myself to the driver's side.

I transfer to my seat and then Jeremy slides my chair in the back of my SUV, tapping the door twice, letting me know I'm good to go.

Katelyn sleeps most of the way there. I see the sign to the entrance of the emergency room when she stirs, moaning.

"We're almost there."

"I'm going to be sick." She wraps her arms around her stomach.

I should have had Jeremy grab a plastic bag or something. "That's okay. Everything's washable." *Or replaceable.*

She shakes her head and a little whimper escapes her mouth.

I turn into the parking lot and pull over. Katelyn opens the door and leans out, dry heaving. I reach over, rubbing her back. From this angle, I can't see if she actually vomited. I haven't heard the tell-tale splatter. It's not like she has anything in her system, but her body seems to think otherwise as it tries to work out what's not there. My phone buzzes and I hit answer on my car screen.

"Everything okay?" Jeremy's voice fills the cab. He pulled up behind us when we stopped.

"We're going to be a minute. You can go park. We'll be there soon."

I end the call as Katelyn sits up and Jeremy passes us. She shuts the door, pulling her legs to her chest and resting her head on her knees. I wait a moment before continuing to the entrance where Jeremy waits for us.

"What are you doing?" she asks.

"You're going to get checked in. I'm going to park and I'll meet you in there." I stop in front of the double doors to let her out.

She bites her lower lip. "I don't want to go in alone."

"Jeremy will be with you," I say encouragingly.

Shaking her head, she says, "I don't want Jeremy. I want you."

Her pleading eyes have me directing Jeremy to the back seat. He gives me a perplexed look through the passenger window, but steps to the back and gets in.

Thankfully, there is a handicap spot close to the entrance. As I park, I ask Jeremy to grab my chair. He wheels it over and then goes to get Katelyn.

We spend over six hours in the emergency room. Jeremy stayed with us until he had to leave for work. Once Katelyn was in an exam bay, doctors gave her fluids through an IV. As they inserted the needle, I thought I was going to pass out. It's not that I have a problem with needles—I've been poked and prodded plenty with my time in the hospital—but something about watching them stick Katelyn made me instantly lightheaded. The nurse came in and made sure she kept down a glass of water before drawing up the discharge papers.

As we wait for them to release her, she slides her hand into mine. "Thanks for being here."

"Of course. You ready to go home?"

She bites her lower lip.

"What's wrong?"

"What if I have to come back here?" she whispers.

And you can't get me here is what she doesn't have to say. It's obvious. It stings a little that it's even a thought.

"Hey." She reaches up, smoothing the creases in my forehead. "I didn't mean to upset you. You were amazing tonight. I'm sure if Jeremy couldn't make it, you would have figured something out."

Yep, called 911, I think. *You suck!* What's worse is that even if my mobility was better, it's not like I would have been able to carry her. We would have been in the same position. *I hate this!*

"Would you be okay coming to my house? I'll be there and my roommates will be around just in case something happens."

"You sure?"

I smile. "Absolutely."

Before my accident, there wouldn't have been a need for anyone else. I would be able to take care of her all on my own. It's infuriating that I need someone else now. I'm grateful for my roommates and the fact they will stop what they are doing at the drop of a hat to help. I just really wish I didn't *need* help.

Katelyn is able to walk to the car on her own. When we pull up to my house, she waits until my chair is assembled to get out. I grab the bag Jeremy packed for her out of the back and wheel around to her. She rolls her blanket into a little ball and tucks it under one arm and then rests the other on my shoulder.

Glancing down, she says, "I have that same tote."

"This is yours. Um, Jeremy preemptively grabbed clothes for you."

"He *what*?" she rasps. Her grip tightens on my shoulder. "He had no right."

"Sorry," I say, wheeling slowly to the house, going her speed. I look up and her jaw is clenched, brows furrowed. When we walk inside, the house is quiet. As I shut the front door, Tyler steps out of his room.

"Hey." He nods at me. "Hi, Katelyn. How ya feeling?"

"I want to sit down." Her hand slips from my shoulder and she all but falls onto the couch.

"I made up the couch just in case it was weird to share a bed, plus germs," Tyler explains to me. "Um, we had some Gatorade so I put that in the fridge and I picked up some Sprite and crackers. Oh…" He snaps his fingers and walks out of the room.

While he's gone, I wheel over to the couch. Katelyn's lying on the couch, huddled under the blanket, fast asleep. I sweep a couple stray hairs away from her face. I rest my palm on her burning forehead and realize we don't have a thermometer.

Footsteps echo down the hall and Tyler reappears. He hands me a package. A thermometer. One of the fancy ones that just glides over the person's forehead. I almost want to laugh with how prepared he was.

Thanks, I mouth.

"I'm going to bed, but let me know if you need anything else, 'kay?"

I nod.

I seriously have the best roommates.

CHAPTER NINETEEN

Katelyn

I wake up to a mostly silent house. The only sound is hushed voices coming from down the hall. I sit up, glancing around the mostly dark living room. A small table lamp illuminates the space. The last time I remember being awake, Dom was sitting at the table in the middle of a virtual meeting, sunlight steaming through the windows. I got up to use the restroom and on my way back to the couch, Dom put himself on mute and asked how I was feeling. I shrugged and laid back down. Looking toward the window now, it's pitch black.

Now that I'm more coherent, I'm ravenous and I feel disgusting. My hair's oily and when I run my fingers through it, they keep snagging on tangles. I also feel like there is a layer of dry sweat coating my skin, which is odd because I've felt like I've been stuck in the Arctic since Monday night. Even though it was a major violation on Jeremy's part to go through my things and pack a bag, I'm super grateful I have clean clothes. I locate my bag leaning against the side of the couch and head to the bathroom. Once there, I look under the cabinet for a towel, but all I find is a first aid kit and cleaning supplies. Sighing, I open the door to find Jeremy standing in his doorway.

"Hey, how ya feeling?" he asks.

"A little better. Um, would it be okay if I showered?"

"Totally."

"Where can I find a towel?"

"Oh, right." Jeremy steps into the hall and opens the little closet opposite his room, pulling out a towel and washrag and handing them to me. He grabs out a toothbrush too. "Feel free to use whatever products are in the shower. Sorry, they all have a manly scent. Uh, there's a comb here as well," he says, pointing to a wide-tooth comb in the medicine cabinet. "If you need anything else, just knock. Do want me to wake Dom?"

"No, he had a long day. He should rest." After spending last night in the hospital with me and then working all day, he needs his sleep. I move to close the door but stop myself.

"Jeremy?"

He turns.

"Thanks for this." I hold up the tote bag.

"You're welcome."

I shower, letting the hot water chase away the chills. After I'm clean, I head to the kitchen, grabbing a can of Sprite and a bottle of water from the fridge. I look around for the crackers, opening a few cupboards, but don't find them anywhere.

I go back to Jeremy's room, knocking on the doorframe. He glances up from his phone. "What's up?"

"Someone mentioned crackers yesterday. Do you know where they are?"

"Yeah." He climbs off his bed and I follow him to the kitchen. He opens the pantry door and pulls out a box of Ritz crackers, handing them to me. I take a sleeve out.

"Is it okay if I take these to the couch?"

"Of course."

Jeremy follows me to the living room. He grabs two remotes from the television stand and hands them to me. "The skinny one is for the volume on the sound bar, and the other one is for the TV. We all have subscriptions to different streaming services so there's plenty to watch."

"Thanks."

Jeremy leaves the living room, and I hear dishes clank in the kitchen. I navigate to Amazon.

"Jeremy, would it be okay if I signed in under my account?" I call out. "Amazon," I clarify.

"Go for it," he calls back.

I sign in and find the episode of *Jane the Virgin* I left off on. I grab my phone to check the time. A little after one in the morning. The voicemail icon sits at the top left corner of my phone. I click on it hesitantly. My supervisor called to see where I was and if I was coming in. I've been sleeping most of the day, I didn't even think about work.

"Oh my gosh," I breathe.

"What's wrong?" Jeremy asks, taking a seat in the recliner. Concern flickers across his face.

"Um, work. I didn't call out."

"Uh-oh. Did you call out yesterday? Maybe they'll assuming you're still sick." He shrugs.

"I was told to take yesterday to recoup. I wasn't excused for today." Tears well in my eyes.

"I'm sure if you explain the situation, they will understand. Plus, you have all the paperwork from the hospital. I wouldn't worry too much."

I swipe away the tears and glance over at him. "It's gonna be fine," he assures me.

Nodding, I hit play. Whether it will be okay or not, I can't do anything right now. The narrator recounts what happened in the last episode. Jeremy reclines with his bowl of ice cream.

I pause the show and look over at him. "Did Dom tell you to babysit me?"

Jeremy looks over, confused. "No."

"Are you usually up this late?"

Jeremy chuckles. "Yep. I go to bed around eight or nine in the morning."

"Why?"

"I work overnights as a security guard for a corporate building in downtown Phoenix. I have the night off."

"Oh." I hit play and the narrator continues.

"Wait, what's happening?" Jeremy asks after the recap.

"It's a little hard to catch you up on. Are you going to be out here for a bit?" I ask.

"Oh, I can head back to my room."

The crackers seem to be staying down; however, my stomach still feels a little queasy. I'm hoping it's just nerves, the memory of puking fresh in my mind. I set the crackers down and take a small sip of my Sprite. "Um, do you mind hanging out here for a bit?" I don't really like being by myself, but I don't want to admit that.

"You sure?"

I navigate back to the pilot episode. "Yeah, let's catch you up." I hit play and then lie down, pulling the blanket up to my chin. A shiver runs down my spine.

"Have you checked your temperature recently?" Jeremy asks.

I shake my head.

Jeremy reaches over and grabs the thermometer. He hits the power button, waiting for a little beep. "May I?"

I nod.

He glides the thermometer across my forehead until it beeps again. "100.2," he says excitedly.

I grimace.

"What's that face for? This is an improvement from earlier this evening."

"It is?" I've been out of it the past twenty-four hours. I have no idea what my temperature has been.

"Last Dom checked it was 101.6. He was starting to wonder if we should take you back in. He'll be relieved to know it's gone down."

We turn our attention back toward the television. Halfway through the episode, Jeremy looks over at me. "Wait, so when does the twin come in?" he asks, referencing the recap from the episode I started.

"Which twin?" I raise my eyebrows, knowing there are a couple sets of twins that make an appearance throughout the seasons.

"So, there really is a lot to catch up on."

"You can thank me later." I wink.

The episode ends with Roman Zazo being impaled by an ice sculpture. Jeremy gasps, as does Dom, who has rolled up behind me.

"What are you guys watching?" Dom asks, rolling over to the side of the couch. He sets his brakes and then takes a couple steps, sitting at the other end of the couch. I slide next to him. He wraps his arm around my shoulder and I tuck myself into his side, inhaling his ocean campfire scent. I briefly wonder what shower products he has in his bathroom and if that's what I smell, or if it's cologne or something else.

Realizing that it's probably somewhere around two in the morning, I sit up, looking at Dom. "Were we too loud? Did I wake you up?"

"You didn't. I just woke up and heard voices. Thought I'd come check on you." His hazel eyes examine me. "Looks like you're clean. How are you feeling?"

"I don't know. Better, I think." My stomach seems to have settled, judging by the fact that I'm still hungry. I reach over, grabbing the sleeve of Ritz and nibble on another cracker.

"Her temperature is down too," Jeremy adds.

"That's good," Dom remarks, bending to plant a kiss on my forehead. "What are you watching?"

"*Jane the Virgin.* Jeremy has a bit of catching up to do."

"Dude, this show is insane, and this is just the first episode. Honestly, I don't even think we could catch you up for the second one. I mean, we could, but a summary would leave out too many details."

"I think I'll survive," Dom quips.

"Will he?" Jeremy looks at me.

I shake my head.

Jeremy reaches over, grabbing the remote and restarting the pilot.

"You guys don't have to watch it again. Just keep going."

"You don't understand. It's better if we just rewatch it," Jeremy explains.

"I think we're taking over Katelyn's space. Maybe we should ask her if she wants to rewatch it or if she wants to rest."

Both of them look at me. I glance between them, pulling another cracker from the sleeve. With Dom here, I feel more relaxed. I pull my blanket over my legs and snuggle closer to him. "You guys can stay."

The first episode ends and the recap into episode two starts. I stand, and Jeremy reaches for the remote.

"You can keep watching. I'll be right back."

"Is everything all right?" Dom asks. Concern flickers across his face.

"Yeah, just gotta go to the bathroom."

Out of the corner of my eye, I see Jeremy do a celebratory fist pump. I look over, perplexed.

"You have to pee. Yay!"

"Um, why does that need to be celebrated?"

"We celebrate these things in this house. Like when someone needs to use the bathroom or even when someone doesn't." He winks at Dom. "We don't shy away from bodily functions."

I definitely need more information but my bladder signals a longer explanation will have to wait. When I return to the couch, Jeremy's not in the room and the show is paused. I hear commotion in the kitchen. I settle back down next to Dom and he wraps his arm around me.

"So, do you really celebrate when someone goes to the bathroom?"

Dom chuckles. "Not *every* time, but when it's a big deal, yeah. Like, in this situation, you were so dehydrated, it's been a bit since you've peed. Going to the bathroom means you're getting better. Yay." He smiles.

I wrinkle my eyebrows. "Why can't we just acknowledge that I'm getting better? Why do bodily functions have to be involved?"

Dom sighs. "After the accident there were quite a few instances where bodily functions marked getting better. It became a thing we recognized. It started when Tyler was finally able to poop. He'd been miserable and on a ton of pain meds which left him really constipated. One day he walked out of the bathroom with a huge grin on his face. He sat down and made a comment about feeling lighter. Jer and I both high-fived him. In my case, it wasn't the fact that I couldn't go, it was the fact that I couldn't stop going."

I stare at him, completely confused.

"I don't have much sensation in that area. It makes it impossible to hold it. The not so glamorous side of my injury." Dom's eyes dart away and then back. "So, if I had an outing or a day where I didn't have an accident, we celebrated."

Jeremy comes back, plopping down in the recliner. "It's weird, we know. After going through what Dom and Ty have, you just roll with it. Make something that sucks into a positive."

"So, wait. Can you hold it now?"

Dom shakes his head. "Not like you can 'hold it.' I had a procedure a little over a year ago to help with that particular issue."

"Oh," I whisper.

"We went a little overboard after his recovery," Jeremy says. "There may have been a cake involved."

Dom's cheeks flush red and he laughs. "It was ridiculous."

"So, congrats on having to pee." Jeremy holds up his hand.

It may be the most ludicrous reason to give someone a high-five, but I can't stop the smile that spreads across my face and do it anyway. I giggle a little. "This is so weird."

"You get used to it," Dom whispers. I cuddle back into his side and we start the episode.

Dom starts dozing off midway through the episode. I shake him awake and tell him to go to bed, pausing the show so he doesn't miss anything.

"Ugh, now I'm gonna have to wait for him," Jeremy pouts.

He sticks his tongue out at Jeremy before turning to me. "Do you need anything?"

"No, I'm okay for now. Sleep good." I kiss his cheek and scoot over.

He climbs back into his chair. "I'm the first door on the right, if you need me."

"Thanks. I'll see you in the morning."

The first thing I do when I wake up is call work and apologize for the oversight yesterday. I let them know that I will not be in today, but I will most assuredly be there Friday.

On Dom's lunch break, he takes me back to my apartment. He escorts me up to my front door, handing me my keys.

"Thanks for taking such good care of me these last few days," I say.

"Absolutely. I'm glad you're feeling better. I hate to leave you, but I have a meeting I need to get back for."

"I'll text you later." I smile.

"You better." His face lights up with a smile of his own. He pushes himself backwards, eyes on me. "Have a restful afternoon, Firecracker."

"Be productive," I say.

He pivots toward his car. I watch, waving as he backs out. He glances over, seeing me in the doorway, giving me a wave back. Closing my door, I take a deep breath. I just spent two nights at Dom's. Eventually, I figured I'd meet Dom's roommates, I just wasn't expecting it to be this soon, and definitely not when I thought I was halfway to death's door. The few times I was coherent enough to watch them interact with each other, I saw a sense of brotherhood there. They all really care for each other, and the moment Dom brought me in, it was like I was just part of their little family too.

You know that won't last long. They'll eventually disappear like everyone does.

CHAPTER TWENTY

Katelyn

Walking into Espresso Yourself, I wave at Stan as I order my usual and then head over to my typical table. After twenty minutes of staring at my screen with no progress made, I glance over at Stan. He did mention if I ever needed help, he would be happy to assist. I swallow my nerves and slowly walk over to Stan's table.

"Excuse me," I say timidly.

Stan looks up. "Hello, Katelyn. What can I do for you?"

"Um, I was wondering if I could ask you something?"

He gestures to the seat across from him. I hesitate before pulling out the chair and sitting down. Stan patiently waits for me to ask my question, but my heart is beating a million miles a minute and I can feel my breaths grow shorter. *Do not panic in front of him!* my mind screams at me. Closing my eyes, I take a deep breath in and then picture a candle in front of me. I slowly exhale, before I look up.

"I'm, um, well, I've been stuck for a bit, and I was wondering if maybe, well yeah, maybe you could see if you could help." *That's a horrible sentence. Way to show him you're good with words*, my thoughts quip. I swallow, keeping my focus on Stan.

He just smiles. "I'd be happy to help. Do you want to bring everything over here?"

Biting my lip, I glance back at my table, then look over at him again. "You're sure?"

"Absolutely. I'm going to grab another coffee, then we can get to work." Stan sounds eager, which makes me feel slightly better about interrupting his afternoon.

As I gather my stuff, I hear Stan laughing at something the barista said. He shuffles back to the table and takes a seat. Once I get situated, he asks, "Do you want to tell me where you are stuck?"

"Well, right now I have the beginning piece, which is the piece you read, and then I have another piece that should eventually be part of the story. I just don't know how to make them connect. I've been working really hard to bridge the gap, but I can't seem to figure it out."

Stan gives me a contemplative look. "I'm betting you're a pantser."

He's right. I hate creating outlines or plotting everything in advance. It's so annoying and a waste of time. In the writing world, if you love to have a whole map of your story laid out before you even begin writing, you're a plotter. If you just write and pray everything comes together, flying by the seat of your pants, you're a pantser. That's me.

I nod.

"Do you have a timeline written down anywhere?"

"No, I just…no." *You can't even write correctly. No wonder you can't finish the book.*

"That's okay. Many who write like you don't write their timelines down, mainly because they don't really know them yet. However, when you're stuck, it helps to have a rough map of key scenes so you can build to them. This might be difficult, but I'd like you to write down all the key points that have happened and all the ones you know you want to happen. It doesn't have to be linear. You can do a traditional timeline or just jot ideas down, whatever feels comfortable for you. Then we can review next week. How does that sound?"

Like homework, I think. "That sounds good."

"Perfect. I think if you can visually see where you want to go, you will be able to map out the path to get there. Sometimes it's hard when it's not right in front of your face. Another exercise that might help you is writing a scene from a different perspective. Maybe choose to look at the scene as a side character, or even the villain. That might open up what's going on around your main character and then you can come back to them with an idea of how they would react."

"Okay, I think I can do that. Do you want me to do both by next week?"

Stan chuckles. "Neither is required. I think a timeline is the most important, but if you struggle with that, then come prepared with a scene. Can you show me the beginning again?"

I open the document and turn my laptop toward Stan. He skims through the first few chapters. He stops when he reaches the middle of chapter three. "Try writing this scene from the young lad's perspective. See what happens."

I read through the scene quickly. Hm, he is a pretty important character. Writing from his point of view might be interesting. Did Stan know that or did he just pick a scene at random? The thought must show on my face.

"I told you I read ahead," Stan comments.

I smile. "You read quite a bit ahead."

"What can I say? It was good." Stan grins. "Well, I should probably go see what Scout has gotten into. I will see you next week?"

"I promise to have something for you."

"I'm sure you will. I look forward to it." Stan collects his coffee cup and heads out.

I sit there for a moment, studying the chapter he pointed out. I'm not sure how to begin telling this story from another person's point of view, so instead, I open a separate document and type up all the major points of the story, adding what I have written and what I know I want to happen. Though I'm not sure seeing them all together is helping me. Now that it's on paper, it feels insurmountable. *You thought you'd magically figure this out? You are not good enough. Give up. Don't waste Stan's time on this garbage.*

Tears spring to my eyes and I close them tight, praying none escape. I take a few steadying breaths, open my eyes, and close my laptop. The goal of asking for help was to get unstuck, not make me give up. Maybe I can ask Stan for advice on how to make this feel less overwhelming. *But admitting it's overwhelming is admitting you're a failure.*

Before I cry in the middle of the seating area, I pack my bag and head out. The first tear falls as I get in my car. Swiping it away quickly, I turn the key and the engine hums to life. More tears fall, and this time, there is no stopping them.

Never, my thoughts whisper. *You will never be a writer.*

CHAPTER TWENTY-ONE

Dom

I'm not sure who's more thrilled that Katelyn is coming to dinner, me or Jeremy. He's been in the kitchen all day perfecting his homemade spaghetti sauce. When I extended the invite to Katelyn, she hesitated before slowly nodding. I think the thing that sweetened the deal and the reason she agreed to come was because we would be watching the new season of *The Circle*.

Sitting at the table now, watching her bite her lower lip, I'm wondering what I can do to ease her anxiety. She's very quiet when meeting new people. It took several conversations for her to relax around me. Maybe there's a bit of social anxiety, but I feel like it's more than that. The number of times she has been close to hyperventilating when a situation becomes stressful is concerning. I watch as Katelyn inhales deep, making a little O with her mouth, then breathes out slowly. She's just far enough away that I can't reach over and give her knee a squeeze, just to let her know everything is okay. I'm afraid if I move, drawing attention to her, it will make it worse.

"So, Katelyn, what do you do for work?" Tyler asks.

Katelyn glances over at him. "I'm currently working in accounts receivable for a label company."

"Do you like it?"

She shrugs. "It pays the bills."

"I know what you mean. I'm currently working for a call center. It's the worst. People are the worst, but like you said, it pays the bills." He shoves a bite of spaghetti in his mouth.

Katelyn looks down at her plate, twirling spaghetti with her fork. "Um, if you don't like your job, have you thought about doing something else?" Her eyes dart back to Tyler.

"Eventually I'd love to get back to riding, but right now it's been a little difficult."

She tilts her head. "Riding?"

"Yeah, I've been doing BMX freestyle since I was, like, eight. So, when I'm not at work, I'm riding a bike or sometimes my skateboard, doing fancy tricks. Except right now." Tyler clears his throat. "Anyway…new topic." His eyes bounce between Jeremy and me for help.

"Okay, you asked for it." Jeremy shrugs and chuckles. "I thought of you last night. My co-worker presented a hypothetical break-in situation while we were monitoring the cameras and it made me think of the time you picked the lock in college."

Tyler and I burst into laughter, the change in conversation seamless. "I thought I was so clever," I say.

Katelyn glances around the table, confused.

"In college, we were all roommates. Your boy here"—Jeremy nods at me—"decided it would be funny to switch our bedroom locks to each of our rooms. I was so furious when I got back to the dorm. I had to wait in the common area until Dom got home from class. As I was complaining, Tyler just stepped out of his room, and Dom's jaw dropped. Apparently, Tyler has a knack for picking locks and when his key didn't work, he just found another way in."

"It totally ruined April Fool's," I say. "Man, that was so long ago."

"A lot has changed since then," Tyler remarks. The table falls silent.

Jeremy reaches for another slice of garlic toast. I notice Katelyn still has a nearly full plate of pasta and a half-eaten slice of bread.

"What do you think?" Jeremy asks, nodding toward Katelyn's plate.

"It's very good." She gives him a slight smile. Her eyes dart to me. "Is it okay if I'm excused? I'll be right back."

"Absolutely," I say.

The minute the bathroom door clicks shut, Jeremy looks at me. "What happened to the girl who slept on our couch for two days? Because that's not her." He throws a look Tyler's way, hoping for backup.

Tyler shrugs. "I didn't really spend much time with her."

Even so, he's the one who ended up with the stomach bug days later. We haven't figured out how that happened.

"We shouldn't be discussing this now. She's going to come back out," I say.

"Dude, this night should be easy for her," Jeremy states.

"Why should it be easy?" An edge creeps into my voice.

"It's not like we're strangers. When she was here last time, she was super chill."

"She also had a fever and was out of it most of the time," I argue.

"Maybe her guard was down because she was sick," Tyler suggests. He glances toward the hallway. "Whatever it was, now is definitely not the time to fight about it."

We fall silent again when the bathroom hinges squeak. Katelyn returns to the table. Twirling a small bite of pasta around her fork, she glances up at the three of us. "Everything okay?"

"Yeah."

Katelyn takes one more bite of her spaghetti before pushing her plate away. The tension in the air is palpable, which she has undoubtedly picked up on.

Bend the rules, you thought. It'll be great. Could this be any more awkward?

"Who's ready for some drama?" I ask, rolling away from the table.

"Sure." Tyler stands and heads into the living room.

"I'm gonna put the food away. Go ahead and start it," Jeremy says, grabbing his plate and disappearing into the kitchen.

Katelyn's eyes trail after him. "Is everything all right?" she asks me.

"Yep. I'm going to help Jeremy with the food. Go make yourself comfortable." I reach for her plate, but she picks it up, taking my plate as well.

"I'll get it. You can go get situated."

"Katelyn, you're our guest. You don't have to clean up."

"It was a good meal, and I should help with something. I'll be in soon," she says.

She walks over to the trash, discarding her remaining pasta and mine, before joining Jeremy at the sink.

"Did you watch any more of *Jane the Virgin*?" she asks as she turns on the faucet. There is a nervous waver to her voice.

"I'd binge it if the other two bozos weren't watching too." Jeremy rolls his eyes.

A genuine smile appears on Katelyn's face. "You got Tyler hooked?"

Jeremy nods. "We made him watch the first couple episodes by himself, but since then, whenever we all have some free time, we're watching."

Convinced she's fine, I let them continue their conversation and make my way to the living room. I park my chair at the end of the couch and shuffle to the far-right seat. Tyler sits on the left side, leaving the middle open for Katelyn.

"How you doin'?" he asks.

I glance over at him, eyebrow raised.

"Look, I can tell she's freaking out tonight, which is making you act weird."

Glancing back toward the kitchen, I sigh. "I think she gets nervous in new social settings." Tyler opens his mouth to say something, but I continue. "Yes, I know this isn't really a new social setting, but like you said, her guard could have been down last time. I just want her to feel at home and I have no idea how to help her."

"For starters, it would help if you relaxed. You've been tense the whole night and she's picking up on it."

From the kitchen, Jeremy suddenly snaps, "That's not correct. Jeez."

The reaction is instantaneous. Tyler bolts from the couch, and I'm quick to follow. The adrenaline makes me forget about my chair. Of course, the minute I reach the kitchen, I'm well aware that I won't be able to stand much longer. Not that I needed to panic. Katelyn is doubled over, laughing along with Jeremy.

"What happened?" I ask, teetering a little.

Katelyn glances over, eyes widening when she sees me standing. She rushes over to me, wrapping her arm around my waist. I loop one arm over her shoulders, leaning on her.

"He was joking. We're good," Katelyn says.

Jeremy nods.

She shifts, bracing herself to hold me upright. I try to stand straighter, taking my weight off her, but my left leg gives, almost taking both of us down. Tyler is quick to catch me.

"I got the rest of the dishes. Thanks for the help, Katelyn," Jeremy says.

"You're welcome." She looks at me. "Let's get you to the couch."

Tyler takes my left arm to assist us.

"I got him," Katelyn states.

"Still, I can help."

"I'm good," she snaps, glaring at Tyler.

He takes a step away, hands up in surrender. "Okay, you got it."

Katelyn and I shuffle back to the couch. Her little frame begins to shake from supporting me. Why didn't she want Tyler to help? As if she hears my thoughts, she says, "I need to know I can do this by myself."

I glance over at her. *Knowing how to help implies long term,* my thoughts toss out. I'm not sure how true that is, but to me, it means she is definitely in this.

Once I'm seated, she sits next to me, breathing heavily.

"You didn't have to do that," I say.

"Then use your chair next time," she snips. "Why did you guys rush in anyway?"

"Jeremy sounded pissed off."

"So?" She shrugs. "I'm perfectly capable of telling him off. I don't need you."

Yep, a little firecracker, I think.

"You're right," I admonish.

"I am." Her eyes dart away from me, her teeth digging into her lip.

I rest my hand just above her knee. "Hey, I'm sorry."

"It's fine," she whispers.

"It's not fine." It occurs to me then that Katelyn and I are alone; Jeremy and Tyler have not come in yet. I'm guessing they think we need some time to talk.

She takes a deep breath. "Tonight is a little difficult for me, but I'm really trying here. Just now, in the kitchen, I relaxed a little. It was nice. Then you and Tyler burst in, and you seemed upset and now…"

A string of curses runs through my head. I screwed things up. *Royally.*

"Don't do that." Katelyn reaches up, smoothing the lines between my eyebrows.

I take a deep breath. "I know you have rules. I guess I just wanted to make sure the night went perfectly."

"I should have never said anything about the rules," she mutters. "It's too much pressure, and now you're trying too hard, and I'm afraid I'm going to mess everything up."

I mutter a curse.

"It's okay. This whole thing is my fault," Katelyn says.

"No." The word comes out harsher than I intended. She jumps. "None of this is your fault. I'm the one who pushed for you to come over. I'm the one who wants the night to go well. I'm the one being extra. You deserve a chill evening, not this crap."

She stills for a moment. "Are we okay?"

"We're good," I say.

"Good." She smiles and calls out an all clear. Tyler and Jeremy, who must have been waiting around the corner, join us in the living room, bringing snacks with them.

"It's nice to see that physical therapy is working out," Jeremy says, plopping down in the recliner.

I reach over, filling a small bowl with popcorn while Jeremy cues up the first episode. "Between time at the gym and PT, I'm slowly gaining some strength back." I was pretty impressed I made it to the kitchen without a mobility aid. I mean, I was screwed when I got there, but to even get there is improvement.

I lean back against the couch and stretch my arm out across the back. Katelyn tucks her legs underneath herself and snuggles closer to me. I give her a small kiss on her forehead. It was a rough start to the evening, but sitting here now, I'm hoping nights like this happen more often.

CHAPTER TWENTY-TWO

Katelyn

What time is your flight? Dom's text reads.

9:35 a.m. If you can't take me, it's okay, I respond.

Stop that. I'm taking you. He sends a kissy face emoji after that.

I had originally planned on taking an Uber since I didn't really want to pay for parking. When I mentioned this, Dom was quick to offer to be my ride. To me, it seems like a huge inconvenience for him. I'm leaving on a weekday and he has work, but he insisted.

Wednesday morning, I'm up hours before I need to leave for my flight. I double-check my bags, making sure I have what I need. I'm so worried I'm going to forget something. Once I feel good that I've packed everything, I sit on my couch, waiting for Dom. I leap to my feet the minute my phone buzzes.

Dom is parked right in front of my walkway. I open the trunk, setting my small suitcase inside.

As I'm buckling up, Dom turns and smiles. "All set?"

"I hope so." I chew on my lower lip.

He reaches over, resting his hand just above my knee. He gives a little squeeze, then backs out. Music fills the silence on the way to the airport.

"So, what do you have planned while you're there?" he pipes up.

"Eliza compiled a list of things she wants to do while I'm out there. I think she wants to go to the beach one day."

"That sounds fun. Do you like the beach?"

I scoff. "Do I like the beach?"

Dom glances over, perplexed.

"Oh, sorry. Yes, I *love* the beach. I'm sad it's so expensive to live near one. I don't think I'd be in Arizona anymore if it were cheaper. There's something about the sound of the waves and the smell of saltwater that is so…peaceful."

"The beach is pretty nice. I could do without the sand, though," Dom comments.

"Did you go to the beach a lot when you lived in California?"

He shrugs. "Less once…" He looks down at his lap, frowning.

"Gotcha."

It falls silent.

"What are you gonna do while I'm gone?" I ask, hoping to break him out of his stupor.

"Miss you," he says without hesitation.

A small giggle escapes my lips.

"I guess I'll just keep busy with work and rely on Jer and Ty to keep me company. But trust me, their company is way different than yours."

"A lot less cuddling I'd imagine," I quip. I laugh outright when he shrugs.

As Dom pulls up to the curb, my heart rate spikes. I'm always a little nervous when I fly. I take a few deep breaths. Dom slips his hand into mine, intertwining our fingers. "The flight will be good. You'll text me when you land?"

I squeeze his hand. "Which time?" I have a layover in Dallas, which only heightens my anxiety.

"Both."

I nod. When I look over, Dom leans over the center console, hazel eyes fixed on me. "You're going to be fine."

I surprise myself when I lean over too, kissing him on his lips. It's a quick kiss, lasting a fraction of a second. When I pull away, his eyes are wide. Now my heart is racing for a completely different reason. "Thanks."

Dom freezes for a moment before straightening. "Uh-huh." His eyes stay glued to me as I get out of the car and retrieve my bag. All of a sudden, a wave goodbye seems odd. I walk over to his side of the car and he rolls down the window.

"See you in a few days." I flash him a smile.

He crooks his index finger, signaling me to come closer. I take a step, leaning into his open window.

"It's going to be a long few days," he whispers against my lips. Then he kisses me again, sweet and quick.

I pull away, noticing the security guard eyeing us. "I should go."

"See you later, Firecracker."

A smile lights my face. I nod and then head toward the sliding double doors, turning just in time to see Dom merge with traffic.

Kissing Dom wasn't planned. In the moment, his hazel eyes boring into me, my body reacted.

It was a bad move. I scowl and shake the thought away. *No, it couldn't have been.*

Two flights later, I land in Savannah completely exhausted. I napped a little on the plane, but not nearly enough to make up for the little sleep I got the night before. Every time I visit, it always baffles me how tiny the airport is with its fifteen gates. I reach the little lobby area, past security in no time at all. As I reach for my phone to text Eliza, I hear her call my name. I look up just in time to see Eliza barreling toward me. Letting go of my carry-on, I squeal, opening my arms to her. We hug, bouncing up and down.

"I'm so happy you're here!" she says.

"Me too."

Eliza glances down at my one carry-on. "Do you have any other bags?"

I shake my head.

"Good. Marc's outside. Let's go." She grabs my bag and my hand and we make our way outside.

Georgia in October is cooler than in the summer. There is a slight chill in the air. At the car, Eliza knocks on the trunk and it pops open. After she sets my suitcase inside, I take the back seat while she climbs into the front.

"Hi, Marc," I say as I buckle my seatbelt.

"Katelyn. Nice to see you."

He checks his mirrors, then backs out of the spot. He reaches over, interlacing his hand with Eliza's. Her fingers tighten and their hands remain that way as we wind onto the highway. I'm a bit envious they can do that. I guess if I drove places, Dom and I could. Dom always drives, though, so it's not a reality for us.

Thinking of Dom brings thoughts of the kiss. Eliza is going to freak when she hears this news. Even though I'm happy to be here with my best friend, a part of me is ready to be home with Dom already.

CHAPTER TWENTY-THREE

Katelyn

It's Thursday, which means Eliza has to work. While she's at work, I stare at all the plot points Stan helped me map out. During our last meeting, he also suggested a small bridge to connect a couple scenes, but progress seems slow. There is still a giant chasm once I get to the middle and I don't know how to get from point A to point B. I think back to the exercise of writing a scene from a different character's point of view. I did take Stan's advice and tackled a scene from the male lead's perspective. It actually helped and gave me some ideas to move forward. Maybe I could do the same thing here. Before diving in, I quickly send Dom a text.

How's work?

Going to lunch. How's Georgia?

Good. Liza and I are going out later.

Any crazy plans? he asks.

Girls night. Can't tell ya. I tack on a winky face emoji.

Dom doesn't respond, so I assume his focus has been pulled elsewhere. I make another cup of coffee and head back to the living room to continue staring at my computer. *Your efforts are futile,* my mind whispers. Turning up my music louder, I try to drown out all of the berating thoughts and concentrate on writing the scene

I'm working on. By the time Eliza walks in, I've written two small scenes and convinced myself not to edit or delete them.

Eliza tosses her keys in the little bowl by the front door. She kicks her shoes off and plops down beside me.

"You smell like French fries," I comment. One of the downsides to working as a waitress.

"Hello to you, too." She nudges my shoulder with hers, glancing at my computer. "Plan on sharing?"

I shrug. "It needs more work."

"You always say that." She pushes herself up.

I roll my eyes.

"Well, you have thirty more minutes to make it perfect. I'm going to shower." She heads toward the bedroom. "What do you want to do tonight?" she calls out.

"Whatever you want," I yell back.

By the time she's ready to go, it's been over an hour. She steps out, hair curled, makeup on, wearing black skinny jeans with a baby pink peplum blouse. Frowning, she shakes her head. "You cannot go out in that."

"Why?" I look down at my dark wash jeans and simple navy blue T-shirt.

She rolls her eyes. "Look, I may live in a small town and there might not be much to do, but we can look cute doing it." Before I have a chance to argue, she spins around and tells me to follow.

Entering her bedroom feels weird, because it's not just hers. She and Marc share this room. There is a nightstand on either side of the bed. Marc's side has a small lamp and a stack of books. Eliza's has an alarm clock and a few cups cluttering the surface.

"These might fit you. Let's see." She shoves three blouses at me before flitting away into the bathroom.

Slipping the first blouse on, my thoughts drift to what Dom would think of me in this. I slip my phone from my back pocket and take a selfie. The red flowy halter top looks really cute. I'm not sure I even want to try the other two on. I pull up my text conversation with Dom and send the picture, adding a little kissy face emoji.

My brain sifts through the few pairs of shoes I brought with me. Now I don't feel so crazy for grabbing options. The black booties will look adorable with this outfit.

"Come in here when you're done, please," Eliza sings.

When I step into the bathroom, she gestures for me to have a seat on the toilet lid. I obey.

"Close your eyes," she demands.

Doing as she says, I ask, "Why are we getting all dolled up?"

"Sometimes it's good to dress up a little. Plus, don't think I didn't see you snap a picture of yourself. Send your sexy selfie to someone?" She smiles, wiggling her eyebrows.

"Shut up."

"What did he think?"

I shrug. "Hasn't responded yet."

"Probably dropped dead from you being so gorgeous."

"I doubt it," I mumble.

"Hey. Look at me." I open my eyes to find Eliza staring at me. "You are beautiful and wonderful. Don't sit and say, 'I doubt it.'" She imitates the way I said it. "He's stupid if he doesn't see how stunning you are. Even more stupid if he doesn't realize how lucky he is to be with you. I mean, you are amazing."

I hold Eliza's stare. "I'm pretty sure he knows that." *At least, I hope he does.*

"Good." She adds a little blush and some powder and then deems us ready for a night out.

Eliza really does live in a tiny town. We found the nicest Mexican restaurant we could for dinner, though being on the East Coast, it doesn't exactly taste like the Mexican food I'm used to. I miss the flavor and the heat. Not that I want to burn my insides with spice, but a little kick is nice.

After dinner, we also did some shopping and then stopped by the grocery store for dessert and wine. Now, we're sitting at Eliza's table, half the bottle of wine consumed and a package of cookie dough open between us. A fly buzzes close to the cookie dough and Eliza swats it away.

"Pesky little thing," she grumbles. Getting up, she grabs a dish towel hanging from the stove handle. She spots the fly and winds the towel up. With a quick flick of her wrist, the towel smacks the trash can.

"Woah, it bounced!"

"What did?" I ask.

"The fly. It literally bounced." She erupts in a fit of giggles, which are contagious.

When Marc walks in from the bedroom, both of us are laughing uncontrollably. "What's going on in here?" he asks.

Eliza tries to explain, but it's all incoherent. I pipe in with little bits of detail, but Marc looks thoroughly confused. He glances between us and then to the bottle on the table. "I think that's enough wine for you," he says, snatching it up quickly and running away.

"Hey, come back here!" She skips after him.

I stay at the table scrolling through Instagram while listening to Eliza and Marc banter back and forth. Eliza giggles and I smile. I love seeing her so happy. I wouldn't be surprised if, in the next few months, Marc popped the question.

I switch to my messages and send a text to Dom.

Hi. Didn't expect to hear from you.

It's quiet in the living room. I peek around the kitchen wall to see Marc and Eliza on the couch, Eliza slowly drifting off on Marc's shoulder. It is 11:40 at night; that's pretty late for her. Though the couch is my temporary bed, I leave them be, take a sip of wine, and resume my conversation with Dom. After several messages back and forth, my phone rings for a video call.

"Hey there. How are you?" Dom asks, a huge grin on his face. I don't recognize where he is. He adjusts the phone, and I see a pillow and wrinkled bed sheets. He must be in his room.

"I'm good. How was your day?"

"Not too bad. Work was a bit of disaster," he says.

I frown.

"It's okay. My girlfriend sent me this stunning picture of her in a little red top. My day got exponentially better after that. It made it hard to care that everything was kind of going to hell in a handbasket."

"Oh no, I'm sorry. What happened to make it so horrible?"

Dom shakes his head. "I'm not talking about work right now. I'm just taking in my beautiful girlfriend. I haven't seen that top."

I shrug. "It's not mine."

Dom frowns and I make a mental note to find a similar top to wear the next time we go out.

"Well, tell me about your day." He shifts and I notice immediately how he grimaces.

"Are you okay?" My heart rate accelerates.

"Yep," he says, but his voice is strained.

Narrowing my eyes, I study my phone. Like if I stare hard enough, I'll be able to tell what's wrong.

Dom shifts again, trying to mask his discomfort. What happened today? Was it from sitting in his chair? Was he up walking around? Did he push too hard during his work out? Did he fall?

"Katelyn? Did I lose you?"

I shake my head. It feels like there is a weight on my chest and it's taking too much work to breathe. I try to suck in as much air as possible as I ask, "You…you, um, said you had a bad day? What happened?"

"We got prints back today for one of our new campaigns, and the font and colors were off, so the hour meeting I had with the printer was basically for nothing…"

I miss most of what Dom says after that, the weight on my chest feeling heavier. "Katelyn." Panic colors Dom's voice. "Katelyn, my little firecracker, you gotta take a breath for me."

"Firecracker?" Eliza's groggy voice comes from behind me.

Setting my phone down, I press my hands to my chest, desperately trying to get oxygen into my lungs.

I jump when Eliza rests her hand on my back. "Hey, what's going on?"

Shrugging, I take a shallow breath. The only thing running through my mind is that I should be there to take care of Dom. Has this been coming for a while? Did I miss something? Was something wrong yesterday? My job is to anticipate and take care of things.

Eliza squats beside me, rubbing between my shoulder blades. She reaches over and picks up my phone, aiming the camera at us. Relief washes over Dom's face the second he sees me.

"Hi there. You must be Dom," Eliza says.

"That's me. You must be Eliza. What can I do?" He looks like he wants to jump through the screen. Part of me wishes he could.

I shake my head. I'm not sure what I need because I don't even know exactly what's wrong. Somehow, I feel like I've failed and I don't have a logical reason as to why or what I failed at.

"Um, are you by yourself? Jeremy and Tyler are around, right?"

Dom nods. "Yes. If I need anything, they're here."

That information eases the weight on my chest marginally. "Okay."

Closing my eyes, I picture a candle. Inhaling slowly, then gently releasing the air, I imagine the little flame sputtering before it goes out. I repeat this several times before opening my eyes, finding Dom already locked on me.

"Are you okay?"

My cheeks flush from embarrassment and tears prick my eyes. I squeeze them shut, hoping none fall. "Sorry," I whisper.

"You don't have to apologize. Do you want to talk about it?"

Glancing at Eliza then back at Dom, I shake my head.

"I'll make sure she's okay," Eliza says.

I reach over, slipping my phone from Eliza's hand and standing. "I just need a minute. Is that okay?"

Eliza nods.

Leaving her in the kitchen, I pace in front of the couch. The movement works out some of the nervous energy. "Sorry I'm not there," I murmur.

"I'd love it if you were here. You could wear one of those sexy nurse outfits." He winks.

"Halloween *is* coming up." A slight grin pulls at my mouth, but Dom's face falls instantly. He catches himself, immediately plastering a smile on his face, but it's not genuine.

He clears his throat. "Do you do anything for Halloween?"

"Just pass out candy. A lot of kids live in my apartment complex. You?" The conversation lets my brain focus on something else, allowing me to breathe.

"No," he states firmly, not explaining further.

"I don't blame you. People are a little reckless on Halloween."

He nods, eyes focused on his lap.

"Dom?"

"People can be careless" is all he says. He looks up again. "Anyway…what are you doing with the rest of your time there?"

"Well, our goal tomorrow is to go to the beach." I glance at the time. "If we want to go, I have to be up early and it's late."

"Of course." He pauses. "You know if you need to talk about anything, I'm here. Seriously. I'll be up for a while."

"I know. I miss you," I sigh.

"I miss you too. Get some rest and I'll talk to you later. I love you."

Eliza steps into the living room with a glass of water at that moment. She freezes and my eyes widen. "I, um… Sleep good. I'll… I…" The words get stuck on the tip of my tongue. "I'll talk to you later." I hang up, left staring at the black screen.

"Woah. Did he just…?"

"We should probably go to bed. Early morning, right?" Whatever look I have on my face stops Eliza from commenting or asking further questions.

"R-right. Sleep tight."

CHAPTER TWENTY-FOUR

Katelyn

Eliza and I are lounging on a large beach blanket, huddled in our sweaters. The weather isn't exactly beach weather, but listening to the crashing waves is peaceful. It always shocks me that the Atlantic Ocean looks more gray than blue.

"So, can we talk about last night?" Eliza asks.

My eyes shift to her face. She's looking down, concern etched on her features. I push myself up, sitting cross-legged. "It's never been that bad," I mumble, studying the blanket's paisley print.

"But something like that has happened before?"

I nod.

"Katelyn, that's not good. Have you thought about mentioning this to your doctor or maybe talking to a counselor?"

"What would they be able to do?"

"Well, there's different coping techniques or medication…"

I shake my head before she even finishes her sentence. "I don't need medication."

"You scared me last night. You scared Dom."

I flinch.

"I'm not trying to make you feel bad." She sighs, rethinking her approach. "I just want to be sure you're taking care of *you*.

You've had a rough few months. It wouldn't hurt to seek some help."

"Liza," I sigh. "I'll think about it." I'm not sure how to explain everything to a doctor without sounding completely mental.

"Thank you. Now, let's talk about what *else* happened last night." A smile lights up her face. "Oh my gosh. That was unexpected."

"Yeah…unexpected…" I murmur.

Her brows scrunch in confusion. "What does that mean?"

"Um, I might have…kissed him before I left."

"Why didn't you tell me?!" She smacks my arm with each word. "I need details. Now. Who initiated it?"

"I did."

"Oh my gosh! You go, girl! And then what happened?"

I shrug. "He kissed me goodbye and then I walked into the airport."

She squeals. "I can't believe it's been over forty-eight hours and you didn't say anything. Now he said I love you!"

I stare at my lap, biting my lower lip.

"Kate?" She brushes my arm. I look over at her. "This is a good thing."

"Is it? What if he doesn't mean it?"

"No way. He said it because he meant it. Though…I did notice you didn't say it back," she says carefully. "What scares you most about this relationship right now?"

Losing him, my brain shouts. I sit there silently.

"I know the last relationship left you with some scars, but what happened then will not happen now. Dom is completely different."

"You barely met him," I mumble.

"Well, I didn't meet the last one at all and I knew he was a jerk. I'm still contemplating killing him for all the hurt he caused." She takes a deep breath, blowing it out in a rush.

Her instincts were right on that one. Eliza shared her concerns about my ex a few months into my last relationship. She tried to be supportive, but every time I brought him up, I could feel her frustration radiate through the phone. When I called her after we broke up, she stayed up way past her bedtime to make sure I was okay. It was a rough breakup, but what happened after just added to the hurt. Several mutual friends bailed on me, leaving me with no one. It's been difficult to trust anyone since. Letting Dom into my life, even a little, has been terrifying.

"Dom was sincere in what he said. He really does love you, and I think you love him. And you already know I'll murder him if he breaks your heart. I say jump into this with both feet. It's going to lead to somewhere good. I can feel it." She beams. "I mean, you already have a cute nickname. How did he come up with that?"

I shrug. "He said I tend to get a little feisty."

"You do! Oh my goodness. I'm already planning what I'm going to say in my wedding toast." She winks.

"No embarrassing stories. You'll scare him."

"He won't be able to go anywhere; he would have already said 'I do.'" She glances down at her phone. "Shoot. We gotta go."

"What? Where are we going?"

"You'll see." She throws a mischievous grin my way.

Dom

Sitting in the cell phone lot, I continue to glance between the clock and my phone, waiting for Katelyn to text that her plane has landed. Ever since I watched her have what I can only describe as a panic attack Thursday night, the only thing I've wanted to do is wrap her in a hug and let her know she's safe. In those minutes where I was left staring at the ceiling of Eliza's apartment while I listened to Katelyn gasp for air, I thought my heart was going to explode. It was the most frightening moment of my life, and I've lived through some truly traumatic events. I was close to buying a plane ticket and flying out there. It didn't matter that it'd be a late overnight flight. I needed to be near her, to hold her.

The one thing that stopped me was Eliza. She was the knight in shining armor in that moment. She picked up the phone so I could see Katelyn and then focused solely on her. She assured me Katelyn would be taken care of, and I believed her. *You put a lot of trust in someone you've never met*, my brain quips, but what else was I supposed to do? Eliza is her best friend, and I could tell Katelyn trusts her. I had to trust her too.

I woke up to several photos of the beach Friday morning, and I hoped those few hours helped her relax. She grew quieter as the day went on and I told myself it was because she was busy enjoying her last few hours with her best friend. My phone chimes with a text from Katelyn and I instantly reverse. A car honks and I slam on my brakes, making me jerk against my seat and sending a radiating pain through my back and down my legs. Taking a minute to check my surroundings, I back out again. My pain, which was manageable, flares up. *Way to go, idiot.*

I breathe a sigh of relief when I see Katelyn standing at the curb, clutching the handle of her suitcase. She places her luggage in the back seat and then slides into the passenger seat, a smile lighting her face. It's almost impossible not to lean over and kiss those lips of hers. However, I'm not sure I can hide my discomfort if I do that.

"I'm so glad you're home," I say, pulling away from the curb. "Me too."

I glance over and notice she's chewing her lower lip. "Was your flight okay?" I ask.

"It was."

She wrings her hands together while she speaks. What on earth is making her nervous? "The beach looked beautiful. Did you enjoy it? What else did you guys do?"

"Yeah, we had a good time. It was a little cold, though. And then, well, um…"

My heart rate spikes. What happened? Is there another reason she was quiet last night? I glance over at her.

"How do you feel about tattoos?" she asks quietly.

"Tattoos?" I repeat.

She doesn't answer. Maybe I didn't hear her right? "Did you say tattoos?"

"Oh, sorry. Yes. Tattoos."

Shrugging, I answer, "I don't mind them. I have one."

"You do?" The shock in her voice makes me chuckle.

"Yeah, I can show it to you later. Why the sudden curiosity about tattoos, though?" *Did she get a tattoo? Please say you got one. That would be so hot!*

"Eliza and Marc got tattoos Friday evening," she explains.

I keep a frown from forming. "Oh, okay. Cool. Where were you while they were getting their tattoos?"

"I was there. I guess this was scheduled before I came out and if they changed it, it would have been months to get another appointment. While we were sitting there Liza kept pestering me to get one too. Their friend, who was the tattoo artist, told me it was rude to sit in the shop and not get one. He was joking. I think." She mumbles the last part.

"So, what you're saying is, you were peer pressured?"

She giggles nervously. "I guess that's a good way to look at it."

Holy cow. SHE GOT A TATTOO. "What did you get?" Her shorts and tank top leave quite a bit of skin exposed, so it has to be in a spot that is covered by her clothes. Or it's small.

"It's not much, and I can easily hide it," she states defensively.

"Are you afraid I'm not going to like it?"

"I don't know," she whispers. "What if you don't? It's permanent."

"Do you like it?"

She smiles widely. "I love it."

"Then I'm sure I'll love it too."

I park in front of her apartment and slowly turn to face her. Her eyes narrow when she catches me wince.

"Are you still in pain? Maybe you shouldn't have come to get me. I could have found another way home."

I take her hand, interlacing our fingers and relax a little bit. She's here. Now, to make sure she doesn't panic over something she can't control. "Firecracker, I'm fine. Just a little sore."

That's a bit of a lie, but she doesn't need to know that.

"Do you want to come in?"

As much as I want to spend time with her, my body is screaming at me. I'd much rather be at home, in bed. Some pain meds and my TENS machine sound amazing right now. But I also don't want to just drop her off and leave. I've been waiting for the moment that I can pull her close and hold her tight. A short moment of holding hands doesn't cut it. "Do you want to come over? I know you just got home, so I understand if you don't."

She glances back at her suitcase. "As long as I can shower at your house. I just want the plane feel off me."

When we arrive at my house, Katelyn grabs some clothes from her suitcase and immediately heads for the shower. A few minutes later, she steps out of my bathroom in shorts and a loose T-shirt, hair still damp. Twirling a strand around her finger, she brings it to her nose, and a smile lights her face. My eyes trail down her figure, searching for her new ink. When my eyes return to hers, she's watching me.

"How are you feeling?" she asks, walking over to my bed.

I pat the mattress and she crawls up next to me. The slightest jostle makes my back and legs feel like they are set ablaze. A hiss of pain escapes through my lips and Katelyn freezes, eyes widening.

"I'm fine. Come here." She's so close. If it didn't feel like I was on fire every time I moved, I'd lean over and pull her to me.

She slides in beside me and I hold my breath as she does. *Come on, drugs, do your job!*

Katelyn's fingers intertwine with mine and I squeeze her hand. "Is there anything I can do?" she asks. Concern laces her tone.

I wink, a little tiredly. "You know what would really help? Seeing your tattoo."

She takes a deep breath and then pulls her hair up. Resting behind her right ear is a little dragon, looking like it's whispering secrets to her. My finger traces the edge of the clear bandage—new skin, I think it's called—and a shiver glides down her spine.

"Well?"

I grin. "It's perfect. My amazing fantasy writer now has her own dragon."

She smiles widely.

"Did it hurt?"

Dropping her hair, she shakes her head. The tattoo disappears instantly. She's right. No one will know if her hair is down, or if she's not standing at the perfect angle. I'm obsessed with the little dragon, though. It's so Katelyn. *I'm going to need that hair up more now.*

Katelyn tucks herself into my side. I wrap my arm around her, holding her close, and breathe a sigh of relief. She's here. She's safe. She shifts and pulls the TENS machine from under her leg. "What does this do?" she asks.

"It's a transcutaneous electrical nerve simulation machine, or TENS machine. It sends little electrical pulses to my nerves to help reduce pain."

"Is it helping?"

I shrug.

"Wait, am I hurting you? I can move."

My arm tightens around her. "Don't you dare." I lean over, kissing her forehead, and she snuggles closer.

"Can I ask what happened? Was there something that could have prevented this?" Her big brown eyes stare up at me, worry etched on her face.

"Pain is kind of a regular part of life now. There are several things I do to manage it. This is just a bad flare-up."

"I know you had physical therapy. Did that make the problem worse?"

"No, stretching and working on my range of motion help quite a bit. It's not fun to do during a flare-up, but I usually feel a little better after." I brush a stray lock of hair out of her face. "I don't want you to worry about this."

"I'm not. I just want to know how to help you."

I smile. "I appreciate that. Speaking of helping..." I take a deep breath. "Can we talk about the other night?"

"Oh." She looks down. "I didn't mean to scare you."

My whole body tenses, which exacerbates my pain. Scare is putting it mildly. I thought I was going to have a heart attack.

"Did something happen earlier in the evening, or was it something I said?"

She shrugs. "You didn't do anything."

"You've had a few instances where things seem a bit overwhelming, and I know you've had some rough days."

Her body tenses.

Inhaling deep, I continue, "I've struggled with depression, have talked to counselors and been on medication. It's not something to be embarrassed by." I don't mention how dark my depression was or what happened almost a year after the accident. She doesn't need to worry about that.

Katelyn pulls away, eyes narrowing. "I'm not embarrassed. It's just…" She glances away. "I can't explain it," she murmurs.

"Sometimes it's hard to put everything into words, especially in a way that someone else will understand," I say gently.

She nods.

"I just really need you to know, I'm here. Always." *I love you* is on the tip of my tongue, but I don't say it again. She didn't reciprocate the feeling when I said it the first time. I'm not worried she'll never feel the same way, but I thought we were at the same point. Maybe I misinterpreted something?

"There's a lot of stuff," she whispers. "What if you find out something and it's too much?"

"Katelyn, nothing is ever going to be too much. Ever."

She holds my gaze before nodding. Even though I'd love for her to tell me everything that she's going through, I know what's it like to struggle putting it all into words. I also understand not wanting to share because of the fear people might judge you or think less of you. I've been there, but how do I get her to feel safe enough to open up?

She rests her head on my shoulder and I comb my fingers through her nearly dry hair. Inhaling, she says, "There is one thing you said that we should probably talk about."

My heart begins beating double time.

"You said a four-letter word I wasn't quite expecting and—"

"I'm not expecting you to say it back right away," I interject. "I want you to say it whenever you feel ready. It was how I felt in the moment. I mean, it's how I feel, but if you aren't in the same spot, that's okay."

"Dom. Hold on." She lifts her head and I shut my mouth. "I was going to say I wasn't expecting it, but I do. Love you, that is. You just surprised me is all. Sorry for not saying it back." She leans in and kisses my cheek, and I nearly die right there from happiness.

CHAPTER TWENTY-FIVE

Dom

"You going to sit there all day?"

My physical therapist's question draws me out of my thoughts. Beside her are several mobility aids, including a few different walkers, arm crutches, and canes. From my seat on the stationary bike, my eyes survey each and then jump back to her.

"Which one speaks to you?"

"None of them."

The goal has always been to be able to walk again, but I'm not sure this week is the time to really try considering exactly three years ago, I was able to walk just fine. No mobility aid needed.

"One has to. Pick one, or I'm picking for you."

Crossing my arms, I glare at her. She mirrors me. When I don't move or make a selection, she drops her arms and walks over to a standard metal walker and brings it over to the bike.

"Let's move to the table." She pushes the walker toward me and then wheels my chair away. I stay seated, studying the walker.

"We can't stretch if you don't come over here," she says. "Besides, it's not going to bite."

I scowl but take a deep breath, grab the walker, and push myself to my feet. The first few steps are steady but then my left leg gives and I grip the walker, cursing. I get my foot under me, balancing more on my right leg. My therapist moves closer to me. *What a vote of confidence.* I know she has to in case I end up needing help, but it's still frustrating.

I'm able to make it to the table on my own, at least. As we work on stretching my legs, I stare at the ceiling, fuming.

"Wow, for someone who wanted to be up and moving, you sure aren't acting like it."

I don't respond. She pushes the stretch deeper than normal.

"Ouch! What the—?" I push up on my elbows.

"You've been coming for months. When we did our initial assessment you told me you walk around some, but you're not steady. Well, you will never improve if you don't actually walk. So, congratulations, you now have a nice pretty walker. I want you to use it for a couple hours a day, just around the house. We'll work on longer periods of time and eventually get you out of the house. Now, lie back."

This is a step to being normal. Stop being a baby. I follow her instructions and finish stretching.

Since it's difficult to maneuver my chair and the walker inside, I text our group chat asking Tyler and Jeremy for some help. Tyler is standing outside when I pull in the driveway. I open the back of the SUV and then assemble my chair.

"Fun new toy," Tyler comments, bringing the walker around. "This is exciting."

"I guess." I wheel inside and grab a water bottle from the fridge. When I turn around, Tyler is staring at me. "What?"

He shakes his head.

"You can set that in my room." I nod toward the walker.

His eyes narrow. "Why aren't you more excited about this?"

"Who said I wasn't?"

"I think it's kind of cool that you'll be up and moving on the anniversary of the accident."

"Yeah. It's great." I roll to the couch, transfer over, and turn on the television.

Tyler snatches the remote from my hand, muting the television. "Talk." When I stay silent, he scoffs. "Whatever, don't talk then." He points the remote at me. "This time isn't exactly fun for me, either. Now, I understand, I'm the idiot who didn't take recovery seriously and ended up with some issues. But I lost things too. My life changed just like yours."

"Just like mine?" I ask incredulously.

"We aren't playing this game." He throws the remote at me and walks out of the room. His door slams a moment later.

Leaning back, I sigh. Tyler's life changed a little. If he would have followed all his recovery procedures, he may not be where he is now. He could probably still ride and do whatever he wants. At least he still has use of his legs. He doesn't need help getting around. He doesn't have to text people to bring items in from the car. He didn't have to retrofit his house to make it functional.

Sitting down for dinner, Jeremy glances between Tyler and me. "What's up with you two?"

"Dom's throwing himself a pity party and I didn't want to attend," Tyler remarks.

Clenching my jaw, I don't comment. There's no pity part, just facts. Next week marks three years since the accident. Three years since my life changed forever, and no matter what I do, I can't get my old life back.

"That's not a good look," Jeremy comments.

"I'm fine," I grumble.

CHAPTER TWENTY-SIX

Katelyn

Closing my eyes, I massage my temples.

"I think this works well. What's the matter?" Stan asks.

Sighing, I open my eyes. Stan turns my laptop back toward me while I take a sip of my latte. "Nothing, I just don't understand why I'm having a hard time. I feel like it wasn't this hard the last time."

"Last time?"

I freeze. "Um, yeah."

"Well, every writing project is different. They each come with their own set of challenges. Would you feel comfortable sharing your previous work?"

The idea makes my heart rate spike.

"The only reason I ask is because I'll be able to get a better sense of your style and your voice. Maybe pinpointing some of your strengths will help us with this project."

Nodding, I sift through my computer files until I find my first story. My stomach is in knots as I attach the document to an email. If I'm sending it to Stan, I might as well share it with a few others. I quickly hit send before I can change my mind and look up at Stan. "Okay, you should have it."

I feel like I might pass out. I focus on taking deep breaths, picturing a little candle.

"I'll read through this next week. Do want to talk about anything for this?" He taps my laptop.

That's a good question. I'm a little over three quarters of the way through now. There are still some gaps in the middle and I don't have a solid ending, but I've finally made progress. Skimming through the scene Stan just read, I shake my head. "I'm fairly confident I know where I'm going right now." I have to throw off the thoughts that say, *This is a silly idea. Why are you trying so hard? You're just adding another story to an already saturated market. It's not going anywhere.*

"I'm glad to hear it. I'll see you next week then?"

I nod. "Thank you."

"You're welcome. You have a wonderful rest of your afternoon."

I work for another hour before I call it quits and head home. As I pull into my apartment complex, my phone rings.

"Hi, Eliza."

"What on earth is this? And why are you just sharing this now?" Marc's voice fills the cab of my car. "I mean, I'm not that far into it yet, but holy cow."

"Hi, Katelyn," Eliza calls from the background, her voice distant.

"Maybe read a little more before you make any judgements," I tell Marc.

"He's gone. He has reading to do," Eliza says, sounding closer now. "I'll have to pry him away shortly so we can get ready to go. Our friends are throwing a Halloween party tonight."

"Fun."

"Yep. Are you and Dom doing anything?"

Now that I think about it, Dom hasn't really mentioned Halloween. I told him I'd basically be free since I usually just stay home and pass out candy to all the kids in my complex. Maybe I could invite Dom over, or maybe they have their own traditions. "I'm not sure yet."

"Well, you should also find out what he's doing for Thanksgiving."

"Thanksgiving? Are you coming out here?"

"Maybe…"

"Seriously?" I squeal.

"We're ironing out a few more details, but it looks like we will be able to make it. I figured it's the perfect time to meet your man."

"I'll ask."

Eliza meeting Dom makes me nervous, but I love them both and it's probably fair that they get to see each other in person after the impromptu video call. Thankfully, I have a few weeks to get comfortable with the idea.

CHAPTER TWENTY-SEVEN

Dom

I feel like an idiot for inviting Katelyn over tonight. I should have just told her to stay home. People are reckless on Halloween, and even though the streets are probably safe now, they won't be later tonight. I glance over at the time; she should be here by now. My stomach clenches.

"What are you doing?" Jeremy asks.

Standing at the window, I debate peeking outside to watch for her car. However, I don't want to see everyone's costumes. We have our house dark and all the outside lights off for a reason. Jeremy steps up and looks out the window for me.

"That's weird. Her car is here."

Jeremy walks outside, leaving me to anxiously wait. When he returns, he's carrying grocery bags. Katelyn trails him. The moment I see her, I know something's wrong.

"Katelyn. What happened?"

She shakes her head. Behind her, Jeremy mimes breathing into a paper bag and then nods at Katelyn. How long has she been outside, and what happened?

I wheel myself in front of her, lacing my fingers through hers. "Hey. I'm right here. You can talk to me."

"I think I'd rather just make dessert," she says, a little breathless. Slipping her hand from mine, she walks into the kitchen. "Um, do you have a mixing bowl?"

After getting her all set up, I wheel myself back to my room to grab my walker, then shuffle slowly back to the kitchen. The thought of food makes me so nauseous, but Katelyn looks more relaxed baking. I shove all my anxiety away and try and focus on her. She studies me for a minute when I enter before focusing back on her dessert.

The walker isn't new to Katelyn. She was adorable the first time she saw me use it. When I made a comment about feeling like an old man, Tyler piped up, "You never know. It could be a huge chick magnet. When I had to use one, women flocked to me."

"He doesn't need a chick magnet," Katelyn had snipped.

"Yeah, I already have a chick," I said. "The question is, is the walker more of a turn-on than the chair?" I raised my eyebrows in question.

"It's a huge turn-on," she said before kissing me.

I walk up behind her. Keeping one hand on the walker, I wrap the other around her waist. "What are you making?"

"Oreo fluff." Her stomach rises and falls as she takes a deep breath. She grabs a tub of whipped cream and scoops it into the mixing bowl. As she stirs, she says quietly, "My mom called me."

"Oh?" Katelyn hasn't talked much about her parents.

"The big change she thought would make everything better didn't." She takes a breath. "Why doesn't she ever think things through? I mean, is it really that hard to take the time to examine what a career change will do and think, hey, maybe this isn't the best move right now?" Her stirring increases as she becomes more agitated. "Apparently, it's extremely difficult. It's *so* much easier to just do whatever feels good in the moment. Ugh, I should have talked her out of it."

"Katelyn, it's not really your responsibility to worry about this. It's her life."

Katelyn stops stirring and twists in my arm. "She never thinks! Then she calls me whenever she's short on rent or needs just a few things to get by like I'm made of money. News flash, I'm not. Jeez, could you imagine if I acted like her? Oh, I hate my job so I'm going to quit and pursue my passion, screw consequences. Ugh! That's not realistic!"

I've never seen Katelyn this worked up. But her rant feels very…familiar. "Wait, is that something you want to do?"

"What are you talking about?"

"Quitting your job to pursue writing."

She freezes, eyes going wide. I don't even think she's breathing.

"What? No," she scoffs. "That's insane and impractical." Her eyes dart away from me.

"I've read what you've written. It's not completely impractical." She finally sent me the completed piece she mentioned a couple months ago, and I'm almost done reading it already. Jeremy has been begging me to send it to him since I haven't stopped talking about it, but I want to be sure Katelyn is comfortable with me sharing it first. It's hard to believe some agent or publisher wouldn't pluck it up in a second.

"Yes, it is," she insists. She steps to the side out of my arm, and I'm immediately hit with the sweet smell of her dessert. That, watching Katelyn panic, and the anxiety around tonight all coalesces into one messy ball in my stomach.

"Firecracker—" That's as far as I get before vomit crawls up my throat. I rush to the sink, stumbling as I do. Luckily, I catch myself.

"Dom? Are you okay?" Katelyn's shaky voice comes from behind me.

I try to answer, only to retch into the sink again

"You're good, man. We're good," Tyler says reassuringly from beside me.

"Katelyn," Jeremy says. Great, are we going to have a whole audience right now? "This happens from time to time. It's been pretty bad this week."

"Usually is," I rasp. "My stupid brain can't seem to remember that the accident—" I swallow the bile threatening to come up again. "The accident is over." Turning, three sets of eyes are all focused on me. Katelyn steps over first, placing her hand on top of mine.

"Pretty bad this week? When did the accident happen?" she whispers.

"Three years ago today," Tyler answers thickly. "A lot changed that night." He turns and walks out. He's right, and I've spent the last week being angry that I'm the one in the wheelchair and he isn't. His life changed just as much as mine did. I will never forget the scream that came from him when he was fully conscious. It will forever haunt my dreams.

"Let's go to the couch." Katelyn follows close beside me. "Are you okay?" I ask her as we sit.

She nods.

"You're sure?" I study her. Those big brown eyes stay fixed on me.

"I'm fine. You're not, though." She frowns.

"This time of year is always hard for me." I inhale deeply. "Halloween night, our friends were throwing a party." I squeeze my eyes tight, not wanting to relive any of this, but it's important for Katelyn to know what happened. She laces her fingers through mine, gently urging me to continue. "Jeremy stopped by for a little bit but had to work so he left early. Tyler and I stayed pretty late. I remember thinking it was peaceful driving home, because not many cars were on the road. The light turned green and I hit the gas, and that's all I remember. From what I was told, we were hit twice. Once from behind and the side. I'm honestly not sure the order, but it was bad. When I came to, I couldn't move. Tyler was still unconscious.

"There were several cop cars, and an ambulance. The amount of flashing lights was overwhelming. I remember I tried to open my door, figuring now that I was awake I should let people know and find out what was happening, but it wouldn't budge. Paramedics finally got my door open and when I went to step out, I realized my legs wouldn't move. I focused on trying to lift my foot, or wiggle my toes, and nothing happened. When I mentioned this to the paramedics at my door they shared a look and I knew that wasn't good. They were working on a plan to get me out when Tyler came to. He let out a *horrendous* scream." My grip tightens on Katelyn's hand. Her eyes don't stray from mine. "He could feel everything."

"Oh my gosh," Katelyn whispers.

"That's always something that has been weird to me. Tyler was in excruciating pain, and I barely felt anything. As they loaded me into the ambulance I remember getting a look at a kid, blood smeared all over the front of him. I thought it was strange that he was standing and not being carted off to the hospital like Tyler and me, but I learned later the blood on his clothes was fake. So, yeah, now we don't really go anywhere or do anything for Halloween."

"Dom," she breathes. A tear snakes down her cheek. "I'm so sorry."

"Don't be sorry." I shake my head. "It's just something that happened." My stomach clenches and because I don't want to throw up all over the floor, I stand and head to my room.

Katelyn

Listening to Dom recount the accident breaks my heart. I sit in silent contemplation until he disappears down the hall, Jeremy doing the same in the recliner opposite me. He knows the story, but rehashing the trauma his best friends went through has to be hard. Especially since it could've easily been him, too, had he not left early. I wonder how Tyler is feeling? Suddenly, a loud crash sounds from the back of the house.

"Dominic," I scream, launching off the couch.

Dom is sitting in the middle of his room, walker tipped over. He looks *pissed*. Jeremy rushes in, extending a hand to lift him up.

"I don't need your help," Dom growls, swatting Jeremy's hand away.

Jeremy backs up, making no additional effort to help.

"Are you okay?" I ask, peeking in beside Jeremy.

Dom lets out a dark chuckle. "Does it look like I'm okay? Jeez, Katelyn, open your eyes. No, I'm not okay. My legs are fu—"

"Dom," Jeremy barks.

Tears well in my eyes before I can stop them. I spin and race from the room, barely registering Dom calling after me. I snatch my purse from the kitchen counter and slip out the front door. The whole time trying to block out another night. Another argument.

Wake up, Katelyn. This little dream of yours is unrealistic. I thought after all you've been through, you'd be a little more practical.

My phone buzzes when I get to the end of the driveway. I miss the call by the time I pull it out of my purse, but it rings again immediately.

"Um…hi," I answer, turning back to the house.

"Firecracker, I'm sorry. Please come back in," Dom pleads. I don't say anything. "Katelyn?" I remain silent. He sniffles a few times before he completely breaks down. "I'm so sorry. I'm sorry. I'm sorry…"

I slowly return to the house, gently closing the front door behind me. Jeremy is standing in the doorway of Dom's room and nods at me as I pass.

"I'm sorry," Dom says again in the phone, not realizing I'm in the room yet.

Quietly setting my purse down, I slip off my shoes and crawl into his bed. He howls in pain, and I hurry to rest beside him.

"Sorry. You're okay." I wrap my arms around him and hold him close. My heart splinters listening to him cry, knowing I can't do anything to help him.

"I'm so sorry." He strokes my hair. "None of this is your fault. I shouldn't have snapped at you."

"I know," I whisper, tightening my arms.

His fingers continue to comb through my hair, which would usually be comforting, but everything is me is screaming to leave. *Open your eyes. Wake up.* The words ring through my head and I can't get them to stop. I'm such an idiot for jumping into this.

Before leaving, I make sure Dom has everything he needs. Jeremy reassures me that he and Tyler will be around. Walking in my front door, I send a quick text letting Dom know I'm safe since

I promised to message him and collapse into bed. The thoughts continue, and I can only pray that I fall asleep quickly.

Open your eyes. Wake up. They're just silly stories. Be practical. You're never going to make it.

You're nothing.

CHAPTER TWENTY-EIGHT

I was so grateful Katelyn came back in but she was tense the rest of the night. She stayed until I was a little more settled. I apologized profusely, telling her none of this was her fault, and it wasn't. When I lashed out, I wasn't thinking. She was worried about me and I took all my anger and frustration out on her. I'd spent the majority of my day upset being in a wheelchair. If it wasn't for some stupid kids, I wouldn't be where I am today. I'd be living a normal life. She nodded and said she understood. Still, I could tell she was putting walls back up. When she moved from the bed, my back screamed at me. A groan of pain slipped out, unbidden.

"Would your TENS machine help?"

I shrugged.

"Where is it?"

"In the drawer." I nodded to the nightstand. She jumped when she opened it and I realized she had caught sight of the postcard. She immediately adverted her gaze, taking a shaky breath, and pulled out both the TENS machine and a prescription bottle. "Are these still good?"

"Yeah." Handing over the machine and medicine, she muttered a goodbye and left.

Tyler walked in a moment later with a glass of water. "Need anything else?"

I shook my head. He turned to leave. "Ty?"

"What?" he asked, back still to me.

"I'm a sucky friend. The accident affected you too and I know better than to compare our situations."

He spun around. "I didn't ask to walk away from the accident. I feel awful that you couldn't, but I don't know how to change that. Sometimes I think you would feel better if I was in a wheelchair along with you."

I cringed. That's the last thing I want.

Tyler continued, "The only thing I know to do is to keep moving forward. We made it through this year, just like we made it through last year, and now, we get to do it all over again. It sucks, but it is what it is."

"You're right."

"I know." The room fell silent. "You sure you're good?" Tyler asked after a minute.

I glanced up at my ceiling and shook my head. "No," I muttered. "I hate this."

"You and me both," Tyler said. "Holler if you need anything."

I nodded and Tyler left.

Jeremy came in before he left for work. When he spotted the prescription bottle of pain meds, he lost it.

"What the hell are you doing with these?" He snatched the bottle off the nightstand. "How many did you take?"

"One."

Jeremy shook his head. "I was just making sure you were okay before I left."

"I'm good."

"Great. I'll be keeping these." He turned and walked out.

Lying in bed this morning, I hear Tyler leave for work. I send a text to Katelyn to see how she's doing but she doesn't respond. I keep telling myself she's getting ready for work and will respond when she has a free minute. Now I'm just wishing Jeremy hadn't seen my pain meds because I could really use some right now.

The front door opens. Probably Jeremy returning home. Dishes clank in the kitchen and my stomach rumbles. When I move to get out of bed, I regret the decision immediately. Leaning back, I breathe deeply, hoping the pain will subside.

"How are you?" Jeremy asks, appearing in the doorway with a plate of food and a mug of coffee.

"Not great."

He brings over everything to the bed. "We really need a little table tray," he comments, setting the mug on the nightstand and handing me the plate. The first thing that captures my attention is the little round white pill on the plate. I grab it and wash it down with coffee. Jeremy watches me but doesn't say anything.

"So, how was work?"

"Work." Jeremy shrugs. "How was your night? Have you heard from Katelyn?"

I shake my head. "I blew it last night. She needed someone who had everything together. She didn't need my mess."

"Why do you think Katelyn needs you to have it together?"

I think back to the conversation about her mom. She has enough to deal with. I don't want her to feel like she has to be responsible for me, too. She needs someone to support her.

Since I don't want to share without Katelyn's permission, I shrug and say, "I don't know. I just do."

"And if you don't?" Jeremy challenges.

When I don't answer, Jeremy crosses his arms. "You don't have anything together; your ducks are not in a row." I go to rebut,

but he holds up his hand. "You and Tyler are both disasters. I also have my own stuff. The great thing is we can all lean on each other at any time. I think you should convey that it doesn't matter what she's going through, that you're here for her. You two can be chaos together."

"Jer—"

"You don't have to say anything. I'm just giving you my two cents." He glances down and then back at me. "I know you're holding stuff in. I'm not thrilled that you had a bottle of pain meds in here, considering what happened before. I'm trying to be chill here, but if something doesn't change…" Jeremy sighs. "You know you can talk to me. And if you can't talk to me, call your therapist. Just don't let everything fester."

I nod.

"If you're not taking care of yourself, you can't take care of Katelyn."

Katelyn

I've been staring at this invoice for so long that it's starting to blur together. I don't even notice someone approaching until I feel a tap on my shoulder. I look up to see Jeff standing behind me.

"Yes?"

"I was wondering if you wanted to grab a bite to eat." He tilts his head. "Everything okay?"

"Yep. Didn't sleep well and I'm not that hungry, but thanks." I turn back to my screen. Jeff lingers. When he doesn't step away, I glance back over. "Is there something else?"

His eyes widen a little at my sharp tone. "A group of friends are getting together this weekend to play games and hang out. I figured I'd extend an invite."

"I'm good. I have plans."

"Oh, of course. Maybe next time. I'll talk with you later, Katelyn."

I give him a courteous nod, turning my attention back to the invoice. I should be calling the client for payment, but my brain can't stop replaying everything that happened last night. Dom messaged me this morning. I don't even know what to say to him. Part of me wants to ask if he's doing okay and double-check that Jeremy is home just in case Dom needs help. However, even asking if someone is there or offering to be available seems like a bad decision. *Open your eyes.* Pressing the heels of my hands to my eyes, I pray that no tears fall.

You were stupid enough to open up, to let him in. Did you expect this to go differently? Did you think you deserve better? You are nothing. You're not lovable. You will never be enough.

My thoughts steal my breath. Breathing in through my nose, I let it out slowly, picturing a tiny flame extinguishing. My heart constricts thinking of Dom teaching me this little coping mechanism. A tear slips down my cheek. I quickly swipe it away, pick up the phone, and dial the number on the invoice. In the cheeriest voice I can muster, I state my scripted greeting to the receptionist.

After work, I check my phone. There are three texts from Dom and a text and a phone call from Eliza. Climbing into my car, I pull up Eliza's contact, needing to talk with her.

"Eek. In just a few weeks, I will be there! Are you excited?"

There is no way I can match her energy. "Yes. I can't wait to see you."

She hesitates. "Is Dom joining us?"

"I don't think so." My lip trembles and I'm happy she isn't sitting in front of me.

"Well, I'll be in town for a week. Maybe we can find another time to meet."

"Um, maybe." I clear my throat. "Is Marc excited?"

"He's excited for the food, not for the flight. He's not a fan of planes," she says and giggles.

She sounds so happy. I'm jealous. Before I burst into tears, I lie and tell her I'm getting another call.

"Tell Dom I say hi. I'll talk to you later. Love you!"

I hang up right after and quickly sweep the tears from my eyes.

My mind runs through everything that happened yesterday. I still need to check in with my mom and make sure she has everything she needs, which reminds me how I let it slip to Dom that I would love to write full time. I'm sure he's going to have an opinion on that, but right now, I'm not sure I want to hear it.

Open your eyes.

I flinch. Ugh, I just wanted to be sure he was okay. Deep down, I feel like I should have noticed he was struggling. I should have been able to anticipate what he needed. Except I didn't. I wrack my brain for ways I could have handled the situation differently but come up empty. Maybe there's nothing I could've done. Maybe we're just not right for each other. He has things he's dealing with and I'm not in a spot to help him.

It's late in the evening, way past Eliza's bedtime, when her name pops up on my screen. My heart starts to pound. Why would she be calling me right now?

"Hi. Is everything all right?"

"Yes, but I don't think you are, and I couldn't go to bed not knowing what was up, so spill."

I sigh heavily. "It's just been a long day. I'm tired."

"Liar," she scoffs.

She's not going to give up until I talk to her. I tell her that Dom fell last night and that I've been worried about him. She's not stupid and she knows I'm not telling her the whole story, but lets it go for right now.

"Well, I'm here if you need me." She yawns.

"I know. You should go to bed. I'll talk with you later."

CHAPTER TWENTY-NINE

Dom

It's late when I text one more time to see how Katelyn's day was, asking her to call me. Three little dots dance at the bottom of my screen, then disappear. I wait but they don't return. I finally crawl out of bed to take a bath and soak my aching muscles. When I return and check my phone, I see her messages.

Day was long.

Hope you're okay.

Not tonight.

Short tiny sentences. Not good. *You are losing the best thing that has happened to you*, my brain states. I can't disagree. Staring at my ceiling, I try and think of how on earth I'm going to fix this.

"What's up?" Jeremy asks from my doorway.

"I don't know what to do," I whisper.

"About Katelyn?"

"I've done everything I know to do. She's not talking to me. Something happened last night and I can't help if she won't talk to me."

Jeremy smirks.

"What?"

"We don't know *anyone* else like that," Jeremy says sarcastically.

"Shut up." I toss a pillow at him. He catches it and launches it back at me.

"Dude, we care for her too. We'll support you in any way we can. As someone who's had experience with a friend who wouldn't open up"—he gives me a pointed look—"it's when they push you away that you draw closer."

"But she hasn't known me for years and after last night…"

Jeremy nods. "Last night was bad. You apologized, though. She can't possibly hold that against you."

I shrug.

"Dom, come on. Give her a little time. Keep checking in with her and if you feel that something is wrong, act on it. Never ignore that feeling. Ever." A look of guilt flashes across his face, so harsh and heavy, that I can't help but nod.

Katelyn

I'm not sure why I came to Espresso Yourself today. My computer is on the table but I haven't even turned it on. I startle when I feel a tap on my shoulder. Stan's brows furrow when I glance up at him.

"Hey there. How are you?" he asks, studying my face.

"Um, okay." My eyes drift to the younger man standing behind him. The man smiles and his eyes crinkle just like Stan's. He also has a similar jawline.

Stan turns. "This is my son, Peter."

Peter extends his hand. "Katelyn," I say, giving his hand a shake.

"I've heard a lot about you. Rumor has it, you're writing the next epic fantasy."

I try to smile but I feel like it comes out more like a grimace. Stan cocks his head. "Peter, would you mind grabbing our drinks? I'll be right over."

"Of course. It was nice to meet you, Katelyn." He gives me a cursory nod and then makes his way over to the counter.

"Katelyn, are you doing okay?" Stan asks.

The lump in my throat prevents me from answering so I just nod.

"Is it your writing? I'd be happy to talk through something if you need it."

"I'm good. Thank you, though. You have a good day with your son." Shutting my laptop, I begin to pack up my bag. Stan stands by the table watching me.

"Pete is good on his own for a moment. Do you need to talk about anything?"

Shaking my head, I step around him. "No, it's just been a long day."

"Okay. Well, hopefully you can get a little rest, and when you feel up to it, I'd love to chat about your other manuscript. I think we can definitely use that to help you with your current project."

"Oh, okay." Tears sting my eyes, and I blink a few times. "I'll see you later."

I rush out before they can fall, but there's nothing stopping them once I climb into my car. *I need to get myself together.*

CHAPTER THIRTY

Dom

Katelyn hasn't responded to a single message today. I glance at the clock. She's probably home or heading home. Making a split-second decision, I wheel myself to my room, grab my keys, and then hurry toward the door.

"Going to Katelyn's!" I call out to my roommates.

"Can you tell her we need more of the Oreo stuff?" Jeremy asks.

I shake my head. "She's barely talked to me. Something's up."

"Apologize again, and then make sure you let her get all her feelings out. It was one bad night, but it can't ruin what you guys have," Jeremy says encouragingly. "Go get her, Dom."

Arriving at Katelyn's apartment, I take several deep breaths and then knock on her door. My heart sinks when she doesn't answer. Pulling out my phone, I start dialing her number when from behind me I hear, "Dom?" I spin to see Katelyn with an armful of groceries.

"What are you doing here?"

"I wanted to talk to you."

"I'm not ready to talk." She steps off the concrete path to pass me.

I turn. "Look, it was a bad night. I really am sorry for what I said and the way I treated you."

She transfers a couple bags from one hand to the other and pulls her keys from her pocket. The lock clicks and she quickly opens the door and sets the bags inside before turning toward me. When I catch her gaze, it freezes my heart. All the walls that she slowly let down are built back up and now seem to be reinforced.

"Katelyn, Firecracker, please talk to me," I plead.

She inhales a shaky breath. "I made a mistake."

"What do you mean? What mistake?"

"With you. With us. With everything. This was a bad idea. I need to open my eyes and realize I'm not cut out for a relationship."

I flinch at her word choice. "Katelyn, I'm truly sorry for what happened and what I said to you."

"I know you are. This has nothing to do with you. I just… I need to be done."

My heart sinks. "Done? I'm not ready to be done. I'm in this. Let me make it up to you."

She shakes her head.

"Katelyn, what's going on? Please talk to me. Would it make you feel better if you yelled? You can. I can take it."

"I don't need to yell. I just realized we each have things going on in our lives and maybe it's more practical to deal with them on our own. Let's face it, you don't need me. I can't help you."

Where on earth is this coming from? "Katelyn, that's not true and you know it."

She purses her lips. "Dom, I can't. I don't think we're good for each other and I need to be done. I'm sorry." Her voice cracks.

"No. I don't believe you. There has to be more and I can't fix what I don't know, so come on. Tell me."

"There's nothing to tell."

Frustration gets the best of me. "You're making this so difficult," I mutter.

"I'm difficult?" Her voice cracks.

"No, I didn't say that."

"I just make situations difficult?" Tears well in her eyes.

"No. Sorry. I just feel that—"

"Go home, Dom! I don't need to be a burden to another person. Now, leave." Turning, she steps into her apartment and slams the door.

"Katelyn, wait!" I wheel myself to the door and knock. "Please, talk to me." I sit there for another ten minutes begging her to come out. Eventually, her neighbor peeks their head out and tells me they'll call the cops if I don't leave. I don't want to cause any trouble for Katelyn, so I do.

The living room is thankfully deserted when I enter the house. I roll into my room, and as I sit alone, there is no way to keep the hurt and anger down. I swear and chuck my phone across the room, watching it shatter into several pieces.

"What's going on?" Tyler barrels in. "What happened?"

Jeremy rushes in a split second later, spotting the broken phone. "What the hell?"

I don't give either of them an answer, just grab some gym shorts and a T-shirt from my dresser. "Don't be in here when I get out," I say, before shutting myself into the bathroom.

Katelyn

I lock down all my feelings as I shut the door. Dom is quick to react, knocking several times before leaving. I'm surprised my phone doesn't buzz with a call or text. After putting my groceries away, I take a hot shower and then curl up on the couch. *Difficult. Such an accurate way to describe you. It's why everyone leaves*, my thoughts relay.

I must fall asleep because when I wake up, it's dark outside. With my guard down, all the feelings from earlier rush in and suddenly, breathing is impossible. It was a mistake to let Dom in. He said it himself—I make things difficult. I didn't even realize he was struggling last night, being so wrapped up in my own problems. How did I not see it? I'm the one who anticipates and helps. I didn't help Dom. He fell and it's my fault. I'm not good for him. I'm not good for anybody. It's better if I stay in my little bubble away from everyone. That way, no one gets hurt.

Tears well in my eyes. I've failed at being a good girlfriend. I'm failing at writing. I'm a complete and utter failure. Not thinking of the time, I call Eliza. It rings and goes to voicemail, so I dial again.

I'm on the third try when Marc answers groggily, "Katelyn?"

"I—I need El—Eliza," I gasp.

"She's right here. Just a moment." There's rustling and then I hear Eliza's voice, threatening death on Marc for waking her. "You can kill me in a minute. It's Katelyn. Something's wrong," he explains.

"Katelyn. What happened?" Eliza asks, now fully alert.

"He—he's gone. I make things too difficult and he left." The dam holding back the tears breaks.

"You're not difficult. Who said that?"

"Dom," I whimper.

"I'm going to kill him." There's a menacing edge to her voice. She blows out a quick breath, collecting herself. "What can I do? What do you need?"

Air would be nice, my thoughts quip.

"Katelyn, I'm here. You'll get through this, I promise. I'm not going to hang up until you're okay."

"I'll never be okay," I whisper.

"You will," she murmurs. "What happened?"

Pulling myself up to a sitting position, I bring my knees to my chest and breathe, trying not to imagine a candle. When I close my eyes, all I hear is Dom's soothing voice and see the little birthday candle with its tiny flame. My heart feels like it's being squeezed in a vice, constricting me further.

"Can't. I can't breathe."

"You can. You're okay. Um…the other day, Marc attempted to make apple pie. It was a total disaster. My kitchen looked like a tornado blew through."

"Why," I gasp, "why was—he making pie?"

"Trying to impress my family with his great cooking abilities. Which is absurd because none of the men help on Thanksgiving. They watch football and eat. I told him he has nothing to worry about."

Marc was out of the country on deployment last year so he missed all the major holidays.

"When do you fly out?" I take a tiny breath, trying to distract myself.

"Early Wednesday. I was thinking I'd come over and help you prep for dinner."

"I wasn't really planning on prepping anything. My mom mentioned she wanted to see me, so I figured I could just have her over for pie or something."

"You should have a turkey dinner. It's the best part of Thanksgiving. What if I come over and prep for dinner and you can still have your mom over for pie?"

"I guess that works."

"Then there's shopping Friday." She sounds so excited. When she lived out here, we were up at the crack of dawn to hit all the good sales. "Or I can come over and we can watch Christmas movies and eat massive amounts of junk food."

I chuckle. "Because the day after Thanksgiving means it's acceptable now?"

"Absolutely. I mean, I think any time is an appropriate time to watch Christmas movies. No matter how other people feel about it."

"She's had our tree up for the past week and a half," Marc yells.

"I have to pee," I announce before putting the phone on mute. Once I've washed my hands, I unmute the phone, throw on my pajamas, and curl up under my bed covers.

"Are you in bed?" Eliza asks.

"Yes. Don't hang up, though."

"I'm not going anywhere. Let's see, what Christmas movies should we watch?" She begins to list off some titles. I snuggle under my blankets, closing my eyes, listening to her. Every now and then, Marc chimes in. A few times they argue about why a movie should or shouldn't be added. She doesn't ask what happened for the rest of the night. Breathing finally comes a little easier and I slowly drift off.

When I wake up, my phone is lying next to me on my pillow. Eliza's name is still on the screen, with the timer for the call running. She never hung up. Hesitantly, I end the call and send her a quick message. I can't think of a good reason to crawl out of bed, so I sink deeper into my blankets. It's late in the afternoon when I finally get up and grab a small snack, curling up on the couch. Eliza messages me throughout the day with little updates on what she's doing.

Later, my phone buzzes and I freeze. *Please don't let it be Dom*, I think as I reach for it. Eliza's name flashes on the screen. I breathe a sigh of relief.

"Hey. How are you?" she immediately asks.

"I don't know." *Dying*, my brain answers.

"It's okay to take time to wallow. Just don't take up permanent residence on your couch, okay? You have a book to write and friends to prepare for."

"Eliza, this—" The words don't make it past the knot in my throat.

"I know," she murmurs.

"I should have never let him in. I was stupid for thinking this could work. Maybe he's right, I make things difficult. It's too hard to be with me. I'm broken and unlovable."

"Katelyn Rose Graham! I *never* want to hear you say that ever again! Do you hear me? You are not broken. You are not unlovable! I don't know what I would do without you. You are my person. Not Marc. You. I love you so much." Her voice breaks. "He is so, *so* dead. Six feet under isn't good enough."

Eliza sniffles and the line goes quiet. "Sorry." Another sniffle. "Are you there?" she asks.

"Mm-hmm."

You are making her worry. Friends don't do that. You are pathetic. She may tell you you're important, but you're insignificant.

"I'm probably just going to go to bed," I tell her. "You should get some rest."

"Katelyn…"

"I just want to sleep," I say.

"Fine, but I'm calling later," she states. "I love you."

"Yeah," I whisper. "Back at you."

CHAPTER THIRTY-ONE

Dom

I'm not doing myself any favors skipping physical therapy, but after the fall I'm not really up for working out. It's taken me all week to get back down to taking just Aleve for the pain. Jeremy has kept a watchful eye on me all week and even though it's been extremely aggravating, it's been a bit of a lifesaver. Not that I'm in the same spot I was, but some feelings have crept back up.

My phone rings and I instantly think it's Katelyn. Of course, it won't be. I sent her a text Sunday morning and a couple Monday. When each of them went unanswered, I stopped trying. Jeremy told me that she just needs space, but the time apart is killing me. It's only been a week and I'm going crazy. I answer my phone before it has a chance to go to voicemail.

"Hi, honey. How are you?" My mom's chipper voice brings a smile to my face.

"Okay. How's it going over there?"

"Good. Your dad's been in the garage all afternoon tinkering. He found these plans for a sled and reindeer that he wants to complete by Christmas."

"I can't wait to see it," I comment. Grabbing my earbuds, I slip them in and then wheel out to the living room.

"Are you sure you don't want to fly out for Thanksgiving? We'd love to have you."

"I'm sure." Ever since the accident, flying has become much more of a production. I have to call the airline in advance for an aisle seat, arrive at the airport *extra* early, and check my wheelchair, which always makes me nervous. I'm terrified they will lose it or damage it. It hasn't happened yet, but I've only flown twice in the past three years. Once my wheelchair is taken at the gate, I have to use a narrow one designed to fit down the airplane aisle and someone needs to push it. I briefly think that I could maybe walk to my seat, but ever since last week, I haven't touched my walker. On the flip side, my dad's blood pressure has been elevated and they didn't want to take the risk of flying until everything is a bit more under control.

Tyler walks in. *Who's that?* he mouths.

Mom, I mouth back.

"Hi, Mrs. Renner!" Tyler calls out.

"Is that Tyler? Oh my, how is he?"

I act as the middle man as they catch up. I'm ready for them to be done, but once Tyler says goodbye and my mom asks about Katelyn, I about beg for him to come back.

"Um…" How do I explain this? "She needed a break."

"What does that mean?"

In order for her to understand, I explain what happened on Halloween.

"Oh, Dominic…"

"I know. It wasn't my best moment. I've owned up to it. When I went to talk to her, she said we were a mistake." Saying it out loud makes my heart ache. I would never call us a mistake. "Katelyn's amazing and I thought we worked really well together."

"From everything you've told me, she's wonderful. She certainly brought joy to your life."

A knot forms in my throat and tears well in my eyes. "Can we talk about something else?" I ask.

"Oh, honey," she says sympathetically. "If it's meant to be, it will work out. Don't give up."

Katelyn

Dom reached out at the beginning of the week. I read those texts over and over again. At one point, I thought about responding but then his comment about me making things difficult runs through my head and I realize there is no response to make. There is no way I'm going to be a burden in someone's life.

I don't have the energy to get ready and I really don't want to change out of my pajamas. I grab my laptop and my mug of coffee and make myself comfortable on the couch. Opening up the writing document, I skim through the last few paragraphs and then just stare. The words blur as tears fill my eyes. *It's so cute that you try. You can't do this. You're going to fail.*

I swipe at my eyes and try and focus. When I saw Stan last weekend he said he thought we could use my other manuscript to help with this. I wonder what suggestions he has. If I didn't feel like I would burst into tears at any time, maybe I would go out. As it is, I barely hold myself together at work and usually have a good cry when I come home.

Maybe the reason I'm stuck at this section is because the main character is out of commission. Sighing, I get up and go grab my notes, pulling out the plot points Stan and I put together. Then I open the document of scenes written in the male lead's point of view. Could I also write this scene from his perspective? As I'm tossing around the idea, my phone buzzes.

Mom flashes on the screen and I hit decline. I'm not in the mood to talk with her right now. On Halloween night she called to tell me she had taken the plunge and gotten a new job. She was settling in and thought her co-workers were nice. However, this job paid slightly less and she didn't take into consideration the pay schedule. After inquiring about her bills and figuring out when her first paycheck would be, we determined she would probably be okay, but she had to be really frugal for the next few weeks.

Not that I thought she would be able to stick to her budget. I spent the next fifteen minutes in Dom's driveway reviewing my finances to make sure if something did come up, I could help her. I was so focused Jeremy startled me when he came out. He didn't pressure me to talk and neither did Dom. It's probably why I felt comfortable enough to open up. I didn't feel like I had to, but I wanted to.

I've read what you written. He sounded so positive and supportive during my rant. Until… *Open your eyes.* I shut that down, not wanting to relive the rest of the night.

Another week passes and I miss Dom so much. It doesn't hurt any less than the moment it happened. I catch myself thinking about him way too often. Wondering what he's up to. How work is going for him. If he's still using the walker. How Jeremy and Tyler are doing. This is why I didn't want to meet friends early. This is why I didn't want to get involved. I was getting attached, and now it's not just Dom that I miss.

I focus back on the spreadsheet in front of me. Due to the end of year, work has been a good distraction. We've been so busy, and after working long days, I usually go home, grab dinner, and go straight to bed. The weekends have proven more difficult. I've skipped my writing sessions at Espresso Yourself. I've barely managed to write anything while sitting at home.

Later, while eating leftover Chinese food, Eliza's name pops up on my phone screen.

"Hey. How's it going?" I ask.

"Ugh, Marc's sick."

"Oh no. What does that mean about your trip?" *Please don't say you have to cancel.* I bite my lower lip.

"Fingers crossed he'll be better before we have to leave."

"Are you worried you're going to get it?" There is no way she can get sick right now. The only thing getting me through is the fact that in another week, I'll be able to see her.

"He's banned from the apartment for the time being and I've taken every immunity booster I can think of. I will not miss this trip."

Thank goodness. Though, it makes me wonder how Dom reacts when he's sick. My heart clenches and I take a shaky breath in.

"Katelyn?" Worry fills Eliza's tone.

"So, you're still coming out even if Marc can't?" My voice cracks.

"Absolutely. I got plans with my bestie, my sister from another mister."

"Good." I take a deep breath. It's going to work out. It has to.

By Saturday, I decide to visit Espresso Yourself. I can't hide in my apartment forever. I bring a book and my laptop, thinking if I don't have it in me to write, I can read. When I walk in, the seating area is empty. I breathe a sigh of relief and make my way to the counter.

I'm halfway through my latte and making decent progress in my book I'm reading when the front door opens.

"Jeez, Peter. It's not funny and we're not five." The woman's short brown bob bounces as she whips her head back to glare at whoever's behind her. Peter, Stan's son, walks in laughing.

"Maria, Peter, that's enough, you two," Stan scolds, following.

A small grin curls my lips watching their interaction. I thought seeing Stan would make me sad, but I'm actually happy to see him. Stan glances around, smiling when he catches my eye. "You two go order, I'll be over momentarily." He joins me at my table. "Hello there, young lady. Haven't seen you in a while."

I glance down at the table. "Sorry, I've just had— I mean, it's been—" Tears well in my eyes and I fail miserably at wiping them discreetly.

"I see. Life's been a little rough."

I nod, eyes still focused on the table.

"Katelyn. Can you look at me?"

I peek up to see Stan staring at me. Even when laughter erupts across the café, Stan doesn't take his focus off me. "Life is like the ocean, beautiful and peaceful one moment, and vile and chaotic the next. You just have to hold on during the tumultuous moments. Have you been writing at all?"

"Now doesn't seem to be a great time," I answer honestly, even though my thoughts carry on about how much of a disappointment I am.

"I find that some of the best scenes come from the most painful moments. Don't bury it. Let it free. If you ever want to talk, you know where to find me."

"Thanks."

"Do you have any plans this Thanksgiving?" Stan asks.

"My friend is coming to town and I'll be meeting up with her," I explain. Stan nods. I'm grateful he doesn't ask about Dom. "What about you?"

"As you can see, my kids are in town. Maria's husband, Troy, and their kids will be here this evening. Peter's wife, Shelia, and their kids will be in tomorrow."

"Sounds like a lot."

"It's going to be interesting. Scout doesn't seem like a fan of people. She's been hiding in my room these last couple days."

Frowning, I say, "Poor thing."

"I love my children, but I think I will be happy to have my space back after this week."

I smile. "I bet you will."

"I'll let you get back to the book. Have a wonderful afternoon, Katelyn."

"You too. Glad I got to see you." And I'm surprised to find that I genuinely mean it.

CHAPTER THIRTY-TWO

Dom

Tyler flew back to Tennessee early Saturday to be with his family. I've tried my best to avoid Jeremy, not in the mood to talk about what happened between Katelyn and me. I'm afraid he'll say that he told me, that I should have given her space. Which, it's a little hard to avoid him when we're in the same car. He insisted we go grocery shopping before he flies out to see his family. I personally think he's lost it. Grocery shopping right now is a horrible idea. It's the day before Thanksgiving and the stores are going to be packed.

"You know, you could fly out with me," Jeremy says, breaking the silence.

"I'm good," I say, not looking up from my phone.

"Sitting at home alone doesn't seem like the best idea."

I take a deep breath before responding. "Jer, I'm good, okay? Don't worry about me. Go enjoy your time with your family."

He tosses a skeptical look my way, but this is my penance. It's my fault I'm spending the holiday alone. *If you would have just shut your dumb mouth, you might have a girlfriend right now.*

As Jeremy drives, I register that we aren't headed toward the grocery store.

"Where are we going?"

"Gotta make one quick stop first."

The second Katelyn's apartment complex comes into view, I shake my head. "What are you doing?"

"Dude, you won't talk. I have no idea what happened, but you miss her. I'm here to mediate. Get you two back together."

I curse under my breath. Jeremy pulls into a spot facing her door. "I'm not getting out of this car."

"Suit yourself." He closes his door and makes his way up the walk. My heart feels like it's about to beat out of my chest. As quickly as I can, I get out of the car and grab my frame from the back seat. It takes a minute to assemble my chair with how my hands are shaking. As I rush to the front door, Jeremy smiles, then knocks on the door.

But it's not Katelyn who answers.

"Hi. Can I help you…?" her friend Eliza trails off, eyes widening when she sees me.

"Hi, Eliza," I say at the same time Jeremy asks, "Is Katelyn here?"

"No." Her eyes bounce between Jeremy and me. "What are you doing here?"

"It's like this," Jeremy starts. "He misses her *a lot* and I'm hoping she misses him enough to talk things out."

Eliza's fury rises with each word out of his mouth. She turns her narrowed eyes on me.

"What is wrong with you?" she seethes. "You took her heart and you broke it into a million pieces! And here I was, stupidly thinking you would be great for her. I mean, I told her this was a good thing and she should jump in." Her voice cracks. "I was rooting for you. You got her to open up and share her writing. Any time I called, I could tell something was different. It was all because of you." She sniffles. "So what is *wrong* with you? Why did you say that she's difficult?"

"You *what*?" Jeremy's head whips to me.

"Oh, you don't know?" A dark chuckle escapes Eliza.

"He's been rather quiet about the whole thing. Care to share?" Jeremy asks.

"Katelyn said that—wait a minute." She turns wide eyes at me. "Did you blame her?"

"No," I state. "And I never said she was difficult."

She crosses her arms. "I'm about three seconds from murdering you with my bare hands. But before I do, I want your side. What do you mean you didn't say she was difficult?"

Jeremy turns to me, raising an eyebrow, waiting.

"Halloween was…not a great night. After that, Katelyn wasn't really responding to my texts or calls, so I decided to come here. She said she didn't want to talk and I told her I wanted to. I told her she could yell or do whatever she needed to do, she just had to talk to me. When she said she couldn't, I may have mumbled she was *making* things difficult."

Jeremy swears under his breath. Eliza stands frozen like a statue. "I'm such an idiot for not controlling my mouth," I mutter.

"You think?" Eliza scoffs.

"If I could take it back, I would. Katelyn is amazing and I didn't mean to hurt her."

Eliza takes a deep breath in and then studies me. "Do you really want her back?"

"Yes."

She turns to Jeremy. "Should I trust him?"

He shrugs. "He has his flaws, but he's a decent human being."

I toss a scowl his way.

Eliza sighs, brow furrowed in contemplation. "I can't make any promises, but I'll see what I can do."

Wait, what? "Are you serious?" I ask.

"Be advised, my boyfriend is in the military. He is highly skilled in a lot of things. If I ever get a phone call again with Katelyn in tears, he will be your worst nightmare. Understand?"

"Understood."

"It won't happen overnight, so you have to be patient. And you better be freakin' worth it. Have a good Thanksgiving." She shuts the door in our faces.

Stunned, I turn back toward the car. We're halfway down the walk when Jeremy says, "Her nice military boyfriend may have assistance if you're an idiot again."

I nod, completely understanding. *Holy cow, I'm getting Katelyn back.* It's a hopeful thought, and Eliza is going to have to use every magic trick she knows to get Katelyn to even consider talking to me. I believe in her, though.

Katelyn

Marc recovered before their flight out. I met up with them Wednesday afternoon on my lunch break, and gave Eliza the key to my apartment so she could prep Thanksgiving dinner. When I got home, she was awfully quiet, giving me weird glances all evening. At first, I thought I was being paranoid, until Marc made a comment about Eliza's day.

"Um, yeah," Eliza says, giving Marc a look. "Katelyn had a visitor while you were at the store."

The pumpkin pie I'm getting ready to place in the oven slips out of my hand. Luckily, I'm able to catch it before it falls to the floor. "Who?"

"We can talk about it another time."

I set the pie on the counter, turning to her. "Who, Eliza?"

"There were two visitors, actually. I didn't catch the name of the second guy."

I swear my heart stops beating for a minute before nearly flying out of my chest. She doesn't mean… "Who was it?"

She stares at me. "I think you know." Her face softens. "Katelyn, what happened between you two?"

Turning, I grab the pie, shove it in the oven, and slam the door. "I'm not talking about this." Eliza slides over from the counter, blocking my exit from the kitchen.

"I don't think you shared the full story, and I want to hear your side."

"No!" Just thinking about Halloween brings an ache to my chest.

Eliza crosses her arms, not moving. Marc steps behind her. "Okay, let's just take a minute here."

I point at him. "Stay out of this."

Eliza's eyes narrow. "Don't get mad at him." She reaches out and I pull back. Dropping her hand, she sighs. "Fine. We have all weekend to talk." She gestures for me to go and I storm straight to my room, bursting into tears the minute the door closes. My phone buzzes twenty minutes late.

Set a timer for your pie. We'll be back tomorrow for dinner. Love you!

I stay curled up on my bed until I hear the timer beep. When I walk out, I see the kitchen is clean. I take the pie out of the oven and set it on a cooling rack. The whole time, my mind wanders. What if I had been here when he came over? Why did he even stop by? Who was with him, Tyler or Jeremy, and why did he have someone with him? What story did he tell Eliza? I'm so mad at

Dom for ruining what was supposed to be a relaxing weekend with my best friend.

Eliza knocks on my door early in the late morning on Thanksgiving.

"Where's Marc?" I ask when I open the door.

"Dropped me off. Thought we might need some time alone."

I step aside and let her in. "What time are we eating?"

"Originally, I thought one, but it might be closer to two. Or we can wait and just make everything after your mom leaves. I figured you needed some time this morning."

"Eliza—"

"I'm guessing you spent half your night wondering what on earth he told me," she says.

I nod.

"Look, if you want to be mad at him, I support you. If you need out of this relationship, I'm here for you, but the thing is, I don't think you want to be out. I think you got scared and instead of being vulnerable and telling him what was going on, you ran."

Tears well in my eyes.

"Look, he's dumb. He should've never said that you were making things difficult. But Katelyn, *making* things difficult and *being* difficult are different things." I open my mouth to argue and she holds up her hands. "I don't agree with how he handled the situation. I'll still help you hide his body."

I smirk.

"So, can you please tell me what happened?"

Hesitantly, I take a deep breath and recount everything that happened on Halloween. Once I start, I can't stop.

"Suddenly, I wasn't standing in Dom's room. I was back at…" I swallow. Eliza's face tightens with anger. She knows what happened in my last relationship. "I was at *his* apartment listening to him tell me how immature I was being about my life."

"But Dom's not him."

"I know," I mumble.

"I was serious about helping you hide a body, no questions asked. Always. However, I don't think I'd be doing my best friend duties if I didn't play devil's advocate. Dom is a good guy. He has his flaws, but he cares for you. Like, it's insane how much he cares for you. I think you should give him another chance. I think you *want* to give him another chance."

I sigh. "I'll…think about it."

By the time we've had a heart to heart, there is no time to make dinner and eat before my mom arrives. I make grilled cheese sandwiches so we're not starving and then we wait for my mom.

During dessert, my mom asks Eliza all about Georgia and how she and Marc are doing. A strange look passes over Eliza's face. I study her for a second, but whatever it was is replaced with a smile in a heartbeat. When my mom directs her questions to me, I tense. She asks about my job and if I'm still writing.

"At least you seem to have more of a social life. You've actually been out when I called," she comments. I want to laugh. If I missed a call recently, it's because I haven't wanted to talk. I'm so happy when my mom leaves.

CHAPTER THIRTY-THREE

Katelyn

Today is Eliza's last night here and we have plans to see each other one more time before she flies out tomorrow. I still have to work, though, and I let out a quiet snarl at this spreadsheet. The client's account is not reconciling and I've reviewed it at least five times now. If I can't figure it out, I might have to escalate the account to my supervisor. After another pass, I make a note to look at it with fresh eyes in the morning and switch to another account. The minute the clock hits five, I'm logged off and out the door to meet Eliza for dinner.

She seems off, though. Eliza only picks at her breadstick.

"What's up?"

"Hm?" She shakes her head. "Nothing."

"That's not how this works. Spill."

She sighs, setting her breadstick down. "Marc's been acting super weird lately."

"Weirder than normal?"

"I don't know. He claimed to have errands to run yesterday and when I asked if I could tag along, he said no. And then today he was gone for like two hours, and when I asked where he had been, he just shrugged and said 'out.' Like, what is that about?"

"It's Black Friday weekend. Maybe he's planning your Christmas present."

Eliza rolls her eyes. "Oh please, that is so not him. He'll wait until the week before and then pick something out. He doesn't plan that far in advance." She goes back to picking apart her breadstick.

"You and Marc have been together for like, what, two years now? There has to be a reasonable explanation for this. It's not like he's cheating on you."

Eliza doesn't respond.

"Um, that hiding a body thing goes both ways. I mean, you have to be more strategic because he is in the military, but it's doable." Thankfully, I get a small laugh out of her. "Look, whatever it is, I'm sure it's not a big deal."

"If you say so. Let's talk about something else."

Leaving the restaurant, I immediately text Marc. I'm not even subtle with my message.

Eliza knows you're hiding something and I need to know what it is.

Three little dots dance at the bottom of my screen, disappear, and then start again.

Wow. Okay. Good to know, but I'm not telling you anything.

So there's something to tell?

You are the worst secret keeper. My lips are sealed. She has nothing to worry about, though.

What on earth does that mean? Do I let Eliza know he's hiding something? Or do I trust Marc and wait to see what happens? On the drive home I convince myself it has to be a Christmas present. Eliza is Marc's person. There is no way he'd do anything to damage their relationship.

At work the next day, I cave and report the account I can't reconcile. My supervisor huffs in exasperation and I feel like I failed. I should have been able to figure it out.

Sitting at lunch, trying to keep my thoughts from recounting my morning and the giant failure I am, I think through my story instead. I was able to make a tiny bit of progress the last time I sat down, but it's been a few days since I've touched it. I have yet to speak with Stan about my other manuscript, so I have no helpful hints from him. *You're failing at everything!* Tears instantly well in my eyes. I quickly gather my lunch, tossing what remains of my salad in the trash, and return to my desk. I pull up my list of clients and work on reconciling another account.

The day doesn't improve. Leaving work, I see I have a voicemail from my mom. Just like I thought, all that planning for a budget didn't stick and she's a little short on rent. Her landlord gave her a grace period, but she needs to have the money by Friday. I can't believe I didn't check up on this when I saw her. I blow out a breath and turn the key. The car makes a strange sound and takes a second to start. *No.* My car cannot die on me. A weight presses down on my chest.

I immediately call Eliza to hear her voice. I need her to tell me I'm going to be okay. That I'll get through this, but the call goes to voicemail. I hang up and call again. When she doesn't answer, I find Marc's number. It goes straight to voicemail.

You're a failure. Insignificant. You aren't helping anyone. Why exist? The loop of thoughts plays over and over. I press my hands to my chest, trying to get air into my lungs. Closing my eyes, I take a tiny breath in and immediately picture a tiny candle. Dom. The thought of him makes my heart hurt.

He cares for you. Like, it's insane how much he cares. Eliza's words ring through my head.

Putting my car in gear, I don't think, I just drive. I have to pull over twice to catch my breath and pray I don't pass out. Somehow, I make it to Dom's driveway and pull the car over. My vision goes spotty when I reach the front door. Before I pass out, I sit down in the entryway and place my head between my knees. I'm not sure how long I sit there for when I hear someone call my name, but it sounds like they're talking underwater. Whoever it is says something else, and then yells. I'm going to pass out. *Would that be a bad thing? What if you never woke up?*

Dom

As Tyler and I pull into the driveway, I spot Katelyn's car parked on the curb. A spark of hope ignites in my chest. Maybe she's here to give me a chance. I'm going to have to thank Eliza. However, I see Katelyn sitting outside the front door. Jeremy's home, why didn't she go in? Tyler grabs my chair, setting it by the car door, and then grabs some boxes from our Costco haul. Trying not to seem too eager, I pull out the paper towels when Tyler yells for me. There's a weird edge to his voice.

"Dominic, now!"

Tyler's panic has me racing to the door. When Katelyn comes into view, my heart stops. Her knees are curled up to her chest, her head hanging between them. As I get closer, I can hear her gasping for breath. I quickly slide from my chair, sitting in front of her.

"Katelyn, Firecracker, you gotta breathe for me." I scoot closer and grab her hands. Her breathing becomes shallower, and she sways backwards. Tyler catches her. He glances at me, worry etched on his face.

"Take a deep breath and picture a candle."

She shakes her head and hurt flashes across her pale face. My heart feels like it's about to explode out of my chest. *You have to fix this!*

Holding her frigid hands gives me an idea. "Firecracker, I'm right here. Can you feel this?" I squeeze her hands. "You're safe. Focus on my hands. Can you tell me how many times I do this?" I squeeze her hands again, three times, and wait for her to respond. "Come on."

If she can focus on something else, it might help snap her out of her panic. It takes me a second to realize she squeezes my hands back. She's still fighting for her next breath but she's responding. "Okay, good. Now how many times?" I pause as she grips my hands. "And now?"

"T-two," she sputters.

She continues squeezing my hands for the next few sets before she attempts to answer out loud again. When she does, she also sucks in a full breath. Tyler quietly stands and motions to the boxes. I nod and turn my attention back to Katelyn. Her breathing hitches when the door hinges squeak.

"It's just Tyler. I'm still here." I squeeze her hands.

"Don't. Leave."

"Never." I tighten my grip on her. *I will never leave you*, I vow to myself.

When she's breathing more steadily, I scoot over to her side. I use one arm to wrap around her shoulders. She leans into me, clutching my other hand, like she's afraid I'll disappear. I kiss the top her head, whispering, "I'm here."

As the sun sets, the temperature drops and she shivers. "Let's go inside," I suggest.

"That's a bad idea. This was probably a bad idea," she whispers.

"I'm glad you came over. Just come inside and talk to me. Please."

Her big brown eyes find mine and after a second, she nods. She stands, releases the brakes on my chair, and pushes it closer to me before resetting the brakes. I climb up and then lead her inside. I push myself toward the couch and then turn to see that she hasn't stepped away from the front door.

"Katelyn." I nod toward the couch. She chews on her bottom lip, debating. Finally, she takes a step in and I breathe a sigh of relief. She sits down in the center of the couch, slips her shoes off, and pulls her knees to her chest. Another shiver runs through her, and I grab the blanket from the back of the couch and drape it around her.

"What happened today?" I keep my words gentle.

Her lip trembles and a tear slides down her cheek. "It's bad." She's so quiet I almost miss her response.

My gut tells me that *bad* is truly bad. I think back to a conversation we had in the first couple months of dating when she said she had a rough day, but this doesn't seem like that. Running away to Australia won't fix this.

"Can you tell me what was bad about it?"

She wipes her eyes and keeps her focus on her knees. "I had to escalate an account at work. Eliza had to go home. My mom can't seem to figure out how to be a grown-up, and I'm failing at writing. I'm failing at *everything*." Her voice catches. The tears fall harder and her shoulders shake. "This hurts too much. I can't do this."

I draw in a deep breath. "I know it's hard right now."

She shakes her head. "It's too *much*. I'm too tired. I don't want to do this anymore. I don't want to fight anymore. I'm just…tired."

"Like, physically tired?" I ask, trying to understand. Not that I need the clarification. *You know what she means.*

She shakes her head.

I brace myself before saying, "You can say it, Katelyn. It's okay."

"Tired of existing," she whispers. My heart cracks with the admission. I pull her to me as she begins to sob. Out of the corner of my eye, I spot movement. Jeremy is standing at the end of the hall, shoulders tense, staring at the back of Katelyn's head. His eyes shift to me. He turns abruptly and heads down the hall. He doesn't quite slam his door but it's loud. Thankfully, Katelyn doesn't notice.

As she cries, I try and think of something that will make her feel better, something to fix everything. But I know from experience, there are no words. There is no magical cure for this. The best thing I can do for her is be here and let her know she's not alone.

"I'm sorry for coming," she murmurs. "I know I make things difficult."

I flinch. "No, you don't," I say adamantly.

"I do, though. I'm messy and broken." Her voice catches and a tear hits my shirt.

"Katelyn, I'm so sorry for ever making you think that. You are perfect in all your chaos, okay? Can you look at me?" She shifts and her beautiful brown eyes find mine. I cup a hand on her cheek. "I want you, Katelyn, every beautifully broken piece of you. Always. I couldn't imagine a world where you didn't reside in it." Her face falls and she buries into my shoulder, tears soaking my shirt. "I love you, Katelyn," I whisper.

CHAPTER THIRTY-FOUR

Katelyn

Once the tears have run dry, I sit up and wipe my cheeks. Dom watches me, those hazel eyes so full of love and worry. "I'm sorry," I say.

"For what?"

"Everything."

"There's nothing to be sorry for. Is there anything I can do?"

I shake my head. "Would it be okay if I go wash up?"

"Absolutely. Are you hungry?"

I shrug. I should probably eat something since I didn't finish my lunch but I don't really have much of an appetite at the moment. Dropping my feet, I stand and make my way to the bathroom. After washing my face and taking a minute to collect myself, I open the door. Jeremy stands just outside in the hall.

"Hi." I look down at the floor.

"Did you mean what you said?" His harsh tone makes me glance up. His face is pinched in anger. My heart clenches. *He heard?*

"Did. You. Mean. It?" he repeats, glaring at me.

My lower lip trembles and I bite it to make it stop. I nod slowly.

He lets out a heavy sigh then steps closer, lowering his head so we're eye level. "If you *ever* feel like that, you call me. I don't care what the status is between you and Dom, you call. I never want my phone to ring again letting me know my friend is in the hospital because they thought living was too hard. That hurts too much." He takes a breath. "Dom's lucky to be alive after pulling that crap," he mutters.

My eyes widen. Jeremy catches himself and looks at me, cursing under his breath. "Look, just, can you promise me that?"

I slowly nod, my eyes filling with tears.

"Come here." He opens his arms and I step into them, wrapping my arms around his waist.

"I'm sorry," I blubber.

He hugs me back. "It's going to get better."

I know he's probably right, but at this moment, it doesn't feel like it.

Jeremy and I walk out to the living room where Tyler is talking with Dom. The conversation abruptly stops when Tyler catches sight of me. I freeze. Jeremy steps around me and takes a seat in the recliner. My gaze passes around the room. "Sorry for messing up your evening."

Dom reaches out his hand, but I stay where I'm at. *You should never have come here. You don't matter. You're worthless. Pathetic.*

"Firecracker." Panic colors Dom's tone. "Katelyn, please come here." When I don't move, Dom shifts to transfer to his chair.

"Don't," I snap. He shouldn't have to help me. I should be able to calm myself down, but breathing becomes difficult as my thoughts continue to pepper me with insults. No, the whole reason I showed up on his doorstep is because he helps. "Never mind, can you—can you come—here?" I ask breathlessly.

Dom places his hands on my hips and tugs me backwards. I lock my knees so I don't fall.

"Katelyn, relax and trust me." He tugs again. This time, I let myself collapse, dropping to his lap. His arms wrap around me and he holds me tight until his hands find mine. "How many times?" He squeezes my hands twice and I squeeze his back. "Good." He leans around me and kisses my cheek. "I'm right here. Can you tell me what's going on?"

I'm very aware that Tyler and Jeremy are in the room, which makes my breathing hitch. I shake my head.

"Can you guys—"

"No. It's—" *I need air.*

"Put your feet up," he instructs.

"Will I hurt you?"

"Not one bit."

I pull my feet up. I manage to place one on his footrest and one on his foot. He doesn't react, just wheels us out of the room. Keeping my eyes closed, I focus on breathing in and out.

"There ya go," Dom murmurs. A door clicks shut, and his arms wrap around my midsection. "In and out, nice and slow."

When I open my eyes, we're in his room. His foot shifts under mine. I swear. "Am I hurting you?"

"I don't want you to worry about me right now."

"But am I?" I twist, trying to see his face.

He chuckles. "I can barely feel you. You're fine."

Putting all my weight on the footrest, I push myself up. His arms slide away, but his hands grip my hips and he helps guide me up. I move over to his bed, sitting on the edge. He wheels in front of me, setting his brakes. His hazel eyes are focused on me. He leans forward and I meet him in the middle, resting my forehead against his.

"I'm failing."

His head shakes against mine. "I don't think you're failing. You had a rough day, but that doesn't mean you're failing." He straightens. "I know it might be hard, but can you try and tell me how you're feeling? Or maybe what your thoughts are telling you?"

My eyes sting with fresh tears and Dom's face blurs. "That I'm worthless and pathetic and no one would miss me."

"Those are all lies. You are smart and talented. You are fierce and tenacious." He brushes a stray hair away from my face. "And I would miss you. Eliza would miss you. Jer and Ty would be mildly inconvenienced." He smirks.

I sniffle. "Everything seems like it's too much. My brain won't shut up."

He kisses my lips. "I know." Another little kiss. "It might be hard to drown your thoughts out at times. When it is, I'll be here to be louder than those thoughts to tell you that you are loved and you're tough. I'll be here to remind you that you are not alone. Always."

I nod. His hand cups my cheek and he leans in close. He presses his lips to mine and I let a small piece of the wall fall as I return it.

Dom

As we sit in my room, my phone chimes. I don't check it until Katelyn settles. When I do, I see Tyler has sent a link for a group order. "Do you want anything from Chipotle?" I ask her. She glances over, shrugging.

"It's getting late. I should go. I've already ruined your evening," she mumbles.

"Hey." She glances over. "You didn't ruin anything. You are more than welcome to stay, or I can take you home. Whatever makes you feel more comfortable." Either way, I'll be with her. There is no way I'm leaving her alone tonight.

"You're sure you want me to stay?"

"Yes."

She fiddles with the hem of her blouse—she must have come straight from work—until she finally whispers that she'll stay. Rolling over to my dresser, I pull out an old pair of sweats and a T-shirt. "Here, why don't you change and I'll go see what the guys are up to." I set the change of clothes on the bed and head toward the door.

"Dom?"

"Yeah?" I turn.

"Thank you."

I nod, closing the door on the way out.

When I roll into the front room, Tyler mutes the television. "How is she?"

"Um, okay for now." It's the most honest answer I can give. "She's going to stay here."

"Cool, cool."

"I added our order to the link you sent. Is someone picking it up?"

Tyler nods. "I was just about to head out." Once he leaves, I transfer out of my chair to the couch. Jeremy glances over at me.

"Are you doing okay?" he asks.

Door hinges squeak from down the hall. "Later?" I whisper.

Jeremy nods as Katelyn appears, taking a seat next to me. I slip my arm around her shoulders. She tenses but I'm not sure what's wrong.

"Katelyn, have you ever seen *Schitt's Creek*?" Jeremy asks.

She shakes her head.

"Now, it's not as intense as *Jane the Virgin,* but it's funny." He navigates to the pilot episode and hits play. The episode is ending as Tyler walks in with dinner.

"Want to come to the table or stay here?" I ask Katelyn.

She sits up. "You can go eat."

"Oh, they ran out of chips. Isn't that the most ridiculous thing you've ever heard? I mean, you're Chipotle, how do you run out of chips? Anyway, I stopped at the store since I know Katelyn prefers eating chips with her bowl," Tyler explains.

Katelyn's eyes widen. "Why would you order me something?"

Good going. You've only had her back for a few hours and have already messed up. "I just thought that if you wanted to munch on something, you could, or you can reheat it later. Or I'll eat it for lunch or something," I say defensively.

Katelyn glances at the table and then back to me. She pushes herself off the couch and sits at her place at the table. The rest of us take ours and everyone except Katelyn silently opens our dishes. Tyler dumps some chips out on a napkin and then slides the bag toward Katelyn. Halfway through my burrito, she finally removes the lid from her bowl and pulls a chip from the bag. She scoops a small bit of rice on the chip and takes a bite. She takes another nibble before setting the chip aside.

"Want to put it in the fridge?" Jeremy asks.

Her lower lip trembles. She pushes away from the table and darts down the hall. I hang my head, cursing myself for thinking I had a clue what she needed. *Way to go, dumbo.*

"Dom?"

I glance up at Jeremy. "I don't know what you're thinking but stop. This is a hard night. I'm assuming you have some feelings?"

I nod. I told Katelyn that she could admit her feelings, but the second she said she was tired of existing, something in me snapped. I've been there. After the accident, my body was broken. I mean, it still is, but at the time I was still getting used to everything. I wasn't accustomed to letting people's stares or comments roll off my shoulders. The pitying looks and the way people changed around me, instantly thinking I couldn't do something for myself, was infuriating. So, when I had had enough, I didn't turn to anyone. I just decided I was done. Sitting here now, I hate Katelyn feels this way, and more importantly, I hate that I can't fix it.

"You're present, and you are doing everything you can. She's going to be fine. Once she's settled, you can come find me."

"Or me." Tyler nods.

It's several minutes before she returns to the table. Jeremy stands, gathers the trash, and clears the table. He returns, pausing in front of Katelyn. "Done?"

She nods.

"The great thing about Chipotle is it reheats well. And here, food is never safe in the fridge. It will get eaten."

Katelyn glances up and Jeremy winks. "I'd say you can put your name on it, but a name doesn't stop anyone."

"It's okay," she whispers. Her eyes shift to me and I give her a small smile.

"What now?" I ask.

Katelyn shrugs. "*Schitt's Creek*?"

"I'm down," Jeremy chimes in.

Everyone congregates in the living room. Jeremy starts the next episode and I automatically wrap my arm around Katelyn. She tenses again and it hits me that even though she was open earlier, there is still lingering hurt. I pull my arm back.

"You're okay." She peeks over, apprehension evident on her face.

Cautiously, I loop my arm around her again, resting it more on the back of the couch than her. She leans closer to me. "It's really okay. I didn't mean to make you feel bad."

"I don't want you to feel uncomfortable."

She looks down. "It's been a lot today. I don't know how to feel right now. If it's too much, can I just say?"

"Yes."

She nods and turns her attention back to the TV. After a few minutes her muscles relax and her head falls to my shoulder. Eventually, her breathing slows to a nice, steady rhythm. When I glance down, she's fast asleep. Jeremy stops the episode and heads out of the room.

"Need anything?" Tyler asks.

I shake my head.

Tyler sits quietly for a moment. "It's been a while since you've thought…" He trails off, glancing at Katelyn. "Tonight was intense. I can only imagine how you're feeling right now. I just want to make sure you're…" He pauses again, swearing under his breath.

"These past few weeks have been hard, and I'm trying to deal with my stuff. But I haven't come close to how I felt when I…you know." Tyler nods. "Right now, I'm just focused on making sure she's okay."

"Okay." Tyler stands. "I probably don't have to say it, but we're here for both of you. If she ever needs anything, she can reach out to either of us."

"Thanks, man."

He nods and heads to his room. When Jeremy comes back out, he's dressed in his security uniform. He sits in the recliner and laces up his boots. "How long you gonna sit there?"

"Don't know," I whisper.

"I could move her to your bed."

"I should probably head home," Katelyn mumbles, suddenly awake. She sits up, rubbing her eyes.

"I'm fine with you staying here. I can take the couch."

She shakes her head vehemently. "I don't want you to do that. I disrupted your night enough. I need to go home."

Taking her hands, I wait until her eyes focus on me. "It's not a big deal. I've slept on this couch plenty of times." She moves to argue but I continue, "What would make you comfortable right now? Don't think about what is fair, just tell me what you need right now, in this moment."

She shrugs.

Transferring to my chair, I take her hand and pull her to her feet, then rest it on my shoulder and lead her toward my room. Thankfully, she follows. I stop at the edge of my bed. "How about this? You lie down, I'll go get ready for bed, and when I come out, you can let me know if you want me to stay with you. Sound good?"

She looks at my bed and then at me. "What side do you prefer?"

"Whichever. I want you to be comfortable."

Slipping away, she scoots to the right side of the bed and sits down, resting her back against the headboard and drawing her knees to her chest. I'd love to know what's going on inside her head, but instead, I do what I said and disappear into the bathroom.

CHAPTER THIRTY-FIVE

Katelyn

The bathroom door clicks shut and my breathing accelerates. Dom has been great and both Tyler and Jeremy have been so sweet, but I feel like a huge burden. Now, Dom is considering sleeping on the couch because of me. What will sleeping on the couch do to his back? I don't want him to be inconvenienced because of me. *Inconsiderate. Failure. Unimportant.*

I close my eyes and take as deep a breath as I can manage through the vice around my lungs. When I do, I get a whiff of sea breeze and smoke. The scent loosens some of the tightness in my chest and I'm able to take a fuller breath. I do it again, but this time, the smoky ocean air is stronger. Suddenly, Dom's breath tickles my ear. "Good job breathing nice and slow. What can I do?"

Peeking my eyes open, I reach out and lace my fingers with his. "Just sit here, okay?"

His fingers tighten in mine. "I'm not going anywhere."

Exhaustion hits me hard and I have trouble keeping my eyes open. Unlinking our hands, I scooch down and pull the covers over my shoulder.

I yawn. "I'm okay with you staying," I say, and fall asleep immediately.

When I wake up, Dom isn't in bed. I'm hoping he didn't wait until I fell asleep and then moved to the couch. I scramble out of bed and out to the living room. Thankfully, the couch is empty. Dishes clank in the kitchen and when I round the corner, Dom is standing to reach the bowls, shirtless. There's a miniature tattoo of Mario running across the little bricks on his left shoulder, along with a scar on his lower spine about two inches long.

"Why Mario?" I ask.

"Holy cow!" The bowl clatters on the counter and Dom grips the edge for support. "Don't do that."

"Sorry. Oh my gosh, I'm so sorry."

"It's fine. I just didn't hear you come in." He sits down in his chair. "Watch your feet." I back up and he pivots toward me. "Morning. How'd you sleep?"

I shrug. "What about you?"

"Not bad. You hungry?"

"Not really. I should actually go home and change before work. Um…thank you for last night. I really appreciate it."

"Of course. I'm always here for you. If you want to come by after work tonight, you're more than welcome to."

"Oh, I don't know if that's a good idea." We're not even together right now. I had no right showing up at his house in the first place, because I'm the one who pushed him away. It's terrifying to think about letting him back in. What if this gave him the wrong idea?

"Fi—" He stops, taking a breath. "Katelyn, I'm just saying, it's okay if you want to. If not, that's fine too. Just reach out if you need anything."

"I will. I'll talk to you later." I grab my purse and keys and head for the door.

"It was a dumb bet," he calls out. I turn. "I was young and stupid, and I lost the bet. Now Mario forever resides on my back."

"Oh."

"Anyway, have a good day."

As I climb in my car, I glance back at the house to see Dom in the doorway. I wave and he waves back. I didn't check my phone after everything that happened yesterday, but I'm still surprised to see several missed calls from Eliza.

CALL ME!! I'M FREAKING OUT, her last text reads.

I immediately dial her. "Oh my gosh. Where were you? Are you okay?" she answers, frantic.

"It was a bad night. I ended up at Dom's house," I admit.

"Wait, what? What happened?"

I take a deep breath. Maybe it wasn't a good idea to call her while I'm driving. I'm not sure how I'll react recounting the day. I'm not pulling over, though; I have to get home and to work.

"Katelyn?"

"Sorry. It's a little hard to explain everything. All I know is that it was lovingly pointed out to me that Dom cares a lot about me, and when you didn't answer last night, I didn't know what else to do."

"Did he help?"

"Yes." My voice catches.

"Good." She breathes a sigh of relief. "How are you? What can I do?"

I pull up to my apartment complex and put my car in park. I have twenty minutes to get ready if I want to grab coffee before work. "I don't think there's anything for you to do."

"Well, I'm here for whatever you need," Eliza assures me.

"I know. Sorry for making you worry. Can I call you later?"

"Absolutely. Oh, wait! Would it be okay if I get Dom's number?"

"Um, I guess."

"Perfect. Okay, I'll check on you later. Have a good day."

After sending Dom's contact information to Eliza and getting ready at home, I pull into Starbucks. Today is going to be a venti-size coffee kind of day. When I walk in, I'm surprised to see Jeremy sitting at a little side table, scrolling on his phone. He glances up, seeing me, and relief washes over his face. Standing, he pockets his phone and walks over to me.

"What are you doing here?" I ask at the same time he says, "Good morning."

"Um, hi. What are you doing here?" I repeat.

He shrugs. "A beverage sounded good. How are you?" He studies my face and purses his lips when he catches the dark circles under my eyes.

"Fine." I step around him and into the line.

"Do you have a busy day at work today?" he asks, following me.

I shrug, glancing over. "Seriously, why are you here? Isn't this out of your way? And aren't you usually getting ready for bed right now? Won't coffee keep you up? And how did you know where I'd be?"

"I'm not even sure which question to answer first. That was a lot."

I narrow my eyes. "Wait, did Dom—"

"Nope," he quickly interjects. "He doesn't even know I'm here. And they also serve tea." He gestures for me to order. I step up to the counter and ask for my usual, an iced coffee with three pumps of mocha. As I pull up my app to pay, Jeremy orders a grande mint majesty and scans his phone.

"Thank you, but you didn't have to do that."

"You're welcome."

We step out of the way and wait for our drinks. Jeremy fiddles with the lanyard on his keys. "Look, I didn't mean to upset you by showing up. I just thought a friendly face this morning after a hard day yesterday would be good. Maybe I'm wrong, though. I think I just needed to see you. You scared me yesterday." He whispers that last part.

He continues playing with his lanyard, not looking at me. "Oh, Dom also mentioned you usually stop for coffee in the morning. I took a guess at the location."

Jeremy's name is called, and he grabs our drinks. He doesn't make eye contact as he hands me mine. When we step outside, I turn and give him a hug. It was a little shocking to see him at first, but for the last ten minutes, I haven't had to remind myself to breathe or try and drown out the negative thoughts.

"Thank you," I whisper.

"No problem."

I pull away. "I should go."

"Yeah. Have a good day." He nods and heads to his car.

"Jeremy," I call. He turns. "Um, could you maybe stop by the next time you work? I mean, you don't…"

He smiles. "I'll see you tomorrow."

CHAPTER THIRTY-SIX

Dom

I'm so screwed. While reviewing notes for my team's pitch this afternoon, I find a few mistakes and make a note to talk with my design assistant. Then I glance at the slide deck and groan, catching another error.

Jeremy walks in, giving me a little head nod. He takes a sip from a Starbucks cup and I give him a perplexed look. He shrugs and walks back to his room.

I think about texting Katelyn. If we were together, I would be texting her every hour. We're not back together, though, and I need to be patient and give her space. Jeremy comes back in, now wearing gym shorts and a T-shirt but still carrying his Starbucks cup. He grabs a bowl of cereal and sits across from me. "How's it going?"

"Sucky." I scowl at my screen.

Jeremy purses his lips. "Need to talk?" He takes a sip of his drink.

"Not particularly," I snap. "Are you drinking coffee?"

"Nope. What's wrong?"

"My design assistant is a moron and kind of ruined this deck that we have to present. I'm not even sure I have time to fix this." I swear under my breath and push away from the table. "Since when do you go to Starbucks in the morning?" I ask as I start the coffee maker.

"Since this morning." Jeremy shrugs. "Um, I saw—"

My phone rings, cutting Jeremy off. "Hello, this is Dominic."

Jeremy finishes his bowl of cereal as the phone call continues. I hang up just as he heads toward his room.

"Jer," I call. He stops, turning. "What if last night was a one-time thing? What am I going to do?"

He thinks for a moment. "Then at least you helped her. As far as what you do next, keep doing what you're doing and be willing to help if she needs you again."

"Should I even broach the subject of getting back together?"

"That's up to you."

I roll my eyes. "Thanks for the advice."

"What would you have wanted?" he asks.

I sit there, silently thinking about it. When I tried to end things, I didn't want anyone. I shoved everyone away. Even if I did think someone could have helped, I wouldn't have been quick to jump back into a relationship that had hurt me. I curse under my breath.

"You're going to have to give her space and time to sort things out," Jeremy says. "Are you sure you're good?"

I shake my head. Jeremy studies me for a minute. "It's gonna be okay. Come find me when you're ready to talk."

I open my mouth, ready to spill my guts, when my computer pings. I scowl at the screen.

Luckily, I'm able to fix a majority of the issues in our presentation before the meeting. As I'm reviewing it once more, my phone rings. An unknown number with an out-of-state area code flashes on my screen. Ignoring it, I return to my task. If it's important the person will leave a voicemail. Except, my phone just rings again with the same number.

"Hello, Dominic Renner," I answer.

"Hi Dom, it's Eliza."

My heartbeat skyrockets. Why on earth would Eliza be calling me in the middle of the afternoon? How did she get my number? "Is Katelyn okay?" I ask, frantic.

"When I talked with her this morning, she was okay. She said she came over last night."

"She did."

"I wanted to call and say thank you for being there last night. That means so much to me and to her, really."

"Absolutely. I'm really glad she came. I mean, I don't know exactly what she was thinking, but I feel like her admitting she doesn't want to exist says enough."

"Wait, what?" she asks, shocked.

Suddenly, I'm not sure what to say. I thought Katelyn would have told her.

"What do you mean she doesn't want to exist? Did she actually say those words out loud, or are you just inferring from other things she said?"

I glance at the clock. I have fifteen minutes to get through this conversation and it's honestly not a conversation I want to breeze through.

"Dom, so help me, if you don't answer I'll—"

"She said those words out loud," I interrupt. "I don't know why she hasn't talked to you about it yet. Maybe yesterday was just too much of an emotional roller coaster and she'll tell you tonight. When she showed up at my house, I did everything I could to make sure she was safe. She stayed the night and I told her she could come over tonight, too. I'm not sure if she will or not, but she's invited. Nothing is going to happen to her, okay, Eliza?"

Eliza clears her throat a couple times before replying. "Thank you."

"How did you get my number?"

"Katelyn. Sorry. She should have asked, but after I couldn't reach her last night, and then she was over at your house, I thought it would be good to have." She hesitates before asking, "So, what does this mean for you guys?"

"It means she felt safe enough to see me. I don't know what happens next."

"Do…do you think she would ever do anything? Like, um…" Eliza's voice cracks and I know what she's asking.

"I think if she had truly thought about it, she wouldn't have shown up at my front door," I say confidently.

"You're sure?"

"Speaking as someone who actually attempted suicide, yes. You don't get help when it's easier to just end everything."

"Oh my gosh." Eliza sniffles.

My computer pings, signaling that my design assistant has joined our team meeting. I curse under my breath. This isn't how I want to leave things. I send a quick message letting them know I'll be a minute late.

"I'm sorry, I know that's heavy. I didn't mean to scare you or to make you worry about Katelyn. I can give you a call back in about thirty minutes or so, but I have a meeting."

"Oh, yeah. Of course. Um, you don't need to call me back. Thanks for watching out for her. I'll let you go."

"I'll save your number. If I feel like Katelyn is in trouble, I'll text you, but I promise that I will not let *anything* happen."

"Okay," she whispers.

I say goodbye and quickly hang up. Jumping on my meeting is the last thing I want to do. I take a deep breath before joining.

As soon as my meeting is over, I head to my room and call Eliza back.

"Hey, Eliza. It's Dom. I figured I'd reach out again. I don't like how our last conversation ended."

"Oh." She's silent and I'm not really sure what to say.

"Do you have any questions for me?" I ask.

"No."

She did say I didn't have to call her back. If she doesn't want to talk, I'm not going force her. "Okay, well then, I guess I'll let you get back to your evening. Have a good night." I reach for the end call button.

"Dom?"

"Yeah?"

"What you said earlier was a lot to process. I know Katelyn has been struggling, I just wasn't aware of how bad it had gotten. I hate being far away," she mutters. "But I'm going to hold you to your promise of telling if something is wrong. I know you'll take care of her. I think it's half the reason I'm not on a plane right now."

"I promise. Um, while I have you, could I get your advice?"

"Sure," she answers apprehensively.

"You're Katelyn's best friend. How do I show up for her and support her?"

"Hmm. Good question. Katelyn's had a lot of practice taking care of others and not a lot of experience with others taking care of her. The fact that she showed up at your house yesterday means she trusts you enough to let you help her. That's kind of a big deal. I guess the only thing I can say is keep it up."

"Thanks."

"You're welcome. Can I ask you a question now?"

"Yes."

"How long did it take for you to feel, um...I don't know the right word. Better? Normal? Nope, better sounds, well, better." She lets out a humorless chuckle.

"It wasn't an overnight thing, but it's not like there's a timeframe or a regiment for these things. Every person is different, and it's gonna take time. Which means that sometimes it's going to suck because there is nothing for you to do." I take a deep breath. "I wish I had a better answer for you."

Her voice wavers. "That's fine. Um, I have to go. You'll take care of my girl?"

"Always. Have a good night."

I roll into the kitchen, where Tyler is hovering over a pot on the stove. He grumbles, fiddling with the temperature dial.

"Haven't you heard, a watched pot never boils?"

He throws a dish towel at me. "Don't be a smart aleck. I don't think this burner is working right. The water should be boiling by now." He moves the pot and hovers his hand over the burner, frowning. He switches burners, then turns. "Who was that on the phone?"

"Eliza."

Jeremy walks into the kitchen at that moment, hair mussed from sleeping. He pauses.

"Who's Eliza?" Tyler asks.

"Katelyn's friend," Jeremy answers. "What did she want?"

"She was checking up on Katelyn. During our conversation I may have let it slip that I attempted suicide."

Jeremy tenses. He was my emergency contact and one of the people the hospital called when I was brought in. He came to visit every day and always seemed so calm. He made polite chit-chat with the nurses and when my parents flew in, he picked them up from the airport and made sure they had everything they needed.

It wasn't until I was discharged that he exploded. He chewed me out for my actions and then didn't speak with me for almost a month. I knew he was getting updates and that sometimes it was him, not Tyler, that wanted to know how I was doing.

"Why would you bring that up?" Tyler mutters.

"She asked if Katelyn would ever think of…" The sudden knot in my throat makes it impossible to finish that sentence. I hate knowing Katelyn has had thoughts like that. She just hasn't acted on them, and I have no idea what I'd do if she ever did. I glance up at Jeremy, but his gaze is firmly fixed on the floor. Tyler is also studying the pot intensely.

"What'd you tell her?" Jeremy whispers.

"I told her I'd do everything to make sure she's safe and that I'd text her if I thought Katelyn was ever in trouble."

"We'll all look out for her," Tyler says.

"Thanks."

Jeremy excuses himself and a little kernel of guilt eats at me, his words from that day playing through my mind. *You should have talked to me! I'm your best friend. What the hell were you thinking? You don't think I haven't noticed, that I haven't been here? That was the most idiotic move you could have ever made! Take me off your emergency contacts. And just know if I get another call like that, I'm not coming.*

I sniffle and Tyler glances over. "It's heavy and we all hate reliving it. You wanna talk?"

"I think I'm all talked out."

"Hey," he says. "All of this sucks, but you have a unique perspective on things. You can use that to help Katelyn. Don't beat yourself up about what's in the past. You're still here. Let's make sure Katelyn also realizes that, even though things are hard, it's worth fighting."

I nod, turning to settle on the couch.

Later that evening, I knock on Jeremy's door. He opens it, gesturing for me to come in, and then grabs his boots and sits on the bed. It's silent.

"What's up?" Jeremy finally asks, glancing up at me before focusing back on tying his shoe.

"Maybe we should do this later."

Jeremy sits up. "How about we do this now."

I clear my throat a few times, but I can't spit the words out. I roll myself back and forth.

"What are you having a harder time with, the fact that you admitted what you did or that you actually did it?" he asks.

"Both."

"At least you're *living* with it. You acknowledged it. I know you're not big on talking about it. Did you tell her what happened?"

I shake my head. "Just that I had tried. And that you don't ask for help when you're done."

"Where's your head at?" He crosses his arms, waiting for my reply. When I don't answer, he sighs. "Dom, man. Come on."

My voice wavers. "I can't believe I made you feel this way."

"What way?"

"Like you're constantly worried the next call you get will be someone saying that your favorite person on the planet is gone. This morning, I felt like I was trying to read between the lines, making sure I wasn't missing anything. I'm so afraid I'm going to overlook what's important."

Jeremy scrubs at his face, letting out a heavy breath. "Like you said, if someone doesn't want help, they won't ask. And even though you know someone really well, it doesn't mean you'll be able to read their intentions all the time. I mean, I knew you were struggling but I didn't pick up on the fact that you basically said goodbye that day. I've replayed that moment over and over again, wishing I did a million things differently."

"Jer, there was nothing you could've done."

He shrugs.

"I'm terrified about how Katelyn is going to react when she finds out. I don't want her to worry that I'd ever do it again."

Jeremy wrings his hands together, then looks straight at me. "Katelyn knows."

I freeze. "How?"

"I let it slip. I told her to call me if she ever felt like she was in trouble, and then I made a comment about your idiotic decision."

I swear under my breath.

"Sorry," Jeremy mumbles.

"It's fine." But it's not really fine, and from the look on Jeremy's face, he knows it. I was going to tell Katelyn eventually, but I was hoping it would be way in the future and not while she was dealing with her own mental health. I take a breath. "How are you doing?"

"I'm just living one day at time."

I study my best friend.

"What? I've never tried to take my life. Stop looking at me like that." I flinch, but he continues on. "Look, it sucks to watch you fall back into some of your old behaviors. I'm not a fan that you're skipping physical therapy, but you've been better at talking so I haven't made a big deal about anything. I hate that when Katelyn said she was struggling, I had some flashbacks. I don't love that I can't magically wave a wand and make all of this better for both of you. It is what it is." He shrugs, glancing at his phone. "I gotta get going. You good?"

I nod.

CHAPTER THIRTY-SEVEN

Katelyn

I'm on my second latte when Stan walks into Espresso Yourself. "Stan," I call.

He looks over and smiles. "Hello, Katelyn. It's good to see you."

"You, too. Um, I'm ready to go through my other manuscript if, um, if that works for you."

"I'll grab my coffee and be over."

Stan orders and then sits across from me. "How's your current project coming along?"

"Not too bad. I've tried working on it a little, it's just slow."

"Well, let's see if we can fix that. Now, your first manuscript is very well done. What I noticed is that you are a character-driven writer."

I shrug. "I guess."

"It's a great thing. It makes it easier for a reader to become attached to your book. It seems to me you really understood your characters in your first manuscript, while in this one, you're still getting to know them."

"Oh." The corners of my mouth pull down.

"Not to worry. They're probably just shy. It's going to take a little more work to figure them out. Have you tried interviewing them?"

"What?"

Stan chuckles. "Interviewing them."

"How do I do that?"

"You sit down with a notebook and some questions and interview your character. Answer each of the questions as they would. This will let you get a good sense of who they are. If you want to be really brave, you can have a friend ask the questions and then you answer like your character."

I bite my lip. "You think that'll help?"

"I think it is one thing that will move you forward. I have a few other suggestions, but it might be best to start there. And if you would like someone to conduct the interview, I'd be happy to assist," Stan offers.

"I'll think about it."

The next day, I sit down and write out interview questions for my main character. Once I have a list, I begin to think through how she would answer them. It's not very easy, though, and I think about Stan's suggestion of having someone else ask the questions. Maybe that will be easier, or maybe he has a question I haven't thought of. I set my interview aside and head to the kitchen for a snack.

My phone buzzes at that moment. It's a text from Dom.

Hey, just checkin' in. Hope you're doing okay. Reach out if you need anything.

It's been a little over a week since I showed up at his doorstep having a complete meltdown. I messaged him the day after and thanked him again for letting me stay and told him I would be okay, declining his invitation to come over that night. I haven't messaged him since, even though I've thought about him every day. But he wasn't the one who said he wanted to be done. That was my decision. I'm not sure how he feels now. Maybe after what I did he doesn't want a relationship. Maybe he just wants to be friends.

I'm a little better. Thanks. How are you? I reply.

My week's been okay. Not looking forward to tomorrow. Monday's stink.

They do. Hope you have a good week.

You too. He sends a smiley face after it.

Dom

"It's been a while," my physical therapist comments when she sees me.

"Yep. I'm here now, though."

"I see that. How's the walking going?"

When I don't answer, she crosses her arms. "You haven't been, have you?" She shakes her head. "Dominic, the only way to improve is to actually do it. Have you decided walking isn't a goal to pursue anymore?"

"No. Yes. I mean, it is. I fell," I admit.

Her face softens. "That's a tad discouraging. There's the old adage, though, that if you fall off the horse, you get right back on."

"Well, I didn't really do that."

She points toward the stationary bikes. "Let's start, then."

After physical therapy, I check my phone to find a message from Katelyn. I've reached out a few times these past two weeks, but this is the first time she's messaged me. I quickly reply and then decide to make a risky move and call her. My heart hammers in my chest as I wait for her to answer. It's on the last ring, about to go to voicemail, when she finally picks up.

"Hi."

"Hey. How are you?"

"Okay. You?"

Rolling my shoulders, I take the plunge. "I was actually calling to see if you want to meet in person sometime?"

The line goes quiet. *I don't think your risk is paying off,* my thoughts quip. The next thirty seconds feels like an eternity.

"Uh, um, yeah?" She pauses. "Yes. I, um, yes, I can do that. Are you sure?"

"I'm one hundred percent sure. I can text you a place to meet."

"That sounds good," she says, a little nervous waver to her voice. "Um, I guess I'll wait for a text. Have a good night, Dom." She hangs up then.

I glance at my screen and smile. It reminds me of the night I first gave her my number. She bolted right after, but she did text me. She might have ended the conversation quickly, but she's not going to stand me up.

CHAPTER THIRTY-EIGHT

Katelyn

My heart sinks when I don't immediately see Jeremy waiting at Starbucks this morning. He mentioned that he has a pretty regular schedule, which means he should have worked last night. I try to ignore the ache in my chest and step in line to order. I'm just finishing up telling the barista what I want when I hear, "I'm covering that." I turn to see Jeremy rushing up to the counter, a few customers behind me throwing him disapproving looks. He ignores them.

"Sorry," he says. He quickly scans his phone and the register beeps.

"Did you want something?" I ask.

He shakes his head and steps off to the side. As we wait for my drink, I study Jeremy's face. His eyelids are heavy and he cracks a yawn. *This is your fault*, my mind reprimands. "Hey, where did that come from?" he asks.

"What?"

He points to his mouth, frowning. "That."

"It's nothing. You know, if this is too much, I'd understand if you can't come."

"Until you say that you don't want me to come, I'm coming. I've had a couple rough nights and work was actually interesting last night, which is why I was late."

"What happened?"

The barista calls my name. I grab my drink and Jeremy and I head outside. We pause at the back of my car.

"We had a break-in. Guy had a weapon. I couldn't leave until all the reports were completed."

My eyes widen, scanning him over. "Holy cow! Are you okay?"

"Yep. But I think the adrenaline is finally wearing off." He yawns again.

"Wow, I'm glad you're safe. Has this ever happened before?"

"Not at this company, no. I've worked various security jobs. Weapons being drawn is just part of the job." He shrugs.

"That's scary." If the situation had gone differently, Jeremy wouldn't have been able to meet me. Would someone have told me? I've never mentioned these meet-ups to Dom. I assume Jeremy has, but still, why would he reach out to me? "Can I get your number?" I blurt out.

He studies me. "Yeah."

He tells me his number. I try to type it into my phone, but my hands are shaking too bad.

"May I?" he asks, extending his hand. I pass my phone to him. As he's typing, he asks, "Did Dom teach you the candle trick?" I nod. "Deep breath, and then gently blow out."

Closing my eyes, I breathe in and release it slowly. Then I do it again.

"Try going a little slower. Really concentrate on the exhale. Now, one more time."

After two more deep breaths, I open my eyes and Jeremy smiles. "Okay?"

I nod.

He hands my phone back. "Now text me so I have your number."

I send a little thumbs-up emoji. His phone buzzes and he grins when he sees the text. He quickly saves my number and then slides his phone in his pocket.

"Kate, I don't want you to worry about this. It happens from time to time. There were two of us there and police arrived quickly. It really was no biggie."

I swallow. "I trust you."

"Good. So, busy day?"

"Not really." Which just means I'll have to find other ways to keep myself busy. It seems like the busier I am, the quieter all those nasty thoughts are.

"You're meeting Dom tonight, right?"

I nod. Dom and I haven't seen each other since the panic attack. When he called to ask if I wanted to meet up, I wasn't surprised. We haven't determined what our relationship status is. Part of me knows he wants to get back together, but there is a miniscule piece of me that is afraid he'll tell me he just wants to be friends.

Jeremy chuckles. "You think it's going to go bad?"

I shrug, biting hard on my lip. "Ouch." I reach up, making sure I didn't draw blood.

Jeremy flinches. "It's going to be fine. Try not to obsess about it all day." He glances at his smartwatch. "You should go."

"I'll talk to you later. Thanks for coming."

"Again, sorry I was late. I'll see you later."

Work is super slow and a few times my thoughts get a little loud, but I'm able to take a walk and calm myself down. The account I had an issue with wasn't my fault, and everything has been corrected. I've tried very hard not to hyperfocus on meeting Dom tonight. We agreed to try a new coffee shop that just opened called Amped.

As I pull into a parking space, I look around and see no sign of Dom's car. I'm twenty minutes early so I try not to panic. At five to, Dom's SUV pulls into one of the handicap spots up front. I take a deep breath and then walk over. His wheelchair frame is sitting on the ground and he's twisted to grab a wheel out of the back seat. When he turns, he jumps.

"Jeez." He places the wheel on and then holds a hand to his chest. "Hi there." He flips his chair and reaches back to grab the other wheel.

"Hi."

He finishes assembling his chair and transfers over. I step back so he can move and close his door. When he turns, he looks up at me. "How was your day?"

I shrug. "Yours?"

"Survivable. Shall we?"

The coffee shop features a grungy rock band vibe. The floor is polished concrete, and there are wooden tables with black iron chairs scattered throughout the center. Over in the corner is a small stage, and there's a giant chalkboard sign advertising a few bands making an appearance this month. Up front by the window are two large black lounge chairs, a coffee table, and a large red couch. Examining the menu, several drinks have different album or artist names.

"Interesting," Dom murmurs, looking around.

Interesting is one word for it. I'm not sure if I'd come here often, and especially not to write. But for some place different or to meet friends, it could be cool.

Dom steps up and orders a "Dark Side of the Mocha." I grab "A Beautiful Chai" with a shot of espresso. Dom pays and then wheels over to a table. I slide one of the chairs away for him.

"Thanks." He smiles.

"Of course. So, um, how are you?"

His hazel eyes fixate onto me. "I've been okay. What's been going on in your world?"

"Just work," I answer.

"Have you been writing?"

"Some. I met up with Stan and we worked together on some things."

"Do the holidays give you more or less time to write?"

"Um, it hasn't really changed," I answer.

Dom pauses, then takes a deep breath. "Shall we address the elephant in the room?" I nod. "I'm not really sure how else to talk about this except to just ask, so do you want to get back together?"

I hold his stare. Panic passes across his features but is quickly gone.

I've had a lot of time to debate if I want to be back in a relationship with Dom. If we had actually had a conversation that night and I didn't shut him out, the breakup might not have happened. There are some moments that are stuck in my brain that make me nervous to jump back in, but overriding those is the fact that he has shown up every time I need him. I think he cared about me before we even fully knew each other, like the first time I met up. He had asked what I was working on and I told him it was nothing. He sounded so sincere when he said it didn't look like nothing. That little look of concern that I've seen from time to time was on his face that day. I was a complete stranger and yet he still worried about me. Why wouldn't I want to be with someone like that?

"I'm nervous, but I'd like to try."

CHAPTER THIRTY-NINE

Dom

Those words act like a blanket thrown over a grease fire, instantly smothering it. The relief I feel is instant. Katelyn is willing to try, and I'm going to do everything I can to not let her regret this decision.

I smile. "I'm so happy to hear that. I want you to know I'm in this. I'm going to let you guide us. If something feels uncomfortable, I want you to say so, okay?"

She nods.

"Would you like to set some boundaries and then we can adjust as needed?"

Slowly, she shakes her head. "We can mostly go back to the way it was. Unless there are boundaries that you need to set."

"I'm good."

Her brown eyes find mine and a small grin slips out. *This beautiful woman is mine.* I take a leap and ask if she wants to come over to the house. She contemplates this for a moment before nodding. "I'd like that."

We finish our coffee and then make our way out. I transfer to my vehicle and then dismantle my chair. Katelyn stands there until it's all in the car. Once it is, she gives a little nod. "Meet you over there," she says, until she stops and turns abruptly. "Wait, is Tyler okay with this?"

I find it odd that she only asks about Tyler. "They know it's a possibility. They're cool."

"Okay." She climbs into her car.

I pull into the driveway just before Katelyn parks on the curb. She doesn't get out immediately, and my heart starts to race. What if she's changed her mind? I'm in my chair and wheeling myself to the house when her car door finally closes. I open the front door and hold it for her. She steps inside, giving me a hesitant smile.

"Look who's back," Tyler says, a smile on his face.

She gives him a little wave, and when she does, I notice her hand is trembling. I lace my fingers with hers. I hate that her anxiety doesn't settle, but surges. This house is supposed to be a safe place.

I'm about to ask her what's wrong when Jeremy walks in. "Hey, hey," Jeremy greets us. He turns toward Tyler. "Did you burn something?"

Tyler rolls his eyes. "Does it smell like I did?"

Katelyn's fingers flex. I squeeze her hand, looking up to find her eyes closed.

"It smells close," Jeremy quips.

Tyler chucks a slice of carrot at him. Jeremy laughs, then turns his attention to us. *Breathe*, he mouths at me. I hadn't realized I'd been holding my breath. I take a deep inhale.

"So, who's your favorite character in *Schitt's Creek*?" Jeremy asks. At this, Katelyn looks up. Her shoulders relax just a little and she tightens her grip on my hand.

"I haven't really watched any more," she admits.

He gives her a disapproving look. "We will have to fix that."

"So, what's for dinner?" Katelyn releases my hand and walks to the kitchen.

"Beef stir fry. I think everything is safe, but…" Jeremy grabs the bottle of sauce, handing it to Katelyn. "Double-check."

She examines the ingredients and nods. "It's safe."

"Phew." He wipes his hand across his forehead.

Katelyn giggles and it's the best sound in the world. Watching them, there is a certain ease to their interaction, how they seem to know what the other is thinking without even saying anything. Jeremy looks over, realizing I'm staring, and a look of guilt colors his features. *That was weird. What in the world is happening right now?*

Dinner is a quiet event. I'm not sure what to think of everything. As everyone finishes, Jeremy suggests an episode of *Schitt's Creek*. We all agree, and I begin to clear the table. Katelyn excuses herself, and as soon as I'm sure she won't hear me, I turn on Jeremy.

"What the heck is going on?"

He rinses off his plate and places it in the dishwasher. He continues loading, not looking at me.

"Jer, come on. Is there something between you and Katelyn?"

His head snaps up. "No," he protests. "Nothing like that. I'd never do that to you. Bro Code."

"Okay, so then what is happening?"

He sighs. "I usually stop and see her in the morning. At Starbucks. It's not every morning, but most mornings after work."

It clicks in my head. Him coming home later these last few weeks. The times I've caught him with a Starbucks cup. "Why?"

His eyes flick to the hall and he lowers his voice. "Because she needed someone and it was one small thing I could do."

"Hi." Katelyn comes back in and we both straighten. Still, her eyes bounce between Jeremy and me. "Everything okay?"

"Peachy keen," Jeremy answers, smiling widely.

Katelyn looks at me, tilting her head.

"Everything's great. Shall we?" I push toward the living room.

She takes a seat next to me on the couch. Pausing a moment, she slowly slips off her shoes and tucks her feet under her.

"Are you mad?" Katelyn whispers.

"There's nothing to be mad about," I answer. Katelyn glances over, and I look into her big brown eyes. "I'm glad that you had a friend." My voice wavers a little and Katelyn frowns. Her lip begins to tremble.

"Hey," I whisper, cupping her cheek. I bend my head, resting my forehead against hers. "I'm happy that someone was there. Of course, I feel like I should have been the one to show up, but maybe I wasn't the right person at that moment. I'm not mad. I'm relieved. You're safe and you're here. Everything is good. We're good." I give her a soft kiss and sit back.

She takes a stuttering breath and curls up against my side. I wrap my arm around her. Jeremy purses his lips, while Tyler looks so lost. His eyes dart between the three of us.

"Katelyn and I see each other for coffee in the morning," Jeremy states. "I'm sure if you want to join, Katelyn wouldn't mind."

She shakes her head. Once the episode is over, I ask her if would like to go talk for a little bit. She nods and I head for the back patio, grabbing a blanket on the way. The weather is beautiful during the day but chilly at night. Katelyn curls herself into a ball on the wicker chair. I pull up to the side of the chair and fan the blanket over both of us.

"Are you enjoying the evening?" I ask.

She nods. "Dinner was amazing. Thanks for having me over."

"Always. Can I ask you a question?"

She nods slowly.

"When we walked in, you reacted. What made you so nervous?"

She doesn't answer right away. "Um." She wrings her hands together. Inhaling deeply, she says, "They all left."

"Who?"

"When my previous boyfriend broke up with me, our friends ditched me too. I never quite got an explanation why. I don't know if he said something to them, or if I did something to make them mad, but one minute they were there and the next they were ghosting me." Her next breath is shaky. "I guess walking in here tonight, I just thought, what if that happens again?"

I chuckle. "Honestly, I think they'd like you more and I'd be the one left behind."

I realize that was the wrong thing to say the minute tears well in her eyes. I mutter a curse. "Hey, I'm sorry. That was a joke."

She swipes a tear off her cheek.

"I'm sorry that happened to you, but Katelyn, if they didn't realize how amazing you are, then they didn't deserve you. It's their loss. Not yours." She shrugs, but I shake my head at her. "You don't have to shrug it off. That left a mark. I want you to know that I'll do whatever I need to do to make this a comfortable space for you. And I said it was a joke, but the guys really like you. They aren't going to just disappear."

"Okay," she whispers. "Can I…ask you a question?"

I nod.

"What would you say if, eventually, I wanted to write full time?"

"I'd say go for it. You are so talented."

Her eyes shine with tears. "You don't think it's impractical? Or that I'm just hiding in a land of make believe?"

Anger flares in my chest. "Who told you that?"

"But do you think that?" she pushes.

"No," I state. "Where did you get that idea?"

"My mom." Her voice cracks. "And…him. I made a comment about wanting writing to be my full-time job one day, and he said that I needed to be practical. He thought it was a stupid idea, especially considering…" She trails off and a tear trickles down her cheek.

Her reaction on Halloween makes more sense now. The minute she realized I had caught on to that dream, she panicked. I want to hurt the people who've made her feel like the talent she has is something to be frowned upon.

"Wait, did I make you feel that way?" I ask.

"What? No!" Her voice pitches up. "I've just been so scared that you're going to realize that my dreams are unrealistic and leave."

"Well, I'm going to disappoint you, then. I don't think it's unrealistic. I think it's a wonderful goal, and I know that one day you'll get there and I want to be someone who helps you."

She wipes her eyes. "Um, on Halloween, when you snapped…I didn't leave because of that. Well, I mean, I did, but it brought on a flashback of another fight and I got scared. And I know you will support me, but that honestly terrifies me. It's not something I'm used to."

"Then we will work on getting you used to it, because you're amazing." I lean over and kiss her cheek.

CHAPTER FORTY

Katelyn

I didn't expect to freak out when I walked into Dom's house. When I opened up and shared that part of my past with Dom, it was really scary, but after our talk, I feel more confident in our relationship.

It's their loss. He sounded so sincere when he said that.

But now, it's time for another scary conversation. I take a deep breath and approach Stan's table.

"Hi, Stan."

"Hello, Katelyn. How are you today?"

"Well, I was actually wondering if I could be Mazey today and you could interview her. Is that weird?"

Stan grins. "I'd be delighted to interview Mazey."

He gestures to the seat across from him. I pull out my interview questions and slide them over. "Feel free to improvise."

Three quarters of the way through the interview, Stan asks a question that is not on my list. As I'm pondering Mazey's answer, the door chimes.

"Well, well, well. It's good to see you," Stan says, smiling.

"It's good to see you, too. It's been a while." Dom rolls up next to me, then reaches out and shakes Stan's hand.

"What are you doing here?" I ask.

"Oh, sorry. Maybe I should've checked first. I thought I'd come see you and grab coffee."

"No, it's fine." I bite my lip. "It's just, um…" I shake my head. "Nothing. It's fine. You're good."

Dom gives me a quizzical look. "If I interrupted, I can go sit at another table until you're done. I don't mind. Or I can take my coffee to go."

Answering these questions in front of Stan is hard enough. Having Dom listen in seems like it'd be overwhelming. A weight settles on my chest.

"Hey, Firecracker." Dom knots his fingers through mine. "I'm gonna go order coffee and then I'll head out. We'll meet up later?"

I shake my head and Dom's brow furrows. I feel antsy and need to move, but I need to be resolute with this, too. "What do you want?" I ask. "I'm stumped on the question, so I'll go order for you and think it over." Dom tells me his order and I excuse myself.

Dom

"This exercise is a little challenging for her, but it will be good, though. Really help her writing," Stan says once she walks up to the counter. I glance over at him. "You know, I spent a lot of years teaching, and every once in a blue moon, I would find a student who had a knack for writing. Very few can do what she can. I believe when Katelyn sees the impact her story is going to make, she will be unstoppable. When she embraces her gift…" Stan whistles. "Watch out, world."

Katelyn moves to the other end of the counter to wait for my drinks. She peeks over at us and I give her a little smile and a nod. "She's something special," I say.

"She is. You take care of her." Stan halfheartedly glares at me.

"I will. I promise."

Katelyn returns with my drink and I thank her. "Okay, I'll let you two get back to it."

"You don't have to leave. Just give us a few minutes to finish this." She turns to Stan. "I have an answer."

I back up and sit at the farthest table from them, giving them as much privacy as I possibly can. When Katelyn stands, I slip out my earbuds and watch the two of them approach. She has a smile on her face and her shoulders look a little more relaxed.

"Are either of you going to be in town over the holidays?" Stan asks.

"I will," Katelyn answers.

"Would you be interested in checking in on Scout? My pet sitter canceled on me and I need to find someone before Monday. Now, before you say yes, I want to warn you, she's a handful. I won't be offended if you say no."

"I'd be happy to check on Scout," Katelyn says, a hint of a smile appearing.

"Thank you. I will send you my address. If you could stop by a couple times a day and just make sure she hasn't completely destroyed my house, that would be greatly appreciated. Actually, if you can come over tomorrow, I'll introduce you to Scout and show you where her food and everything is."

Katelyn nods. "Yes. Let's do it!"

CHAPTER FORTY-ONE

Katelyn

Dom pulls up to Stan's house, agreeing to come along with me for my first time visiting. My eyes instantly shoot to the front door, which is tucked into the corner of a little patio. If there's a step to get into the house, Dom won't be able to get in. I turn to ask Dom about it, but he's already putting his chair together. Once he's out of the car, he glances in. "Are you coming?"

As we approach the door, my heart rate accelerates. There is a little step on the patio and not enough space to get momentum like at Espresso Yourself. I reach out and hit the doorbell, my mind working overtime to figure out an accommodation for Dom. The front door creaks as it opens.

"Hello there. Come on in." Stan smiles and steps aside for us.

I glance back at Dom. His eyes shift to the step and then to his lap.

"Something wrong?" Stan asks.

"Um, no. Well…"

Stan peeks out. "Oh. I didn't think about this. Hm. Maybe the side door would be better. The walkway is gravel, though."

"It's okay. Actually, it looks like I can step in. Katelyn will have to carry my chair, but I think it's doable."

I flash back to the night Dom fell. The loud crash, Dom's harsh words. *Open your eyes.* I slam my eyes closed as my breathing grows erratic.

"Katelyn? Are you all right?" Stan asks.

Dom's fingers knot in mine and he squeezes my hand twice. My fingers don't—*can't*—respond. I'm stuck in the past. What if Dom falls here?

With my eyes closed I try and picture a birthday candle, the flame extinguishing with a slow breath. I think I got it when Dom speaks.

"Firecracker? Would it be easier if you get the tour and then meet me in the car?"

"What if you fall?" The question slips out before I can stop it. "It would be my fault," I admit.

"Katelyn, look at me."

I open my eyes and turn to Dom. His hazel eyes are wide and full of guilt. "It would *not* be your fault."

"What would work best for you?" Stan asks. "I'm happy to assist in any way I can."

"Do you have a chair or stool? That way, I can sit while Katelyn brings my chair in."

"I can do that." Stan walks away and comes back with a wooden dining chair. "Where would you like this?"

"Just to the side of the door is good."

Stan sets it down on the left side. Dom wheels up and glances in, spotting the chair. "Perfect."

When he stands, his legs shake slightly. He grips the doorframe and lifts his right leg, then his left. When he is securely in the dining chair, I bring his wheelchair in. Stan closes the door behind me.

"Sorry about that," Dom says.

"Don't apologize, young man. Are you okay?" Stan's voice sounds muffled.

Dom nods.

"What about you?"

Dom nudges me and then nods toward Stan, but my eyes don't stray from him. He clears his throat. "Are you okay?"

"Why are you asking me? Are you?" My breaths are shallow and little dots cloud my vision.

"I just said I was," he says calmly and slowly. "Stan is making sure we both are."

"Oh, yes. I'm…" I sway a little. Dom catches my waist and tugs me toward him. I fall into his lap.

"Deep breath for me," he whispers.

"I'm fine," I lie. I try to stand but he holds me firmly in place.

"Not yet. Just breathe." His breath tickles my ear. "So, how long have you lived here?" he asks Stan as his hand trails up and down my spine.

"I've been here for almost ten years now."

The rhythm of Dom's hand matches the rate of my breathing. "The living room seems cozy."

"I think so. Though, my favorite room is my office. I think Katelyn will appreciate it."

I look over at Stan, my curiosity piqued, when something furry brushes against my leg. I yelp and look down. An orange tabby, not quite full grown, turns and rubs up against my leg again.

"Hi, Scout." I reach down and pet her head. At this, a purr radiates through her tiny body.

"She's very sweet when she wants to be," Stan remarks.

Scout stands there for another second, letting me pet her, before darting off down the hall. The bell on her collar jingles the whole way. A moment later, there's a crash. Stan sighs and then looks over at me. "How are you?"

"Fine." I go to stand and this time, Dom lets me. I line up his wheelchair and he transfers over. "It was just a stressful situation. Sorry for the drama."

Stan's brow furrows. "A little drama keeps life interesting. Shall I show you where the litter box is?"

The litter box is kept in Stan's small laundry room. Extra litter is stored in the cabinet. In the kitchen, Stan shows me where he keeps Scout's food and gives me instructions for feeding her. I'm trying to pay attention when I hear Dom say, "Well, hi there."

I step out of the kitchen and glance into the living room. Scout stands in Dom's lap, staring up at him while he runs a hand down her back.

"He's taken, little missy," I say.

As if she heard me, Scout nestles down on his lap and Dom laughs. "I don't think she's threatened."

Dom

Scout has been curled up on my lap for the last ten minutes. Stan finishes showing Katelyn where the food and treats are, and then he takes her down the small hall.

"Oh my…" Katelyn breathes.

I gently wheel myself forward, glancing around the corner and spotting an open door at the end of the hallway. The back wall is covered in bookshelves. Katelyn must be in heaven. She makes a slow circle, her eyes alight with wonder. Stan chuckles and steps out. "I'll let you peruse," he says.

"That's quite a collection," I comment.

"Some are mine, but a majority are my late wife's. She was the reader in the family." Stan is quiet for a moment. "May I speak with you?" He nods back toward the living room.

I reverse into the room and Stan takes a seat in the rocking chair. "That isn't the first time that has happened, is it?" he asks.

I glance back toward the office, then look over at Stan again. I shake my head.

"You handled it very well. It's hard to remain calm when someone you love is panicking."

"Sounds like you know from experience."

Stan nods. "My oldest granddaughter has severe anxiety. The first time she had an attack in front of me, I was anything but calm. I wanted to fix everything for her that instant. Watching her mother calmly set her down and talk soothingly to her was incredible. After that, I asked my daughter-in-law to teach me all her techniques so if I was ever alone with my granddaughter, I could help her. It can be very difficult."

"That's an understatement," I mutter.

"How often does that happen?"

I shift in my chair. I don't want Katelyn walking in on this conversation. Scout stirs in my lap from my movements. She stands and stretches before bouncing away and running down the hall. "What are you doing?" Katelyn asks. "Oh no, wait!" There's a loud clatter before a jingle and a flash of orange darts through the room.

Footsteps echo down the hall and then Katelyn emerges, sheepish. "She knocked over the stack of books on your table. I picked them up, but if you had them in a particular order, well, they aren't anymore."

"It's a daily occurrence," Stan says. "I'm just glad she didn't try to scale the bookcase. She does that as well. When you're in there, you really have to watch her."

"I will. Thank you for letting me in. It's beautiful."

"I thought you'd like it. You're more than welcome to spend as much time as you want in there."

"Thank you so much. Well, I guess we should let you get back to your afternoon. You ready?" she asks me. When I hesitate, her head tilts slightly, her eyes darting between me and Stan.

"Would you mind giving us a minute?" I ask. Katelyn bites her lip, hesitant.

"I bet Scout would love some treats," Stan suggests.

"Um, okay." She walks to the kitchen and then calls for Scout. The little cat dashes out from behind the couch and into the kitchen.

I look at Stan. "I'm not quite sure if it has escalated. We were…apart for a while. I think today was a product of what happened when we—" A knot forms in my throat and I have trouble getting the words out. I try and clear it. "What happened today was partly my fault. I wish I could fix it, but I'm not sure I can." I take a deep breath to steady myself. "She's going to be back in a moment. Would it be possible to talk about this another time?"

"Of course. Please let me know if I can help in any way."

I nod. Katelyn walks in from the kitchen, Scout trailing her. Stan laughs. "You've made a friend."

She glances down. "I guess so."

I wheel myself over to the dining room chair and transfer over. Katelyn moves my chair to the patio and sets the brakes. As I step down, Katelyn keeps her arm outstretched, ready to catch me. "It's not your job to catch me," I say, but grasp her arm anyway once I let go of the doorframe. I take a step and then sit in my chair.

"I wasn't going to catch you. It doesn't mean you can't lean on me for support, though," she points out.

I knot my fingers through hers and kiss the back of her hand. "Thank you."

Stan follows us out. "Thank you for coming over. I'll leave the key under the mat. If you have questions, I'll leave my number and the cell numbers for my son and daughter on the counter."

Katelyn nods. "Got it. I hope you have a great holiday."

"You as well. What are you two doing?"

"I'll actually be at my parents," I say.

Katelyn's face falls slightly, but she's quick to plaster on a smile. "It's just me. When I'm not here, I'll be working or at home."

"Well, I hope it's enjoyable."

Katelyn shrugs. "Have a good day." She turns and heads toward the car. I follow her out, saying a quick goodbye to Stan.

He stands in the doorway until we're out of sight. Katelyn waves as we drive away. Once we round the corner, she looks over. "What were you and Stan talking about?"

"When?" I ask, fingers tightening on the steering wheel.

"When Stan banished me to the kitchen."

"He didn't banish you to the kitchen."

Katelyn sighs in frustration. "Was it about me?"

"Yes," I admit. I'm not going to lie to her. "He was just concerned."

"Because I overreacted."

"You didn't overreact. You *reacted*." I don't want her to feel bad about what happened this afternoon. More importantly, I don't want her to suppress her feelings in the future. I'd like to find a way to manage her anxiety so that doesn't happen again, but I can't force her to do something she's not ready to do.

When we come to a stoplight, I rest my hand on her knee. "How do you wish it went?"

"I wish I wasn't broken." Her voice wavers. "I wish Stan didn't see me this way. I wish *you* didn't see me this way. I wish everything wasn't so overwhelming and my thoughts weren't so loud."

I give her knee a squeeze. "Katelyn—"

"It's fine. Don't worry about it."

Right before we left Stan's, Jeremy had texted saying he placed an order for pizza. I thought it would be easier and cheaper if I just picked it up. Now, I'm thinking delivery would have been better. As I pull into a parking spot, I catch Katelyn wipe her eyes.

"I'm sorry about earlier. You reacted because of me," I say.

She turns to me. "That's not true."

"What happened on Halloween wasn't your fault. I need you to know that."

"Yeah, but—"

I shake my head. "There are no buts. You couldn't have prevented it; it just happened. It's not anyone's fault, okay?"

She nods. I move to get out of the car, thinking Katelyn probably needs a minute to herself, but surprisingly, she climbs out, too.

Entering the pizza parlor, the girl at the cash register is bent over the counter, intently focused on something. She glances up and sets her pencil down. "Hi, how can I help you?"

"We have an online order for three pizzas. Should be under Jeremy."

She looks up the order on the computer and then heads toward the back. Katelyn studies the papers on the counter while she's gone. When the girl returns, she slides three boxes toward me. I reach up and set them in my lap.

"That's really good," Katelyn says, pointing at the papers.

The corner of her lips quirk up. "Thanks." She glances down at them for a moment. "Actually, could I get your opinion on something?" When Katelyn nods, the girl shuffles some more papers around. "Which one do you think looks better?"

"Oh man, they are both amazing. If I had to choose, I'd pick this one." She points to the page on the left.

"Can I see?" I ask. The counter is just high enough that I'm unable to see over it.

The girl holds up two sketches of a blouse. Both look similar, except the one on the left has long bell sleeves that add a little flare to the top. *Katelyn would look spectacular in that*, I think.

"Wow."

"Seriously, Mac, are we recruiting customers to help with homework now? Is it not enough that you torture us?" a guy says, walking behind the counter. I catch his name tag, Chris, as he passes.

Mac scowls. "I was just getting some quick feedback."

"Let them go enjoy their pizza. You have other issues to deal with."

Mac gives Chris a questioning look. He nods toward the dining area, to a young girl maybe sixteen, clearing dishes off a table. "She loaded all the napkins backwards. Again. I mean, it's not that hard and yet…"

Mac sighs. "I'll take care of it."

"Isn't it fun being the boss?" Chris quips, continuing on into the back.

Katelyn looks at the sketches again. "He said homework. Is this for class?"

"These aren't. I was just doodling." Mac shrugs.

"Holy cow. These are just doodles? These are amazing."

Mac smiles. "Thanks." She looks over Katelyn's shoulder and her smile widens. Focusing her attention back on us, she asks, "Can I do anything else for you?"

"We're good. Thank you." I pivot while Katelyn takes one last look at the sketches, says a quick thank you, and turns. Behind us is a tall gentleman, eyes only for Mac. We quickly move out of his way. When I look back, Mac glances around the dining area, making sure the coast is clear, before leaning over the counter and kissing him.

It's a quiet ride to the house. Once I park, I assemble my chair and Katelyn grabs the pizzas.

"Hey," I call and she turns. "I'm sorry, about earlier. I didn't mean to upset you. Stan just wanted to make sure you were okay. His granddaughter has anxiety and he recognized some of the signs."

"I don't have anxiety," Katelyn snaps. Her face grows hard.

"Sorry," I murmur. If Katelyn doesn't think she has anxiety, what does she think this is?

"The pizza's getting cold" is all she says and heads inside. Once she sets down the boxes on the table, Jeremy and Tyler already congregating over them, she grabs a slice and walks right past me to the couch. Jeremy's eyes bounce between Katelyn and me.

"Everything okay?" he asks. "What happened?"

I'm a colossal idiot, I think. I shake my head. "It was just a bad afternoon. Everything's fine."

CHAPTER FORTY-TWO

Katelyn

Tyler plops down on the couch next to me, his plate piled high with pizza. "I hear you watch *Love is Blind*."

I nod.

"Perfect." He grabs the remote and starts one of the older episodes.

Dom slides in beside me, groaning. "Come on, man."

"You know you're in just as deep as I am," Tyler quips.

The couples have been on several blind dates now and the last two couples get to meet for the first time. As the doors open for one couple, revealing their match, Tyler leans over. "Do they stay together?"

I shrug. "You just have to keep watching."

"Maybe if you told him, we could change it," Jeremy grumbles.

The episode is ending when I stand and clear the plates. I grab a bottle of water and return to the couch, tucking myself into Dom's side. His arm wraps around me. The minute Dom implied I had anxiety, my brain instantly rejected the idea, but the more I think about it, maybe he's right. But I don't think it's just anxiety, and what if that's part of the problem? Either way, it means I'm broken. Tears prick my eyes and I blink hard.

Dom kisses the top of my head. He leans close, whispering, "Too bad that top was just a sketch, because you would've looked beautiful in it. However, you look gorgeous in sweats and a T-shirt, too. It doesn't matter what you're wearing or what you do, you will always have my attention. I love you. Even when you feel like you're a mess. I love you in all your chaos. It makes my life fuller." He kisses the top of my head again. "You're safe."

I lift my head to find his hazel eyes staring at me. "Here, come here." He transfers to his chair and I follow him to his room. Rummaging through the bottom drawer, he pulls out a pair of sweats and then holds up a T-shirt. I nod, and he hands them to me. "I'll let you change."

"Dom?"

"Hm?"

"What if it's more than anxiety?" I whisper.

He pauses, then closes the bedroom door. "Then it's more than anxiety." He shrugs. He stops in front of me and laces his fingers through mine. "Firecracker, whatever's going on, I'm here for you. You don't have to face anything by yourself."

I take a seat on the edge of his bed. "Did you ask for help?"

"Not right away. I learned that was a bad decision," he mutters.

"Jeremy eluded to, um…"

He nods carefully. "That was before I asked for help, before I started treatment, and before I was ever on medication." He takes a deep breath. "It was about a year and a half after the accident. I had recently moved into my apartment and was learning how to be independent again. I hated that I had to relearn how to do things or adapt to things. I wanted my old life back, and when I learned I could never return to it, I decided it was easier to not live at all.

"I had leftover pain meds. I popped those and a few others, thinking it wouldn't hurt, and laid down on the couch. I woke up in the hospital. My parents were on a plane and Jeremy was sitting in my room. I was told a faulty fire alarm went off in my apartment building, and emergency personnel were checking in with all the residents to make sure everything was okay. I guess they checked my apartment and found me unresponsive. And now, here we are." He clears his throat. "I guess some higher power or the universe or whatever decided I needed to be here. The more time passes, the more I'm grateful that I am."

"All the time?"

He lets out a humorless chuckle. "Most of the time. Life is hard, but I do know I would've missed out on some great things. Just because it's hard doesn't mean you give up. I'd love to tell you that as soon as I was on medication and started talking to a counselor, it got better, but I can't."

I frown.

"It took work. Just like adjusting to my new life took work. What sucked is that after my attempt, Jeremy wasn't around. He was the one that pushed and pushed and suddenly he wasn't there anymore. I think that was a lightbulb moment for how royally I had screwed up." His face falls a little. "That relationship took work, too."

Tears well in my eyes, and he squeezes my hands. "I know it seems like a lot, but I promise the work is worth it, and you won't be alone. I'm right here."

I lean down and kiss him. Resting my forehead on his, I breathe in his ocean campfire scent and a sense of peace washes over me. "Thank you."

"Always." His lips brush against mine. "I'll let you get changed." Giving me one more quick kiss, he turns and heads out the door.

When I walk out, Dom is back on the couch making a case as to why the couple on screen isn't going to last until the end. Tyler scoffs and begins his counter argument. There's commotion in the kitchen, so I leave them to it and round the corner to see what Jeremy's up to.

"Should I let them know who's right or let this play out?" I point toward the living room.

Jeremy rolls his eyes but doesn't say anything. Instead, he pulls out a carton of dairy-free ice cream and Hershey's syrup. I smile at his thoughtfulness. He dishes out two bowls of ice cream and leans in close when he hands one to me, whispering, "You're going to have to keep your mouth shut. I have money on this."

I giggle as I follow him back to the living room. Dom gives me a questioning look as I tuck myself into his side. "Where's mine?" I hold out a large spoonful, which he devours. After a second, he winces. "Cold."

Dom pulls into the parking spot in front of my apartment. I turn in my seat. "What time is your flight tomorrow?"

"It's early."

"That's not a time," I say.

Dom grimaces. "Tyler's dropping me off at four."

"I could meet you guys at your house and ride with you."

He shakes his head. "That would mean you'd have to be up at three thirty in the morning and go to work right after. I'm not making you do that."

"You're not *making* me. I want to. You took me to the airport," I point out.

"That was different."

"How was that different? Please. It's really not a big deal."

He cups my cheek in his palm. "I love that you want to see me off, but I would rather you get plenty of sleep. I promise I'll check in often."

It makes sense, but I don't like it. Dom must catch what I'm feeling from the look on my face because he asks, "Would it make you feel better if you pick me up?"

I nod.

"Okay. I'll send you my flight details." He leans over and kisses me. "I'll see you in a week."

"I already miss you," I whisper.

"Me too. Here's hoping the time will fly by."

CHAPTER FORTY-THREE

Dom

The flight to my parents' house thankfully goes smoothly. I've been texting Katelyn throughout the day, and she responds when she can. All I keep thinking is that it was a mistake to leave her. What if something happens while I'm gone? I should have checked if she had vacation time and invited her, or maybe I should have just canceled my trip. My mom would have thrown a fit, though. I text Jeremy to see if he met up with her for coffee this morning.

She changed her order this morning.

I roll my eyes. I don't care about her order. *How was she? Did she seem okay?*

She was fine. Three little dots then appear at the bottom of my screen. *Are you going to survive this week?*

Not sure.

"Kids and their phone these days," my dad comments from the driver seat. I look up to see him glance at me through the rearview mirror.

"Sorry. I'll put it away."

"Were you checking in with Katelyn?" My mom looks back. Both my parents picked me up from the airport this morning.

"I was texting Jeremy. About Katelyn," I tack on.

"How are you and she doing? It's only been a short time that you've been back together."

"We're good."

She smiles. "Hopefully we'll be able to meet her soon."

When we arrive at the house, my dad grabs my chair from the back and I wheel inside. After the accident, they discussed me moving back. They were already getting quotes for remodeling their house so it would be accessible to me, but I was adamant I would be fine on my own. They still did some work on the house for when I come to visit, though. They outfitted all the entrances and exits with ramps and, in some cases, widened doorways. They also added a second master bedroom to the main floor with all the accommodations I need.

Of course, they weren't so sure about me living on my own or as far away as I was after the suicide attempt. My mom had stayed out in California for two weeks and checked in multiple times a day once she was back home. I think she felt better knowing Tyler and Jeremy were there when she couldn't be, just like I feel better knowing they are both there for Katelyn now. I still wish I was with her, though.

Rolling into my room, the first thing that catches my attention is the walker standing by the bed.

"You've mentioned you're working on your mobility. I thought it might be helpful to have," my mom says from behind me. "Will this work, or should we get something else?"

"This works. Thanks."

She pats my shoulder and I look up at her. She smiles at me. "I'll let you get settled."

Early Christmas Eve morning, I use my walker to get to the kitchen. Christmas music plays quietly as my mom hums along from the stove.

"Smells good," I greet.

My mom turns to me, smiling. My dad does the same when he walks in. He claps me on the back. "Well, this is nice to see."

I'm glad my parents are overjoyed at seeing me standing and walking. After my fall, I almost gave up, just like I did a couple years ago. Only now, I have hope for the future, and maybe, sometime soon, Katelyn will be able to see that, too.

Katelyn

Christmas morning, I'm woken up by a text from Dom. I send back a little GIF of Santa, wishing him a Merry Christmas. I'm so excited he'll be back home in two more days. I miss him.

Since I didn't make any plans today, I brew a cup of coffee and pull out the Mazey interview, reviewing my answers. As I do, I see areas in the manuscript where her character could definitely be developed, but there are still pieces that don't work from her point of view. Maybe I should do an interview for the male lead, too. How will that help, though? The story is told from Mazey's view only. But…should it be?

In the late afternoon, I drive over to Stan's. I grab the key from under the mat and let myself in. "Hi, Scout," I call. A little bell jingles as she sprints in from the dining room. I bend down and give her a little pet before checking her litter box.

I giggle as I fill her food bowl. The whole time, she stares at me aggressively. As soon as I put her bowl down, she scarfs the food like her life depends on it. Her bell clinks against her bowl and I leave her to it, taking a seat in Stan's office, which is more like a mini library.

I pull up my Kindle app just as my phone rings. I smile. "Hi."

"Hey, Firecracker. Merry Christmas."

"Merry Christmas. How's your day been?"

"It's been good. I kind of miss the Arizona weather, though. It's cold here. I'm also missing you a ton."

My smile widens. "I miss you too."

"So, what did you do today? Did you see your mom?"

"Nope. I did a little writing and then came to check on Scout." I did text my mom, but after Thanksgiving, I've been a little angry with her. I loaned her money to cover rent and she said she would pay me back, but in all the times she's said that, it happens maybe a quarter of the time.

"And how is she?" As if she knows she's being talked about, she walks into the room and hops on my lap. He laughs. "Cute."

"What did you do?"

"Presents this morning, and then tomorrow we're going out with my extended family to Hershey Park. Should be fun."

"That does sound fun."

"Yep. Anyway, just thought I'd check in. I can't wait to see you. Love you."

My heart skips a beat. We haven't said that to each other since getting back together, but we haven't really been back together that long. "Um, yeah. Okay. You have a good…" I take a breath. "Have a good night. I love you too," I blurt and immediately hang up.

CHAPTER FORTY-FIVE

Katelyn

Leaving work Thursday, I hop in my car and turn the key to start it. It emits a horrible clicking sound, and then it falls silent. I try again and still nothing. The only person I can think of to reach out to is Jeremy. I breathe a sigh of relief when he texts that he's on his way. I lock my doors and wait in my car. A few minutes later, I jump when a knock comes on my passenger side window. Jeremy waves, and standing behind him is Tyler. I unlock my doors and Jeremy slides into the passenger seat. "Your knight in shining armor has arrived."

"Um, hello, what am I?" Tyler says.

"My squire," Jeremy tosses out.

Tyler sneers at him then looks over at me. "What's the problem?"

I turn my key to demonstrate the stupid clicking sound.

"Pop the hood," Jeremy says, climbing out of the car. I search for the little hood lever and pull. "Okay, turn the key again."

Once I do, Jeremy comes around to my side and leans into my open window. "I think you need a new battery."

I chew my lower lip. "How much is that going to cost?"

"It depends, but you're probably looking somewhere in the ballpark of three hundred dollars."

"Three hundred?" I squeak. "And what if it's not the battery?"

"I'm ninety-nine percent sure it's the battery. It's a super easy fix. We take this one out, get a new one, and then you're good to go," he says.

"Great." My chest tightens. The money I gave my mom for her rent would've covered this. I have plenty of money saved and I'll be fine, but this wasn't planned. I try and take a deep breath in.

"Kate, it's okay. Let's go get a battery."

As we climb into Jeremy's truck, he asks me what my favorite band is. When I say I don't have one, he asks for my favorite song instead.

"You're going to laugh," I say.

"I promise, I won't. What is it?"

I tell him and he searches Spotify. "Ordinary" by Alex Warren begins to play.

"Why would I laugh at this?" Jeremy asks. The chorus starts and he glances at me through the rearview mirror. "Seriously?"

I shrug. "It's a catchy song." Between the music and listening to Tyler and Jeremy banter from the front seat, the tightness in my chest loosens and I'm able to relax a little.

Once the new battery is put in, my car starts just fine. I thank Jeremy and Tyler for coming to my rescue and head home.

Dom

It's a two-hour drive from my parents' house to Hersheypark. As we approach the entrance, I spot my aunt Sheryl and her family. Suddenly, someone comes up behind me and pushes my chair. I quickly pull my hands away from the push rims.

"Long time, no see, man." My cousin Dylan pops up from behind me. "How's it going?"

I take a deep, slow breath. I'm furious, but he probably doesn't realize how inconsiderate this is. "Fine," I say. "You know, I'm perfectly capable of getting myself from point A to point B. I don't really need help." I try to keep my words light, but a hint of anger slips through.

"Right. Sorry." He lets go and comes to walk by my side. "How's life?"

"A bit different since you last saw me."

"That's right, I hear you're off the market now. Is your girl here?" he asks, looking around.

I shake my head. Once everyone arrives, we wander around the park for a couple hours and then regroup at our cars to drive through Hershey Sweet Lights, an attraction containing two miles of Christmas lights. I send a quick text to Katelyn to see how her night is going.

My car has a new battery. Jeremy and Tyler are lifesavers.

At that same moment, Jeremy's name flashes on my screen. I quickly answer. "Hey, man. What's going on over there?"

"Not much. Have you talked to Katelyn?"

My back straightens. "I hear you guys are lifesavers. What happened?"

"Nothing big. Her battery died and we got her a new one. Everything is good." Jeremy's attempt to be cool is pathetic.

"But…?"

"There were a couple moments where it seemed like she was really anxious. She kept biting her lip or wringing her hands, but she never had a full-blown attack." His exhale is sharp. "Man, I feel like I'm tattling. Katelyn should be telling you this."

"No, it's fine. I appreciate you calling. Where is she now?"

"Home. I wouldn't have let her go if I didn't think she was okay," he says defensively.

"Jer, I trust you. Thanks for taking care of her. Tell Tyler thank you for me, too."

We say goodbye and I immediately call Katelyn.

"Hi there," she answers.

I release a slow breath and try to keep the worry out of my voice. "Hi. So, a new battery? What happened?"

She tells me the story, even explaining how nervous she felt, and then it's silent. I glance out the window at a cute little igloo with three penguins. "Katelyn?" I ask.

My mom peeks back at me. I give her a small smile.

"I was thinking of making a doctor's appointment," she admits quietly. "If I let you know the details, would you mind coming?"

Relief hits me, sharp and quick. "Not at all. Send me the details when you have them."

"Thanks. How's your night?"

"Actually, let me show you." I hang up and then FaceTime her. I turn my camera so she can see all the lights.

"Pretty," she sighs.

CHAPTER FORTY-SIX

Katelyn

It was so nice to talk with Dom last night. The light tunnel was magical, and at the end of the call, his mother called out a hello. He reluctantly turned the camera and I said a brief hello. When he came back on, he looked thoroughly embarrassed. It was adorable. Now, sitting in the cell phone lot, I glance at the clock on my dash. It's a quarter past seven and his flight was supposed to be in at 6:35. I've tried texting and calling him and I haven't received an answer. I'm about to call Jeremy when my phone buzzes with a text from Dom.

SORRY! THEY LOST MY CHAIR. TRYING TO FIGURE IT OUT.

What does he mean they lost his chair? How do you lose a wheelchair? How is he supposed to get around?

The next message he sends is full of profanities. The airline is currently on the phone with the airport in Pennsylvania trying to locate his wheelchair, and at the moment, they have no leads. Jeremy rings me shortly after.

"Hey, I've been made aware there's a situation," he says. "Dom has a spare wheelchair here and it sounds like I'll be heading that way shortly with it."

"Oh. That's good that he has an extra."

Jeremy lets out a low whistle. "Don't tell him that. He hates this chair. He just never wanted to be without a backup in case anything ever happened to his good one. He's livid."

And he's all by himself. I pull out of the cell phone lot and drive to the parking garage. I don't care what I have to do to get to him. He should have someone with him.

"Do you want to head home and I can let you know when we're on our way back to the house?" Jeremy asks.

"Nope. I'm going in. Maybe it will help to have someone," I determine. On the line, Jeremy is quiet. "Is that a bad idea?"

"That's actually a great idea, but he's really upset and this is a sensitive subject, so don't take anything personally if he lashes out."

"Got it. I guess I'll see you when you get here?"

"Guess so."

I hang up and rush inside. I stop at the first ticket counter I see. I quickly explain the situation and am directed to guest relations. There, I have to rehash the situation all over again, and it takes forever for them to contact an associate that will escort me to the gate. I still have to go through security, which adds another fifteen minutes. I shift from foot to foot, antsy, and as soon as I'm through, I ditch my escort and bolt for Dom's gate. As I approach, I hear him yelling at the employee at the desk. He's sitting in one of the airport wheelchairs that have to be pushed by someone. The few people walking by slow slightly to see what the commotion is about.

"Hi," I say breathlessly, finally arriving at his side.

Dom's head whips my way. My anger flares when I catch sight of his puffy red eyes. I lace my fingers through his and then turn toward the counter. "I'd like to know how the hell this happened and what you're doing about it."

The guy at the counter sighs. "As I explained earlier, we are unsure of what happened. We are currently trying to locate the wheelchair, and when it is located, we will do everything in our power to make sure it is returned in a timely manner."

"Okay, and in the meantime? I believe he deserves something for this inconvenience."

Dom squeezes my hand. I don't tear my eyes away from the worker. They lost his freaking *wheelchair*. They should be bending over backwards to make sure he's taken care of.

Another employee walks up. "Good news, I've located your wheelchair. It will be on the next flight out and will arrive this evening around midnight."

Dom swears, releasing my hand. He goes to push himself back, only to realize he's not in his chair. He swears loudly then closes his eyes and takes a deep breath in, pinching the bridge of his nose.

"We'll get the whole story later. This is quite a blunder on the airline and one that should *never* be repeated. I think it would be wise for you to consider some sort of reimbursement due to all the trouble this has caused."

"I'm never flying with them again," Dom mutters.

"That's just for starters. In regards to the chair, do we have to come back for it or will it be delivered?"

"Oh hell no. I will be here to pick it up. I want to make sure it's mine and that they didn't mess that up as well."

I nod. "I guess that settles that," I say. My phone buzzes. Jeremy is here and will meet us wherever we need him to. "We will be back around midnight to pick up the chair and to speak with your managers about this incident. Thank you." I step behind the wheelchair and squeeze the handle, pushing Dom away.

"What the hell are you doing?"

"We're leaving."

"I can't leave. I still have to grab my bag and I don't have my wheelchair!"

I find an empty gate and take a seat, angling Dom toward me. Taking a shaky breath, he closes his eyes and inhales deep. I take his hand, interlacing my fingers through his. Glancing over at me, he opens his mouth but quickly slams it shut, shaking his head.

"You're really mad right now and I completely understand. Let's get out of here, maybe grab some food, and then come back and get everything straightened out."

"But my—"

"Jeremy has your backup chair," I explain calmly.

He grimaces.

"I know it's not your favorite, but it's something. He'll meet us at baggage claim and we'll go from there." I lean over and give him a kiss before standing, walking around and pushing him again. On our way to baggage claim, he clenches and unclenches his fists. A few times his arms twitch, like he wants to push, but he knows he can't.

Jeremy is waiting at baggage claim for us with Dom's spare chair and his bag. As we make our way to the parking garage, it seems like Dom has to work a bit harder to push this chair and I know it's not doing anything to calm him. I rest my hand on his shoulder and he glances up. I give him a smile. *Sorry*, I mouth, squeezing his shoulder.

When we reach my car, he crooks his finger and I bend down. His hands find my waist and draw me in for a deep kiss. When I pull away, I'm a little lightheaded.

"Thanks for showing up," he says, a bit breathless.

"Always." I give him a quick peck on the lips. "Let's go get some food."

We're back at the airport a little after midnight. The manager of the airline, the assistant manager, a customer service representative, Dom, and I are all crammed into a small office. By the time we finish our conversation and examine his chair for damages, which thank goodness there are none, it's a quarter to two.

"I'm so grateful you were here today," Dom says.

I pull into his driveway and then look over at him. "I'm glad. How are you doing?"

Dom shakes his head. "It's one reason I hate flying. I hate this stupid chair," he mutters.

"That's fair."

His head whips toward me. "What do you mean?"

"That what happened today *sucks* and hating your chair seems like a fair statement."

He pinches the bridge of his nose, swearing under his breath.

"I'm right here," I say. I reach over and rest my hand just above his knee, and he knots our fingers together.

CHAPTER FORTY-SEVEN

Dom

Sitting in the exam room waiting for the doctor, it's unsettling to watch Katelyn gnaw on her lower lip like she is. She pauses and I see her chewing has left her skin raw and cracked. It must hurt. I glance at my phone. We've been back here for thirty minutes and no one has come in yet. I'm about to go find a doctor when Katelyn climbs off the exam table. She pulls one of the plastic chairs closer to me and sits, lacing her fingers through mine. This is a very different Katelyn than the one at the airport a few weeks ago that demanded free airfare and waived luggage fees for all the hassle I had to deal with. Not that the airline did anything. Showing up at the airport in the first place was amazing, but then in the car? She didn't try to come up with something to make me feel better; she just seemed to understand the situation and agreed with me. Suddenly, I didn't feel like I was completely alone.

I kiss the back of her hand. "This is a good thing. I'm right here," I say, repeating the same thing she told me then.

"I don't know how to do this or what to say. How do I tell them that I'm not only physically tired, but also emotionally tired? Is that even a thing? I mean, part of the reason I've never made an appointment is because I don't know how to describe this, and if I do describe it, I sound like I'm crazy."

I pivot so I'm facing her. She looks over at me, eyes wide. "I can't do this." Her voice cracks.

"Yes, you can. I think you tell them exactly what you just told me. There is both physical and emotional fatigue. I'm sure your doctor will ask more questions to get a better sense of what is going on. We'll figure this out."

Katelyn opens her mouth to say something but there's a knock on the door. A female who looks to be in her early forties with a blunt bob and oval glasses walks in and smiles. "Hello, I'm Dr. Goodwin. You must be Katelyn." She extends her hand. Katelyn nods, quickly shaking the doctor's hand.

"And you are?" Dr. Goodwin turns to me.

"I'm Dom, her boyfriend." I shake the doctor's hand firmly.

"Wonderful. So, what brings you in today?"

Katelyn inhales sharply and her hand begins to tremble. I squeeze it tight, letting her know I'm right here.

"Sometimes it feels like there is a weight on my chest that makes it really hard to breathe, like my lungs are being constricted. Um, a lot of times my brain just keeps thinking lots of thoughts and then it makes the weight worse. And I'm tired, and not just physically," Katelyn explains. Her eyes dart to me and then to the doctor.

She reacts calmly. "Can you describe a situation where it's become hard to breathe?"

"Um, the most recent time was when my car died. It was a super simple fix but it wasn't something I had planned for. It happens a lot when I didn't plan or anticipate something."

"Can I let you know something I observed?" I ask Katelyn. "Is that okay?

She nods.

"When we first started going out, she was really quiet. It took her some time to open up. I understand that's normal, but then we went out with my friends and the new social setting seemed to trigger something."

Dr. Goodwin nods. She continues to pepper Katelyn with a ton of questions. She listens attentively, jotting down little notes. Every once in a while, Katelyn squeezes my hand and I squeeze back.

"You're dealing with some tough stuff," Dr. Goodwin says. She looks down at the iPad in her lap and purses her lips, tilting her head. "I'm going to recommend speaking with a counselor or a psychiatrist. They will be able to help you dig deeper and find the root of what is causing this worry. I don't want to say anxiety yet. I'd rather a specialist determine if that's the case and where you're currently at."

"Will that take a long time?" Katelyn asks, her voice wavering.

"It depends on when you can get in to see someone. I think after a visit or two we can confer and then decide where to go from there."

"Where would we go?" I ask, then wince and turn to Katelyn. "Sorry, this is your appointment."

"No, it's a good question." She looks at Dr. Goodwin expectantly.

"Well, depending on what a counselor determines and what I've observed, we will decide if we want to introduce medication or if weekly therapy sessions are better. It may even be a combination. We can also take a look at hormones and vitamin levels to see if any of those are out of balance. There are a lot of options and we want to make sure to choose the right one." Dr. Goodwin smiles kindly.

However, Katelyn frowns. "Got it."

It hits me that Katelyn wasn't expecting to come in and be told that there are additional hoops she has to jump through. She was expecting a remedy today that would make her feel better. She stands and thanks Dr. Goodwin for her time.

"I'll send you home with a few recommendations for counselors and psychiatrists. As soon as you have an appointment, call my office and schedule a follow-up with me and we will come up with a plan. We will figure this out."

Katelyn nods and walks out the door. She's silent the whole way to her apartment. As I assemble my chair, she says, "I'm sure you have a ton of work. You can go." Her voice is flat.

Who cares about work? I think. There is no way I'm leaving Katelyn like this. I continue to put my chair together but her hand reaches out and stops me.

"Seriously, Dom. You can go," she reiterates, but her voice trembles.

I push her hand out of the way and finish assembling. I transfer over, grab my backpack from the back seat, and wheel toward her front door. When I don't hear footsteps following, I turn.

Katelyn still stands at my car, eyes closed, breathing in and out. I roll back to her and grab her hand. I place it on my shoulder and then head back to her apartment. This time, she follows. Her shoulders shake as she unlocks the door and she no more than kicks off her shoes before she tucks herself into the corner of the couch and sobs. Setting my backpack on the floor, I sidle over to the couch and pull her close to me.

"I want to fix this. I don't want to be b-broken anymore."

"Who said broken was a bad thing?"

"If something is broken, you throw it away. It's useless."

I stroke her hair. "Actually, if something breaks, it can be repaired, and it may end up looking more beautiful than before. And even if something can't be repaired, it can be repurposed. Things that break are never useless."

Katelyn cuddles closer to me, her tears soaking my shirt. After a while, she shifts her position.

"You should go," she sniffles.

"I'm fine here."

"What about work?"

"I have to check in with my team around four. That's it."

Her brown eyes shimmer with lingering tears. She uncurls herself and stands. "Are you thirsty? Or hungry?"

"Maybe a water."

When she returns from the kitchen, she sits beside me, handing me a glass of water. "Does it have to be silent for you to work?"

"Not necessarily."

She bites her lower lip, wincing a little. "Is it okay if I watch TV while you work?"

"Absolutely."

I scoot over and grab my backpack from the floor, pulling out my laptop. Katelyn cues up *Gilmore Girls* and then walks out of the room. Returning with a pillow, she curls up on the chaise and hits play. It's fairly easy for me to tune out the show, but I keep glancing at Katelyn. At one point, her eyes flutter closed and it takes a moment for them to reopen. After another ten minutes of fighting it, she's fast asleep.

I remember those days, when it was easier to sleep than to deal with everything. For me, I was tired of dealing with the pain from the accident and feeling like I was never going to be "normal" again. Relearning to do simple tasks was exhausting.

I push a stray hair out of Katelyn's face. My heart aches for her. I wish I could wave a wand and make all of this better, but the only thing I can do is be here for her and walk with her through this. I know from experience that it gets better. She just has to hold on.

CHAPTER FORTY-EIGHT

Katelyn

"I don't know how anyone finds joy in this," Dom says from the dining room. I sit up a little and look over the back of the couch at him chopping garlic at the table.

"You know you can just buy minced garlic."

He glares at me then goes back to chopping. "How's the book?" he asks.

"Really good."

We drift back into silence, and I continue reading. After my appointment with my general practitioner, I called the few counselors and psychiatrists she recommended. The only one who could get me in quickly was Dr. Raja, a psychiatrist. The appointment was only an hour but ever since, my brain hasn't shut off. She asked a lot of questions about my childhood. When I made a comment about feeling more like the parent, she nodded and wrote something on her notepad. She wants to see me one more time before conferring with my doctor. After tossing and turning all night, I got in my car and drove over to Dom's house. I reconsidered once I got there and was about to pull away when Jeremy arrived home. He waved and then motioned for me to roll down my window.

"Good morning. What brings you here?"

"Couldn't sleep," I admitted.

"Well, come on in." Jeremy led me inside, knocked on Dom's door, and then promptly shut himself in his room, probably falling asleep immediately. Dom poked his head out, his hair mussed, and in nothing but boxers. His eyes widened when he saw me.

"Morning, Firecracker. Is everything all right?"

I shrugged. He wheeled himself to me and knotted his fingers through mine. "What can I do?"

I shrugged again. "I just didn't want to be alone. Is it okay that I'm here?"

He kissed the back of my hand. "Of course."

This is where I've been ever since. I decided to skip going to Espresso Yourself, but made sure to email Stan to let him know I wouldn't be there and attached the new scenes I wrote since the interview we did.

"Hey, can you come here?" Dom calls. I turn, finding him no longer at the table. I slip in my bookmark and head for the kitchen. Dom is standing by the stove. He pours a cup of milk into a skillet and then carefully lets go of his walker. With one hand he grabs the cutting board and with the other he slides the minced garlic off with a knife into the skillet. He sets everything down quickly and grabs his walker.

"Can you add the cream cheese?" He nods to the tub.

"Sure. Are you all right?"

"Yep." He leans over and kisses my cheek.

I was surprised to see him come out with his walker, but he said his physical therapist wanted to see him use it more. Apparently, he's up to a couple hours each day.

The alfredo sauce is almost ready and the noodles are boiling when Tyler comes around the corner, limping. He grabs a Gatorade out of the fridge, but the next step he takes, he hisses in pain. Dom clamps his mouth shut.

"Are you okay?" I ask.

"Fantastic," Tyler answers sarcastically. He hobbles toward the living room and a loud curse follows. Dom flinches.

"What's going on?"

"His hip has been causing him a lot of pain lately. He's been going to PT, but it hasn't been helping much. At this point he's probably facing another surgery," he whispers. Dom looks down and when he looks back up, his hazel eyes glisten with unshed tears. I'm stuck on how to make this better.

I rest my hand over his. "What's on your mind?"

He shakes his head. "Just wishing I could change the past."

"A lot of people wish they had that superpower." I lean over, pressing my lips to his.

"Get a room," Jeremy drawls from somewhere behind me.

I begin to pull away but Dom deepens the kiss. I wrap my arms around his neck. Jeremy fake gags. When Dom leans back, he has a smile on his face.

"There is no need for that so close to the food." Jeremy tosses us a look of disgust. "Smells amazing, though."

"And it's ready to consume," Dom says.

In the living room, Tyler slides my book onto the coffee table. Under his breath, he mumbles something about Morgan and if she has read it. Dom and Jeremy share a look and I wonder what that's about.

As we eat, we watch an episode of *Schitt's Creek*. Now that I'm paying attention, the show is quite hilarious.

Tyler scoops a bite of pasta into his mouth. "This is good, by the way."

"It's because Dom minced the garlic by hand," I tease. Dom pinches me lightly and I giggle.

I've just finished my pasta when my phone rings. It's Eliza.

"Hi." I stand and walk toward the front door.

"Firecracker." I pause, telling Eliza to hold on. "You can go in my room," Dom says. I give him a quick peck on the cheek before heading down the hall.

"Hi there. What are you up to?" Eliza asks, sounding glum.

"Just watching TV. What are you up to?"

"Not much," she sighs.

"What's going on?"

"I think we're moving. I'm not really sure where or when, but Marc was notified today that it's a possibility. Ugh…I like it here."

"I know you do, but hey, maybe you'll move closer to me." I'm trying not to get my hopes up. Marc could be stationed anywhere. I just don't want to consider that they could move even farther away.

"If we move, I have to say goodbye to the beach and the frequent trips to Disney. And my friends and my job. I actually like my job!"

"It might be hard, but you're a people person, Eliza. You're going to make new friends wherever you go. When will you know for sure?"

"It's the army. Who knows?" she whines. "Okay, I don't want to think about this anymore. What's up with you? How are you doing?"

"I'm okay." I try to sound happy.

"No, you're not. What's going on?"

"My appointment is next week Tuesday." My voice wavers and I clear my throat. This appointment will give me a diagnosis and lay out a treatment plan. Thinking about it causes my heart rate to spike.

"I know you're nervous, but I think you'll feel better when you have some answers. I'm so proud of you for taking this step. It's a good thing."

"I hope so," I whisper.

"How are you and Dom?"

"We're good. He's been very supportive through all of this." Today, he's been my lifeline. I've felt so much better just being around him.

"Good. I'll kick his butt if he steps out of line," she threatens.

I laugh. "I know you will. So, you'll keep me posted on moving?"

"Yes. Ugh, the military sucks sometimes. At least it's not a deployment."

Marc has only been deployed once so far, and it was torture for Eliza. She kept her plucky attitude, though. Luckily, she and Marc were able to stay in contact and video chat often. He was also stationed in an area that was peaceful compared to others, which made her feel marginally better.

I spend a few more minutes on the phone with her and then head back out to the living room. It's impossible to hold in my laughter when I round the corner and all of them are engrossed in an episode of *Love is Blind*. Tucking my feet under me, I lean against Dom. He wraps his arm around me.

"How's Eliza?" he whispers.

"She might be moving."

His eyebrows lift in surprise. "Back here?"

I shake my head, my mouth pulling down at the corners. Dom pulls me closer to him and I breathe in his smoky beach scent. Once the episode ends, I catch Tyler shift, then inhale sharply. He takes a few deep breaths and then quickly stands. Jeremy watches him.

"I'm fine," Tyler grumbles, hobbling out of the room. "See you guys tomorrow."

It remains quiet until I hear Tyler's bedroom door shut. "Who's Morgan?" I ask immediately. Jeremy smirks and I feel Dom's chest rumble as he chuckles.

"Morgan is a coworker he's completely infatuated with. We're just waiting for him to make his move," Jeremy explains.

"What do you know about her?"

"Just that they started hanging out at lunch a few weeks ago. Apparently, she likes books. Oh, and she has chatted with Tyler's cubicle buddies about *Love is Blind*, too," Dom says.

"That's it?" I ask incredulously.

Dom shrugs. "Should we know more?"

"Obviously." I take my phone out and pull up Instagram. Thinking for a moment, I find Tyler's Instagram and search through his followers. There are a couple of Morgans but only one who works for the same company Tyler does. Morgan Giles. "This must be her."

Dom peers over my shoulder and Jeremy rushes over, plopping down on the couch to see my screen.

"Woah, she's way out of his league," Jeremy states.

"He's got some game," Dom corrects, slapping Jeremy's arm. "I mean, I don't know if it's enough to score with her, but he has a chance."

"A slim one," Jeremy says, taking my phone and scrolling through the pictures.

Eventually, Dom begins to doze on the couch and I take that as my cue to head home.

CHAPTER FORTY-NINE

Dom

I'm working through e-mails after lunch before I head into an afternoon full of meetings when my phone rings. Katelyn's name pops up on the screen and my heart beats double time. I immediately answer.

"Hi, Firecracker."

"H-hi," she stutters. "Do you h-have—" She doesn't finish. Instead, she gasps for air.

A knock sounds on my door and one of my team members pokes their head in. "We're all set up in the conference room. You ready?" I hold up my index finger.

"Do you—have to—go?" Katelyn asks between heaving breaths.

"I've got a few minutes. Have you tried the breathing techniques you've been practicing?"

A month ago, Katelyn had her doctor's appointment and was diagnosed with depression and severe anxiety. The doctor recommended that she continue seeing her psychiatrist at least once a week and take prescribed medication. She didn't have any reaction to it at first, but now, instead of making her feel more calm, it only seems to have exacerbated her anxiety.

I quickly type out a message on Teams to let everyone know I'll be a few minutes late.

"Mm-hmm. Not—" She doesn't finish.

I quickly google ways to calm anxiety and the 3-3-3 rule pops up. "Firecracker, I'm here. You're not alone. Can you tell me where you are?"

Another knock comes but I don't acknowledge it. My only priority right now is Katelyn.

"Out—outside. Dr. Raja said i-it would help."

"Okay, that's good. Is there a bench or something around? Somewhere you can sit?" Her ragged breathing has my heart pounding.

"Yes."

"Let's try this. Close your eyes and tell me three things you can hear."

She remains quiet on the other line. I start to panic but then she says, "A plane. A lawn mower." There's a pause. "The leaves rustling."

"Perfect, now name three objects you see."

"I see a car, the grass field across the street, and…asphalt." Her breathing slows slightly.

"Now, wiggle three body parts. Since I can't see you, can you let me know what body parts you move?"

"Um, my toes. The fingers on my right hand. Does blinking my eyelids count?"

"I'll count it."

I sit there listening to Katelyn breathe in and out. "It smells like weed out here," she mumbles.

"Weed, as in marijuana?"

"Yep. I mean, not enough to get a contact high, but someone was definitely out here earlier."

"I guess that's one way to get through your work day."

She giggles and my heart rate slowly returns to a normal rhythm. I glance at the clock and the message I didn't realize that came through.

"Katelyn, I'm so sorry. I have to let you go. Are you okay?"

"Yes. Sorry to bother you."

"You didn't bother me. You can call me any time. Um, my afternoon is full of meetings and one of them will be a little difficult to step out of, but I will if I have to."

"No, no, I'll be fine. Thanks for answering. I love you."

"You're welcome. Love you, and I'll talk to you later."

Katelyn

Walking into Espresso Yourself the following Saturday, I see Dom and Stan deep in conversation already. I walk over, resting my hand on Dom's shoulder. He glances up, smiling, but it quickly shifts when he notices the dark circles under my eyes.

I'm fine, I mouth, leaning down to give him a quick kiss. "Hi, Stan," I say, straightening.

"Hello, Katelyn. How are you?"

"Okay. I have a question for you, but…" My eyes bounce between Stan and Dom. "Did I interrupt?"

"Not at all," Stan says.

"I'll grab my coffee and come back, then?"

"Perfect."

By the time I get my coffee and return to the table, my stomach is in knots. *This idea is ludicrous. You are not talented enough to pull this off. Give up!* I slide into the chair next to Dom and his fingers entwine with mine. I shove my thoughts away and pull out my computer.

"I was thinking…" My voice wavers and I take a moment to recollect myself. "You know that exercise you suggested about writing a scene in someone else's perspective?"

Stan nods.

"I've done that with a few scenes so far and it helped, but I'm not sure how to write the scene in the main character's perspective. I think it works better in his point of view." My eyes flick to Stan and then down to my lap. I'm scared to see his face when I ask the question. What if he says it's good but his expression conveys otherwise? But Stan just sits, patiently waiting for me, so I blurt it out. "What if I write this from two points of view?"

"That's an intriguing idea. How would you lay that out?" Stan asks.

I glance up. He looks at me and raises his eyebrows. "Would you bounce back and forth between the two characters? Would one character receive more page time than the other? Are you limiting the points of view to just two characters?"

I swallow and tighten my grip on Dom's hand. "I was thinking the majority of the story would be told from the main female character, but a few chapters would be told from the male lead. Is that dumb?"

Stan shakes his head. "I'm just wondering why I haven't seen these chapters yet. Are you able to send them to me next week?"

I nod and the knot in my stomach loosens slightly.

"Perfect. Unfortunately, I have to get going now, but I'll be waiting for those, young lady." Stan gathers his cup and scoots off the bench. "Oh, would you be interested in watching Scout again? The grandkids have spring break coming up and I wanted to travel out there to spend the week with them."

"I'd like that."

"I'll send you the dates. You two have a wonderful afternoon."

The door chimes as Stan leaves. Dom turns to me. "How are you?"

I'm about to say I'm fine, but I've been working on being open with people I trust so instead I answer, "I haven't been sleeping good. I hate that I feel *more* anxious now."

"I'm sorry."

I shrug. "One day at a time, right?"

"Right." He kisses my cheek. "So, dual point of view? That sounds interesting."

I bite my lower lip. "I hope so."

"It's going to be brilliant. I can't wait to see your name on the *New York Times*'s Best Seller list."

I give him an incredulous look. "That's never going to happen."

"What are you talking about? An epic fantasy told in multiple points of view. It's going to soar to the top. I'm sure of it."

"Dom."

"Katelyn, you're so freaking talented and you have so many great teachers. I mean, haven't you said that to be a great writer, you have to be a great reader?"

"Stephen King said that," I mumble.

"Okay, well, you're *always* reading. I think by now you have a good sense of what works and what doesn't. For instance, sparkly vampires don't work."

I roll my eyes. "I feel like some would argue that point. I mean, how are they supposed to be?"

"I don't know. Like the ones from *The Lost Boys*."

My brows wrinkle in confusion. *Since when are there vampires in Neverland?*

Dom gasps. "*The Lost Boys*? Classic 1987 movie with Corey Feldman, Corey Haim and—oh my gosh, that's where I've seen him!"

"Who?"

Dom snaps his fingers a few times. "Um, the grandpa. Lorelai and Rory. *Gilmore Girls*. The grandpa is a vampire."

"Okay…?"

"Do you know how long that's been bugging me?"

I shake my head.

Dom laughs. "Way too long. Anyway, my point is, you can do this. I'm sure you've already been applying things from what you've read without realizing it. Your book is going to be amazing! I can't wait to read it."

I stare at my computer screen. "You make it sound like it could also be unoriginal."

"What? No!" Dom grips my chin gently and turns my face toward his. "You are unique, and your story will be one of a kind. What I meant was that you know how to convey emotions better than some because you've seen how so many other authors do it. You know what it takes for a place to come alive because you've read books that let you get lost in that world. You're not just copying and pasting. I know because I've read some of it, and it's incredible."

I shake my head. *You're a copycat, a wannabe. You're not going to make it.* Suddenly, a weight settles on my chest. I close my eyes, then inhale, hold, and exhale, all for four counts. I do this a few times before I lift my head. Dom's hazel eyes are trained on me.

"I'm good," I assure him. *No, what I have is original*, I tell myself, and the thoughts disperse.

"You've got this," he says resolutely. "I have total faith in you, and when your name appears on the Best Seller list, I'm going to say I told you so." He taps my laptop. "But I won't be able to say that if you don't get to work."

CHAPTER FIFTY

Dom

Catching up with Stan this afternoon was exactly what I needed. Not only did we talk about Katelyn, I opened up a little about my past, explaining that because of my experience it was easier for me to relate to what she was going through. Stan pointed out what Jeremy did a few months ago—it'll be hard to take care of Katelyn unless I take care of myself first. I've been trying to commit that to heart and prioritize myself, too.

The rest of the afternoon was spent watching Tyler freak out about the date tonight. He finally gained the courage to ask Morgan out, but made it a double date with Katelyn and me. Now, Tyler, Katelyn, and I are waiting in the lobby of an escape room when a woman with blonde, chin-length hair walks in. Her blue eyes survey her surroundings. When she catches sight of Tyler, a grin breaks out on her face.

"Sorry I'm late. Traffic."

"No biggie." Tyler shrugs. His smile is huge. "Morgan, this is Dom." He gestures to me. Morgan reaches out and shakes my hand. "And this is Katelyn." The two of them shake hands.

"Shall we?" I ask.

The attendant leads us to a wooden door. "A shadow passes overhead, but you're not concerned. You're here for the treasures hidden inside this crumbling stone castle. The rumors of the dragon haunting the grounds is not a deterrent. Entering the castle"—the attendant opens the door, stepping inside, and we follow—"the once ornate floors and furniture are covered in layers of dust. Clues throughout the castle will lead you to the suspected treasure, but a roar sounds in the distance." At this, the speakers play a dragon roar. "Will you be able to find the treasure before you become the dragon's next meal? You have one hour to find out. Good luck." The attendant backs out of the room and closes the door.

"Will we even be able to spot the dragon? Maybe it's like Zezura, and can blend into its surroundings," Morgan comments.

Katelyn chuckles. "You've got a point."

"Oh, man. I love that you got that," Morgan says.

Katelyn's eyes light up. "Yes, I am obsessed with those books."

"Um, I hate to interrupt, but I'd rather be out before we even have to worry about a dragon," Tyler says.

We get to work solving clues. The girls chat about books while we investigate. At one point, I roll over to Tyler and tease, "If worse comes to worse, you can just pick the lock, right?"

"I mean…" He shrugs.

After a half hour, a louder roar rings through the speakers, followed by a thirty-minute warning.

Tyler reads a clue out loud and then turns to Katelyn. "You should be an expert on dragons. What does this mean?"

Morgan looks up from the drawer she was rummaging through. "Why would she be an expert?"

"Because apparently she reads about them, and she's been writing about them." Tyler glances my way. "Right?"

I study Katelyn, who isn't saying anything. When I catch her wiggle her fingers and then roll her shoulders, I realize she's running through the 3-3-3 rule. As I lace my fingers through hers, she answers, "I don't think I'm an expert. Read it again."

"'Once whole, his dwelling place now lies shattered. Frightened and alone, the beast finds shelter among dragonets but isn't quite like them.'"

"Dragonets?" Morgan asks.

"Small dragons," Katelyn comments. "Wait, small. It's a baby!"

"It hatched," Morgan pipes up. She glances around the room. "Got it!"

On one of the shelves of the bookcase is a broken egg. When Morgan assembles the four pieces, each piece has a number outlined in different colored rhinestones.

"I think I know what that goes to." Katelyn releases my hand and walks over to a lock on one of the desk drawers.

Tyler comes and stands by me. Morgan reads off the numbers and Katelyn enters them into the lock. She shakes her head. They try a different combo and the lock clicks open.

"We'd be so screwed without them," Tyler comments.

We find the treasure with minutes to spare. As we're walking out, Morgan turns to Katelyn. "So wait, are you really writing about dragons?"

"Um, I mean, I'm writing a book with a dragon in it."

"Can I read it?" Morgan asks excitedly.

"It's not done yet, but…I do have another story," she says carefully. "No dragons, but it does have Fae. I can send it to you."

"Yes, please!"

"While you're at it, can you send it to Jeremy? I may have talked about it a lot and now he really wants to read it," I say.

She laughs, sounding nervous but also slightly relieved. "Sure."

Katelyn

Sunday afternoon, I sent my first manuscript to Morgan and Jeremy. I like Morgan. Talking about books with her helped me a lot during the escape room. There were several moments during that night my anxiety spiked. I think about it while sitting in Dr. Raja's office now.

"How's your week been?" she asks me.

"It's been fine." I shrug.

"And what does fine mean?"

It frustrates me when she does this. She doesn't let me get away with filler words, instead making me spell out exactly what I'm feeling. When I explain what happened Saturday evening, the corner of her mouth pulls down. She makes a note on her notepad and looks back up at me.

"And how is everything going with your mom?"

My automatic response is to say fine, but I know she'll just push me to put it into words again. "I spoke with her last week. She told me everything was going well. I did ask her about her finances and made sure she had everything she needed."

"It's sweet that you do that, but remember what we've talked about. She is an adult."

"And I need to let her make her own mistakes and also get out of them."

Dr. Raja nods. "Exactly."

Near the end of our appointment, Dr. Raja reviews her notes. Looking up at me, she asks, "How would you feel about switching your medication? I'm not sure what we're currently doing is working."

I bite my lower lip. "Um, I'm willing to try. Do you think it will help?"

"There's only one way to find out."

CHAPTER FIFTY-ONE

Dom

"Are you sure you don't want help?" I call out from the couch. Tyler has been in the kitchen for the past twenty minutes getting dinner prepped and all I've heard is the banging of pots and pans interrupted by quite a bit of cursing.

"I'm fine!"

Sighing, I grab my walker and shuffle into the kitchen. Tyler rolls his eyes when he hears me approach.

"What are we eating anyway?" I ask.

"Food," he answers flatly.

The front door opens and we both turn. Katelyn walks in, looking a little flustered. "Hi, Tyler." She gives him a little nod then leans into me for a kiss.

I place my hands on her hips. "How's Scout?"

"Ugh…she's a menace," Katelyn grumbles. She slides her phone out of her purse and pulls up a picture of Stan's living room, specifically zooming in on the curtains in the window… and the little claw marks running down them.

"Stan's response was funny, though." Switching to her text messages, she finds Stan's text thread and shows me the latest message.

Thou shalt join his brethren in paradise.

I laugh. "Sounds like it's happened before."

"It's a good thing she's cute."

"Are you guys finished?" Tyler snaps.

"Do you need something?" I narrow my eyes at him.

He covers a pan with tin foil and sticks it in the oven. He shifts and grimaces. "Could you watch this? Then in like fifteen, twenty minutes make the quinoa? Morgan's gonna be here in about an hour."

After our double date, Tyler went out with her several more times and invited her over for game night tonight. It's her first time at the house, though, so his nerves are through the roof.

"Sure, man."

Tyler nods and uses the counter and then the wall for support as he makes his way to his room. I told him he could use the walker, but he doesn't want to use it until it's absolutely necessary.

Katelyn joins me on the couch. She asks how I spent my day, and I tell her about the latest gossip at work. As I stand to finish dinner, Katelyn's eyes trail me, worry flitting across her face. Leaning over, I kiss her on the lips. "I'm good."

"Sorry. I know."

"Don't apologize. I just need you to know." She smiles at me and I leave her on the couch.

When the doorbell rings, I turn to answer the door, only to see Tyler has beaten me to it. He grins widely when he opens it. "Hi, Morgan."

"Hi. Oh, it smells good in here. Thanks for having me over."

"Of course. Feel free to make yourself at home."

Tyler joins me in the kitchen. Soon, chatter drifts in from the living room. Tyler pulls out the pan from the oven and is removing the foil when both girls squeal, erupting in a fit of giggles.

Tyler glances over at me. "I wonder what that's about?"

I shrug and call out that dinner is ready. The girls walk into the kitchen, still engrossed in their conversation.

Jeremy turns the corner. "Wait. If you're talking about what I think you are, I need you to stop. I'm only halfway through."

Everyone turns.

"I was bored at work the other day." He shrugs. "I took Katelyn up on her book recommendation."

Katelyn bursts into laughter and the sound melts my heart. It's been a while since she's been this relaxed. "Morgan, this is Jeremy. He apparently has been sucked into the fantasy world."

"One word. Dragons. And there is fighting and it's brutal. You can't make fun until you read it."

"He has a point," Morgan agrees.

The first half of dinner is filled with talk about books. Suddenly, Morgan points her fork at Katelyn.

"Oh my gosh! I finished it."

Katelyn startles. "Finished what?"

"Your book. I'm actually halfway through a reread. The world is incredible, and your FMC is outstanding."

"What's an FMC?" Tyler asks.

"Female main character," Morgan explains.

"Hold on, you already finished?" Jeremy asks. "I apparently need to step things up. I'm only halfway through." He looks over at Katelyn. "I'd have to agree, though. Your female character is fierce."

Katelyn blushes.

"So, where are you in the publishing process?" Morgan asks.

Katelyn shakes her head. "Nowhere."

"Girl, why not? This book is phenomenal! You should definitely publish this."

After dinner, Katelyn clears the plates while Tyler sets up the game Ransom Notes. I watch her from the dining table. All the raving about her book made her quiet.

"Too much book talk?" Jeremy asks from beside me.

"I don't know."

"We'll try and cool it."

I nod, and Katelyn joins us at the table again. Once we're all seated, Tyler explains the game. The premise is to lay out a prompt card and then, using the little magnetic word tiles, create a response on our trays to answer the prompt within ninety seconds. The five of us gather our words and Tyler flips over the first prompt.

We make it around the table once, and Katelyn is clearly kicking our butts. We're all gathering new word tiles when she suddenly blurts at Morgan, "Do you really think it would be worth sending the manuscript to an editor?"

Morgan nods. "*One-hundred* percent!"

Katelyn reaches for my hand and I knot my fingers through hers. She takes a deep breath in and holds it, letting it out slowly. Tyler starts the time, and the new round begins. I'm more worried about Katelyn than my tiles, and I don't think she's focusing either until she lays three word tiles on her magnetic tray. The timer beeps.

She leans over and glances down at my empty tray. "You're not going to win like that."

I shrug. To me, Katelyn will always come first.

CHAPTER FIFTY-TWO

Katelyn

It's been a few weeks since I started my new medication and I've been feeling better. Maybe tonight is just a bad night, a fluke. Staring at my ceiling, I wish my thoughts would quiet, or that there was a way to let all these roiling emotions out.

You could cut them out. My heart skips a beat. I immediately reach for my phone and call Dom. I'm not surprised when he doesn't answer—it's almost one in the morning. I run through all the things Dr. Raja suggested I do and then text the only person I know who is up at this time. As I wait for a reply, I grab my pillow and blanket and move to my couch. I turn on the television when my phone starts buzzing.

"Hi," I answer.

"You're up late," Jeremy says. "What's going on?"

"I couldn't sleep and, um…" My voice quivers. There is no way I can tell Jeremy what I was thinking.

"Katelyn, are you safe by yourself?" Worry laces his every word.

"I think so."

"What are you doing right now?"

"Sitting on my couch." I pull my knees to my chest and cuddle under my blanket. "I was going to watch TV."

"What have you been watching?"

"*Gilmore Girls*. I've seen it a million times so if I fall asleep I don't have to go back and catch up."

"It's a comfort show."

"Yeah, kind of."

Jeremy says something that I can't make out.

"What was that?"

"I was just talking to my coworker."

"Oh. If you have to go, that's okay." The last thing I want is for him to get in trouble at work. If he's at work, that means he'll be at Starbucks in the morning. That makes me feel a little better.

"I'm good. What are you reading right now?"

"I'm in the middle of *Blade Breaker*."

"That sounds interesting."

"It's good so far. It's the second book in the Realm Breaker trilogy."

"Nice. What's the series about?"

I hear conversation in the background. "Jeremy, I'm—"

"Not hanging up this phone until you hear a knock on your door. Now, are you going to tell me about the books I added to my TBR or do I have to read the description?"

Without giving spoilers, I tell Jeremy about *Realm Breaker*. He asks which characters are my favorite so far and I tell him it's Domacridhan and Sorasa Sarn.

Chuckling, he says, "Of course one of your favorites is named Dom."

"Are you reading anything right now?" I ask.

"I've been listening to the Fireborne series because someone said I should."

"Do you like it?"

"Yeah, but I'm not sure how I'm supposed to feel about this Powers character."

I'm about to reply when a knock at my door startles me. I shuffle over and peer through the peephole. Tears instantly spring to my eyes as a distorted Dom pulls out his phone and mine buzzes a second later.

"Katelyn?" Jeremy asks.

Sniffling, I say, "He's here. You can go."

I don't give Jeremy a chance to reply. I hang up and swing the door open. As soon as Dom is inside, he shuts the door behind him and pulls me into his lap. I bury my face in his shoulder and draw my feet up on the footrest.

Dom rubs my back soothingly. "Shh, I'm here."

We settle on the couch. My head rests in his lap and he gently combs his fingers through my hair.

"Do you want to tell me what happened tonight?" he asks quietly.

"No," I whisper.

His fingers freeze momentarily and then he returns to a slow rhythm.

"I'm not sure how," I explain. "I've already emailed Dr. Raja. Hopefully she responds in the morning."

"Good. Do you want to stay out here or go in your room?"

"I'm good here."

Dom's presence quiets everything and I'm able to fall asleep. When I wake up, Dom's not on the couch. Sitting up, I glance around my apartment and see his chair over by the bathroom. After a few minutes, the bathroom door opens and Dom walks back over to the couch, using his chair for support. He runs his thumb under my eye, his forehead puckering in worry. I lean into his touch.

"I should probably get ready," I whisper.

"Do you have any sick time? Maybe it would be better to take a day to rest."

"It's too quiet when I'm here by myself. Work is a good distraction."

Dom doesn't love the thought of me working on so little sleep, but he understands the need to be occupied.

He joins Jeremy and me at Starbucks. The second I see Jeremy, tears prickle my eyes. I'm so grateful he saw my text and called me last night. Even more appreciative that he found a way to wake Dom. I wrap him in a tight hug as soon as we reach each other.

"Morning." His arms loop around me. "How are you?"

"Tired, but here." I pull back and smile. "Thank you for keeping me company last night."

"Anytime." He claps Dom on the back. "How's it going?"

"I need coffee."

As we wait for our drinks, they tuck me between them. I soak up these minutes of feeling safe and am already counting down the minutes until I'm back in Dom's arms later tonight.

Dom

It's been a week since I showed up at Katelyn's doorstep at two in the morning. Apparently when Jeremy couldn't get ahold of me, he called Tyler, who about gave me a heart attack when he woke me up. Tyler hasn't woken me up since, but I find myself jolting awake from time to time and checking my phone. I keep telling myself if she's in trouble, she'll call someone. She was able to speak with her psychiatrist the next day and doubled up on her appointments for the next couple weeks. For now, they aren't changing her meds.

Now, on Katelyn's doorstep again, I'm praying she answers quickly because I feel like I have to pee even though I went to the restroom right before I left the house. I've been going to the bathroom way more than necessary today. On the drive over, a few chills ran down my spine, and that only happens when I'm running a temperature.

"Hi." She smiles when she answers the door. "You're early."

"Uh-huh. Excuse me. I need to use the restroom." Careful not to roll over her toes, I squeeze by her and head to the bathroom.

When I come out, I find her in her room, sitting on the floor in front of her mirror. I tap her door frame, and she looks up.

She furrows her brows. "Everything okay?"

"Everything's great. You excited for tonight?"

Her eyes scale my figure, and she tilts her head. "You don't look so good. I'm fine with ordering food and staying in."

If we stay in, it'll ruin the surprise. One I've been very proud of keeping for the past week. "Really, Firecracker, I'm fine. I can't wait to go out with you."

She comes to stand in front of me to kiss me. I pull away quickly, hoping she doesn't notice my elevated temperature.

The second we enter the restaurant, I spot the surprise immediately. It takes Katelyn a little longer as her eyes roam around the room, but then she does a double take.

"Oh my gosh. Eliza!" She rushes over. Eliza barely gets to her feet before Katelyn plows into her, wrapping her in a hug. "What are you doing here?" Katelyn asks. She then whips around and points at me. "Did you know?"

I nod. When Eliza reached out to let me know that she and Marc would be in town and she wanted to surprise Katelyn, I was on board. From there, she sent me information for a reservation at Top of the Rock restaurant in Tempe.

She turns back to Eliza. "Why didn't you tell me?"

"I thought this would be more fun." Eliza shrugs, grinning. "And I was right."

The hostess comes to the front and calls our party to a table. Once we're settled, Katelyn turns her attention to Eliza. "So how long are you here?"

"We'll be here for a few days. Taking advantage of the time Marc has off before we move."

"Wait, so you're officially moving?"

"Yep. We have to be in Oklahoma on May sixteenth."

"Wow. That's, like, three weeks away."

"Yeah. It's all right though. It's closer to you." Eliza's smile widens. "I also thought it would be better to show you this in person instead of over a video call." She holds up her left hand, her ring finger sporting a simple gold band with a single diamond in the center.

The squeal that erupts from the girls hurts my ears. Marc leans away from Eliza.

"Oh my gosh, I'm so excited for you! When did this happen?"

Eliza looks at Marc. "Last Friday. This jerk"—she smacks him playfully on the shoulder—"told me we were just going to grab a quick bite and then come home to watch a movie or something. I looked like a total slob."

"How did he do it?"

"Do you want to tell it?" she asks him.

Marc shakes his head. "It's all you."

"I had just come home from work, so I changed into leggings and a T-shirt. He walked in from work too and then asked if I was hungry. We decided to grab sandwiches from this cute little deli in town, and when we got back, he surprisingly turned on *How to Lose a Guy in Ten Days*. He hates that movie, but he knows it's one of my faves. We cuddled on the couch and at the end of the movie, he told me that he had finally found out he was being restationed. As I processed the news he got down on one knee and said, 'I figure if you're going to be following me around, we might as well get hitched. What do ya think?'"

"Awe," Katelyn sighs.

"I mean, I'll follow this man anywhere. He's my forever. Now, here we are."

Katelyn beams. "Here you are."

"Congratulations," I say.

"Thank you." Eliza gives me a little nod. "I wanted to tell you in person and Dom helped me make it a surprise. He's a keeper."

"I think so, too." She rests her hand on my knee, but instead of smiling, her brow furrows. Reaching up, she places her hand on the back of my neck and the chill of her touch sends a shiver down my spine. She kisses my cheek too, and her lips linger. When she pulls away, I know she's aware I have a fever. I subtly shake my head. I'm not going to be the reason we cut this celebration short and she loses time with her friend.

I excuse myself before the food arrives to use the restroom. As I pull back up to the table, I catch Katelyn's eyes trailing me. I give her a small smile as I secure my brakes. The girls make plans to spend tomorrow afternoon together and Eliza insists we all meet for dinner before they have to fly back out.

"We'll see. Dom has a busy weekend," Katelyn says and grips my hand.

As soon as we're in the car, Katelyn turns to me. "Dominic, why on earth did you tell me you were fine? You are not fine!"

"It's nothing contagious. I'll get some antibiotics and be good as new."

"How do you know?"

"It's a UTI. They happen." I shrug. One of the many downsides of having to use a catheter.

"Oh." Her anger fizzles out. "Is there anything I can do?"

"Nope. Plenty of fluids and rest. And I'm up for dinner with Eliza and Marc."

She pins with an exasperated look. "You are *resting*." The second I pull up to her apartment, she leans over and gives me a quick kiss. "Text me when you get home. I'll check on you tomorrow."

CHAPTER FIFTY-THREE

Katelyn

Leaving the restaurant last night, my phone buzzed, but I was too worried about Dom to check my messages. I think about the text from Marc now while I wait for Eliza at Espresso Yourself.

You would have never been able to keep your mouth shut if I told you that over Thanksgiving I had asked for her dad's permission to marry her. It was the one chance I had to do it in person and I had to take it.

My jaw drops. *You've kept this a secret for months!*

I know. And Eliza thinks I can't plan stuff.

"Oh my gosh." I chuckle. She had picked up that something was off, just not in the way she thought.

"Hey, hey," Eliza calls out, walking in.

"Hi." I give her a quick hug.

She spins around, taking everything in. "This is where you come every Saturday?"

"Almost, yeah."

"Do you have a regular table?"

"I usually sit over there." I point to my usual table, and my eyes flick to Stan's empty one. My shoulders droop a little. I was looking forward to introducing Eliza to him, seeing how I've mentioned him a few times already, but he's not here today. I hope he's okay.

Waiting for our drinks, Eliza gives me a curious look.

"What?"

"Is everything okay with you and Dom?"

"Yeah, why?"

She fidgets with her engagement ring. "Something seemed weird last night. You kept watching him and by the end of the night, you seemed upset."

I'm not sure Dom would appreciate me sharing his medical dilemma with her so I shrug. "We're fine."

"Katelyn, if something is up…"

"He wasn't feeling good last night. I was just worried."

"Okay, but if anything changes, say the word." She's still looking at me skeptically.

"I know."

Eliza nods seriously and starts fiddling with her ring again.

"Do you have a date or anything yet?" I ask.

She glances down at her finger, wiggling it. The diamond sparkles under the florescent light. "I was thinking sometime in the winter, but I'm not sure."

"Are you going to come back here or stay in Oklahoma? Or get married in another state?"

She chuckles. "We're going to come back here. Both our families are here, and so is my maid of honor." She nudges my shoulder.

"Wait, seriously?" I squeal.

"Duh, who else would it be?" Her smile lights up her face.

After hours of talking wedding details over coffee, I head to Dom's. I knock and then walk in. Tyler and Morgan are on the couch watching television.

"Hey, guys."

Tyler gives me a little nod and Morgan turns. "Hi, Katelyn. Publish that book yet?" she teases.

I shake my head, rolling my eyes.

"I'm waiting!" she calls after me.

Dom's door is ajar. I push it open a little to see Dom fast asleep on his bed. I tiptoe in, lightly kiss his cheek, and then turn to leave. I'm almost to the door when I hear, "Where are you going?"

I spin. Dom's pulling himself up to a sitting position.

"I'm sorry. I didn't mean to wake you."

He pats the bed. I slide my shoes off and crawl up next to him. "How are you feeling?" I press my palm to his forehead. He feels warm, but not too hot.

He shrugs. "How was your afternoon?"

"It was great. I love when Eliza visits."

Dom scooches off the bed, grabs his walker, and goes to the bathroom.

"You seem to be moving around really well," I say as he slips back into bed.

"Up to about four hours a day." He leans in and I meet him, pressing my lips to his. His arms slip around me, pulling me closer to him. I'm breathless when we separate. I lay my head on his chest and breathe in his smoky ocean scent.

We cuddle together on Dom's bed until my phone buzzes. It's an email from Stan. It's weird that he's emailing me so late. When I click on it, my heart stops. "Oh my gosh."

Dom's hand slides down my back. "What's wrong?"

"It's Stan. He's in the hospital. They need someone to check on Scout."

I scamper off the bed and grab my purse.

"Hold on. I'll go with you."

"No, it's fine. You aren't feeling well."

He transfers to his chair, wheeling around the bed to block my path.

"Dom, Maria got my email from her dad's account. She said that he's been in the hospital since this morning. I need to go." I try to step around him but he pushes forward.

"Firecracker, take a breath. Let me come with you. We will make sure Scout's okay."

I chew on my lower lip. Finally, I nod. "Be quick."

Dom

Katelyn immediately kneels down and lifts the doormat. When she stands, panic is written all over her face. "It's not here. He always leaves a key under the mat. We can't get in."

I lace my fingers through hers, noticing the slight tremble. "We'll find a way to get in."

"How? I've tried calling the number Maria provided in the email and I can't get ahold of anyone."

"I have a solution." I pull out my phone and send a quick text. Twenty minutes later, Tyler pulls up to the house.

"What's he supposed to do?" Katelyn's voice pitches. She looks back over to Tyler's car. Her eyes widen as he approaches, using a cane for support.

"Hey, hey. Whose house are we breaking into?" Tyler teases.

"We are not breaking in," Katelyn says firmly, narrowing her eyes at him.

"Okay, so why am I picking the lock?" Tyler raises his eyebrows in question.

"You're *what*?" She turns to me. "That's the solution?"

"We need in. He can get us in." I shrug.

Tyler leans his cane against the wall and lowers down. He pulls out a little set of lockpicking tools and starts working. I squeeze Katelyn's hand and she closes her eyes, exhaling slowly before taking a steady breath in. I count silently to four and she exhales again.

"I saw you staring," Tyler says, interrupting her breathing. Her eyes pop open. "Please tell me it's sexier than a walker."

"What does Morgan think?" Katelyn asks, then looks around. "Where is Morgan? Did we just ruin your date?"

"No. She left shortly after you guys. She thought it was a bit of a turn-on, though." Tyler smirks, tapping the cane, but then his face turns serious. "I have surgery on May eighth," he murmurs.

"That's soon," I remark.

"Twelve days," he says. There's a click and Tyler turns the handle. "Eureka!"

As soon as Tyler is standing, Katelyn pushes past him and enters the house.

"How you getting in?" he asks me.

"Just like he did last time," Katelyn calls and then peeks her head out. "Will that work?"

I nod and motion Tyler to go in. Katelyn brings my chair in and then closes the door. She calls out for Scout, but nothing happens. When Katelyn reaches the end hall, she gasps, her hand flying to her mouth. "Oh no. No, no, no, no, no." Suddenly, she's running.

Tyler limps over to the hall and swears. I'm right behind him, and suddenly looking down into Stan's wide open office. A shelf full of books is now on the floor. Katelyn picks one up, its corner completely chewed off. A little jingle comes from behind me. Scout saunters past and rubs against Katelyn's arm.

"You are in big trouble, young lady." Katelyn gently pushes Scout away, but all she does is jump into my lap instead and fall fast asleep.

The entrance to the office is too narrow so I can't enter, but I sit outside the door to keep Katelyn company. She picks up the books and places them back on the shelf, turning the one with the chewed corner out so Stan can see it. When she finishes, her lower lip trembles and her eyes shine with tears. She takes a deep breath and walks over to pet Scout.

"Troublemaker," she murmurs.

Katelyn steps to the door and I reverse so she can get out. As she passes me, she gives my shoulder a squeeze. A moment later, a bag rustles from the kitchen. Scout perks up and then darts off the chair, bell ringing as she races to the kitchen. Tyler peeks into Stan's office.

"Who reads this much?"

"Smart people," I deadpan.

"Rude." Tyler pulls the door closed, punching my shoulder as he walks by.

On our way out, Katelyn locks the deadbolt and messages Maria to let her know she was able to stop over. As soon as we're in the car, I look at Katelyn.

"What?" she asks.

"Feel better?"

She bites her lip, but then catches herself. She purses her lips and nods. Reaching over, she places her hand on my forehead. "How are you feeling?"

I shrug. "This little bit of activity has made me feel worse and the antibiotics haven't really kicked in yet."

"I think we should cancel dinner tomorrow."

I shake my head.

"But—"

"Nothing," I cut her off. "I'll rest and drink lots of fluids. I can handle dinner."

She frowns. "I bet you five bucks your temperature is higher and all you did was drive me to the house."

"I don't want to take your money."

Her eyes narrow. I wink and give her a cheesy grin.

When we get back to the house, Katelyn goes straight to the bathroom and grabs the thermometer. She slides it across my forehead and it beeps. "99.7."

"That's not even a temperature." I grin.

"Dominic, is that higher?"

I shrug.

Huffing in frustration, she places her palm on my forehead. "You feel warmer than earlier."

Taking her hand, I kiss her palm and then the back of it. "It's not a big deal." I let her go and wheel to my room. Her footsteps follow.

I quickly change, slipping on a sweater because I have chills. Sliding into bed, I crook my finger, and she joins me. I hand her a five-dollar bill. "When I checked this morning, it was 99.2."

She pockets the money and then curls into my side. "Do you need anything?"

"I'm good." I drape my arm around her.

"You know, you've mentioned from time to time that you wish you were normal. Now, this might not help, but everyone gets UTIs. That isn't something exclusive to wheelchair users." I look at her questioningly. "It might happen more often, but literally everyone on the planet is susceptible."

I grin. "You're right."

"Just thought I'd point it out."

I kiss the top of her head. "It actually makes me feel a little better."

I turn on the TV and then pass the remote to her and let her pick a show. As she searches for something to watch, I replay the last couple hours in my head. Katelyn had moments when I thought her anxiety was going to overpower her, but she breathed right through it. *This is her figuring it out*, I realize. I'm happy to see her new medication seems to be helping.

I sigh and her beautiful brown eyes flick to mine. She grins and nestles closer to me.

CHAPTER FIFTY-FOUR

Dom

Before they fly out Monday, we decided to meet Marc and Eliza at LumberjAxes in Tempe for dinner and axe throwing. We find the elevator, and as we step in, Katelyn's phone rings. Her brow furrows.

"Hello, Maria," she answers.

Maria? Stan's daughter.

"Wait, I can't understand you."

There's a brief pause and then Katelyn's phone crashes to the ground. Her knees buckle.

"Katelyn," I yell, unable to catch her.

She curls over herself, her shoulders shaking violently. The elevator door opens and a group begins to step in, only to freeze at the scene before them. They back out and let the doors close. I grab her phone and realize the call is still connected.

"Hello? This is Dominic."

"Hello, Dominic. This is Troy. Maria's husband." He clears his throat. "As I just told Katelyn, Stan passed early this morning. He had a stroke."

My heart stops. I barely register what Troy is saying. I place my hand on Katelyn's back, letting her know I'm here.

"I'm…so sorry to hear that." My voice cracks. "Um, how is Scout?"

A whimper comes from Katelyn.

"Peter and his family have been staying at the house. Scout is fine as far as I know."

"Okay. Thank you for the call."

"I know Katelyn had a great friendship with Stan. We felt she should know. There will be a service in the next week or so. I can send the information over if you would like to attend."

"That would be good. Thank you. I'm sorry again."

I hang up the phone and slide it into my pocket. I'm not sure how many times the elevator has gone up and down. Leaning over, I tug Katelyn's arm. "Firecracker, can you stand?"

She pushes herself up off the floor, but she's not quite stable. I pull her into my lap and her feet automatically find the footrest. She turns, burying her face in my shoulder. As I push us out of the elevator, her arms wrap around my neck and she holds tight. The minute we are at the car, I set my brakes and loop my arms around her waist.

"Eliza," Katelyn sniffles.

"What?"

"Marc and Eliza. They're waiting. I have to, um…"

Right, we were meeting people. They are probably waiting on us. "I'll call her."

When Eliza answers, I take a deep breath and explain the situation. Hearing the news again brings a fresh round of tears from Katelyn. I wrap my arm tighter around her.

"Oh my goodness. How's Katelyn? Where can I meet you?"

"I can text you my address. I'm going to take her there."

"I'll see you guys shortly."

Thankfully, it's quiet when we enter the house. Katelyn doesn't say anything, just walks to my room. A tear snakes down my cheek and I quickly swipe it away. She doesn't need to see me cry right now. She needs someone who is steadfast, but another tear escapes. Jeremy steps out of his room and the minute his eyes land on me, he rushes down the hall.

"What's wrong? What happened?" He inhales sharply. "Is it Katelyn?"

I shake my head as more tears fall. I close my eyes tightly and pinch the bridge of my nose. I knew Stan, but Katelyn was the one closer to him. He was helping her with her novel. She lost so much in a millisecond. I can't fall apart right now. *Pull yourself together, man!*

"Seriously, dude! What the hell happened?"

Door hinges squeak, and then Tyler is there, too. "What's going on?"

It's difficult to take a breath. *You need to check on Katelyn.* I'm frozen, though.

"Stan d-died," Katelyn says quietly from my doorway.

"Who?" Jeremy whispers to Tyler.

I will myself to sit up, but startle when Katelyn wiggles her way onto my lap. Looking up, her face blurs with fresh tears. I feel awful for her witnessing this. She cups my cheek, leaning her forehead again mine.

"You can be sad, too," she whispers.

And I break. I wrap my arms around her and pull her close.

Katelyn

My world stopped the second Troy took the phone from Maria and told me Stan had passed away. I had no idea how I was going to keep going. In the fog, I remembered Eliza and Marc, but it still shocked me when they arrived at Dom's doorstep. The minute Eliza stepped inside, I was a puddle of tears. She sat with me all night, reluctantly leaving early Monday to go pack and catch her plane. I called out sick to work and then went to Dom's room.

For the past week, I've basically lived at his house. The only time I went home was to pack some clothes and grab my laptop. Dom encouraged me to take more time off work, but I didn't feel like it was an option. Plus, my brain could focus on something else for eight hours a day. Except, I burst into tears when Jeff came over to my desk to say hello and ask how I was. I barely got the explanation out before bolting from my desk.

Services for Stan are held two weeks after his passing. Even though Jeremy had never met him, he still comes along with Tyler, Dom, and me. Several of Stan's former students are in attendance and a few give a speech. Listening to all the stories makes me happy and sad. He was such an amazing teacher and mentor. I have no idea how I'm going to finish my book without him.

Driving to the graveside service, it's quiet in the car. Dom parks and assembles his chair. "You can go ahead. It might take me a little bit to get over there."

"Me too," Tyler says. He had surgery a week ago and has been using a walker to get around.

"I'm fine."

"Katelyn." Dom's voice cracks. "I don't want you to miss anything. Seriously, go."

I shake my head.

"I can walk with you," Jeremy offers.

I look at Dom. "We're going together."

The cemetery grounds are uneven, but Dom navigates it well. The whole trek, I rest my hand on Dom's shoulder. We arrive at the burial plot just as the pastor steps up to the podium. As soon as we're there, Dom takes my hand and knots our fingers together. Jeremy stands on my other side, with Tyler next to Dom. The graveside service feels like it's over in a blink, and then we're back in the car.

CHAPTER FIFTY-FIVE

Katelyn

A few days after the funeral, I receive a call from Maria asking if I can come over to Stan's house Saturday. They had been sorting through Stan's personal effects and his will. Apparently, he left me a couple things and Maria wanted to make sure I received them. But once I arrive, I can't bring myself to climb out.

Dom rests his hand on my knee. "I'll be right here the whole time."

We enter the house and the ache in my chest makes it difficult to breathe. Scout runs right up to me. I immediately scoop her into my arms and squeeze her tight. She relaxes for a second and then wriggles to be put down. She darts out of the room as soon as her feet hit the floor.

"Come have a seat," Maria says. She heads for the dining room.

I slide one chair away from the table, making room for Dom, and then take a seat. Peter and Maria sit across from us.

"Thanks for coming," Peter says.

"Of course. I'm so sorry," I say. I reach over and lace my fingers through Dom's.

"Thanks," Maria whispers. She clears her throat. "He left a couple things for you." She lifts a stack of books on the table and slides them toward me. "My parents loved books. They loved sharing books more. He wanted you to have these."

My eyes catch on the chewed corner of the book on top and my lip trembles.

Maria continues, "I also went through his computer and there were a few documents you had sent him that he made remarks on. He may have returned some of these already, but I'll go ahead and forward everything he has, just to be safe."

I nod.

Maria and Peter share a nervous look.

"Now, the next thing is a huge commitment, and we understand if it is too much," Maria prefaces.

"What is it?" My stomach tightens in knots and the air starts to thin. Dom squeezes my hand twice. I squeeze back and take a deep breath.

"Both of us have full-time jobs and families to take care of. A pet doesn't fit in our lives right now," Peter says.

My eyes widen and I immediately look for Scout.

He nods. "Scout seems quite taken with you and we know she would be in great hands. If you want her, she's yours."

My eyes well with tears and I nod.

It feels surreal walking out with Scout in my arms. Dom carries her bowl and food in his lap. She's surprisingly quiet the whole way back to Dom's. Her ears twitch and her eyes take in everything. As we near his house, my chest grows tight.

"Katelyn? What's wrong?" Dom asks, panic lacing his words.

"I'm not prepared for this. How am I supposed to take care of her?" I run my hand down Scout's back.

Dom parks and then takes my hand. I look over to find his hazel eyes pinned on me. "You're right. You didn't plan on this, and there are a lot of things that you'll have to figure out."

"Should we have even brought her here? Maybe we should have gone to my apartment."

"You're over here all the time and she seems content in the car. You can bring her over whenever you want, and if you stay here, she can stay, too. It's fine."

"You're sure?" My heart is beating a million miles a minute.

"Absolutely. Take a deep breath for me."

I exhale all the air out of my lungs and then take a deep breath, hold it, and let it out slowly. Scout looks at me when it ruffles her fur. I click my tongue at her, smiling.

"You're going to find a way to make this work because you love her. She has food and all her immunizations. You have some time to figure out a budget and how to work everything she needs into your life. You're okay."

I lean over and give Dom a kiss.

As soon as I step into the house, Jeremy sits up straighter. "What on earth is that?"

"A cat," Dom answers.

"And what is it doing here?"

"Jeremy, this is Scout. She's mine." I smile.

"And I repeat, what is it doing here?"

"Katelyn's over here a lot lately. We thought it would be good for Scout to acclimate to both houses," Dom explains.

Jeremy scowls.

"Oh my gosh, who is this?" Tyler asks, shuffling over with his walker. He reaches out and pets Scout's head.

"This is Scout."

"You're so cute," he coos at her.

Jeremy swears. "I can't believe my life."

I don't know why, but at that, I burst out laughing. When I compose myself, the guys are looking at me like I've sprouted another head.

"Sorry, I don't know why I'm laughing."

"Laughing is good," Jeremy says.

"I love hearing you laugh," Dom comments. Suddenly, it turns into tears. Scout wiggles and I set her down. She immediately darts down the hall, making herself at home.

When Morgan shows up, she's immediately infatuated with Scout, but who wouldn't be? It might be too soon to think this, but Tyler and Morgan are so getting a cat when they're married. We watch Scout walk along the back of the couch, stopping to sniff every few steps.

"I'm sorry to hear about Stan," Morgan comments solemnly.

"Thanks."

"Tyler told me he was helping you with your current manuscript."

A lump forms in my throat and I blink back tears. I nod.

"I know it might take some time, but when you're ready, I'd be happy to help with whatever you need. I'm actually an English major."

Dom clears his throat, and when I look over, his eyes are red. I turn my attention back to Morgan. "I'll keep that in mind."

Dom

It's been two months since Stan's passing. Katelyn and Scout basically live here with the three of us. It didn't take her any time to make a plan and work Scout into her life.

As it turns out, Jeremy is allergic to cats. He grumbles constantly, but secretly, I don't think he minds taking Zyrtec every day. He's constantly playing with Scout when she's here, like now. There's a little jingle from Scout's bell as she pounces on the ribbon that Jeremy is waving, keeping her busy while Katelyn works.

Her Saturdays have looked quite different these last couple of months. When I look over her shoulder where she sits at the table, I see her mouse hovering over her manuscript.

"It's okay if you take a little more time," I murmur.

"I don't know how to do this."

"Do what?"

"Write through this pain. Stan told me to write through the pain." Her voice cracks and tears well in her eyes. "And I don't think I can."

My chest tightens at her sorrow. "It's okay if you leave this for a little while longer. You've been working on your first manuscript more. Maybe keep focusing on that."

A month ago, Morgan encouraged Katelyn to send her first manuscript to an editor. It would help Katelyn focus on something else and keep her writing.

"There's nothing to do right now. It's still with the editor."

"Right. Do you know when you'll hear from her?"

She shrugs. "Another week, I think."

I sit, pondering what Katelyn could do in the meantime. "Could you write like a prequel or a novella for your first manuscript?"

Katelyn looks over, surprised by the suggestion.

"What? I pay attention when you and Morgan talk."

A hint of a smile appears. "Seems like it." She turns back to her screen.

"Think about it." I bend down and kiss the top of her head.

A week later, I'm sitting on my floor, wheelchair parts scattered around me, doing regular maintenance to keep it in good working condition. I've been doing great at using the walker and have even walked around outside of the house a few times, but I still feel more comfortable in my wheelchair depending on how long we're out.

From the front room, I hear a squeal, and my heart rate accelerates. Katelyn rushes into my room, sliding a pile of bolts over and plopping down next to me.

My eyes trail the movement. "Oh, sorry, is this okay?" she asks.

"Yep." I scoot over a little, giving her more room. "What's going on?"

"Read this," she says breathlessly.

I take her phone from her and read the email.

Katelyn,

>*HOLY MOLY! It was such a delight to work on this! Thank you for trusting me with your book baby.*

The email goes on to detail how the edits were made and performed, and that Katelyn can accept or decline any changes. The editor also raves about the characters and the world. I look over at Katelyn, who's beaming.

I whoop excitedly, wrapping her in a tight embrace. Her laughter quickly turns to tears and I know who she's thinking about. Her arms slip around me and she holds me close. "He's so freakin' proud, Katelyn," I whisper.

She only cries harder. A tear slips down my cheek, too. Eventually, her arms drop and she pulls away, wiping her eyes. I hand her phone back to her.

"I should call Morgan."

"I think she's coming over. She'll probably be here in another hour or so."

Sure enough, an hour and a half later, there's a knock at the door and then Morgan calls out a hello. Katelyn bounds over to her to tell her the news, and the squeal that comes from the two of them bursts my eardrums.

"I told you!" Morgan exclaims. "Have you looked at it yet?"

Katelyn shakes her head.

"Well, let's do it."

Katelyn walks back to the bedroom and grabs her laptop. The two of them sit at the dining table, hovering over the notes.

"Wow. There is so much here. Oh, this is interesting. I like this." There's a pause. "Katelyn?"

Making my way over, Morgan watches Katelyn with worry. I gesture to Morgan's chair and she nods, getting up so I can sit. Katelyn's eyes are closed and I panic when I realize she isn't breathing, but then she slowly exhales. Her eyes remain closed for a moment longer before they open, seemingly searching for something. Then she whispers, "My toes." Her fingers wiggle. "My fingers. My shoulders."

She goes through the 3-3-3 rule one more time before her eyes shift back to her laptop screen. "This is a lot."

The page on screen is littered with little red marks and a few comment boxes. If just this page seems overwhelming, I can't imagine thinking about the whole document. Katelyn reaches over and closes out of the document, then quickly leaves the room.

"I guess we're done for today?" Morgan says.

"Just give her time."

I wait for Katelyn at the end of the hall. When she comes out, she walks over and wraps her arms around me, resting her head on my shoulder. With one hand on the walker for balance, I wrap the other around Katelyn, holding her tight.

"What advice would Dr. Raja give you?"

Katelyn takes a breath. "If something seems too big, make it small."

"Can you do that with your manuscript?"

She nods against my shoulder. "I was also thinking that maybe I could skim through for all the positive comments. That way, I can go back to those if I need to. I don't know."

"I love that idea. You're going to figure it out," I say resolutely. She lifts her head and I give her a kiss. "I have total faith in you."

EPILOGUE

Dom

I lied to Katelyn when I said I had a business trip. I tried to convince her to take a few days off work and come out with me, but she wanted to save up her vacation time for a writing conference she's been looking at. Thankfully, she agreed to travel for the weekend. Otherwise, this trip would have been for nothing.

I've tried to remain calm all morning, but I knew the minute I suggested coffee, I'd start panicking. As we approach the coffee shop, Katelyn lights up with recognition.

"Oh my gosh, this is where we first met."

"It is."

Unlike the day we met, the seating area is mostly empty. Our table is vacant. "Why don't you take a seat, and I'll order?"

"I can stay with you."

"No, really. I'm fine. Go sit," I say hurriedly. She gives me a confused look. I try to compose myself. "Sorry. If you want to, that's fine. I'm just saying you can sit."

She tosses out another puzzled look my way and heads for the table. I breathe a sigh of relief. My plan won't work if she's not at the table.

I order our coffees and text the group chat. When my name is called, I grab our drinks and approach the table.

I gesture to the open handicap spot. "Mind if I…?"

Katelyn regards me like I've completely lost it, until realization hits her and she laughs.

"Yes. I mean, no. I mean…" She giggles. "You're ridiculous."

My hands are shaky as I set our coffee on the table. Katelyn's brow furrows.

"It took a while to get your name," I start. My voice trembles, but I push through, pulling out the ring box from my pocket. "I'm hoping it won't take as long to get a yes."

Her jaw drops and her eyes widen. Voices come from behind me, the group entering a little too early, but Katelyn's big brown eyes don't stray from mine. I open the box to show her a halo cushion cut ring. "So…?"

"Yes," she breathes.

Her answer brings me right back to when she saw me again at the grocery store, saying my name for the first time. I take the ring in trembling fingers and slip it on her hand. Cheers and whistles erupt and Katelyn glances over my shoulder to see Eliza, Marc, Tyler, Morgan, and Jeremy holding Scout.

Eliza is at the table instantly. "Eek. Oh, man. You did a good job," she says, examining the ring.

We leave the coffee shop before we're kicked out for being too rambunctious. Especially because pets aren't exactly allowed inside, either. We stroll down the boardwalk instead. Katelyn rests her right hand on my shoulder and continuously wiggles her left hand, watching the sunlight catch on her ring.

I have no idea who to thank for the series of events that lead me here—from the accident to the job change—but I'm sure happy they did. I look around at this amazing group of people, my eyes landing on my beautiful fiancé. If my decision to end everything had panned out, I would have missed all this. Katelyn's beautiful brown eyes slide to me and I smile.

Katelyn

When Dom first brought up a trip to California, I declined. He had flown out for work and I figured he wouldn't have much time to hang out. Plus, Morgan and I had been working through my second manuscript, which I finally began working on about a month ago. Morgan was so patient with me, sitting silently as I bawled my eyes out while we reviewed a few scenes. Stan's handiwork is so evident that my heart aches knowing he won't be here to see the final product. Especially as I review the second point of view. Now, when Mazey looks over the chasm, she isn't alone. Morgan and I have been making great headway, and I didn't want to ruin our flow. However, Dom was persistent and I conceded to meeting him on Friday and spending the weekend with him.

Now, sitting in our king-size bed, the beautiful California sun streaming through our window, I check my e-mail for any responses to the queries I sent out for my first manuscript. I decided I'd query agents, and if nothing comes of it, I'd go the self-publishing route. Dom has been nothing but supportive.

Dom glances over my shoulder. "Anything?"

I shake my head.

He kisses my cheek. "It'll happen." He clears his throat. "So, coffee?"

Looking over at him, his shoulders are tense, and he looks worried. *When do I ever say no to coffee?* "Of course."

I'm giddy when he brings us to the coffee shop where we met. Walking in, I glance around, flashing back to that moment Dom rolled over to my table. When he insists I take a seat, I look at him, perplexed. Instead of arguing, I do as he says. I hear his name called, but as he approaches the table, he slows a little. "Mind if I…?"

It takes me a moment, but then I laugh and recite the words I did when he first asked me that question. Though all lightness flees when I notice his hands trembling as he sets our coffees down. My eyes scale his figure but there are no visible issues. I'm about to ask what's wrong when he says, "It took a while to get your name…"

My heart stops when he pulls out the ring. I'm barely able to get the yes out. His hands quake as he slides the ring on my finger. Suddenly, the coffee shop is extremely loud, and I lift my eyes to find all our friends gathered by the entrance. Eliza rushes over, pulling my left hand toward her. We make a quick exit so our excitement won't disturb the few patrons and the employees.

Walking down the boardwalk, my chest tightens at the thought of all the changes this will bring. I exhale all the air out of my body then take a slow breath in, hold it, and exhale again. My eyes shift to Dom, his hazel eyes already trained on me. His smile instantly erases the tension I feel. Leaning down, I give him a quick kiss, thinking about how lucky I am to have him in my life. He is my safe place, my calm. I know if I have him by my side, I'll be able to face whatever life throws at me.

Acknowledgements

First to my Heavenly Father. I prayed A LOT about this story, and it wouldn't have been possible without Him.

To Chandler, for letting me know about the Kindle Vella competition. Katelyn and Dom's story was born right then. I knew each Kindle Vella "episode" would be in a different point of view. I was so sad when Amazon decided to discontinue Kindle Vella, but I knew their story wasn't over yet.

To all who tuned in to each Kindle Vella "episode." I knew I couldn't leave you on a cliffhanger. Your interest and encouragement are the reason this book exists.

To Tim, who edited all Kindle Vella "episodes" before I released them. He is the best little brother! I'm so fortunate he is also a night owl. I'd call late in the evening asking what one of his comments meant or ask him to read through a re-write and he'd jump on it. Shout out to Mikalah as well. I'm not sure how many out-of-context sentences you had to hear this time. I'd apologize, but let's be honest, I'm not sorry and I can't say it won't happen again. I'm still writing, and I know I'll still go to him for advice.

To Jared for providing "Dark Side of the Mocha." What he has yet to realize is Amped will appear in future books and I'm going to need a whole menu...

To Wheels2Walking for all the YouTube videos about life in a wheelchair. Richard Corbett, the creator of this channel, was extremely open about his injury and his experience. I watched and re-watched several videos to help shape Dom's story.

To Whitney Lynn, my sensitivity reader. She knows what it's like to live life in a wheelchair and was super helpful in making sure all my research was accurate. When it wasn't, she was gentle in letting me know where I went wrong and how to correct it.

As always, thank you to Makenna Albert for your extraordinary editing skills. This time she completed two different edits and I'm so grateful!

To Ary, who created the original artwork for Katelyn and Dom. See the next page to see her amazing work.

Finally, to you. Yes, you. I wouldn't be able to live out my dream if you didn't pick up this book. Thank you!

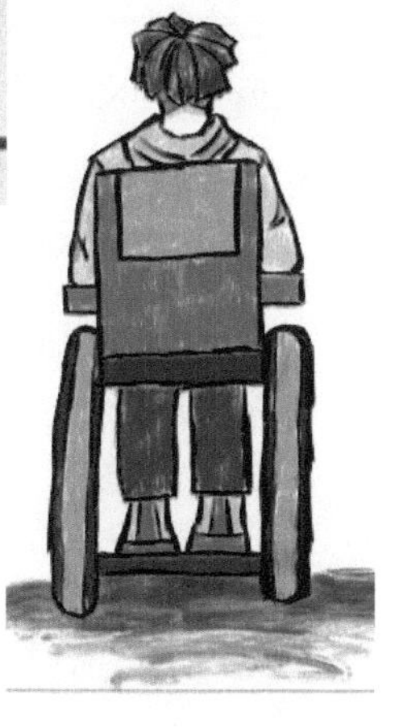

Karen Ramsey is an Arizona native. She recently resigned from her job to pursue writing full time. Since growing up in church, she feels her life is powered by faith and caffeine keeps her going. She often wonders if there's a Starbucks Anonymous and should she attend, seeing as how she visits multiple times a day. Her debut novel *Enjoy the Little Things* was published in 2023.

These Broken Pieces has a playlist!!!

Books / Shows / Movies

Books

- Harold and the Purple Crayon – Crockett Johnson
- Alexander and the Terrible, Horrible, No Good, Very Bad Day – Judith Viorst
- To Kill a Mockingbird – Harper Lee
- Dragon's Kiss – E.A. Winters
- Realm Breaker – Victoria Aveyard
- Fireborne – Rosaria Munda

Shows

- *Friends*
- *Jane the Virgin*
- *Love is Blind (US & UK)*
- *The Circle*
- *Schitt's Creek*
- *Gilmore Girls*

Movies

- Harold and the Purple Crayon
- The Lost Boys

A Note to Readers

This book focused on topics of depression, self-harm, and suicide. If you are struggling with any of these, *please* reach out to a trusted friend, family member, or help hotline.

You are not alone!!

Call/Text 988

Confidential. Free.